Siren's Mark

Siren's Mark

LUX RAVEN

LACONIA
PRESS

For the sick girls...

*because even on your worst days, you're
still main-character material.*

*You deserve adventure, heat, and someone
who looks at you like you're magic.*

Content Warning

This book is part one of a duology, meaning it tells the first half of a larger story. While this installment has its own arc and resolution, it does end on a cliffhanger. The full story concludes in book two with a **guaranteed happy ending.**

Now, onto the serious stuff. This book contains **explicit sex**, **alcohol use**, and **violence**. There are mentions of a death by suicide, though it's not depicted or detailed.

I believe in content warnings because mental health matters. If certain topics are difficult for you, I want you to have the information you need to make the best choice for yourself. Below, I have included a more detailed list of potential triggers. If you prefer to avoid mild spoilers, you may want to stop reading here.

෴

Story includes: homophobia, sexual harassment, blood & gore, emotional abuse in childhood, death by suicide (mentioned, not depicted or detailed), medical gaslighting and trauma, death, illness, hospitals, ableism, memory loss, and emotional abuse & manipulation (not between the primary couple).

If you have any questions about specific triggers, please feel free to reach out to me directly at luxravenwrites@gmail.com. Your well-being is important, and I want you to engage with this story in a way that feels safe for you.

1

 ZANE

An immortal walks into a hospital.

I don't have the punchline to this one yet, but it feels like it's got to be a joke.

The wind shakes the barren trees that line the walkway toward the building's automatic sliding glass doors.

I pull out my phone to re-read Kami's texts.

Kami

In hospital - Need you to meet me

Not dead btw

Of course she didn't include her room number.

I hate hospitals. They're just monuments to the fragility of humans; a constant reminder that illness and death are around every corner. How do they even live like that—knowing that at any minute it could all just end?

My eyes scan over the building directory until I find the words 'Information Desk' and head in that direction.

The lobby has that typical bland hospital look: white, barren walls and taupe carpet. I've never understood why everything in hospitals is white and beige—the two colors that are impossible to get blood stains out of.

A few people are queued up at the desk, with many more seated in what appear to be the world's least-comfortable chairs.

Me

How do I get to your room?

I guess I'm going to have to wait like everyone else.

I stand behind an older man hooked up to a machine that he rolls along with him. They really shouldn't make sick people stand here waiting like this.

I glance back at my phone; still no response.

As I look up, the girl approaching the counter catches my eye. She seems out of place in this room of ailing, elderly people. She looks about 25 and, at least on the surface, in perfect health. Her hair is dyed a vivid shade of purple and she's dressed in a leather jacket, skinny jeans, and combat boots. She's an anomaly.

Who are you?

"I get that," she says to the grumpy-looking woman behind the desk, "but I've literally been here four times this month. Do you really need the same forms again? I mean, I'm already in your system, right?"

The receptionist glares at the girl through the rim of her glasses. She mutters something about hospital policy and the girl lets out a frustrated sigh before grabbing a pen and sitting down with the forms.

Before too long, it's my turn and I approach the desk.

"Hello, love," I say, giving the woman my best charming smile. Thanks to the glass barrier between us, I can't just use my powers this time and will have to rely on my other gifts.

"Primary complaint?" she asks in a monotone voice.

Okay, I guess I'm a little rusty.

"Uh… I'm looking for Kami Selim. She called me asking me to meet her here but I don't know her room number," I say.

Her eyebrows lower and she gives me a look that is equal parts judgmental and unimpressed.

Apparently I'm a lot rusty.

"I can't give you patient details, sir," she says.

"I understand," I say. "Could you at least tell her I'm here?"

"Sorry, I can't confirm whether or not this patient is even in the hospital."

Bloody humans. I should have known better. People only help you if there's something in it for them.

As I ponder a way to get past this woman, my phone vibrates in my hand.

Kami

207

———•———

AVA

If I have to fill out this stupid form one more time, I'm going to lose it. If I didn't have diabetes last week, I don't have it this week.

Name, birth date, Social Security number, new/returning patient…

Really? Feels like deja vu. A frustrated sigh escapes me as I write them in—again.

Heart condition? Asthma? Lung disease? Certainly not since I filled this out on Thursday. I take my pencil and just draw a line down the "No" column then flip the page.

Name and birth date. *Again??* I'm struggling to resist the urge to be sarcastic here. What happens if I put a different name on the second page?

I think for a moment before I settle on writing *"Stop asking me."*

"Not why I'm calling," I hear a man's voice say in a British accent. "Her room number is 207. But I'm not sure what to do from here. What do we have to say at a hospital here?"

He's tall and almost offensively good looking, with shaggy brown hair and a thin layer of neatly trimmed facial hair. He's wearing a thin grey T-shirt that clings to his skin with a shoulder tattoo peeking out on one side and another tattoo on his opposite forearm. I watch as he paces across the lobby with a phone to his ear, clearly uncomfortable and speaking in a hushed voice with his back turned to the receptionist.

"Like, do I have to tell them I'm family or some shit?" he asks into his phone.

Oh, he's visiting someone. He's probably worried about being let in.

"I mean, I can't exactly provide proof of that," he continues.

I should help him.

I go over to him, reaching to tap him on the shoulder, but he turns around before I do. That was weird; he must have heard me coming. He looks quite surprised by my intrusion but smiles.

"You don't need to be family," I say. "And I wouldn't bother talking to the receptionist anyway. She's legitimately the worst."

Fucking Janine. I swear that lady hates me.

I point to a cluster of signs and say, "Just follow the arrows to B Campus, and then the numbers leading up to your friend's room. That whole family thing is more of a bad TV medical drama rule and not actually an issue these days. Besides, if you act like you have permission to be there, you could probably start a fire and no one would question it."

"Thanks," he says with a small laugh.

"No problem," I say. I walk over to the nearest chair and sit back down. His eyes seem to follow me as I walk away.

Yeah, sure Ava. The super hot guy is definitely staring at you because he's interested and not because you just weirdly intruded on his conversation.

I catch the tail end of his sentence as he returns to his phone call. "…this girl was helping me find Kami's room."

At least he didn't say 'this weird girl wasn't minding her own business.'

He looks irritated at the person on the other line and walks down the hall, mumbling in a harsh tone.

"Ava Reynolds?" a nurse calls.

"That's me," I say, walking to her.

"Okay, come with me. I'm going to get you started on your MRI prep."

"Oh and I can take your paperwork," she adds, gesturing toward my clipboard.

"Oh, uh… yeah," I say, and reluctantly hand it over. I was planning on wussing out and changing some of my sarcastic answers but I guess I'm committed now. I just hope she'll do me a favor and won't read it right in front of me.

———•———

ZANE

Room 205… 206… There it is. 207.

I peek around the corner to see a battered figure laying in the hospital bed. It's Kami. Her long brown hair is still flawless as ever, despite her face and arms being covered in dirt and debris. She's holding onto a gaping wound in her abdomen that has soaked through a layer of gauze. Her hands are stained red with blood.

"Hey," she says, with a bit of a groan.

"What the hell happened?" I ask.

"Long story involving a very bitchy Seer and a kheru knife. I'm fine, or at least I will be. That's why you're here."

"Why did you come to the hospital instead of me in the first place?"

"Well, I was knocked unconscious and they brought me here by ambulance. I guess they tried to put an IV in me…"

"Shit. I imagine that went well…"

"They broke a fair amount of equipment before I regained consciousness. But it's fine, I suggested they forget everything they had seen."

That's a relief. I'm not exactly prepared to answer the 'why does this woman have magic skin' question.

"Fuck that parking lot, man," Kieran says as he steps into the room.

"You finally found a spot?" I ask.

"I made one," he huffs. "If I didn't see a soul in that parking lot for twenty minutes then it's safe to say there's not gonna be anyone there to give me a damn ticket."

Kami rolls her eyes.

"Oh good," she says. "You brought your pet."

Kieran returns her eye roll and crosses his arms. "Nice to see you too, Kami."

"Alright, let's not start this again," I say, stepping in between them.

"He's an Incubus, Zane," Kami says with irritation. "They're demons. Bottom-feeders. He's just leeching off your powers and you get nothing out of the deal."

"Oh suck my cloven hooves," Kieran spits.

"I'm seriously over this back and forth between you two," I say. "Kami, we need to get you healed before you bleed out."

"Aww," Kieran says, "You haven't done your little magical make-out session yet? So glad I could join for this."

Kieran rolls his eyes and sits in the corner. Kami looks as though she's about to go for Kieran's jugular, so I seize the opportunity to grab her face and pull her in for a kiss.

It's been a while since I've had to heal another Siren like this. The feeling is a combination of distant and familiar. I feel her lips warm and watch as the color returns to her golden-brown skin.

"How is it?" I ask, gesturing to the bandages on her wound.

"It was good for me," Kieran interjects, suggestively raising his eyebrows with a smirk.

Kami shoots him a glare before standing up and inspecting her stomach. Her wound is no longer visible. She runs her hands carefully along her smooth abdomen.

"Yeah, I think we're all good. Thanks, Z."

"So," Kieran asks, "are you all crazy in love with Zane now?"

"Siren venom only has that effect on humans." Kami scoffs. "For other Sirens it just has the healing effect."

"So what happened, anyway?" Kieran asks, looking at Kami. Kami is cleaning herself off at a nearby sink. The sink is gradually filling with blood-dyed water.

"I was chasing a bounty and ended up in the woods off Route 28. I ran into a Seer that I have a history with…"

"History?" I ask.

"I may have slept with her sister. I honestly don't entirely remember; I just know that she's hated me for the last 40 years or so. Anyway, apparently she was expecting me—*Seer* and all, go figure—and she greeted me with a kheru knife to the spleen."

"Those can hurt a Siren?" Kieran asks.

She rolls her eyes and scoffs.

"Yes," I say. "It can pierce a Siren's skin. Works on most other Immortals too. Not demons, though."

A nurse appears behind us with a concerned expression. She must have heard the tail end of our conversation.

I quickly grab the nurse's wrist and she furrows her brow at the touch.

"There's nobody here," I say. The woman nods along. "You're imagining things. Forget this conversation."

The nurse pauses a moment, then seems to drift off before walking away.

Kami scoops up her coat and bag in a quick motion.

"Alright," she says, swinging her bag over her shoulder. "Let's get out of here before we have to work over the whole staff."

2

 ZANE

Kami said she'd handle her own ride home, so Kieran and I head back to the car. I push the elevator button while Kieran eyes a curvy blonde doctor at the nursing desk.

"So Kami's charming as ever," he says, reluctantly pulling his eyes from the doctor's *assets*.

"Yeah, you know how she can be. She's just looking out for me. She hasn't had a lot of positive experiences with demons in the past. She thinks you all have ulterior motives."

"Ah come on, can't a bro have a supernatural wingman?"

I chuckled. Supernatural wingman isn't exactly the title I would have come up with, but it's a very Kieran thing to say.

"She thinks I'm reckless," he says. "She's right, in a way. Or she was. It goes without saying that I've made some bad decisions. I wasn't looking to out myself or draw any unwanted attention. Certainly not to lead it your way."

He looks at me with concerned eyes, almost guilty. I'm not really looking to have a gushy moment right now.

"I know," I say.

"I hope you don't think of me as a leech," he says with a serious expression.

"No, mate, not at all. Honestly, we're good."

For an Incubus, Kieran is very young. Kami expects everyone to have their shit together right away, but sometimes I think she's too far removed from her past to remember what that learning stage was like. God forbid I take him in because I have compassion for him.

When I first met Kieran, he was starving. He would kill anyone he could lure because he needed everything he could get. It's sick that Incubi don't have any powers to help them lure their prey like we do, yet they need to feed off human sexual energy to survive.

The elevator dings before the doors open to reveal the girl with purple hair. She has some paperwork rolled up in one hand and a bright pink bandage wrapped around her elbow. She must've just had a blood test of some kind.

Her grey eyes catch mine as we step into the elevator and she smiles awkwardly.

"Hey," she says. "So you found your friend?"

Kieran immediately inserts himself between us before I can answer. "Hey Zane, aren't you going to introduce me to your lovely friend?"

I see his eyes widen as a deep, dark smile washes over his face. I've seen this look before when he has spotted his prey.

"I'm Kieran," he says, reaching out for a handshake.

"Ava," she responds.

I feel an uncomfortable pressure in my chest as their hands meet. This girl has just come from a blood test and told the receptionist she had been here many times recently. Whatever's going on with her, she's not someone he should be targeting. She could get hurt, or worse.

The elevator stops and I firmly pull Kieran by the arm out of the elevator.

"This is us," I say. "Bye."

I'm getting him away from her. Now.

———•———

Kieran is quiet, but fuming, leaving a minute for the elevator doors to close as he slowly walks toward the car.

"What the hell was that, man?" Kieran snaps. His eyes are wide with fury and his body is tense. He punches a nearby cement pillar and a chunk crumbles off.

"Kieran, stop," I say. "That girl is sick."

"So?!" He growls, his hand tugging on his hair at the root.

He's still pissed. When an Incubus feels threatened they can be difficult to calm down. Their hunger is intense and all-consuming. Of course it doesn't help that this is Kieran I'm dealing with; he even had a temper when he was human.

"She's too fragile. We have no idea what might happen if you feed on her."

"Sure you don't just want her for yourself?" he asks, his eyes tight and accusing.

"I heard your heartbeat back there. It jumped when you saw her."

"I don't do that anymore, you know that. Involvement with humans is way too complicated for me. The moment we kiss they're infatuated. It's never clear what's real."

His expression softens, his fists slowly unclenching.

"You know you can just have sex with them, right?" he says.

"Yeah, I'm aware. It's just, that can be difficult in its own right."

His shoulders lower and his chest deflates.

"Because you get involved?"

I chuckle. Kami would have found this particularly funny. I don't get *involved* with anyone. I hardly get involved with other Immortals. Feelings are messy and I've never been a fan.

"Because my nature takes over. I start making bad decisions and someone always gets hurt."

Kieran lets out a loud laugh. "I know how that goes."

At least he's laughing now and not trying to kill me.

He smiles and gestures towards his red pickup truck, two of its wheels resting precariously on the concrete curb. He unlocks the doors as we walk toward the car.

"So you actually think it's dangerous?" he asks. "If someone is sick, I can't feed off them? I could hurt them?"

"I honestly don't know, but it's not worth the risk."

My mind goes back to the purple-haired girl with grey eyes.

Is she really sick? What could be wrong with her that she has to go to the hospital so much?

I don't want Kieran to hurt her. I don't want anybody to hurt her.

<hr>

AVA

A soft buzzing wakes me from a dead sleep.

Where is that coming from? What time is it?

The sun has set outside but the clock in the kitchen is glowing. 7:30. Great, I napped for three hours.

I follow the buzzing to a soft light coming from my phone on the coffee table. The caller ID says 'JEN'.

"Hey," I answer, half asleep.

"Heyyy!!" she chimes. "How was your appointment, hon?"

"Oh uh… same old, pretty much. They poked me with needles. Got to wear a super-chic hospital gown. Sat in a tube while a magnetic machine composed its own truly atrocious EDM music. It was a dream."

"Still no answers?" she asks.

"Not yet," I say. "They'll get the results in a few days, but I'm not super hopeful. Everything is pretty much always negative. It's been a year; I doubt this is going to tell them anything."

"I'm sorry, hon," she says. "How's your pain today?"

My shoulders, neck, and back are tight and sore. My legs are achy and my knees hurt every time they bend. But for me, this is a pretty good day.

"Not too bad," I say. "I took a long nap; I think that was good for me."

"That's awesome! You should come out with me tonight then!"

I sigh. Going out sounds fun, but it also sounds like a giant hassle. Plus I'd have to wear uncomfortable shoes.

"Pleeeeaaase!" she presses.

"Okay," I say, "But I'm wearing flats."

"Girl I don't care what shoes you wear," she says. "Oh, and bring Mike."

Bring Mike? What?

Jen has never been Mike's biggest fan, in part because he always makes me feel guilty when I hang out with my friends. Her sudden change of tune is suspicious.

"There's this super hottie I've been trying to casually run into at this bar, so if things go well maybe we'll turn it into a double date," she adds.

Ahhh, now that sounds more like Jen.

"Okay, what time?" I say. Mike is such a pain to talk into going out somewhere, but hopefully the promise of beer will talk him into it.

"Meet you at Pike's Tavern in an hour? I'll text you the address."

After confirming a few details we hang up and I text Mike. After three hours of napping, I'm still tired, but I need to get out of the house.

Here goes nothing.

———◆———

ZANE

It's crowded here tonight. I'm used to Kieran tending bar most nights but there's someone new behind the counter tonight: a pretty, full-figured brunette that he's undoubtedly chatting up while grabbing our drinks. He knows better than to prey on a colleague. That could get messy.

He returns with a couple of beers and a large glass of what looks like Coca-Cola.

"Is that a soft drink?" I ask.

"There's soda in there, yeah. But uh, it's like 90% rum."

Yep, that's Kieran for you.

"Ahh, I see," I say. "So planning on taking it easy, then, eh?"

For an Incubus, it takes about five times as much alcohol to get the same level of drunk as a human, and it burns off faster. Sirens, on the other hand, respond to alcohol much like humans do, although we don't suffer the same health effects.

"Gotta keep my wits about me," he says with a smirk. "I'm on the hunt."

He laughs and takes a hefty swig of his beer.

"Alright tiger," I say. "Who's your target tonight?"

He scans the room for a moment before focusing on a table with a curvy, Asian hipster girl that looks about 25 and a smug-looking, slightly older guy in a shiny navy bomber jacket.

"I hope you're looking at the girl," I say as I take a sip of my beer. "That guy looks like a right prick."

"Yeah I agree—all the more reason to liberate her. She definitely doesn't seem into him either, which makes my job easier."

I look back at the two of them. There's no way they're together. She's dressed in a black dress and knit black beanie with long, thick wavy hair. He's got that classic 'trust fund kid' look complete with pristine white sneakers that probably cost more than most people's cars. They're awkwardly staring in opposite directions and both keep checking their phones.

"Something tells me you're in the clear there anyway," I say.

"I dunno, man," Kieran says. "I've seen plenty of cool women who were with total dicks."

"And you presumably *liberated* them?"

"What can I say? I'm a good samaritan."

I laugh, almost choking on my beer.

"Well then, let's go save the poor woman," I say with a smirk.

We grab our drinks and approach their table.

Kieran tosses his head back so his shoulder-length black hair falls out of his face. Incubi can control how they look in just about any way, shapeshifting into their prey's ideal. Kieran doesn't stray much from the look he had when he was human, partly as a preference and partly because he was naturally gifted with good looks.

At 6-feet tall with a wide, sculpted build he's imposing to most people. We're about the same height but he's much thicker and more muscular than I am. If he had my tattoos he might be too intimidating, but instead his long, messy hair, warm brown skin, and subtle goatee make him look like he stepped off the cover of a romance novel. If I could choose a look to entice people, especially women, I'd definitely go with Kieran.

"Hey," he says to the girl. "My friend and I have a debate going. He says he thinks you're a local. I say there's no way. I would've seen you around before."

Oh god, that was slick and so cheesy at the same time.

She smiles and blushes, batting her eyes behind heavy black eyeliner. This is going to be too easy. Kieran might not even need me.

"I'm actually from here. Just moved back last year."

The guy next to her rolls his eyes. Luckily he doesn't seem interested in beating the shit out of us, so that's another strong sign that they're not together.

"That's crazy," Kieran says. "I can't believe I haven't seen you around before. I'm a bartender here and I'd remember *you*."

If I had a dollar for every time he's used that line...

"Really??" She asks. "You bartend here?? I'm Jen by the way." She leans in and seems to be genuinely interested.

Wow, it's looking like all this girl needs is a couple of free drinks. She shakes hands with Kieran before extending a hand to me.

"Zane. Pleasure to meet you," I say.

Jen lets out a squeal and says, "Ooh, British! Real accent I take it?"

"No, love, just watched too much Monty Python as a kid and I'm afraid it stuck this way."

By the tentative looks I'm getting in response I can tell they're unsure if

I'm kidding.

Sharp bunch, this lot.

"Yeah, it's real. Lived in London for a long while."

I extend my hand to introduce myself to the douche.

The douche nods back. "Mike," he says.

They're an odd pair and have captured my curiosity. They're not together… right?

"So you two together?" I ask him while Jen and Kieran chat and giggle at the other side of the table.

"Uggh…" he grunts. "No. She's my girlfriend's friend. We're waiting for her and she's *late*, which is just typical."

His face twists into an irritated expression and he gulps down some of his beer.

"I don't even know why I'm here," he continues. "She always tries to make me do this stupid shit with her and her friends."

He rolls his eyes and chugs more beer. *This guy seems delightful.*

"What stupid shit would that be?" I ask. "Coming out to a bar?"

"Yeah, just… everything. And of course she's just leaving us hanging here. I have shit to do."

What. A. Wanker.

"What is wrong with you, Mike?" Jen interjects. "She's like ten minutes late. We're not torturing you. Stop making me regret inviting you."

"Who's late?" Kieran asks, trying to follow the conversation.

"Speak of the devil!" she says, jumping up and reaching for someone behind me.

"Ava, this is Kieran and this is… oh shoot. I'm sorry, what was your name?"

I turn around to see those grey eyes staring back at me, both of us slightly shocked. I feel my heartbeat begin to hammer in my chest. I'm hoping Kieran doesn't notice after last time.

Why do I care if Kieran thinks I like this girl? I don't.

What is she doing here, anyway? Did Kieran somehow find her and invite her? But this girl—Jen—she knows her.

The turning gears in my mind finally tick into place.

That means… she's the douchebag's girlfriend?

Nope. Nope. No way. That's not acceptable. She's not dating this guy.

Ava and Jen are looking at me as though they've asked me a question. Did they?

"It's Zane," Kieran interjects. "His name is Zane. Hey there, Ava!"

Oh crap. Kieran is not an acceptable option either.

"Are you guys stalking me or something?" she asks. By the tone of her voice, it's not clear if she's joking or serious.

"Well, I work here," says Kieran. "So I'm pretty sure *you're* stalking *me*."

That predatory smirk returns to his face.

That's it. I'm gonna kill him.

3

Where do these guys keep popping up from? First the hospital—twice. Now here.

"You work here?" I ask.

"Yeah," Kieran says. "I'm off tonight, though."

I've never been to this particular bar before. I'm pretty sure the only reason Jen chose this place was that she was hoping to run into someone she has her eyes on.

"How do you guys know each other?" I ask.

"We just met," Jen chimes in, pulling up a barstool for me between her and Mike.

"Hey," I say to Mike, giving him a kiss on the cheek.

"You're late," he says, not even making eye contact.

Oh good. It's gonna be one of those *nights.*

"Sorry," I say. I'm not even fifteen minutes late, but in this case I would rather just apologize than let it turn into a whole thing.

"Have a seat, guys!" Jen says to Zane and Kieran, gesturing to a couple of empty stools on the opposite side of our table.

Zane has a stern, tense look to him as he takes his seat. Between the eavesdropping earlier and this chance encounter, it's more likely he thinks *I'm* the creepy stalker.

Well, this is awkward.

"So, Ava," Mike says with an irritated voice. "Clearly you and these two are already acquainted." He scoffs and takes a sip of his beer.

This is going great so far.

"Yeah," Jen interjects, attempting to lighten the mood. "How do you guys know each other?"

"Uh, we don't really," I say. "We just bumped into each other at the hospital earlier."

"You had *another* appointment?" Mike asks.

"Yeah, it's no big deal. Just tests and stuff. Don't worry about it."

I try to leave Mike out of most of the details. Every time I tell him they don't have a diagnosis for me he just complains and insists I need to try harder. I'd rather not deal with that right now. Besides, I don't exactly want to share my private medical information in front of these strangers anyway.

Mike gives me a suspicious look as he takes another swig of his drink.

"And now you're all here," he says. "Crazy coincidence."

"Must be fate," Kieran says with a flirty smile.

Kieran certainly isn't helping my case with Mike tonight.

"Kay," Mike says, grabbing his beer and pointing toward the pool tables in the back of the bar. "Well, I see Jason back there. I'm gonna go play pool."

He walks off in the direction of the pool tables. Jen has resumed conversation with Kieran, but I can't help but notice Kieran's eyes on me.

"What's his problem?" Zane asks.

"Mike? Oh uh, he's just a little awkward with people sometimes."

"Does that include you?" he asks.

Mike is sensitive and sometimes insecure. It always seems worse when he has to meet new people. Yeah, okay, sometimes he's a dick too. But honestly, so am I.

"No, he's just complicated," I say. "It takes time to get to know him."

"I'll pass on that, thanks," Zane asks with an eye roll.

"What does that mean, you'll pass?"

"I mean I don't think it's worth putting in that much effort getting to know someone like that. If you start off acting like an arse, it's not my job to wait until you're tolerable."

He smirks and takes a sip of his drink.

"He's not an ass, or 'arse.' Whatever. And I think you're being an *arse* for saying that anyway."

He looks up from his drink, looking slightly vulnerable. For a moment, his brown eyes catch the light in a way that makes them look an almost-otherworldly shade of green. Damn, this guy is good looking. That chiseled jaw, perfectly placed freckles across his cheeks, elaborate designs inked into his arms…

What was I saying?

"You certainly aren't the first person who has said that," he says with a smile. "So you might have a point. I just speak my mind is all."

"I have a bit of that foot-in-mouth problem myself. I still prefer honest people over phony ones, so I guess if you're an ass that's okay as long as you're straight up about it."

He smirks at me and looks down at his drink. His smile is incredibly charming and he seems to know it. I follow the line of his jaw to his neck and down to a tattoo on his bicep. It seems to be a harp with a snake wrapped around it.

"I like your tattoo," I say. "A harp?"

He looks down for a moment. "Yeah, thanks," he says. "It's uh… kind of a long story."

"So you don't play the harp?" I joke.

He chuckles. "No, it's kind of a juxtaposition thing. The beauty of the song pulls you in, but the snake is waiting to bite you. It's kind of supposed to represent the danger in beautiful things."

"Or the beauty in dangerous things?"

"I haven't put it that way before, but I like it."

Kieran suddenly turns to join our conversation. "So what are we talking about?" he asks in a singsongy tone. He seems like he's had a bit too much to drink.

"Tattoos," I say.

"Yeah?" he asks. "What's the rose mean?" He points to the rose tattoo along my wrist.

"Oh, well, I read that the rose is a symbol of both life and death. I liked the paradox. Plus I was a super moody teenager and it seemed fitting for my dark, twisted soul."

Kieran laughs and I notice a few tattoos on his arm.

"What about yours?" I ask.

He looks confused for a moment.

"I didn't even notice those!" Jen says, at a volume she only thinks is appropriate because she's a bit tipsy.

"Oh yeah, uh… these are just random designs really. No meaning or anything." He blushes and looks down. Zane's mood has suddenly shifted and he's now casting a glare in Kieran's direction

"Hey Jen," Zane says abruptly. "What type of drink is that?"

That was weird. Why is he suddenly asking about her drink?

"Oh, it's um…" She looks down to remember what she ordered. "…a Manhattan I think."

Zane reaches for Jen's hand and casually brushes it.

"Would you mind if I try some?" Zane asks.

She seems flustered, but smiles and passes him her drink. He takes a sip and hands it back to her.

"I was interested in trying it, but yeah, not for me," he says.

Kieran is eyeing Zane with a questioning expression. There seems to be a silent conversation happening between them. Jen takes another sip of her drink and Kieran quickly resumes conversation with her. The whole interaction seems a bit odd, but everyone is already moving on.

A smile comes across Jen's face and she's blushing hard. With a giggle, she leans over to whisper in my ear.

"Aaavvvaaaaa…"

She points toward the bar. A buxom bartender with a shoulder-length messy bob is pouring beer out of the tap.

"That's herrrrr!!" she whispers not-so-subtly.

This must be the woman she was telling me about. I didn't realize she was a bartender here, but it explains why she's been getting so chummy with Kieran.

"Isn't she beautiful??" she mumbles, practically drooling. "I'm going to talk to her."

In an instant, she stumbles off her barstool and walks over to the bartender. *What the heck?*

This is not like her at all. Jen has always been somewhat of a slow mover, but the liquid courage must be having a serious effect on her tonight. Zane and Kieran look at each other a bit stunned before Kieran bursts out laughing.

"Well, that's not how I saw this going!" he says through his fit of laughter.

———◆———

ZANE

Okay, that—in hindsight—was not my smoothest move.

I watch as Jen approaches the bartender. She's rosy-cheeked and her eyes are wide, pupils dilated from the venom I left behind from my sip of her drink.

What am I doing? Why am I desperate enough to keep Kieran away from this girl that I'm willing to practically throw him at anyone else?

I turn back to the table. Kieran is still chuckling as he sips his drink. He looks up at Ava like he's sizing up his dinner.

Nope. Nope. Nope.

"So your friend has a thing for the bartender?" he asks with a laugh. "And by bartender I mean, *not me*."

He chuckles again and allows his arm to rest on the table, exposing his newly 'tattooed' skin. He's acting like he's not going for her but his body betrayed him. Even though he didn't intend to, his body was shifting ever so slightly to make him more attractive to his prey. I've rarely seen him lose control in this way. He must be really interested in this girl.

"Yeah, I guess so!" she says, with a slight blush appearing on her face. "Jen told me we were coming here because she wanted to run into her crush, turns out it's the bartender. I don't know what came over her just now. She's usually a, um… slow mover?"

Ava's expression turns to one of shock and disgust as she stares over my shoulder. I look to see Jen and the bartender kissing in an aggressive way that is slightly hard to look at, practically prying each other's lips open with their tongues.

Yeah, that's awkward.

"Wow," she says, her face reddening. "Yeah, I guess she had a little more to drink than I thought."

She uncomfortably chugs the rest of her drink, trying her best to look away from the bar.

"It looks like you could use another one of those," Kieran says. "What are you drinking?"

"I don't know," she says. "They ordered drinks before I got here. This is, um… not the best. Maybe a rum and coke instead?"

"You got it," he says, smiling back.

I don't want him buying her a drink, but I'd rather stay here with her than leave them alone together.

"So, love," I say. "Based on the way you downed that drink, would it be safe to assume you're not having a great time?"

"Sorry. It's not personal," Ava says with a sigh. "I don't go out a lot and I kind of thought I'd be spending time with Jen and Mike tonight and well…"

"You're stuck with me," I say with a smirk.

"No, no," she says in a flustered, apologetic tone. "I didn't mean it that way; I just meant… sorry."

She sighs and bites her lip, looking downward and fiddling with her glass.

"So you're British?" she asks, clumsily changing the subject.

I resist the urge to make another sarcastic remark.

"Yeah, sort of. I've lived in a lot of places, London for the longest. I guess I picked up the accent."

"I dunno, not sure I hear it," she says, a cheeky smile flashing on her face.

"Oi, a sarcastic one. I like you."

"Back with drinks!" Kieran says. "Gotta admit, it was hard to, uh, get the attention of the bartender."

He gives us a wink and chuckles. "Had half a mind to try and get an invitation to that party, but it seems like they're having plenty of fun on their own."

4

While waiting for Jen to tear herself away from the hot bartender, I tossed back a couple more drinks. I'm definitely going to regret it tomorrow, but right now the pain has dulled and I prefer to be drunk if I'm going to have to deal with Mike's attitude tonight.

Mike reluctantly agreed to drive me home, making it pretty clear that it was a burden to him, but he said he didn't want me to have to call an Uber.

"So are you going to ignore me the whole ride home?" I ask.

"I'm not ignoring you," he says.

"Okay, well, you're not talking and you ditched me to play pool all night. Plus you have that pissed off look on your face."

"*I* ditched *you*? I'm pretty sure the only reason I came there was for you. And then you start flirting with these guys that you mysteriously seem to know and it comes out that you had a hospital appointment that you didn't tell me about—I felt totally blindsided by the whole thing!"

As much as I want to be irritated I have to admit that it probably did feel bad from his side.

"I only know them because I showed one of them how to find his friend's hospital room. And I wasn't flirting with them. I'm sorry I didn't tell you about the appointment; I honestly didn't think you would have wanted to know.

He sighs, still staring ahead at the road.

"I promise. Nothing was going on. There's no conspiracy."

His shoulders seem to relax a little, as though just maybe he hears what I'm saying.

"Okay," he says begrudgingly.

After another stretch of silence, he lets out another sigh and says, "So what was this appointment for?"

"Just another round of tests. They did an MRI and took more blood."

"And? What did they find?"

"It's too quick to tell. I think it's mostly to eliminate a few worst-case-scenario things. I doubt they'll come back positive."

"Worst case scenario? Like what?" he asks, the concern in his voice rising.

"Um, brain tumors, cancer, the big dangerous things. I think they're just trying to cover their asses."

"Mmm…"

His face is stern, agitated. His lips pursed in a tight line.

"What?" I ask.

"It's just interesting, that's all." The way he says it implies his attitude is back.

"What about it?" I ask.

"I just… I didn't realize this was so serious."

"I don't know… I hope not. I just want to find out what's going on at this point. If it's serious I guess I'd rather know than be ignorant. I just need an answer."

I look out the window, watching as we pass one streetlight after another along the suburban, tree-lined road.

"I just wish I had known before," he says, letting out a sigh. "I wish you had told me."

"What do you mean?" I ask. "I am telling you."

"I mean before all…" He pauses to gesture between us. "…this."

He can't possibly be saying what I think he's saying. He wishes that he knew how sick I was before our relationship because he wouldn't have dated me?

No. Hell no. He doesn't mean that.

"What do you mean by that?" I ask.

"I mean I wish I had been able to make an informed decision. When we started dating, I didn't know you were sick. You didn't tell me you had all these problems."

My heart suddenly drops.

"Why?" I ask. "Do you not want to be with me?"

"I'm not saying that. I'm already in love with you. It's done now."

"Wow, how romantic," I say, my voice becoming more and more full of anger.

"I mean, I love you now so whatever. I'm just saying I would have liked the choice."

"You would have chosen not to love me?" I ask.

"I dunno… Maybe."

I'm angry. I'm hurt. All of these feelings of being broken come bubbling to the surface. Nobody wants the sick girl. No—not sick—broken. People feel bad for sick people. A sick person has a name for the thing that makes their body betray them. They put a label on it and people love them and take care of them and wish them well. When your body aches for no reason to the point of exhaustion, when unexplained dizzy spells and nausea interrupt your life, and every test comes back negative, you're not sick. You're just broken.

I can't tell if I feel like throwing up because of the alcohol I overindulged in tonight, because of the things Mike is saying to me, or because my stupid body is yet again failing me.

My head is spinning and all my insecurities are laid right there in front of me. *He's right. Nobody wants this. Nobody wants me.*

"Yeah," he says after a long pause. "I probably would have."

"Fuck you!" I snap at him.

"Oh that's real charming, Ava." He scoffs.

"I wasn't aiming for charming. I was aiming for *FUCK YOU!*" I scream.

"Hey, whoa! Calm down. I'm with you, aren't I? I love you now. I'm already in this."

"Well, allow me to let you out of this then," I say, my voice dripping with rage.

I don't care if I'm broken or unlovable or whatever the fuck I am; I'm so pissed and I'll be damned if I let Mike see me cry over the cold, heartless words coming out of his mouth right now.

"I don't want to be let out, that's what I'm saying. I'm attached to you now."

"Oh, well if you're *attached*," I say with sarcasm, "Pull over."

"Ava," he says in a serious tone. "I'm not letting you out to walk alone. It's like, another three miles to your apartment."

"Let. Me. Out."

"No," he says. "You're being immature right now. Let me finish driving you home and we can talk about this."

I'm furious and I feel tears rising in my eyes.

"Let me the fuck out right now, Mike, or so help me I will jump out of this moving car!"

"Jesus Christ. Fuck. Fine."

He pulls over with a swift motion. I swing open the door and jump out.

"Oh, come on, Ava. Get back in the car, please? I love you."

"Go fuck yourself," I say with my middle finger in the air as I walk away.

Knowing Mike, he's going to follow me home, or attempt to coax me back in the car. I just want to be alone but I don't know how to get him to leave.

His tires screech against the pavement as he turns his car around and peels off in the other direction.

So much for that theory. He definitely just left.

The tears suddenly fall out of my eyes all at once, as if the dam has suddenly broken. I erupt into a heavy sob.

After ten minutes of walking, the ache in my muscles that was dulled by the alcohol is back with a fury. Everything is throbbing. Am I going to have to call an Uber to pick me up with tear-stained cheeks on a random section of road just to drive me the last couple miles to my apartment? Fucking great.

I reach for my phone, but find nothing but the empty pocket of my jeans.

Fuck. I left it in Mike's car.

———•———

ZANE

I was feeling a bit better after Kieran paired off with that girl for the evening, but now that I'm driving back these negative feelings are rushing back.

Why do I care this much?

I don't know this girl, so why am I wrapped up in her? Why was I desperate to get Kieran to go for her mate? Why did I want so badly to make him go away so I could have her to myself?

If I didn't know better, I'd say this was exactly what Siren venom does. That intense obsession, that craving for someone. A deep, all-encompassing attraction that takes over your brain, forcing you to make decisions you'd never make in your right mind.

The only problem is that Siren venom doesn't work on Sirens.

This feeling is equal parts intoxicating and nauseating. I've had passion before, maybe even love once or twice. But never with a human, and never—never—this instantaneously.

Her grey eyes flash into my mind.

Fuck. I'm so screwed.

I shake out my shoulders and toss my head side to side in an attempt to refocus. I turn and watch as the traffic lights ahead all light up green, undoubtedly due to it being 2 am and my car being the only one on the road.

I look ahead toward the park and see a figure walking in the distance. My eyes focus on what seems to be purple hair.

Ava.

Fuck, no way. Nope. I've lost the plot and I'm full-on hallucinating this woman now. As I pull closer, I swear it looks more and more like her.

Why would she be walking along the road in the middle of the night? I thought she went home with her boyfriend.

Did something happen? Is she in trouble?

My mind immediately flashes to the worst case scenario.

Did he hurt her? Did she have to run from him?

I'm instantly filled with rage, my blood boiling beneath my skin. I hear a loud crack and look down to see a three-inch chunk of steering wheel in my hand. Fuck.

I try to regain composure and slowly pull up next to her, rolling down my passenger side window.

"Ava?" I call. "Are you okay? Do you need a ride?"

She turns to me and I see her flushed red face, her eyes teary and raw.

I'm going to kill that bastard.

"Heyyy," she says, her voice weak and heartbroken. "I um… I'm okay. I just… it's a long story. I lost my phone and my house is close so I was just walking back but I'm just… I… yeah I'm fine."

I can't stand to see her like this. She looks completely gutted—devastated beyond measure. I'm not about to leave her alone.

"It's no trouble, love," I say. "You said your house is close, anyway, right? It's really not a problem."

"Oh, um… I…" she stutters. She looks at me with uneasy eyes. After running into her twice already today, I most-definitely look like a stalker.

"How 'bout I let you borrow my phone then?" I suggest. "You can call your mates or order an Uber?"

I reach across to the window and hold out my phone. I have no intention of letting her call a ride, but I need to get her closer.

Alright, yeah now I'm realizing why she might think I'm a creep.

She reluctantly walks to the car and grabs for my phone. As our hands touch, I stare into her grey eyes.

"It's safe to let me take you home," I say.

She pauses for a moment, then releases my phone from her grasp.

"Actually," she says, "yeah if you wouldn't mind, I could really use a ride home."

I reach over and open the passenger side and she hops in. She gives me a little half smile and mentions her flat is up ahead in a couple of miles.

"So what happened?" I ask. "I mean, you don't have to tell me. I don't mean to pry." I'm not used to having to ask for something politely, but I don't feel comfortable charming her with my powers. I want our interactions to be genuine. I want her to want to tell me.

"Well, let's just say you may have been right about Mike being an '*arse.*'"

The way she put air quotes around arse makes me chuckle, but then I consider the implications of what she just said and my rage returns.

"Did he hurt you?" I ask through a clenched jaw.

"No, nothing like that. We just had a fight."

"And he left you on the side of the road?!"

"No, no. I mean, he did—but I explicitly insisted he did."

The thought of it makes me smirk a bit. I imagine her slamming the door and stomping off in a fury. That suits her. I wonder how he set her off.

"What did he do for you to feel that way?" I ask.

"He just said something shitty. It's not a big deal, I just really didn't want to be in the car with him.“

"So, are you two broken up?"

Yesss. Brilliant.

"Yeah? I don't know," she says softly. "We kind of left it in a weird place. Oh, turn here."

I turn down her street.

"That's me, the brownish-grey building." She points to a small apartment building and I pull up.

I step out of the car and walk around to open her door. I offer my hand to help her up and the moment we touch I'm lost again in her.

Something's not right. In the quiet, I can hear her heart beating, blood traveling through her veins, oxygen filling her lungs. But there's a wrongness to it that I can't quite pinpoint. As soon as she stands up she wobbles and falls, my arms catching her before she hits the ground.

"I'm okay, I'm okay," she said, almost as if she's convincing herself.

"I think you've had too much to drink tonight," I say. "You need to rest. Here, I'll walk you to your door."

———◆———

AVA

Zane carefully leads me up the steps to my apartment. It's so embarrassing that I just practically fainted over there. It's hard to say if it's a dizzy spell or if I'm just drunk. He certainly seemed to think it was just the alcohol. Maybe that's because to him, I'm not broken. I'm a normal girl and everything's fine. I'm not the girl nobody wants. I'm not damaged. I'm not a burden.

The feeling of his hand on my lower back ignites my nerves as he gently guides me up the stairs. In the light of day he's handsome, but up close, shrouded in a haze of alcohol and emotion, he's incredible. I want to be the normal girl he sees right now. One that someone would want.

I grab my keys and unlock my door. I turn back to him, a subtle smile on his face. *I could be that girl. Just for this moment.*

I reach my hand to his cheek and he seems startled—anxious almost—but doesn't pull away.

"Ava, I..." he says. He looks like he's trying to express something, struggling to find the words. It's as if he's having a battle inside his head.

I lean in closer.

In an instant, his lips crash into mine and I'm overcome with a sense of euphoria. Tingling spreads from my lips to the base of my spine and my whole body feels relaxed.

His kiss becomes more intense, more urgent—almost desperate. He pushes me into the house and slams the door behind us. My body collides with the wall as he sinks his hands into my hips and presses his chest to mine.

He scoops me up, my legs wrapping around his waist as he kisses my neck.

His eyes again seem an intense, radiant green as they meet mine.

I lean to kiss him and he freezes, pulling me off him in a sudden swift motion. I don't know why he's stopping now, but I'm not ready for this to end.

I try to pull him closer but he recoils, quickly putting the room's width of distance between us.

"Sorry, Ava," he says through shaky breaths. "I-... I can't."

"You can't what?" I say, but as the words leave my lips he's out the door. The sounds of his footsteps echo through the hall as he practically sprints down the stairs.

I'm shocked, hurt, upset. But I also feel a peace that I haven't felt in a long time.

That is, until Mike pops into my head.

Oh crap. Mike.

5

 ZANE

Fuck fuck fuck fuck fuck.

I rush into my car and slam the door with such force that the car shakes violently. I sink my fist into the dashboard; the blades of the air conditioning vents snap as a small section of console crumples under my touch.

Fuck.

What just happened?

Why did I have to kiss her?

I've spent a lifetime building up the strength to defy my urges, but in just seconds alone with this woman my resolve shattered.

It's been years since the last time I felt compelled to kiss someone. Decades since I actually went through with it. And a human? Almost never. For me, physical touch is a means to an end—a transaction.

With a human, my kiss takes away their inhibitions. It sends them into a fog of lust toward whomever they're attracted to. In Sirens, a kiss helps the body repair. But it's always clinical, controlled.

In my youth, I would let my urges get the best of me. I'd take advantage of humans for whatever I wanted, without regard for who it harmed. But I knew it was never real, and that made it all feel empty. So now I keep my distance from humans.

Yet tonight, this one girl slipped past all my defenses. A lifetime of building self-control and discipline was all but meaningless against a pair of grey eyes.

It plays over in my mind again: her gentle hand against my face, the sudden surge of adrenaline, her lips connecting with mine, my hands intertwined with strands of purple hair…

Fuck.

My senses are on fire, my chest feels heavy, and my mind is clouded with need for her.

I start my car and drive over to Kieran's. The odds of him having a girl over are good, but I can't be alone with my thoughts right now.

———◆———

As I knock on Kieran's door, I find my fist banging more intensely than intended. I'm trying to be cool, but my heavy breathing and the frantic drumming in my chest will almost certainly give me away.

"Hey bro," he says with a confused look as he opens the door. "What's going on? Aren't you supposed to be sleeping or something?"

"Yeah, er… sorry mate, do you have company?"

"Nah," he says with a shrug and a gesture to come in. "What's up? You're…"

He pauses and his eyes narrow as he takes in a deep breath.

"You were… with Ava?" he asks, with a tone that could easily read as confusion or anger.

He can smell her on me—of course he can. I didn't think it would be that obvious. He has had his eyes on her since he first met her in the elevator. I can see his chest puffing up as a mixture of hurt and rage flash across his face.

"Did you just…" he says, stumbling through thoughts. "But… I wanted… You said you weren't interested. You said…"

"I know. I'm a bloody idiot. I don't know what happened."

His expression seems to soften and a smirk almost appears.

"Holy hell, man!" he exclaims. "You like her!"

I can't tell if this is better or worse than Kieran trying to beat the shit out of me. His grin is growing increasingly more smug by the second.

Yep. This is officially worse.

"I don't…" I start to say. "I mean, I didn't like her. I made a mistake. I shouldn't have, but… she needed a ride home and I gave her one, then she came up to me like she was going to kiss me, and I just had a moment of weakness."

"*You?*" Kieran says. "*You* lost control? The big bad Iron Siren? Mister Will Power—Mister Don't-Get-Involved—suddenly lets a human seduce him?"

"It was a kiss, alright? One lapse."

We each take a seat on either side of his rust-colored sofa as Kieran switches the TV off with the remote.

"You reek of arousal," he smirks.

"Oh, piss off."

"Still, dude. This is big. You've never had a relationship. I've never seen you show any interest in anyone. I know you've had a few flings in the past with other Immortals, but…"

"Calm down, mate. I'm not gonna marry her. I'm probably never even gonna see the girl again."

"Can you even *have* a relationship with a human?"

"No," I say. "But I wasn't going to."

"Do you just make them perpetually lust-crazy or what?"

"After a while, in theory, a Siren's kiss can drive a human insane."

The thought sends an uncomfortable feeling to my stomach. I mean, I don't want a relationship with this girl. This is just a fluke. I just don't like the idea that it would be impossible.

"Ahh," he says. "That's right. Going mad, crashing their ships into the coastline and whatnot."

"*In theory*," I say. "I've heard it as a rumor, but I've never known anyone who has tried to stay with a human for very long."

"How much credit can you really give those nonsense old legends, anyway? Didn't they also make you all out to be sexy ladies with fish parts?" he says with a laugh.

I roll my eyes. The mermaid thing just won't die. Sirens have had wings since the dawn of time, yet somewhere along the line some wanker saw a manatee and had to rope us into his weird fish tales.

"You're supposed to be a three-foot-tall, furry elf," I say with a smirk.

Kieran lets out a laugh.

"Touché," he says.

I spend the next twenty minutes explaining what went down after I left the bar: finding Ava after her fight with her boyfriend, driving her home, the kiss.

"So, what makes this girl so special, then?" Kieran asks.

"Nothing," I say.

Liar.

Everything about her seems special to me. Her grey eyes. The way she walks the line between being tough and sensitive and doesn't seem to care what anyone has to say about it.

"So you just kissed her, got her all lust-crazy, and then bailed?"

"I mean, that's not exactly how I'd put it, but yeah."

"You got her all worked up, and then you left her there. Alone."

"Yeah," I repeat. "So what?"

"You do realize the boyfriend is probably going to come back, right? And now she's all dosed with Siren venom and good to go."

My heart stops.

"Oh, bloody hell."

Kieran breaks out into a fit of laughter.

"First you set up her friend at the bar, and now you're hooking these two up," he says. "Aren't you just a little supernatural matchmaker?"

My fists tighten until my knuckles are pure white. I can't get the image out of my head now—that cunt from the bar touching her, exploiting the effects of my venom on her system. My head feels feverish and I want to punch through a wall. *She can't be with him. Fuck no.*

"I'll kill you," I say, my voice thick with rage over a low growl.

"Jesus, man, calm down. I'm not the one who got you in this situation, am I?"

I try to relax, but I feel my blood pressure rising.

"Yeah, I know, alright?"

"Man," he sighs. "This girl has really got you under her spell. If I didn't know any better, I'd say *she* was the Siren."

"Very funny."

"Either that or you're getting high off your own supply."

He's not wrong. This is precisely what our venom does to humans. It makes them lose control, causes a single-minded obsession with the object of their affection, and heightens their arousal.

No, that's not possible. I can't be affected by my own venom.

Can I?

———•———

AVA

I'm jarred awake by the shrill ring of my doorbell.

Ugh. What time is it?

According to the clock on my nightstand and the light peeking through my curtains, it's almost noon. I drag myself out of bed, my muscles aching to a degree that should really be reserved for being run over by a monster truck. Lifting myself to stand is an impossible task and my head is pounding from my unfortunate choice to overdo the drinking last night.

Oh god. Last night.

I walk out into the living room and up to the door.

My mind flashes back to the fight with Mike. Kissing Zane. Zane bolting out the door.

Good job Ava—you're walking man repellent.

The doorbell chimes again. I know who is on the other side of that door and I really don't want to open it, but I know I don't have a choice.

I open the door to reveal Mike standing with his hands in his pockets, a slouched posture, and an apologetic expression.

"Hey," I say.

"Hey," he replies. He holds out my phone. "You left this in my car last night."

"Thanks," I say, grabbing it.

"Can we talk?" he asks.

I nod and invite him in. He sits in a chair in the corner and I take the sofa. My memory flashes again to last night, Zane and I in this same room. I cringe at the awkwardness of this whole moment.

"I'm sorry," Mike says. He looks at me like those words will solve everything.

"You told the truth. That's all I can ask of you."

"So we're good?" he asks.

I sigh and shrug.

"I mean… no. I'm sorry, but how can I be with someone who thinks being with me is a mistake? Who thinks loving me is a mistake?"

"I didn't say that. You just put me in a position where I fell in love with someone, and now I have to worry about you and worry about losing you."

"I don't think it's just that, Mike. I think you don't want a girlfriend who has problems. Who can't go out with you any time you want. Who has to take the elevator instead of the stairs. You see me as broken, and because you do, I do."

"Maybe that's true," he says. "But I'm not saying I'm leaving you. I said I love you. I said I'd stay because I love you."

"I don't want to be with someone who sees me as a burden," I say. I can feel tears building in my eyes.

"Are you breaking up with me?" he asks, looking almost more furious than hurt.

"I'm sorry, Mike, but yes. I am."

His eyes fill with anger and his expression hardens.

"You think someone else is going to love you?" he snaps. "We got together before this stuff got really bad, and you think you can just go out and find someone now who's not going to see this stuff as a liability? You're worse off now than you've ever been. I decided to stay with you. Nobody else is gonna make that choice."

His words cut to the bone. They feed that little voice inside my head that tells me I am fundamentally damaged. That I'm more trouble than I'm worth.

"Then I'll be alone," I say, "but I'm not staying with someone who thinks that they're stuck being in love with me."

He stands up and stomps his way to the door.

"Fine," he says. "I couldn't have tolerated you for much longer anyway."

He slams the door behind him.

6

"Heeyyyyy! Where have you been?!" Jen's voice says on the other end of the phone.

"Hey," I say, trying not to sound like I've been crying. "Sorry, I left my phone in Mike's car."

"What's wrong?" she says, her tone suddenly serious.

"Mike and I broke up."

"Oh," she says. "I'm so sorry, honey. What did he do?"

"It… he just… he didn't love me the way I think he should have."

"Damn right," she replies, matter of factly. "I'm sorry, hon. I don't mean to be insensitive. It's just… I tried so hard to like him. I *really* did. But from day one I just thought he did not deserve you."

"Thanks," I say. I don't know whether or not she'd still feel that way if she knew everything that happened last night with Zane. On the shitty girlfriend scale, I'm pretty sure making out with a handsome British stranger after denying flirting with him is kind of top-of-the-charts.

"What?" Jen asks. I guess she's now progressed to just straight mind reading.

"I don't think he's entirely at fault here. Or a least, I'm not blameless."

"What do you mean?"

"I uh… I kind of made a mistake. You remember that British guy, Zane, from last night?"

"Yeeahhh…?"

"Well he ended up driving me back to my place and we sort of… kissed."

"Woohooo! Yessss!" she cheers. "Wait, I swear you said Mike was taking you home."

"Yeah, it's a long story, but… woohoo? You're not disappointed in me? I'm not a giant whore-y whoreball from whoreville?"

"Okay," Jen says with a giggle. "First of all, I'm totally going to use that in the future. Whore-y whoreball from whoreville? That's amazing. Couldn't have done it better myself. Secondly, that guy was ridiculously good looking and honestly I've been 'Team Anyone-But-Mike' for quite a while now."

"Is that so?"

"Yeah, but you can't tell your friend that you hate who they're dating. It's a one-way ticket to your friend never talking to you again."

"I wouldn't do that," I say.

"Come on, I wasn't about to open that can of worms. People always shoot the messenger on those kinds of things."

"Fair enough…"

"So, how was it? Macking on the man candy?"

"'Man candy?'"

"I mean he's got that accent, and he's pretty great-looking…" she says. "For a dangler, that is."

"Okay new subject!" I say. "If we're talking details… how was your make-out sesh with Miss Bartender?"

"Ohmygod Ava, sooooo good!"

I feel like I'm about to regret having asked…

———•———

ZANE

I approach Kami's crisp white, Spanish-style estate. The entrance is flanked by elaborate topiaries. The rounded double doors are made of thick, dark wood and are almost twice as tall as most. A wrought iron chandelier hangs above. As I press the doorbell, a regal chime echoes on the other side of the doors. After a moment, they swing open.

"Well look what the cat dragged in!" Kami says, pulling me in for a hug. Her eyes catch Kieran standing behind me and her expression changes immediately. "Oh. You brought *him*."

"Aww, Kams," Kieran says with a grin. "If ya missed me you could've just called!"

She glares at him and I can tell she's debating whether or not to sock him in the face for calling her Kams. She seems to decide against it and guides us both inside. The estate is massive, with lofted ceilings, marble floors, and antique furniture.

"This is your place?" Kieran asks.

"Sort of," she says. "It was given to me to use as long as I want it."

"Given to you?" he asks.

"If you haven't noticed, people tend to give me what I want," she says.

"Damn, Zane, why don't *you* have a mansion?" he asks.

"Not everybody wants a mansion, Kieran. Besides…" I say, giving Kami a bit of a glare. "Some of us like to be *discreet*."

She looks like she's considering snapping at me but again decides against it. It seems we've caught her in a good mood.

"So, you weren't very specific in your text. You had something you wanted to discuss?" she asks.

"Yeah, uh…" I pause for a minute.

Where do I even start?

"Zane's in loooove!" Kieran teases.

"Piss off, mate."

Kami looks at me, gobsmacked. "What??" she asks.

"I'm not in love," I grumble. "I just… what do you know about Sirens being susceptible to venom?"

"We aren't," she says matter-of-factly. "Why are you asking?"

"He's in luuurrrhhhvvvl!" Kieran says. *He's being a right git today.*

"Seriously, I *will* end you."

He waves his hands in the air in surrender.

"You're in love with another Siren?" she asks. "Who??"

"I'm *not* in love," I huff. "But uh… I'm just wondering, is it possible? Could I be affected by my own venom?"

She takes a moment and gives me a once over and looks deep into my eyes.

"No dilated pupils," she says. "No sweating. Heart rate sounds normal. Even if it was possible, and honestly it's not, you don't have any of the classic signs. Why did you think you might be?"

Kami has always had lovers, some more long-lasting than others, but I've spent most of our lives hearing about *her* relationships. Now that the circumstances are reversed, it feels foreign.

If I told her it was a human I was feeling these things about, she would surely tell me what I already know: it's impossible. Humans are too fragile. Every time I kiss her she could be inching closer to insanity. Even if that weren't true, she's mortal and she will age and die.

"I just felt kind of… out of control for a moment," I answer.

"He's obsessed," Kieran adds. "He lost control and he kissed her. Then he showed up to my house with his heart racing, breathing heavy—he was a mess."

Kieran chuckles at my expense.

"Wow," Kami says, her jaw slack with shock. "*You* lost control? Holy crap. Wha-… who is she?"

"She's human," Kieran answers.

"Human?" she asks, her eyes growing wider still. "Wow."

"I know," I say. "It's a bad idea. I get it."

"No," she says. "I'm just surprised. Your past affairs were always Immortals. And everything with them was so intentional, careful. Ever since, well… you know. I'm just surprised it's a human who's having this effect on you."

"It's impossible anyway," I say.

"It's not impossible. It's… difficult. I've done it once or twice, that is, had a relationship with a human."

"You have?" I ask.

I knew she had relationships that I didn't know about. It never occurred to me they might be with humans.

"Yeah," she says. "But uh… it's tough. You can't kiss them without triggering that lust instinct. It's hard to tell what's real, if any of it. And you have to be careful with what you say when you touch them. Our touch can make them suggestible even when we don't mean to."

"What about the whole madness thing? Is it real?" I ask, unsure if I want to know the answer.

"I don't think so," she says. "I mean those relationships only lasted about six months or so each. Maybe with more time it could have. But I don't think it's real. I've never heard of it happening to anyone in real life."

"That's good news then!" says Kieran. "You can stop losing your shit and just ask her out. Or just get it out of your system and have sex with her already."

"I already told you," I say, "I'm not interested. It was one mistake, alright?"

"Oh please!" he says. "You're obsessed. You're going crazy. You're jealous as hell."

"I'm not jealous."

"Oh yeah?" he says. "Then you won't mind if I take a shot at her?"

I feel an instant tension in my chest and my jaw clenches. He's trying to get himself killed, I swear.

"Go for it," I say through my gritted teeth. He wouldn't dare.

"She a good kisser?" he asks, taunting me.

"Get fucked!" I say. The words launch out of me with a fury.

"Maybe I will," he quips, with a cheeky smile.

Before I can think, my fist connects with his jaw and he's launched across the floor. The look on his face is one of disbelief. Kieran and I have fought before, but he's always been the one to start it. I turn to Kami, whose face is equally stunned. Kieran bursts into laughter.

"Daaayyummmnn!" he says. "That wasn't a bad punch, Zane! Have I finally found a button to push in you?"

I do my best to recover my cool demeanor and force my fists to loosen.

"Sorry," I say, offering him a hand up. "I uh… I don't know why I… sorry."

Why did I hit him? Am I jealous? Why do I care?

I've known this girl for one day, and she has a boyfriend anyway.

Kieran stands, readjusting his clothing and brushing the hair from his face.

I look over to Kami, who seems curious. I notice a bandage on her arm that I hadn't seen when we came in. Was that from yesterday's incident?

"What happened there?" I ask. Anything to change the subject at this point.

"Oh, yeah," she shrugs. "I got sliced by a Harpy last night."

"How did you even run into a Harpy?"

"I was asked by a rather powerful Immortal to track down a fugitive who was rumored to be in Port Charlotte. I asked a few of my contacts for information and they led me to that Seer and a Harpy who might have been helping this guy. As you might have guessed—the Harpy wasn't super interested in talking either. These Immortal jobs are the worst because I can't use my powers, so I have to bargain whatever I can or hope I can hold my own in a fight."

"You should have asked me for venom," I say.

"I had just asked you earlier that day," she says. "Besides, I need to be able to handle myself every now and then."

"If you're going to keep ending up in these situations, why don't I give you some extra venom for emergencies?" I suggest.

"That's a good idea, actually," she says, stepping out into the kitchen.

"Wait," Kieran interjects. "Why have you never offered *me* that?"

Giving my venom to an Incubus is asking for trouble, even if he is my friend. He can still be reckless and, by his nature, he's overwhelmed by his urges. Although, some would say that about Sirens too.

"Because she needs it to live. You need it to get laid."

Kieran rolls his eyes at me. "I need to get laid to live!" he says.

"You're not starving any time soon."

He huffs, crosses his arms, and slumps into an armchair.

Maybe Kieran does act like my pet.

Kami returns with a small vial in her hand.

"Here," she says, tossing it to me. "If you wouldn't mind."

I press the vial under my tongue and wait until it's about half full before capping it and handing it back to her.

"Thanks," she says with a mischievous expression. "Now you can get back to defending your *girlfriend's* honor."

———•———

AVA

Ever since Jen met her new girl, she has practically dropped off the face of the earth, so when she asked me to join her for drinks at Pike's, I reluctantly agreed.

I don't really want to risk running into Zane after the incident last weekend, but she assured me Shayna would be bartending this weekend so there's no reason for them to be there. Then again, she was bartending the last time too. I still don't know why Zane took off that night and honestly I'd rather just pretend the whole thing never happened. He probably thinks the worst of me since he knew I was dating Mike when I kissed him.

As I walk up to Pike's, I scan my periphery constantly. This part of town has always creeped me out. The buzzing neon sign above the door triggers memories of last weekend. Meeting Mike and Jen here. Running into Zane and Kieran, before I even knew their names. The fight with Mike. Then Zane and the kiss.

Pike's is equal parts trashy dive and cozy hometown pub. The walls are plastered with a collage of framed patron photos, kitschy signs, and graffiti. The main area has a classic wood bar with red stools and scattered tables to match. The back room holds two pool tables where big burly men who look like they belong in a biker gang are playing pool.

I look around and let out a sigh of relief as Kieran and Zane are nowhere to be found. That's one awkward conversation I don't have to have tonight. Shayna is tending bar while Jen sits on a stool looking longingly in her direction.

"Hey!" I say, sitting beside Jen at the bar.

"Heyyyy! There's my little whoreball!" she says.

Oh great, so that's gonna be a thing now.

"I'm so sorry I've been so absent this week," she says. "I know you're going through a breakup and I meant to check in, but work has been the absolute worst and I had to pick up three extra shifts."

Jen is a lab tech at a local company that does forensic testing for a handful of police departments in the state.

"Hopefully that's not because there's a serial killer on the loose," I say, mostly joking.

"No!" she giggles. "We're just short-staffed! Although, there were two weirdly similar deaths that we've done a bunch of testing on and can't figure out. Isn't that spooky?"

"I'd rather not know about that."

"Okay," she says with a laugh. "You asked!"

Jen catches me up on her and Shayna. It turns out they haven't seen each other much either. I thought I was getting blown off, but it turns out Jen's work really *was* taking up all her time. Shayna intermittently swings by to chat and grab us more drinks. Jen tells me about her obnoxious coworker and the latest episode of The Bachelor. I tell her that I haven't seen Mike since he dropped off my phone but have heard from friends that he's been talking about me behind my back. Jen has a few choice expletives to assign him.

"So what's the deal with Zane? You gonna call him?" she asks.

"I don't have his number," I say, hoping she doesn't feel the need to pry for details.

"You kissed, but you didn't get his number? How does that happen?"

"Well, he kind of left quickly."

"Left quickly? I don't understand. What does that mean?"

"Well," I say. "We kissed and it got kind of intense and then just… he just took off, Jen. It was so weird. I feel like I must've done something wrong."

"He didn't say anything?"

"He said 'I'm sorry, I can't.'"

"Can't what? Can't kiss you? Can't have sex?"

"I don't know… I think he meant because I have a boyfriend."

"He's probably gay," she says. "I mean, he's incredibly pretty—like weird-pretty. Sure, he doesn't seem all that gay, but he's British so that totally throws off my gaydar."

"I did not get the impression he was gay," I say. "You just think everyone's gay."

"Yeah, girl. Everyone *is* gay! It's not my fault the hot Brit probably polishes bats for the other team."

"What's that now, love?" a familiar voice says behind us.

The color drains from Jen's face as she realizes she's been busted.

Well, this is awkward.

7

"Uhhh…" Jen says with wide eyes. "Nothing."

Yep. This is reeaaally awkward.

"Have a theory you care to share?" Zane asks.

Jen seems to be internally debating how to handle this.

"Just talking about this lame-ass guy who made out with Ava and then panicked and bailed on her. Gotta be gay, right?"

She must be drunk enough to have hit the 'particularly bold' threshold. My cheeks feel hot with embarrassment. Zane raises his eyebrows and smirks.

"Fair dues," he says, taking a seat next to me at the bar. "That guy does sound like a lame arse."

He smiles at me and I instantly melt.

"What do you think, Ava? You think you might give this bloke a second chance?"

I can't even think straight when this man is talking to me, let alone smiling at me.

"Um… I guess we'll see."

In a moment, Kieran appears and slings his arm around Zane's shoulder.

"What's up, ladies?" he asks. "This guy giving you a hard time?"

"Hey Kieran!" Jen says. "How's it going?"

"Better now," he says, smiling at us both. "We weren't planning on staying long, I was just grabbing my paycheck, but if you gals are here I could be persuaded to stick around."

This guy is such a smooth talker. Kieran looks at me for a moment and touches a loose strand of my hair.

"You know," he says. "This purple is quickly becoming my favorite color."

Zane's eyes narrow and I see that same green shade in them that I saw the other night.

"Hey," he says, with a hand to Kieran's chest. "Pretty sure nobody asked."

"Touchy touchy!" Kieran says, taking a step back. "It's nice seeing you, Ava."

Kieran smiles then leans in to me and whispers, "I'd love to get to know you better, but my friend here is literally crazy about you, so I better not." He walks away toward the bar's back office.

Zane is crazy about me? Is that what he means? My chest fills with warmth and butterflies.

"What was that about?" Zane asks.

"Nothing," I say. I can tell it's already driving him nuts not knowing, but after he ducked out on me so suddenly last weekend I'm happy to get a little revenge. He shifts uneasily in his seat.

"Do you want to go somewhere?" he asks. "I feel like it's impossible to talk in here."

I don't know why I feel like agreeing to this, but I'm drawn to him.

"Where?" I ask.

"I know a place."

———※———

Zane pulls his car into the Powell Center parking structure. His cobalt-blue Challenger with racing stripes along its hood was out of place in the Pike's parking lot, but in this area of town it's just one of many flashy cars.

The Powell Center is the tallest building in the city and houses the big financial offices and law firms. He hops out and makes his way over to the lot attendant. By the time I reach them, the attendant is scanning a card at the elevator.

What are we doing here?

We step inside the elevator and my mind is lost as to why we're here. Does he work here? Did he say what he does for a living? I can't remember. The floor numbers continue to climb. 22… 23… 24…

"Where are we going?" I ask.

"Well, I'd tell you, love," he says with a grin. "But that would spoil the surprise."

I'm pretty sure he's not leading me here to be murdered in this high rise office building. Pretty sure. We continue upward, passing 30, then 40.

The elevator finally dings as we reach level R. Does that mean roof? I mean, if you were going to kill someone, I feel like throwing them off the roof would be a pretty good way to do it. But he's not going to murder me—right?

Pretty sure.

The elevator opens to a barren concrete rooftop overlooking the shining city below.

"So love, what do you think?" he asks.

"It's beautiful," I say. "How do you know about this place? Do you work here?"

"No," he says. "The, uh, attendant lets me up here sometimes."

"Are you friends?"

"In a sense."

"Ah, so we're going with the brooding and mysterious answers then?"

He laughs. "I wasn't aiming for that, no. I'm trying to answer your question honestly. You said you prefer people to be honest."

He does seem like he's choosing his words carefully. Why would he not want to tell me how he knows this guy?

"So then you and the parking guy are… together then?"

He chokes on a laugh.

"No. Me and the parking guy are not *together*. I take it your conversation with Jen led you in this direction?"

"I uh… maybe?"

He steps closer to me until we're just inches apart, putting one hand on my hip and bringing the other to my neck. He pulls me in closer, his lips nearly touching mine.

"Do you think I'm gay, love?"

I struggle to find words. All I can think about is how his hand feels at my waist, his touch on my skin.

Nope. The signals I'm picking up are pretty much the opposite of gay.

"I… uh… no. Not particularly."

"Good," he says with a smile as he steps away. "Just wanted to make sure you know where my interest lies." His eyes roam across my figure. With most men, this would be an unwanted intrusion, but with Zane I find myself wanting every last bit of his attention.

I'm speechless. One look from him has obliterated my ability to form a coherent sentence.

"I have a way with people," he says. "I've only met that bloke once or twice. I just talked him into letting me up."

"Really?" I ask. "Don't buildings like this have super tough security?"

"Like I said, love. I have a way with people."

"I guess you do," I say. I can't deny he certainly seems to have a way with me. We both sit down on the ground with our backs against a cement structure of some kind.

"So if we're asking questions, does that make it my turn?" he asks.

"I guess so. What do you want to know?"

"Where are you from?"

"That's your big deep question?" I ask with a laugh. "I grew up here in Port Charlotte, went to college in California, and came back here a little over a year ago after I got my degree. What about you?"

"Oh yeah, um… a little bit of everywhere. I was born in Greece but I didn't stay there long. Lived in England for a long time. One of my mates ran into some trouble over there and she asked me if I wanted to come to the States with her a few years back, so we did."

"What kind of trouble?" I ask. "Like, with the mob trouble?

"No," he says with a laugh. "There was a group of people there that weren't pleased with her. We needed some time away from all that."

"For someone who says they're not talking about the mob, you sure sound like you're talking about the mob."

He laughs again.

"I'm pretty sure it's my turn," he says.

"Fine. Ask away."

"Why are you with that guy?" he asks.

Oh geez. I really didn't expect that.

"Sorry," he says before I have a chance to answer. "It's none of my business."

"I'm not," I say. "With him, that is."

"Is that because of…"

"No, no. It was uh… a long time coming."

A smile creeps into his expression. If he's trying to look disappointed, he's failing miserably.

"Well, love, I want to say I'm sorry about that, but I'm not. Not one bit."

"Yeah, I can tell. You're clearly real torn up about it."

"Well, you know how I feel about him. And I think I've made it pretty clear how I feel about *you*."

I feel my cheeks redden and I rush to change the subject.

"So my turn. What do you do?"

"That's such an American thing to ask," he says.

"Well, I am an American, so I guess that makes sense then."

He pauses and wrings his hands for a moment.

"I don't technically have a job right now. I've been investing money and I used to be involved in several different things back in England, but I'm not officially working right now. What about you?"

"I do freelance coding and web design," I say.

"Ahh, so you're a nerd then."

I roll my eyes and playfully sock him in the shoulder. He turns and his eyes meet mine.

"What's something you love to do?" I ask.

"Hmm…" he says, combing a hand through his hair. "I collect coins. I like to keep coins from all the places I've lived and traveled."

"So you're a nerd then," I say with a smirk.

"Oi!" He laughs. "Cheeky girl."

When he smiles at me, all the feelings I felt on Friday come bubbling to the surface.

"Why did you leave Friday night?" I ask. The second the words leave my mouth I want to scoop them up and shove them back in.

His eyes widen and his mouth pinches shut.

"Was it because I had a boyfriend?" I ask.

My stupid mouth just keeps spouting out words.

"I uh… I think it was my turn," he says.

"Oh yeah, okay. Right, sorry."

"Why were you at the hospital the other day?" he asks.

Great, the one question I didn't want him to ask. Now it's out there. There's a voice in my head, maybe even Mike's voice, telling me he'll never accept me if I tell him the truth. That I'll cease being a normal girl in his eyes. That from here on I'll be the poor sick girl, not the sexy love interest.

There's yet another voice that tells me I've made a point about honesty now and I can't very well just lie. That voice is also saying, *'Fuck Mike and his bullshit.'*

"I went in for some blood tests. I've been having a lot of unexplained muscle pain and exhaustion and other stuff."

Well, it's out there now.

"Did they figure it out? With the tests?" he asks.

"I think you have to answer my question first."

He sighs and then smirks.

"Touché," he says, letting out another sigh. "Well, I didn't give a shit about that douche, I'll tell you that."

He sighs again, this time long and heavy, as he runs a hand through his hair. "I left because I'm a coward. Because I felt something with you that I hadn't felt in a really long time and I didn't want to take advantage of you."

I want to ask him what it was that he felt, but I know he's going to insist on me answering his question first. So instead, I lean in close and kiss him.

8

I can't believe I'm back in the doctor's office again. I've already waited twenty minutes in the lobby, another ten for the doctor to arrive, and another ten after the doctor left to order another blood test.

You know what sucks? Blood tests.

But of course this doctor wants to do yet another one.

You know what it's gonna test positive for? Blood.

I hear a tap at the door and a nurse wheels in a cart of blood testing supplies.

"Hi! Ava?" he says, reading from his clipboard. "I'm Trevor. I'm going to be taking some blood for your tests today."

The nurse is clean-shaven with short, shaggy, golden-blond hair. He has chiseled features and a tall, fit frame under light grey scrubs. He seems absorbed in looking over my chart and grabbing vials.

"So we're gonna take about three of these today," he says as he holds up an empty vial about the length of my pinkie.

Oh, joy.

He catches my eyes for a moment and smiles.

"I like the purple," he says, pointing at my hair.

"Oh, thanks," I say.

As he draws my blood I find myself looking away, still not quite able to stomach the sight of the whole thing. He seems to sense my discomfort and tries to make conversation.

"So it seems like they're testing for a lot of unpleasant things. You must be feeling pretty lousy," he says.

"Yeah," I say.

"That really sucks, I'm sorry. But you know, we see a lot of people in here and sometimes it takes a while to get answers, but there's always an answer."

I hope he's right. Sometimes it feels like there's no light at the end of this particular tunnel—just more blood tests.

"What do you do for a living?" he asks.

"I'm a web designer."

"Do you like it?" he asks.

"I do, yeah. I enjoy it and I get to work from home and set my own hours, which is helpful with all this going on."

"That's awesome," he says. "It's so important to find something you love to do."

"It's killer on the joints, though," I joke.

"You know, I help out with this occupational therapy program where they give you help setting up your work station and walk you through ways to help improve your posture and mobility for work. Would you like me to grab you some information on that?"

"That would be great, thank you!"

He pauses for a moment and applies a bandaid to my arm. He looks up at me with a smile as he adjusts his latex gloves.

"Have you heard of a band called Blue Panic?" he asks.

"Yeah," I said. "They were one of my favorite bands when I was in high school."

I can't believe this random nurse knows such an obscure punk band.

"I saw them last year and the lead singer had the same color purple hair," he says. "You totally remind me of her."

I smile. *The cute nurse thinks I look like a super hot rocker chick? Oh yeah, I'll take that.*

"Well, it was great meeting you Ava," he says, wheeling the cart out of the room.

What the heck is up with this hospital and the cute guys, man? Who needs Tinder when you have a rare, undiagnosable health condition.

I step out of my car and take a moment to check my reflection in the car window. I anxiously straighten and tug at my outfit a bit: black jeans, black ankle boots, a white fitted tee, and my favorite burgundy leather jacket. I'm aiming for casual, cool-girl-who's-totally-not-freaking-out-or-overthinking-this vibes. It's been a while since I've been on a first date—if this even counts as a first date.

Is it really a first date if you've already had an aggressive make-out session with the person?

Twice?

I check the time on my phone—12:23 pm.

Okay, he said he'd be here at 12:30, so if he's anything like Mike he'll be at least five minutes late, which…

I freeze when I see Zane just outside the café entrance. He's casually leaning against the wall in a nice black jacket and dark-wash jeans. He looks up and when his eyes meet mine, he straightens and seems to tuck something behind his back.

"Hey," I say as I walk up. "That wasn't suspicious at all."

He combs a hand back through his hair and lets out a breathy laugh.

"You caught me," he says, pulling out the arm he had tucked behind his back. He's holding a single rose. "I was second-guessing this particular gesture. It's a bit cliché, right?"

He looks almost nervous, which catches me by surprise. This man does not strike me as the type to doubt himself, yet here he is tentatively holding a rose out for me.

"It's very sweet," I say, reaching out to take it from his hand. "Thank you."

He shoves his hands in his pockets and smiles.

"I wasn't sure if that was something people still do… flowers and all that." He pushes the door open, gesturing for me to enter first. I walk in and he follows behind me. "It's been a few decades since my last proper date."

"A few decades?" I laugh. "I know what you mean. It feels like that for me too."

"Right." He gives me a tight smile and sweeps a lock of hair behind his ear.

We're shown to our table and Zane pulls out my chair for me. We spend a moment chatting over the menu and the waiter is back soon to take our orders. I'm doing my best to act cool when all I can really think about is how unreasonably pretty this man is.

As the waiter walks away, Zane slips off his coat, revealing a red plaid button up layered over a black tee that fits tight over his sculpted chest.

Okay, this man is too beautiful to be out on a date with me. Am I being pranked?

"So your friend Jen is pretty intense," he says.

"Intense?" I laugh. "That's one way to put it."

"In a good way. She speaks her mind. I like that. And she's clearly very protective of you. It's good to have friends like that."

"Seems like you and Kieran are close."

"Yeah, he can be the same way. Though Jen seems a bit more ready to throw hands—which, if you know Kieran, is really saying something."

"So true," I say with a laugh. "How long have you and Kieran been friends?"

"Oh we've been friends for… very… long."

I can't help but chuckle a little at the weird way he says it.

"Is that your way of saying you two used to date?" I ask.

He cringes and scrubs a hand over his stubbled chin.

"No. Hell no." He shakes his head and sighs. "I swear I'm not usually this bloody awkward. Just a touch rusty. I'm not used to people asking questions of me and… answering them."

"And you're still trying to claim you're not in the mob?"

"You clearly enjoy giving me hell, don't you love?" He leans back in his chair and crosses his arms over his chest with a playful half smile. "I see why you and Jen get along."

"That was definitely not an answer," I say. "I can't tell if you're question-dodging because you're really hiding some deep dark secret or if you're just trying for the brooding and mysterious vibes."

His brows jump and he tilts his head.

"Alright then, no more dodging. Ask me anything."

"Okay, ummm… what's the last crazy thing you did?"

"You mean, besides snogging a woman I had just met and then disappearing?"

I can't help but laugh at that, even though a blush is creeping up my neck.

"That's not something you usually do?"

"Never." He lets out a sound somewhere between a huff and a laugh.

"The '*snogging*' or the running away?"

"Both. I'm usually very… in control of my emotions. My mates love taking the piss about it."

"How so?"

"They make fun of me for being reserved."

"Isn't that normal for British people?" I ask. "Or is that just a stereotype?"

"For Brits, yes. For me and the groups I used to hang out with, it was quite uncommon. Our culture was very… passionate, fiercely protective, quick-tempered. It's said that we burn hotter than most."

"That doesn't seem like such a bad thing."

"It's complicated. It's something that I've tried very hard for a long time not to be."

"Maybe it's worth embracing," I say. "You said it yourself, being *intense* can be a good thing."

He hesitates, his gaze distant.

"I suppose it's just fear. When you burn that hot, you can burn people without meaning to."

"You're doing a terrible job of convincing me you're not in the mob."

"I must be rustier than I thought," he says with a soft laugh. "I've never had to work so hard to convince a date I'm neither in the mafia nor homosexual."

"Then you should probably stop saying things that gay mob bosses would say."

"Boss, eh? I guess I've moved up in the organization."

"I'm assuming the ranking is done based on who is the most broody."

"I knew it would be of use some day." His eyes crease at the edges as he smiles and takes a sip of his drink.

"Well, for the record…" I say. "At the risk of overstretching your metaphor, maybe fire is another one of those things that is both beautiful and dangerous. And you can either fear the danger or appreciate the beauty in it."

He sets his drink down, his eyes fixed on mine.

"You might be right."

9

 ZANE

As I walk through the door I'm hit with the familiar sights and sounds of Pike's. I head toward the bar and wave at Kieran as he serves another customer.

"Well look who's still alive!" he says, sliding me a beer. I haven't been to Pike's for a couple of weeks, pretty much since the night that we ran into Jen and Ava.

"Yeah, yeah," I say. "I've been busy, alright?"

"Jesus, you can say that again. I'm fucking starving, man. Your new girlfriend is officially getting in the way of your wingman duties."

"She's not my girlfriend," I say.

Fucking Kieran.

"Yeah, okay, man. Sure, she's not your girlfriend. She's just a girl you obsess over and you punch your best friend out when he makes a pass at her, and you're out with her so much I haven't seen you in weeks… but sure, yeah, she's not your girlfriend."

"I've only known her a couple weeks."

"And yet you're leaving me to fend for myself pretty much the entirety of those two weeks. The sex must be fuckin' fantastic."

I feel my jaw clench and I fight the urge to chuck this beer directly at his face.

"I wouldn't know," I say through my gritted teeth.

He looks at me, gobsmacked. "You don't know?"

"No, I don't know, okay? That proof enough for you that she ain't my bloody girlfriend?"

His jaw drops and the corners of his mouth curve up as though he's about to laugh.

Fucking Kieran.

"Holy shit, bro. You haven't closed the deal? Either you're really, truly interested in this girl or you've seriously lost your touch!"

"Piss off, Kieran."

"Whoa," he says teasingly. "Somebody's sensitive. Did I touch a nerve? Your powers not as effective with the ladies as they used to be?"

"Powers are just fine, mate. Don't need 'em anyway."

"Yeah right! Have you ever even seduced a woman without your powers?"

He's really testing me tonight.

"You serious? This coming from the bloke who's starving without me?"

"Hey!" he snaps. "I'm alive, aren't I? Obviously I have more game than you do if you haven't closed the deal with Ava."

The beer bottle shatters in my hand, the shattering glass attracting eyes from around the room. Kieran quickly grabs a towel and pretends to look at my hand for wounds.

"Wow, so subtle there, Z," a woman's voice says. I turn to see who it belongs to and meet Kami's grin. "You have to watch yourself. You know what happens if we get outed. Best case we get heat on us, worst case we attract attention from someone who wants to kill us. After all of these disappearances around town, it's probably best if you don't go around smashing bottles and making yourself a prime suspect."

"Don't blame me. This twat is trying to start something," I say nodding toward Kieran.

"He's a demon," she says. "That's kind of his M.O."

Kieran chuckles to himself, wiping beer off the counter.

"We're having a debate, here, Kami. Incubus versus Siren, who has more game?" he says.

"Please," she says. "Sirens. Hands down..."

"Without powers," Kieran chimes in, cutting her off.

"Oh ." she says, pausing for a moment. "Then I guess it depends on the individual."

"Me versus Zane," he says as he pours us each a shot.

"Oh, you're really underestimating Zane, here," she says. "You forget he's dated mostly other Immortals, a lot of Sirens in there too. He can't use his powers on them. Plus he's got the whole brooding, bad boy thing."

"Come on," he says. "I can do brooding bad boy." He rolls up his sleeves to reveal tattoos on both arms. He still has the tattoos he used to impress Ava.

"Why the fuck are those still there?" I ask.

"Why, bro? You got a problem with them?" he asks, all but egging me on.

"When did you get those?" Kami asks. "You shift them on?"

"Yeah, uh… Kinda did it by accident," he says.

"Ahhh, met a girl—or guy—who's into tattoos, I take it?" she asks.

"Girl, yeah."

For a moment he looks embarrassed. *Is he still trying to get to Ava?*

I feel heat rising in my chest.

"And you still have them?" she asks. "Just sleep with her and move on. Talk about no game… I'm sure Zane would've gotten the job done and moved on by now."

"Oh, I think you'd be wrong about that," he says with a mischievous grin.

I'm about to test the concept that an Incubus can't be killed. I'd like to see how he survives his head being ripped off.

I grab one of the shots off the counter and down it.

"That's it. You wanna play? We'll play. Pick anyone in this bloody bar. You and me, no powers. First one they invite back to theirs wins."

"Oh, it's on!" he says, scanning the room. "Blonde, black dress."

Leave it to Kieran to choose the most over-the-top-looking woman in this place. She has long, bleach-blond curled hair, heavy makeup, and a skin-tight dress that leaves nothing to the imagination. Her chest is practically spilling out. I should've known—she's exactly his type.

<hr>

Kieran and I have been chatting this girl up for 20 minutes and I'm so bored I almost don't care who wins.

Almost.

After the way Kieran has been getting under my skin today, if I'm not going to sock him in the jaw, I'm at least going to win this stupid game. I can't remember the last time I had to really try, let alone compete, for someone or something.

The blonde is currently laughing at some dumb joke Kieran has made. I'm clearly not winning at the moment; I need to bring it back. *Ugh. This girl is so not my type.*

She's not Ava.

Bloody hell. My stupid brain. Where did that come from?

I try to refocus on the conversation, but my eyes catch Kieran's inked forearms.

Are you fucking kidding me? He's chatting up this girl and he's still got Ava on his mind?

I want to tear the flesh from his bones, but right now I'll settle for winning this.

I stare at the girl, focusing until my alcohol-induced haze morphs her dull blue eyes into a soft grey, her blond hair into a vibrant purple. Her eyes meet mine and for a moment I forget she's this stranger in a bar.

"Sorry, love. I'm just so bloody captivated by you. I got lost for a moment."

She shifts in her seat, a blush creeping over her cheeks.

"Wow, um…" she bats her eyelashes, and for a second the facade fades and she's back to the random blonde.

Fuck. Focus.

"You've just got my head spinning," I say. Suddenly the words are pouring out of me and I can feel my subconscious speaking for me. "I just can't think straight. All I know is… I want to listen to every word you've ever wanted to say. I want all of you."

Part of me knows that the words coming out of my mouth are insane. I don't even know what I'm saying or what I mean. I'm too drunk to think straight.

Does she believe me? Does she believe these words are for her? Is this even what this woman wants to hear or is my brain just desperate to get the words out?

She leans closer to me, her eyes intense. It seems that my words are having their intended effect. She feigns a look of shyness while aggressively tracing her hand up the inside of my leg beneath the table.

"Hey, is that Ava?" Kieran's voice says.

I shoot up from my seat as though I've been fired from a cannon, knocking over the barstool and someone's drink as the table shakes.

Fuck fuck fuck.

My eyes scan the room but I don't see any sign of that purple hair. I look back to see Kieran helping the blonde clean the spilled drink off her dress with a napkin.

Fucking tosser.

10

My phone buzzes on the kitchen counter. I open it to see two missed calls from Jen and three missed text messages.

Zane

Hey love. What you up to?

Headed to Pike's later with Kieran. Will I see you there?

Jen

Grrl answer ur phoonnnee

Ugh. I'm so tired and all this hanging out with Zane and going to the bar with Jen has me even more worn out than usual. The only downside about pretending to be a normal twenty-something is that my body is not in on the secret and insists on reacting like an arthritic 70-year-old instead.

My phone rings again. This time I answer.

"Finally!" Jen's voice says on the other end of the line.

"Yes, Jen. And I've missed *you* too!"

"So what is up with you and that Zane guy?" she asks. Jen never asks a question like that if she doesn't already have an opinion to share.

What *is* up with us? We've been going to movies together, grabbing coffee, chatting on the phone. One time he joined me at the laundromat while I waited for my clothes to dry. We've been texting and calling each other a lot. We've kissed, but only twice, and each time I was the one who had to make the first move. Is this just a friendship where early on I tried to kiss him two times and he was too polite to turn me away? But then he keeps making all these suggestive comments and seems to be flirtatious.

"Hello?" Jen's voice echoes. "Earth to Ava?"

"Yeah um… sorry. I don't know, Jen, I guess we're friends?"

"But you guys make out, right?" she asks.

"Well," I say. "I kind of initiated it both times."

"Okay so you two are basically free agents, right?" she asks.

No… I mean… are we? I mean… I guess?

"He has insinuated that he's not the player type," I say, my voice sounding more unsure than I intended. "So I think he's just dating me. But I don't know, Jen, that's not a conversation we've had yet."

"Hmm," she says in her judgey, something-is-definitely-up-but-I-don't-want-to-say-what kind of voice.

"What's the 'hmm' for?"

"Shayna was just telling me that the other night at the bar, Zane and Kieran were competing over a girl."

My heart drops. I can't think of any words to respond with.

"I mean, that's okay, right?" she asks. "Since you're not officially together?"

I can't find the words to respond. *Is he just one of those guys who tries to pick up a new girl at the bar every night?*

"Yeah, totally…" I mumble. Despite my attempts to sound unaffected, my voice comes out shaky and dejected.

"I'm sorry honey," she says. "I really didn't mean to upset you, I just thought you should know. It seemed like you guys might be heading in the direction of something more serious. I'm sorry, should I not have told you? I thought it was the right thing but now I feel bad."

"No, no… Thank you for telling me. I mean, it's not like we're exclusive or anything. We hardly even kiss so I mean… I guess I thought there was something there but… it doesn't matter."

I feel tears welling up in my eyes.

"Aww honey," she says. "Are you crying?"

"No, I'm fine," I say, my wavering voice betraying me.

"You know what, he's a total idiot. I think I was right about him being gay anyway. You're gorgeous and wonderful and anyone who doesn't see that is a giant idiot. If you were a lesbian and I didn't see you as my sister, I would date you so fast!"

I laugh. "Thanks," I say, "I guess."

"You're damn right, 'thanks,'" she says. "I'm quite a catch!"

"Would you be up for hanging out tonight?"

She takes a breath and pauses. "I told Shayna I was going to visit her while she's working tonight. I was gonna ask if you wanted to come out with me but… I don't want to put you in an awkward position if we end up running into Zane and Kieran."

"Yeah, Zane actually asked me to come by, so I know they'll be there tonight."

I feel sick thinking that he just hits on whatever girls are in that bar. Zane and Kieran are just players and I should have known better. Guys that good-looking are always massive tools.

"Oh my god, I have the best idea," she says. I know her well enough to know that this tone of voice is always the precursor to a truly evil plan.

"What idea?"

"We know Zane is gonna be at Pike's. Why don't you show up looking out-of-this-world hot, and then totally ignore him all night and make him jealous?"

My brain knows instantly that this is a bad plan. A very bad plan. This is childish, incredibly immature, and a ridiculously passive-aggressive way to handle a problem. My petty heart, however, is cackling with delight.

Let's make the bastard squirm.

———•———

Jen pulls up to the bar and I'm suddenly filled with a mixture of nausea and regret. Jen talked me into tight leather pants and a loose, somewhat-sheer white v-neck tee that shows a fair amount of cleavage.

She assured me that as a 'connoisseur of women,' she determined this was the hottest possible outfit. I was debating wearing a tight dress, but she insisted this was more me. And she's right, but now I'm worried that this outfit isn't attention-grabbing enough.

"Get out of the car, you super fox, you!" she shouts.

I oblige, if only to avoid her loudly calling me a super fox in the parking lot again. I haven't responded to Zane's texts all day, so he doesn't know I'll be here. I'm suddenly feeling embarrassed. This is crazy immature of me.

I follow Jen in through the front door and immediately spot Kieran and Zane sitting in the corner with two beautiful women.

What is this, a meeting of the way-too-attractive people's club?

I'm hit with a pang of jealousy that quickly kicks my vindictiveness into high gear.

Fine. He doesn't want me? Good. I don't want him either.

Jen and I approach the bar as Shayna pours a couple of beers from the tap. I can sense Zane's gaze in my peripheral vision, but I avoid looking his way.

"Hey there!" Jen says to Shayna.

"Hey, sexy mama!" Shayna says back with a sly wink.

Oh my god, you two, get a room already—can't you see I'm having an awkward moment over here?

Shayna takes our orders and returns with our drinks. Jen and I make small talk for a bit, but it's not long before I feel a presence behind me. Zane must've come over from their table. *Maybe he was interested after all?*

"Hey," the voice says. I turn to see a tall, thirty-something man with dirty blond hair, a five-o-clock shadow, and a cocky grin. He must have just gotten off work at some sort of corporate job because he's wearing a suit with the tie loosened.

"I love the hair," he says.

I catch Jen's grin out of the corner of my eye. She seems pleased with how her plan is working so far.

"Thanks," I say, taking a sip of my drink as Shayna hands it to me. I forgot how much getting hit on is the worst. This is why I don't go to bars. Now I remember.

He seems slightly tipsy already and his smile is devilish.

"Those pants are awfully tight," he says.

Eww. This guy is already giving me the creeps. Before I have a chance to respond, he leans in closer.

"I bet it feels real good to take them off," he says in a low, heavy voice.

"Hey mate, piss off," a British voice says behind me. Part of me is still hurt by Zane's hitting on other women, but another part of me is so glad he's here right now.

"Oh, shit," the guy says. "Is she your girlfriend?"

Of course he's asking Zane rather than asking me directly. *What a charmer.*

"No!" he says, in an almost aggressive way. *Ouch.* Thanks for that.

"Then mind your business, *mate*," the guy says, mimicking Zane's British accent and poking him in the chest with his index finger.

This guy seems like he has a death wish. I can see every muscle and vein in Zane's neck and arms practically ready to burst. His skin has turned five shades redder and his eyes are narrow and vivid green.

"You fucking serious, you prick?" Zane says, knocking the guy back with a shove to his shoulders.

I step in between them to calm things down, my hands raised.

"Hey, hey," I say. "To your corners, okay? Don't fight, it's fine. Just calm down."

The guy walks away in a huff to join a group of guys in the pool room that seem to be his friends.

I take a hefty swig of my drink and finish it off. As if she's reading my mind, Shayna brings some shots over for each of us. I quickly down one of those too.

Zane is clenching his jaw hard, his hands balled into fists. He grabs his shot and Jen's and downs them in quick succession.

"What the hell, Zane?" I ask.

"What the hell? Seriously? You ignored my texts, didn't even tell me you were coming tonight, and then I try to save you from this creep and it's 'What the hell?' to *me*?"

"First off," I say. "I don't need to tell you I'm coming to a bar with my friend. Secondly, I didn't ask to be saved from anybody."

Did I want to be saved? Yes. But that is not the point right now, and he doesn't have to know that part.

"Oh, did I interrupt your night then, Ava? Did you want to go fuck him?"

Kieran is now standing behind Zane, wide-eyed and clearly not expecting to have stumbled upon this particular conversation.

"And what if I did?" I snap.

I don't—because, *eww*—but he doesn't have to know that.

"Wow, okay," he says, combing a hand through his hair. "Then excuse me for intruding."

"Speak for yourself! You and Kieran seem to have dates for the evening."

"You're right. I don't know why I'm here trying to save your sorry arse when I could be fucking one of them. You're not worth my bloody time."

His expression is cold and his eyes are glowing green. I feel the urge to cry, but I refuse to give him the satisfaction of knowing his insult had its intended effect.

"Don't talk to her like that, you snobby British dick!" Jen spits.

This is getting way out of hand and I feel all the eyes in the room on us. Kieran is trying to deescalate the situation, talking in hushed tones to Zane. The tension dies down for a moment and the bar patrons seem to return to their conversations.

"So if I'm not worth your time, Zane, then why do you keep calling me? Why do you keep talking to me? Why are you getting jealous?" I ask. I struggle to keep my voice from sounding teary.

"You seriously think I'm *jealous*?!" he asks, like it's a ridiculous thought.

"If you're not jealous, then what was that?" I ask.

"I felt sorry for you," he says, with no expression in his face.

I hate him. I wish he had said anything but that. That's why he let me kiss him but he didn't try to kiss me. That's why after I told him about being sick he didn't make a move. He felt sorry for me. I was sick, I was broken, and that was all he saw in me.

I can feel tears about to spill from my eyes, and I feel the overwhelming urge to do something stupid.

Fuck it. It's either this or cry in front of this entire room of people.

I make a beeline for the back room with the pool tables. The blond guy from earlier catches my eye as I approach. I walk up, grab his tie, and pull him in for a kiss. He's shocked but more than happy to join in.

I feel his hands instantly roaming around my ass and taste vodka on his lips. His kiss is aggressive and sloppy, but missing the fire behind Zane's. The man's friends make cheering noises behind us. He grabs a firm handful of my ass, and I feel simultaneously disgusted and pleased with myself at the thought of the visual Zane is getting right now.

Suddenly, I feel myself being pulled off of him in a flurry of motion. In an instant, Zane is on top of the guy, his fist connecting with his face. Kieran and one of their lady friends are pulling Zane back and Jen is tugging me away.

"Time to go, time to go, time to go," Jen repeats frantically, guiding me further toward the door.

I watch a wooden stool go flying across the bar. It hits the wall at lightning speed and splinters like it had gone through a wood chipper.

Did that come from them? Could someone have possibly thrown a stool that hard?

I suddenly feel woozy. The combination of the alcohol, stress, and one of my more potent dizzy spells hits me and I know in an instant that I am going down fast.

I watch as the edge of the doorframe speeds closer and closer toward my face. I see Jen's blurry face. And blood.

11

 ZANE

"Well, that was fun," Kieran says with a chuckle.

Fun is not the word I would use. I rest my head in my hands. The hospital lobby is surprisingly quiet, even for 11 at night.

I'm such a fucking twat.

This girl has made me bloody crazy. When I look at her, she somehow—against my will—manages to make me feel things.

Kami sits beside me, draping her legs casually over the metal arms of the blue upholstered chair.

"Okay, what the heck, Zane?" she asks.

"I dunno. Fuck." I sigh.

"You lost your shit back there, man," Kieran says, grabbing a magazine and taking a seat in the corner. "I'm supposed to be the one with the temper."

"She makes me so goddamn angry that I just want to fucking…"

"Strangle her?" Kami asks.

"Kiss her," I say. The words leave my lips before I have a chance to filter them out. Kieran lets out a laugh in the corner.

I shoot him a deadly glare. "If you want to keep your tongue, I suggest you shut your fucking mouth, Kieran."

He mimes zipping his mouth shut. *If only he could do that for real.*

"And you thought the best way to make your feelings known to her was to say shitty things to her and get into a screaming match in a bar before beating some guy she was kissing to a pulp?" Kami asks.

Well sure, when you say it like that, it sounds like a bad plan.

"Kieran's right," she says. "Your game is shit."

Kieran tries to muffle his laugh. I'm seriously thinking about giving him an impromptu tongue-ectomy.

"I don't know how to do this, Kami. I know how to talk to every bloody person on the planet. Immortal, human, everyone. Everyone but her."

"You're used to always getting what you want," she says. "Me too. I get it."

She's right. I hate the idea of Ava wanting someone that's not me.

Does that mean I'm jealous?

No.

Yes.

Fuck.

"So kiss her or work your touchy voodoo, man," Kieran says. "Can't you just make her like you?"

I've controlled people with my powers in the past, used a kiss or two to stir up a little romance. But Ava is different. I want her to actually want me, not just because she has to.

"I want it to be real with her," I say.

"Jesus, Zane," Kami says. "This girl has really done something to you."

You have no bloody idea.

"Well," she says. "You should probably start by not telling her you're gonna go fuck other girls. Didn't appreciate that by the way. Ew… No thank you."

"Yeah, sorry, I was caught up in the moment. She seemed jealous of you and I wanted to use it against her."

The words sound disgusting as they make their way to my ears. *I'm a giant fucking twat.*

"You know, you could have tried telling her we were just friends."

"Yeah, but I'm a giant fucking twat."

"Well at least you know it," she says with a smirk.

"And you could have done it without making a mess in the bar for me to clean," Kieran adds. "Management is already pissed about the whole incident. You're gonna have to work your Siren magic on a bunch of people before you can come back to Pike's."

"Yeah," Kami says. "Throwing a stool was pretty much the opposite of subtle. You can officially no longer give me crap for being obvious with my powers when you're out there juggling furniture for a crowd of twenty."

"Hey guys," Jen says as she walks in. "She's fine, a little embarrassed about everything, but totally okay."

I feel like my heart just beat for the first time in over an hour.

"The doctors think the alcohol and stress made her lose her balance and that caused the fall. The cut on her head is just a surface wound and they don't think she has a concussion. They said the head just bleeds a lot and it looks scarier than it is. I told her you guys were here, but uh…"

I'm pretty sure the words about to leave her mouth are something akin to 'but you're a total fucking twat and she doesn't want to see you.' Or whatever Americans say instead of twat.

"Yeah," Kami says, giving me a comforting pat on the back. "We don't expect her to want to chat right now. We just wanted to know she's alright."

"Are you gonna stay with her?" Kieran asks Jen.

It's killing me that he's suddenly all caring and sensitive right now.

"No, uh," she says. "I asked, but they said they don't allow people in the patient rooms this late. They're gonna watch her overnight, but she'll mostly be sleeping anyway. I'm gonna grab a bag of her things and swing by to pick her up in the morning."

Jen lets us know she's heading out. Kami and Kieran nod and gather their things. They both seem to know better than to ask me if I'm coming with them.

AVA

A bit of sun is peeking into the hospital room window. I can't believe it's already morning. The nurses kept me up all night, clicking buttons on my monitor and waking me up to check my vital signs. The lack of sleep, my drinking last night, and this stupid cut on my head have created the perfect storm for a monster headache.

Oh god. Last night.

Tell me I didn't do that. Tell me I didn't get into a screaming match with Zane in the middle of the bar, make out with that creep just to make him jealous, and then smack my head on the way out and end up in the hospital.

I touch my head and feel a bandage over what seems to be a stitch or two. I know they gave me a few stitches, but it was numb until now.

Ouch.

"Hey," a voice says from the doorway.

It's Zane. His broad shoulders and shaggy hair are instantly recognizable in my peripheral vision.

"Um, hey," I say.

I'm trying my best to pretend I'm not thoroughly embarrassed right now, both by my behavior last night and the tumbled-in-the-dryer-for-three-hours look I have going on right now.

What happened last night? Did Zane punch that guy because of me? Because I kissed him? *Oh god, why am I so awkward?*

"So, love," he says, looking down at his shoes and combing a hand through his hair. "You took a bit of a dive last night, eh?"

Kill me now, please.

"Yeah, I lost my footing I guess… How did you get back here?"

"I told you, love—I'm good with people."

Yeah, I remember hearing all about his way with people. I remember seeing it with his *date* last night. Why is he even here?

"Well, um… thanks for checking on me. I'm fine."

"Could I say something?" he asks.

"You've kinda got me as a captive audience here," I say, gesturing to the machines I'm hooked up to.

"I'm sorry," he says.

"For which part?" I ask. "Saying I'm not worth your time? Saying you felt *sorry* for me? Or laying out the guy who I was making out with?"

"I…" he pauses. "Fuck… all of it? Or… hell, maybe not that last bit."

He runs his hand through his hair again, tugging on the ends.

"Okay," I say. "Good to know."

I'm not giving him the satisfaction of accepting his apology. I don't care if I'm being petty.

"Why are you so frustrating?" he asks, his voice strained as he pounds a fist hard against the wall.

"How am *I* frustrating?"

"It's like you're constantly trying to infuriate me."

"How am I doing that?"

"By not accepting my apology. By getting mad when I try to help you. By kissing that prick in front of me."

"You and I, we're not together, okay Zane? You made it pretty clear I'm not your girlfriend. Besides, you had your own date to attend to."

I feel my eyes getting teary again. *Damn it, why can't I be more badass right now?*

"She's just a friend, okay? I was…" He sighs. "I guess I was jealous. I don't know. I've never been… *that* before."

I know I shouldn't find that romantic, but I kind of like it. Not that I'd admit it.

"Jealous?" I ask.

He sits down at the edge of my bed.

"Yeah, I… I've never had… competition before. I've never had to share what I wanted."

"Someone's a bit full of himself," I say with a scoff.

"You're right. Perhaps I've got a bit of an ego problem." He lets out a long shaky breath and runs his hand through his hair. "I like you. Really, truly like you, Ava. And for me, that's… rare. I haven't dated in bloody ages and when I thought you were entertaining that bloke's advances, I suppose I got a bit—alright, *very*—jealous."

"I kind of figured that out when you tackled the guy to the floor."

He huffs out a soft laugh.

"Did that give me away?" he asks, a small smile tugging at his lips.

My heart flutters. The man really does have a great smile.

"You said you felt sorry for me."

"Is that what I said?" He cringes and rubs a hand down his face. "I'm such a bloody arsehole."

"Yep."

"I don't feel sorry for you, love. If anything, I feel sorry for myself."

"Yourself?" I lift my eyes to meet his.

"I'm the only one here who made an arse out himself last night; possibly ruined something with an incredible woman."

His eyes lock onto mine with a silent question: *did I ruin things with you?*

"Are you insinuating that I should forgive you?"

"Insinuating? No. Hoping, praying… begging maybe. Is it working?"

"Maybe."

"I've realized I'm not the best at dealing with my emotions when it comes to you. I haven't wanted something so much in a long time and I'm low on practice. I'm hoping you'll see that and take pity on me."

"And what do you want?" I ask, hoping I know the answer.

He turns and leans toward me, brushing a strand of hair from my cheek. This is the first time he's ever looked like this before, almost a little shy.

"Isn't it obvious, love? I want what any man with any sense would want. I want you."

12

"I want you??" Jen squeals. "He actually said that??"

Jen turns to me in shock, her hands slightly turning the wheel. I grab the wheel to steady it.

"Geez, Jen, watch the road!" I shriek.

"I'm sorry, I'm just stunned. Like, what kind of Jane Austen crap is this? People don't say this stuff in real life. Especially men! So, are you guys *a thing* now?"

"I don't know…" I say with a shrug.

Are we a thing? We had this whole conversation, but then we never really got into details. It seems like we are… maybe a thing? Or on our way to becoming one?

"How do you not know?" she asks.

"Well, you walked in during our conversation and we never really got a chance to finish it."

"My bad. I didn't expect you to be having this intense moment in the hospital at 7:30 in the morning. Really, I should've known."

Jen has always had quite a penchant for sarcasm.

"I'm not blaming you," I say. "I'm just saying I don't know. I think we're not-not a thing."

"Well that's helpful," she says. "You've gotta keep me updated on your not-not boyfriend then."

I roll my eyes and rest my forehead on the passenger side window.

"Ow!" I yelp, having just leaned directly on my wound.

"Don't put pressure on it!" she scolds. "You just got stitches! You could pop them!"

"I didn't do it on purpose! And it was only two stitches; it'll heal fast."

She chuckles for a moment.

"Shayna said the bar is gonna be closed tonight while they clean up. Sounds like it was a real mess. You're gonna have to watch who you kiss, or lover boy's gonna tear up the whole town."

"I don't plan on kissing random strangers anytime soon, thanks. I've learned my lesson."

"And you've got the wound to prove it!" she says with a laugh.

"Oh, shut up. You're just gonna mock a poor, helpless, injured lady?"

"Only because she totally has it coming for all the times she has mocked me."

As we pull into the parking lot of my apartment building, I notice a familiar white Range Rover in the parking lot.

Shit.

It's Mike.

———◆———

"If it's Mike's car, then why isn't he in it?" Jen asks as we step out of the car.

We turn the corner toward my apartment and I instantly recognize Mike's silhouette in front of my door.

"Hey," he says softly. His hands are tucked in the pockets of his jeans and he's shifting awkwardly back and forth.

"Hi Mike," I say.

He seems to register that I have a bandage across my forehead.

"Jesus Christ, Ava, what happened?!" he gasps.

Jen pulls me aside and asks me if I want her to stay or give us some privacy. I tell her to go and she leaves as I turn my attention back to Mike.

"Hey," I say as I unlock the door. "Come in, we'll talk."

Mike follows and closes the door behind us.

"What's with the bandage on your head?" he asks as I plop my keys on the counter by the door.

"I slipped," I say. I'd rather not get into the other details with Mike.

"Are you okay?" he asks softly, lightly touching the bandage with his hand.

"Yeah, I'm fine." I shrug away. Mike's touch feels foreign, unwelcome. The few weeks that we've been apart feel like a lifetime.

"I'm sorry, okay? I know things were tense and we both said some things."

"Did we, Mike?" I ask. "I feel like I remember *you* being the one 'saying some things.'"

"Come on, Ava, I'm trying."

"You're right. I appreciate that you're trying to make amends."

"So we're good?" he asks.

"I mean, I think I need some time. But maybe in a while we could try being friends."

"Friends? Are you serious?" he asks, his tone shifting from kind to aggressive.

"What do you expect, Mike? We didn't break up because of what you said in the heat of the moment. We're not what each other needs or wants."

"I expected you to come to your senses and stay with the only person in the world who loves you and has stayed with you through everything."

I want to tell him he's not the only person who loves me. I want to tell him that he doesn't deserve a medal for staying with me. But I'm exhausted and confused, and I don't want this conversation to keep going on all day.

"Well, then you expect wrong," I say.

"Are you fucking someone?" he asks.

"Oh my god, Mike. Are you serious? You've always been so freaking sure I'm cheating on you."

"Because you flirt with every fucking guy you meet!"

That's such crap.

"We're not together, Mike. So if I flirt with someone, it's not your business is it?"

"Did you fuck the British guy?" he asks.

I feel a pang of guilt. I didn't have sex with Zane, but I can't say that nothing happened between us.

"You did?" he asks, attempting to read my expression. "Of course you did."

He stomps over to the door and slams it as he storms out. I lock it behind him and drop to the floor, my back against the closed door.

Freaking men.

As I sigh, I feel a vibration in my pocket.

Mike

cheating skank

Way to make me not regret leaving you.

ZANE

I knock on the door and hear footsteps descending the stairs.

I can't believe I'm dating again. Dating a human, no less.

The door opens to reveal Ava in a green blouse and short black skirt. Her hair is wavier than usual and one side is pinned up with a barrette. She smiles as our eyes meet.

"Hey," Ava says.

I feel my heart thumping in my chest.

What kind of magic is this girl working on me?

"Hey," I reply.

"So, where are we headed?" she asks, grabbing her purse and draping it over her shoulder.

"I thought, er..." I start to say, but I'm at a loss for words. Those grey eyes have practically drained my focus and I find myself momentarily questioning my every move.

Is this what humans feel when they're affected by venom? It's horrible.

"Table?"

"Did you literally just say table? As in the piece of furniture?" she asks with a laugh.

I'm distracted, but I'm not *that* distracted.

"The restaurant is called Table," I say.

"That sounds familiar," she says.

"It's good. We should get going; I made a reservation."

I open the door to my car and let her in before getting in on the driver's side.

"I forgot how cool your car is," she comments.

"Thanks. It's the newer version of the Dodge Challenger. I like the classic look."

"That's like, really expensive, right?"

I smirk. Money isn't hard to come by when you can have anything you ask for.

"I guess," I say. "Money isn't really a big deal to me."

"Ahh, so you're super-rich then?"

"You could say that."

"Wow. Rich people never admit they're rich. You must be, like, really *really* rich."

I can't help but laugh. Ava always tells it like it is.

"Americans are always about money, aren't they?" I ask.

"I don't care if you have money," she says. "I'm just being honest. You have a lot of money for someone who doesn't have a job. It's weird."

She's got me there. I'm probably coming off like a drug dealer right now.

"What happened to your dashboard?" she asks, pointing to the crumpled fist-sized dent I left in a fit after that first night we kissed.

I'm trying to think of a good excuse for such a specific mark. Chemical spill? On second thought, maybe one that doesn't make me sound even more like a drug dealer.

"My air freshener exploded," I say.

What the hell am I talking about?

"It uh… I had an oil air freshener thing and it got too hot on a sunny day and it exploded. Weird fluke thing," I explain.

Yeah, that doesn't seem suspicious at all.

AVA

The doors open to an expansive restaurant with high ceilings and a giant lit-up tree in its center. I get the impression Zane kind of undersold how expensive this restaurant is. A woman walks up to us and immediately recognizes Zane, welcoming us both and seating us right away. Our table is secluded and by the window. I wonder if he requested this spot specifically, since it's definitely the best seat in the house.

The host hands us our leather-bound menus—which of course, don't even list the prices. I'm pretty sure this is one of those places you don't come to if you even think to ask about the price of your meal.

She takes our drink orders and steps away.

"So this is uh… fancy," I say.

"Yeah, I thought… it's really good. And when we had coffee that one time you mentioned you really liked French food. I thought you'd maybe like it."

He seems more unsure than usual and is kneading his hands together a bit.

"It seems great," I say. "How do you know about this place?"

"I know the owner."

"Oh, wow! Are they a chef?"

"No," he says. "They just like good food."

"This place must be pretty new. I've never heard of it before."

"Have you always lived in Port Charlotte?"

"I lived here during high school, moved back after college."

I figure I'll leave out the part about moving back because I couldn't afford to live in San Francisco and still pay my extra medical bills.

"Do your parents live here?" he asks.

Should I also leave out the dead mom and drug addict dad? Yeah, probably.

"Nope," I say. "What about yours?"

"My parents?" he asks. "Yeaahhh… that's a complicated story I rather not get into."

He looks embarrassed, so I reach out to hold his hand. He freezes at my touch and his eyes widen.

I don't get this guy. He'll kiss me and will say he wants me, but then I have to make all the moves and he flinches every time I do.

"Fuck…" he mumbles.

"Shit, sorry," I say, pulling my hand away. "I didn't mean to overstep. I thought…"

"No," he says, grabbing my hand between both of his. "Love, I didn't mean it like that. I… I'm just nervous, I guess. I'm just feeling… It's complicated."

"Nauseous?" I ask.

"No," he says with a laugh. He pauses, clenching his jaw for a moment before his eyes find mine. "I'm… losing control a little."

"As in, you're going to murder me?" I ask.

I'm joking of course. Mostly. *I hope.*

He lets out another laugh.

"No," he says. "I'm just… losing my ability to stay away from you."

Wow. That was smooth.

"I feel like if you wanted to stay away from me, you could've just not invited me out tonight," I say.

"True," he says with a smirk. "Maybe I lost that ability a long time ago."

13

 ZANE

I take a sip of what I think is a martini then hand it back to Kieran.

That is really not my drink.

"There you go," I say. "Have fun."

"Thanks, bro," he says with a devious look in his eye.

I wash it down with another sip of my beer. Kieran delivers the glass to his latest conquest—a thin-yet-muscular gentleman with curly hair sitting several stools down from me. I give it five minutes max before they disappear to the back room.

It's probably time for me to head home anyway. I might text Ava and see what she's up to, if she's still awake.

"So, if it isn't the British dude who fucked my girlfriend…" a slurring, drunk voice says from behind me.

I'd assume he was talking to Kieran if he hadn't said British. I don't bother turning around to engage with whoever this is.

"Oi, you got the wrong 'British dude,'" I say.

"Do you fuck that many men's girlfriends that you've lost track?" he says with a drunken mumble.

"Mate, you're clearly pissed off your arse."

Kieran chuckles to himself, but his laugh seems to fade and his expression morphs into a devious smirk.

"Oh, this just got interesting," Kieran says. He turns to his latest target and says, "Don't you go anywhere, gorgeous. I just have to see how this goes down."

What does Kieran think I'm going to do? I bust up a guy in the bar one time, and now he thinks I'm going to get into a fistfight with every drunkard I meet.

The guy leans into the bar next to me and sets a beer on the counter. He's got a smug, basic-white-guy face that I can't seem to place.

"You know what, you did me a favor. Apparently Ava is a massive whore anyway."

Oh fuck. This twat is Mike.

"You don't know what you're fucking talking about," I say with an eye roll.

He's trying to get a rise out of me, but I didn't have sex with Ava—let alone when they were together—and I especially don't care what this wanker thinks of her.

"Oh yeah?" he asks. "So you want me to believe you didn't fuck my girlfriend?"

Kieran is watching with a sly smirk. He's just waiting to see if I'll lose my cool.

"I don't think you have a girlfriend, *mate*," I say, taking another sip of my beer.

Kieran busts up laughing.

"Yeah, thanks to some British son of a bitch who doesn't respect other people's property," he snaps.

"Again, pretty sure you don't have any *property*." I turn slightly toward him to make eye contact and smile.

"If I wasn't *fucking clear*," he says, jabbing my shoulder with his fingers, "when I stuck my dick in her that made her *my property*."

In a flash, I've got the collar of his shirt twisted up in my fist. He struggles to breathe as the fabric tightens around his neck.

"Okay, okay," Kieran says, putting a hand on my chest and turning to address Mike. "This has been fun, dude—it really has—but you *seriously* have no idea what you're doing here. I'd prefer not to have to clean your brains off the walls."

Kieran leans into me and whispers, "Remember what Kami said? About trying not to draw unwanted attention?"

I loosen my grip on Mike's collar, his face already a deep red. His eyes are bulging with panic. I exhale hard and release him. He takes several steps back and readjusts his shirt.

"Leave Ava the fuck alone," I say.

As he steadies himself, his courage seems to rebuild.

"Don't worry," he says with a smirk. "There's nothing I could do to her that I haven't already done."

I see red. My hand grips his arm tight by the wrist and I'm overwhelmed with options.

Do I break his arm? Choke him? Kick his kneecaps in?

"Zane," Kieran says sternly with a hand on my shoulder. He seems slightly baffled, out of his element as the voice of reason between us.

Fuck! Fine!

"Alright, *Michael*," I say, tightening my fingers around his wrist. I scan the room for a moment. "You see that big bloke in the corner with the neck tattoo?"

He nods, his drunken boldness instantly replaced with fear.

"You see that girl he's got his arm around?" I ask. "You're gonna tell her, in excruciating detail, how you want to fuck her. And you do want to, don't you, Michael?"

He nods and I release his arm. Kieran's eyes go wide and Mike walks toward the back corner of the bar.

"Damn it, Zane," he says with a hand combing through his hair. "That wasn't really what I meant."

A rumbling of voices in the corner grows louder and louder as I down the last bit of my beer. Kieran's look of frustration turns into a medley of shock, horror, and amusement.

"You're helping me clean up," he says to me, before returning to his date for the evening.

I hear a loud crash behind me and can't help but smile.

———◆———

AVA

My vision is hazy as I try to find my phone to check the time. It's pitch black outside, maybe 1 or 2 in the morning?

"What is it about you, Ava?" I hear a voice ask.

I jump and sit straight up in a panic.

Where did that come from? Is someone in my apartment?

A male figure is seated at the corner of my bed.

Oh god, I'm definitely going to be murdered.

The man turns and I recognize the face—it's Kieran.

"Uh… what are you doing here?" I ask.

"It's okay, Ava," he says. I don't know why, but I'm not as scared now, maybe because I know it's Kieran.

How did he even get in? Could Jen have given him a key?

"So what is it?" he asks. "What makes men lose their minds over you?"

"I um… they don't? I don't think they do."

"They do, Ava," he says, inching closer to me.

I'm in a bit of a fog as I try to wake up. Why is Kieran here?

"Are you great in bed, Ava?" he asks. "You must be."

His hand wraps around the back of my neck, the other bracing himself on the bed. His touch is oddly cold.

"Kieran?" I ask. "What are you doing?"

"I just want to try something," he says, leaning into me.

He pulls me in and our lips meet. His lips are cold too, but it feels nice at the same time. He closes his deep, dark eyes and I feel his long hair brush against my shoulders. I'm so exhausted; I'm practically powerless to resist.

"I'm starting to get it," he says, breaking our kiss. "But I'd like to gather a little more information."

His other hand moves off the bed and slinks around my waist.

"Kieran," I say. "We shouldn't. I… I can't think straight right now. What time is it?"

Without answering he pulls me toward him so that we're both on our knees atop the mattress. He kisses me again, slipping his icy tongue between my lips. He's freezing to the touch, but somehow I'm feeling almost overheated. His hand moves from my waist to grab a firm handful of my ass. I'm dizzy and exhausted, but the feeling is still intense. Not as intense as it is with Zane, but still good.

Zane.

Oh my god—Zane. What the hell am I doing?

I pull away sharply.

"No, Kieran," I say. "I don't want this, this isn't right. Zane and I…"

"Relax," he says. "Zane doesn't do relationships anyway, right? You don't have any responsibility to him."

"I…"

Zane doesn't do relationships? I mean… I know we haven't explicitly said we're exclusive, but it feels like we are.

"I can't," I say, pulling away and covering myself with the blanket. "Why are you here, Kieran?"

"I'm not," he says with a smirk.

Suddenly, I open my eyes to an empty room.

Holy crap. Did I just have a sexy dream about Kieran?

14

AVA

My ears are ringing and there's a throbbing, dizzy sensation deep inside my head that I can't quite explain. I'm so frickin' sick of this. I feel nauseous and can't decide if grabbing a snack would make it better or worse.

Is it just me, or is going to the doctor the absolute worst possible thing to make a person do when they're sick?

Seriously, I can use my phone to have food delivered to me in twenty minutes. I get a car in four minutes to drive me wherever I want. I can download a book in ten seconds. I can stream a movie almost instantly. All these things can happen just because you might be feeling lazy. But if you're genuinely in pain or really, truly feeling like hell, they have you make an in-person appointment. You have to physically drag yourself into the office, wait half an hour past your appointment time in an uncomfortable chair, then get poked and prodded and generally annoyed, only to then be told that you'll need to go get tests or medicine or something else that you almost certainly don't have the energy for.

Can't I just send someone on my behalf? My weight and blood pressure have never given them any incredible insights anyway.

Of course my appointment had to be at 9:30 in the morning. I'm exhausted enough at noon but this is just cruel. I hardly got any sleep last night.

I flash back to the dream last night, Kieran kissing me... *Oh god. Can I just wipe that whole unfortunate fantasy from my brain now, please?*

"Ava Reynolds?" a voice calls from the doorway.

I stand up and see the same blonde nurse who did my blood tests last time.

"Hey!" he says. "I remember you! Web designer girl!"

"Yep, that's me!" I say. "But that's my superhero name, so don't tell anyone my secret identity."

He laughs a bit more than my lame joke deserves.

"Don't worry, Ava," he says with a smile. "Your secret's safe with me."

He winks and leads me back to the patient room.

"So it looks like you're here to discuss some results with your doctor. Have there been any changes, any new symptoms we should make note of?" he asks.

"Um… I mean, I keep getting these dizzy spells. My ears start throbbing on both sides and I feel nauseous. I'm not sure if they're worse or not, but they certainly keep happening."

Like right now for instance. Uggh.

"Okay," he says. "I'll make a note in your chart. Anything else?"

Does the perpetual 'my body is on fire' sensation count? Oh no wait, that's not new.

"Just the same stuff," I say.

"Okay, Web Designer Girl," he says with a smile. "The doctor will be in shortly. You keep fighting the good fight!"

He steps out of the room and closes the door. As the pattering of his steps recedes down the hall, I swear I recognize a familiar voice. It sounds like Mike. I crack the door a bit and look out. Sure enough, I hear Mike's voice.

Why the heck is Mike here, anyway? Is he looking for me?

He's walking along the hall as a doctor talks to him.

"I'll put in that referral for the plastic surgeon," the doctor says.

Mike turns briefly as he rounds the corner and it's just enough to catch a glimpse of his face. He's covered in bruises and has surgical tape over his nose. It looks like it's broken. Once they round the corner, they're out of view.

Holy crap, what the hell happened to him?

———•———

I sit in my car in the parking lot, rubbing my eyes as I struggle to overcome my dizziness enough to start driving. My phone rings through my Bluetooth-connected stereo.

"What's up, girl??" Jen's voice says from the other end of the line.

"Hey," I say, not exactly selling the I'm-totally-healthy-and-not-dying vibe I was going for.

"Awww," she says with sympathy. "Feeling bad today?"

"I'm okay," I lie—not for her benefit, but for mine. I'm just plain tired of saying I feel bad all the time.

"Then what's up?" she asks.

"Kind of weird question," I say, "but have you heard anything about Mike getting into a fight or accident or something?"

"Whaaatt??" she asks. "No! What happened to Mike?!"

"I have no idea. I just spotted him in the hospital just now and he looks like he stuck his face in a beehive. His nose was all taped-up and swollen, his face had a bunch of bruises, and he had giant swollen spots under each eye."

"Whoa!" she said. "You think *Mike* actually got in a *fight*??"

"I don't know, I only saw him real briefly but I heard him talking to the doctor about a plastic surgeon."

"Oh daaanng! He must be super fucked up!" she says. "Do you think he had a run-in with your boo?"

Eww. I hate that word.

"No," I say. "I do not think he 'had a run-in' with Zane. It's not like they hang out in the same circles anyway. No chance they'd ever cross paths."

"What about Pike's? If Mike came looking for him that's where he'd go, right?"

"Oh, I mean," I pause. Could Mike have come looking for Zane? That would make sense if Mike thought I cheated with him.

"Shayna did tell me there was a big fight the other night over some girl. She's here, I can ask. Hold on."

Oh geez. Could Zane and Mike really have gotten into a fight?

I decide to text Zane.

Me

Did you get in a fight with Mike?

"Hey babe!" Jen says to Shayna. "Who got in that fight the other night at Pike's?"

Shayna's voice replies in the background, but I can't make out her words.

Zane

Did someone say I did?

Me

Answer the question, Zane

"If I showed you a picture could you tell me if it was the guy who got beat up?" Jen asks Shayna.

Zane

Did somebody hurt your pretty-boy ex?

I can't say I would think of Mike as a pretty boy, but I think that's just Zane's not-so-subtle way of dodging this question and throwing a dig at Mike in one go.

Me

Did you?

"Yeah, that's the guy," I hear Shayna confirm. "They put his picture on our Banned Patrons list."

"I'm putting you on speaker, 'kay?" Jen says. "Shayna, tell Ava what happened."

"Well," Shayna says. "I wasn't there, but I heard about it after. This dude was all up in the face of this other guy. I guess the other guy was pretty big with tattoos and whatnot."

Uh oh. This other guy sounds familiar.

"Anyway, apparently Scrawny here decides to stir up shit and says a bunch of inappropriate stuff about the tough guy's girlfriend and the guy goes off on him and beats his face in."

Oh my god. I'm honestly shocked Mike had the guts to say stuff like that to Zane. He must've been incredibly wasted.

I bury my face in my hands and cringe. I always thought guys fighting over me would be hot, but this is just embarrassing and stressful. What the heck do I do with this information?

Zane

I was a good boy, love ;)

Oh really?

He probably has no idea I'm getting the straight details from Shayna right now. I do not appreciate being lied to.

"It was quite the story around the bar the last few days. Your friend here apparently has balls of steel!"

"He's not a friend," Jen says. "More of an enemy, really."

"Ahh, in that case, you'll be happy to know that it sounds like this guy got a serious beatdown and is forbidden from the bar."

"What about the other guy?" Jen says. "Anyone we know?"

"Uhh…" Shayna pauses. "I know he's a regular and that's pretty much all I heard about him."

I can't believe Zane is lying to me.

> **Me**
> I've heard different.

> **Zane**
> Then you heard wrong. If pretty boy got in a fight, it wasn't with me.

> **Me**
> Why are you lying to me rn?

"Oh my god, I knew it!" Jen shouts. "It was totally Zane!"

"What?" Shayna says, shocked.

"This guy is Ava's ex-boyfriend!"

> **Zane**
> I'm not bloody lying to you.

"Um…" Shayna says uneasily. "I dunno…"

The two exchange heated whispers and I hear a click.

I think Jen just put me on mute.

"Guys?" I ask.

A call from Zane pops up on my screen, but I decline it.

"Guys?" I ask again. There's another click followed by white noise.

"Ava," Jen says. "Don't be mad but uh, Shayna seems to think the girl they were fighting over was there with them."

I feel anger building in my chest. My ex and the guy I thought I was dating were fighting. Over a girl. And that girl wasn't me.

Ouch.

Zane

We should talk. Come over?

Me

Be there in 10

15

 ZANE

Who the fuck told Ava I got in a fight with Mike?

It has to be Kieran. As far as everyone else knows, Mike got in a fight with that random guy.

Did Mike say something? What could he possibly say?

'Zane convinced me to go get in a fight with this other guy so it's really his fault'? I'm sure that would go over well. 'How did he convince me, you ask? I assume he has touch-based hypnotic powers.'

I'm being paranoid. There's no way she knows. Mike probably just lied to her.

I hear footsteps approaching my door, followed by a knock.

"Hey," I say tentatively as I open the door. She looks upset and her heart is beating rapidly beneath her skin.

Fuck.

"I know you got in a fight with Mike," she said. "Why did you lie to me?"

Fuck.

"I…" I run my hands through my hair, tugging slightly. "I didn't lie to you. I just didn't tell you everything."

She looks furious, but also hurt.

Does she know what I am? How? She's going to leave me, isn't she?

"And the part you left out was the part where you broke his face?" she asks, exasperated.

"Whoa whoa," I say. "I didn't do that. I mean, I'm not blameless here but I *did not* hit him and I *did not* break his face."

She looks at me with questioning eyes. I can tell she's struggling with whether or not to believe me.

"I don't know what's worse," she says, "the fact that you're lying to me about punching him or the fact that you punched him because he was saying sexual things about your girlfriend."

I'm taken back by the way she just threw the word 'girlfriend' out there. Part of me is pissed at the context but another part still wants to smile.

"You know that he said those things about you?" I ask. "Who told you that?"

"Oh please, Zane, save it! I mean your *other girlfriend*, the one who was there with you—the one you were fighting over?"

Wait… What?

"I'm… I…" I stutter, trying to wrap my mind around what she's saying. "I did what now?"

"You heard me. I know what the fight was really over."

"Wha-…" I say. I'm at a loss for words. "What are we talking about right now? I'm bloody confused."

"Shayna told me everything, okay?" she said, her eyes filling with tears.

Shayna? Shayna wasn't even there that night. What would she know about…

Oh my god.

Fucking… She heard a rumor? That's what's happening right now.

I reach out to touch her shoulders, pulling her to look toward me. Her arms remain tightly crossed and her eyebrows are furrowed.

Of all the things I thought would screw me in this relationship, a random rumor about me having another girlfriend was not one of them.

"I don't have another girlfriend. It's just you, love. This is clearly a misunderstanding. Please," I beg, "please believe me."

She seems lost in thought.

"Okay," she says, her expression softening into an almost smile.

"Okay?" I ask.

That was weirdly easy.

Oh fuck. She's human. I just charmed her.

"Shit," I say under my breath.

"What?" she asks.

"I just, I meant to explain more… I feel like you're believing me for the wrong reasons."

"What reasons?"

"You're… I'm… fuck. I don't even know," I say. I feel like I have to be truthful with her, if only to make up for accidentally manipulating her. "Can I just say… The guy who punched Mike wasn't me. They were fighting about that guy's girlfriend, not you. But I got into a… *mostly verbal* argument with him before that. And that was about you."

"So wait…" she says, her eyes narrowing. "He did say sexual things about me? Because you implied that he did."

"Yeah, he was just trying to get under my skin," I say.

And it worked. If Kieran weren't there to stop me, Mike would be dead ten times over.

Sure, he was trying to make me jealous, but it was more than that. He wanted to claim her. He wanted to make it clear that she was his possession.

If I had been the one who beat him, he wouldn't have gotten back up.

I feel my blood heating up again and I try to distract myself to calm down. Almost on cue, Ava smiles at me then looks down and blushes and I'm instantly lost in her.

"You embarrassed, love?" I ask.

"I didn't mean to say that I was… that we were… *you know*. I mean I know we haven't talked about it."

"What? You mean when you called yourself *my girlfriend*?" I shoot her a teasing grin.

"I wa-, I mean… I said that mostly for dramatic effect."

"Ah, well love, if you're gonna keep having jealous fits, it would probably work better if you were my girlfriend."

"Yeah?" she asks. "Wait a minute, I'm not jealous!"

I wrap my arms around her and pull her into me.

"Yeah, baby, sure you're not," I tease.

I lean in close and kiss her on the lips. Her lips are soft and warm and I melt into her. I pull back for a moment to brush a strand of hair from her face.

Her eyes dilate instantly and her heartbeat speeds up. She takes a sharp breath in and her lips part slightly.

Aside from our first kiss, this may be the only other time I can recall that I've kissed someone without thinking about the effect it would have on them.

She instantly wraps her arms around my neck and I lift her onto the kitchen counter. Her legs wrap around me and everywhere our skin touches is electrified.

I can't help but be pulled in by every kiss. She has never needed venom of her own to have this effect on me. I'm all but powerless to resist her.

She reaches her hands under my shirt, her nails raking across my bare back. My every nerve is on fire.

She tugs up on the bottom of my shirt. My brain and my body are fighting at every turn.

I need her. I need her now.

No. She's on venom. She's not in control.

I'm not in control.

I hold my hands up over my head, letting her peel off my T-shirt. My hands wrap immediately around her ass.

Yes. More. All of her.

What am I doing? I'm taking advantage.

I look into her eyes; her pupils are so wide you can hardly see any grey.

"Fuck!" I accidentally let the word slip out as I set her back onto the counter and pull away in one fast motion.

My body is bloody furious with me. My skin is burning, every nerve screaming to resume contact with Ava. I want her, but I can't… not like this.

"What are you doing?" she asks as I run to the fridge. She's staring at me with a look of intense confusion.

What are you doing? My body echoes the question. *She wants you. You want her. You need her.*

I grab a water bottle out of the fridge and throw it to her.

"Drink that," I say, grabbing two more and placing them next to her on the counter.

Venom wears off a lot faster if you chase it with water. *Now if only that would work for me.*

"Okay, um… yay hydration and all, but I thought we were in the middle of something," she says, standing up and walking towards me.

She trails her fingertips along my chest and I back into the closed fridge.

Yes. Keep going. This is bloody amazing

You can't be certain she wants this.

I jump back in a moment of clarity and send a deep dent into the stainless steel fridge.

"Oh, uh, I… I…" I say with a stutter. "This fridge is super cheap."

I knock things off the counter, stumbling backwards over my own feet as I attempt to pull myself away.

"I'll be right back," I shout, running down the hall. "Drink those waters, okay?"

I slam the bathroom door behind me and see my reflection in the mirror. A pair of glowing green eyes stare back at me.

FUCK.

16

I pull my car into the parking lot outside Zane's apartment.

I finally got Zane to invite me over to his place again. For someone who is always so eager to see me, these past few weeks he's been intent on avoiding us spending time alone.

I'm probably being paranoid, but I swear it's always something.

'My apartment is a mess right now.' 'I have to get to bed early.' 'I'm just really dying to check out this new movie.' 'I figured it was rude not to invite your friends.'

What happened to guys always wanting to get women alone any chance they get?

My phone buzzes in my pocket.

Jen

Sooo, tonight's the nite??

Thanks, Jen. Like I wasn't already nervous.

Me

Don't jinx me Jen

Jen

Are you there??

Me

Not yet.

Jen

Bow chicka BOW WOW

Me

Stoppp. You're stressing me!

Jen

Come on, he's totally into u you just
need to seal the deal! What r u wearing?

I snap a quick photo of my jeans and low-cut maroon tank top under a black cardigan before I step out of my car.

Jen

Cute but I meant *underneath*

Plz no picture of that. Don't
wanna think bout u like that

Me

Ewww stopppp

I'm not about to tell Jen, but I am wearing a matching black lace bra and panty set under this. You know—just in case.

I step out of my car and take the elevator to Zane's floor. His apartment is simple but very nice and has a gorgeous city view from the 14th floor of his building.

"Hey baby!" Zane's voice chimes as I open the door.

"Hey!" I say, leaning in for a kiss. He shifts to kiss my forehead instead.

Damn it.

He's wearing a white shirt that is tight along his skin in all the right places.

"Hey Ava!" a voice says from the living room.

Oh great. Kieran's here.

"I hope you don't mind," Zane says, "I invited Kieran to hang out with us."

Damn it, Zane.

"Yeah, cool," I say.

Not cool. Not at all cool.

Zane offers me a drink as I sit down on the leather sofa next to Kieran. He's playing some video game on Zane's television. It looks like he's playing as some kind of beast with the head of a bull with a big sword slicing through crowds of monsters.

I haven't seen Kieran since the—ahem—dream I had. It feels weird to hang out with them both now.

"Wait," I say, scrunching my eyebrows as I inspect Kieran's arm. "I swear you had tattoos, didn't you?"

"Oh uh, yeah," he says with a quick glance to Zane. "Those were just temporary ones. You know, those wash off ones."

"Oh, okay," I say.

They certainly looked real. *Weird.*

"Come on, a real Minotaur would thrash these civilians!" Kieran shouts.

"Yeah mate," Zane says with a chuckle. "'Cause you and I both know plenty of *real Minotaur*s." He raises his eyebrows at Kieran.

"Yeah you know what I mean," he says with a weak laugh. "If Minotaurs *did* exist. They would definitely be able to handle this mess. Obviously there aren't real Minotaurs though."

Kieran pauses the game and his eyes meet mine and his smile widens, looking devious as usual.

"Sorry, Ava," he says, a smile creeping across his face. "Am I paying attention to a video game when your beautiful face is right here?"

I blush and shrug. Zane's jaw tenses and his expression becomes hard.

"I'm a taken woman now so your compliments will get you nowhere," I joke.

"Uh, what now?" he asks, looking over at Zane whose expression is stern. "Does grumpy over here know that? 'Cause if this is the first time you're telling him, I'm pretty sure you and I are about to see one hell of an apartment-demolishing rampage."

"Uh," I mumble.

Zane didn't tell Kieran that we were together? Why not?

"Oi, piss off," Zane says with a huff.

"Well I'll be damned!" Kieran says. "I guess our boy here has calmed down over you. I'm shocked he's not snapping his chair in half. Zane's not usually the jealous type so I was kind of enjoying watching him go postal every time someone glanced at you."

Kieran laughs as Zane walks to me, handing me a can of soda.

"So who's the new boy toy?" Kieran asks.

I look to Zane to see if he's going to chime in, but he's avoiding my eyes.

"Uh," I say, stalling for time. *Should I just say it?*

Our conversation is interrupted by a knock at the door.

"That's probably food," Zane says, jumping out of his chair and over to the door. In a split second, he returns with bags of Chinese takeout and proceeds to place everything out on the dining table.

I follow him to the table with Kieran close behind me. I unbutton my cardigan and shrug it off my shoulders, hanging it on the chair as I sit.

"Perfect," I say. "I'm starving!"

Kieran sits across from me, his eyes wide and honed-in on my chest. I really only had Zane in mind when picking out this outfit, but here we are.

"Damn, Ava," Kieran mutters, licking his lips. "I'm feeling pretty famished myself."

I'm assuming he didn't mean that the way it sounded, right?

A sharp crack reverberates through the room. We look over to Zane as his fist is resting on the freshly cracked marble of the kitchen counter.

"Leave," Zane says with a rumbling voice. His eyes shine a vibrant green under the kitchen lights but his pupils seem deep and dark.

"Oh shit," Kieran says. "I guess I spoke too soon about him calming down."

Kieran jumps up and darts toward the door, his hands held up in a defensive position. Zane's expression is pure rage. I guess that possessive streak didn't really go away.

"Come on," Kieran says as he continues to back away. "I mean, I am who I am, bro. Besides, she's got a boyfriend now anyway, so why do you care if I…"

His eyes shift rapidly between Zane and me.

"OH." Kieran's eyes widen. I guess he just did the math. "You… and… OH. So much for not being the relationship type, huh?"

Wait, isn't that what he said about Zane in my dream?

Okay, I'm definitely being paranoid now.

Zane lets out a low grumble that sounds almost like a growl and takes a single firm step toward Kieran.

"Wow," Kieran says. "I'm uh… I'm late for a thing anyway. A thing where I don't get the crap beaten out of me in your kitchen."

He grabs his black jacket from the entryway and, with a quick wave goodbye, slips out the front door.

———•———

ZANE

That fucking wanker.

Yeah, he's afraid of me now, but he wasn't afraid enough to ogle Ava's tits five seconds ago.

Anger like I've never felt is pumping through my veins and I can hear my heartbeat pounding in my ears.

"Zane?" Ava's voice says softly from behind me as I feel her hand rest on my shoulder. "It's okay, he didn't mean that. He was just being flirtatious. He didn't know."

Oh he bloody well meant it. She doesn't know just how much he meant it.

"Here," she says, guiding me over to the couch. "Come sit."

I can feel my body relaxing at her touch. She sits on the couch and pats the seat next to her.

"Ahh, uh," I mumble. I want to sit next to her, but the closer I am to her the more I want to touch her, kiss her, and when I'm all pumped up like this I struggle to control myself even more than usual.

Her face looks sad, dejected.

"You don't want to sit with me?" she asks.

If she only knew how ridiculous that thought is. All I want to do is be with her.

"Of course I do, baby," I say, sitting beside her.

I reach an arm around her shoulder and pull her in. Her warmth on my skin is simultaneously soothing and electrifying.

She looks into my eyes suspiciously.

"What color are your eyes?" she asks.

Oh crap. She noticed that?

A Siren's eyes only change color when they're at their most uninhibited, when the body and mind fight and the mind loses. When rage or lust pushes them to the far edge of the human-to-animal spectrum.

I guess I really have been losing it around her a lot if she's noticing it enough to ask.

"Oh, er, they're hazel. Why?"

A lie, but it's an easy way to explain if she has seen them flip from brown to green. I was lucky that my Siren eyes were a reasonably human shade. Kami's eyes turn a bright gold and I've even known some Sirens whose eyes become purple or red.

"Huh," she says. "That makes sense, I guess. Sometimes I swear they look really green."

She looks into my eyes and her lips part just slightly. Damn, she doesn't even realize what she's doing to me.

Kiss her. Take her. Now.

"Yeah they do that," I say, leaning over to kiss her on the forehead.

My body is furious with me. She sighs and pulls away.

Shit. That is definitely not the sound a woman makes when she's happy with you.

"Zane?" she asks. "Why do you do that?"

"Do what, love?"

"Kiss my forehead."

God damn it. Was that wrong? I thought girls liked that sort of thing. *How am I literally built to seduce women but I keep fucking up with Ava?*

"I… You don't like it?" I ask.

"No, I do, it's just that I feel like you're avoiding kissing me."

Well there it is, I've officially been made.

What do I say to that?

Well, love, it's a simple answer really. I'm just a mythological creature with the ability to hypnotize people with my touch, and when humans ingest my venom they're overcome with lust. I've never had an actual relationship, let alone with a human, and I have no idea what I'm doing with any of this.

Simple, right?

"I just… Fuck, Ava, I want to kiss you more, I do! I jus-… with us, things start moving really fast when we're kissing and I want you to be… aware of your choices."

Yeah that made sense. I sound mental. *Fuck.*

"You want *me* to be aware?" she asks. "So you're aware and I'm not?"

She's got me there. My brain has never been less present than when I'm kissing her.

"Yeah well, that's a bloody good point. I uh… I can't quite say I'm entirely capable of controlling myself with you either, but it's different."

You know, magical powers and all. Fuck.

"What's different?" she asks.

"I just want to be sure you want… whatever happens."

"I do," she says. Her lips part and she leans in just close enough to almost kiss me.

Fuck. Those eyes, those lips… I'm officially done for.

I close the remaining distance between us and our lips meet. I hear a quickening thump as her heart begins to race. My hands snake around her waist and pull her closer. I tumble on top of her, kissing along her neck toward her shoulders. Her fingers tug lightly on my hair.

Fuck that feels good.

Her cheeks are flushed and her skin is dewy under my fingertips. Her pupils are wide with lust. Every indicator tells me that this isn't her—this is the venom.

"This," I say, pulling back, "is exactly what I'm talking about, love."

I bloody hate myself right now.

"What part of this," she says, pulling off her top, "says 'I'm not ready' to you?" She grinds into me and kisses my neck.

Fuck it, I can't say no to that.

"Bloody hell, Ava," I say, practically growling through my teeth. I relax into her and kiss her, my tongue slipping past her lips. The sound of my own heartbeat is drowning out hers.

I need her.

She doesn't want you, she wants the Siren.

"Fuck," I snap. "Ava… Is there anything, right now, that you wouldn't do?"

She pauses for a moment. Her eyes are full of lust and I feel her fingers tracing across my abs then tugging at the hem of my shirt.

I reach down to stop her hands.

God damn it Zane, you're an idiot.

"Ava," I said sternly.

"What was the question?" she asks.

"Right now, what could I ask you to do that you'd say no to?"

Who cares. I need her, now.

"I'll do whatever you want, Zane," she says, leaning in for a kiss.

"Fuck," I mumble, pulling myself off of her and readjusting my pants.

"That is precisely my point, love," I say, kissing her on the forehead.

Way to cock block yourself.

"Zane, come on, really?" she says. "So you're just never gonna kiss me or have sex with me?"

Zane, you're a giant fucking twat.

"Babe, I'm not saying never," I say. "I just have to figure this out first."

"Figure what out?"

"How to… how to make sure you don't do something you'll regret."

"And what if I want to do something I'll regret?" she asks, her hand tugging at the button on my jeans.

"Damn it, Ava," I say with a smile. "You're just here to test my self-control, aren't you?"

I step back from the couch. She's right, I can't keep doing this. The fact that I've resisted her this long is a bloody miracle.

"How about this," I say, "have a couple glasses of water and we'll finish dinner. If you're still set on it come morning we can revisit this conversation."

"In the morning?" she asks.

"Well, love, I can't exactly just send you home now, can I?"

17

 ZANE

I step out onto the balcony to avoid disturbing Ava, who is fast asleep on the couch. I hold my phone to my ear and listen to the ringing.

Pick up, damn it.

"Zane, what the hell?" I hear Kami's voice whine at the other end of the line. "Are you seriously calling me at this hour??"

"Right love, like you never call me in the middle of the night for a random favor."

"Okay, sure," she says with a yawn. "But you never call me this late."

"Well, I am now."

"So what's the emergency?"

"It's not exactly an emergency but, uh…"

"Did Ava already break up with you?"

"No," I say. "But thanks for immediately assuming that."

"My bad," she says. "What's up?"

"Ava wants to have sex."

"Oh my god Zane—what are you, a teenager? Do we need to have *the talk*? Should I tell you about the Sirens and the bees?"

"Kami you're not as funny as you think you are."

"I'm hilarious and you know it," she says.

"I've been trying to avoid being alone with her but… I'm struggling to control myself."

"Oh wow," she gasps. "This is good!"

"How is this good?"

"You're letting loose. No more tightly wound, can't-let-my-guard-down Zane.

You've been holding yourself back for so long. You're finally being who you are: a true Siren."

"We can have my coming out party later, love. I'm losing my fucking mind over here. My eyes have been sparking green so much that she's starting to ask questions. I can't even think straight when I look at her. I'm turning bloody feral, I swear."

"Men are so melodramatic," she says with a sigh. "You could always try aster. Or anything with aster in it. Personally, I like absinthe."

Aster is a spice that calms the passions of Sirens. I've always prided myself on never needing it.

"First off, who has absinthe just hanging around in their pantry?" I ask.

"I do."

"Of course you do," I sigh.

"Honest answer, Zane? You just need to feed your urges. You're a Siren. Just have sex with her. Don't make it more complicated than it needs to be."

"How? How do I do this? How do I know if she really wants to?"

"Well first off, venom doesn't make people do anything they don't want to do. It just brings your desires to the surface. It's an aphrodisiac, not hypnosis," she says. "Secondly, you could just ask her."

"Ask her what?"

"Ask her what she wants to do before you guys get all hot and heavy. Then you're double sure."

"I… huh… maybe that would work."

"Well it's better than sporting a perma-boner." Kami was never one for subtlety.

"Ahh that's enough, thanks. I'm hanging up now."

"You called me, remember?"

"Bye, Kam," I say as I end the call and set down my phone.

I peek through the glass door to see Ava fast asleep.

I'm going to have to try something eventually. Otherwise, this girl is going to kill me.

———⦙———

AVA

I wake up on Zane's couch, tangled in his arms with my head on his chest. He's now wearing a black T-shirt and grey sweat pants. I borrowed one of his shirts and a pair of boxers to sleep in. He's still fast asleep and through the window I can see the sunrise.

Ow. Pain is shooting up my back, but I don't want to move. This just feels too perfect.

Zane's chest rises with a deep breath as he stirs awake.

"You're so beautiful, baby," he mutters drowsily, his eyelids just cracked open.

I just woke up after sleeping in my makeup and on most days I would assume I look like crap right now, but the way he says it makes me feel like the most gorgeous girl who has ever lived.

He stretches before wrapping his arm back around my shoulders.

"So," I say. I think it's time we had that talk.

"So?" he asks.

"I believe I was promised a talk."

His eyes widen and he seems to jolt up a bit.

"Bloody hell, you really don't waste any time, do you love?"

"I'm a girl who knows what she wants," I say, leaning in for a kiss. He puts a hand to my lips to stop me.

"Want me that badly, do you?" he asks.

I hate his cocky attitude. Why is he like this? I'm hot so why won't he have sex with me?

"Oh whatever," I say, untangling from him and getting up off the couch. "Get over yourself. If you don't want me, nobody's forcing you to do anything."

He follows me as I straighten my clothing and look for my sweater.

"Baby," he says, grabbing my arm. "I didn't mean it like that, I *do* want you."

"Then what's your deal?" I ask, crossing my arms. He sighs in response. It suddenly occurs to me that I may have been insensitive.

"Are you a virgin?" I ask.

He explodes into a fit of laughter.

"You think…" he stammers between laughs, "think that I… am a virgin?"

His laughter gets louder. He's so full of himself.

"Okay, that's enough ladykiller, it's not that funny." I cross my arms and shoot him a glare.

"I'm sorry," he says as his laughter settles. "I just… I'm not a virgin, no."

"So you just sleep with everyone but me?"

"Love, I do not just… no… it's not like that." He huffs and runs his hand through his hair.

"Then what's your deal?"

"I've just… never cared very much what anyone really thought of me…" He lets out a long sigh and his eyes meet mine. "…until you."

"Until me?"

"Yeah. Being with you confuses me," he says. "I want you to *really* like me, to *really* want to be with me, to *really* be attracted to me. I don't want to cloud that."

"And you think having sex will cloud whether or not I really like you?"

"Yeah, I guess," he sighs.

"Well I do really like you. And I'm telling you that. And I'm attracted to you."

"Alright, love, so you want to have sex with me?"

"There's that cocky attitude again…" My eyes narrow.

"What do you want me to say?" he says in a frustrated tone. "That I want you? That you're fit as fuck? That it takes everything I have to resist you even for one fucking second? 'Cause if you need me to swallow my pride here and make it clear that I'm bloody obsessed with you, then I will."

His eyes flicker between green and brown and he seems a combination of shy and exasperated.

"I…" I try to speak but I'm at a loss for words. "You… Then why try to resist me?"

"Because I care about you," he says, seemingly startled by his own words.

Our eyes meet and he smiles.

"You want me to fuck you?" he asks in a low, soft voice.

Duh, dude. Duh.

"Yeah," I say. "That's kind of my point."

"Right now?" he asks, approaching me.

Wow. Okay, to the point then.

"Yes," I say, stepping closer and tracing my hands across his chest. He shivers at my touch. I attempt to kiss him but he puts up a hand to stop me.

"Nuh uh uh," he teases. "I have a few more questions. Do you want me to…"

He bends down to kiss my neck.

"…use my tongue, love?" he asks.

My skin tingles as his lips touch me.

"Yes," I say softly.

"Do you want to…" he says, moving to the other side of my neck, "use yours?"

Dayumm. I feel the blood rushing to my face at his words.

"I um…" I'm suddenly feeling shy.

Damn it, Ava, you're an independent, sexually liberated, adult woman. You can do this.

"Ye-… Yes," I mumble. Not exactly the confident, sexy tone I was going for, but I got the word out.

"Well then," he says with another kiss at my collar bone. He grabs my ass and presses his hips into mine, letting out a breathy moan as he does. "You're about to get what you want, baby."

Zane's lips crash into mine and my body feels electric. The pain in my back and neck eases and all that's left is ecstasy. My nerves are on fire and every touch feels ten times more intense as a wave of heat rushes through my body.

His hands grope along my body as I wrap my legs around his waist. He grips my ass, lifting me and carrying me back to his bedroom.

"Fuck, baby, you're so sexy," he says between kisses.

He lowers me onto his bed and climbs on top of me as I pull my shirt off. He kisses along my collar bone and down my chest until he reaches the pair of borrowed boxers I'm wearing, tugging them off me in a swift motion.

I pull his shirt off over his head, revealing his flawlessly sculpted body. His eyes are shining a brighter green than I've ever seen them and his expression is wild with lust.

His kisses become increasingly ravenous and I slip my hand beneath the waistband of his sweatpants and stroke him. A growl resonates deep from within his chest and he lifts my body further along the bed until his mouth is between my legs, kissing me through my panties.

Damn. This boy is gonna kill me, I swear.

He grabs my panties with each hand and tears them in two as if they were made of paper

"Oops," he says with a smirk.

In seconds, his tongue is on me and I feel an incredible sensation radiating from his touch. I'm overcome with waves of pleasure rippling out through my body. I've never felt better in my life.

This is what I've been missing with him this whole time??

I'm barely coherent, my vision is fuzzy, and I feel like I'm floating, riding through one wave of sensation to the next.

"Zane…" I moan. He squirms and his back tenses.

"Fuck, baby," he sighs. He kisses my stomach and works his way up to my chest. He rises further until his eyes meet mine, radiating a green glow. "Say my name again."

"Zane," I say through heavy pants.

In what seems like an instant his boxers are off and he's on top of me, slipping a condom on. A low guttural moan escapes his lips as he buries himself in me.

I see sparkles at the corners of my vision and I drift in and out of pure pleasure.

"How do you want it, baby?" he asks.

"I... I..."

Words, Ava. Words. What are words again?

"You want it fast, baby?" he asks, thrusting into me rapidly.

"Or do you want it... nice... and... slow?" He reduces his pace, slowly pushing in and out of me with each word.

My muscles have turned into pudding and now he's asking me to form a sentence?

"Ff... fffasstt," I stutter.

"Fast, baby?" he asks, a smirk spreading across his face. "I'm really glad you said that."

He increases his pace again, pounding into me as the pressure between my thighs increases.

"Because," he says, his breath catching. "I've been waiting... too long... to have you. I wasn't sure I was gonna... be able to... take it slow with you, baby."

I let out another moan as pleasure overpowers my brain. My legs shake and my whole body tingles.

"Zane... Oh god..."

My vision goes white. He continues, his pace quickening slightly as deep moans emerge from his chest.

"Ffuuckk," he yells, releasing into me with a shudder and collapsing on top of me.

We both rest for a moment entangled in each other.

"Ava... Fuck..." he says, his voice strained.

I giggle.

"Are you..." he asks, raising himself onto his elbows to look me in the eyes. "Are you okay?"

"I'm better than okay," I say, basking in the floating-on-a-cloud feeling.

"So," he lets out a sigh. "You don't regret it?"

Is this boy crazy?

"No, dumbass," I say. "This is not my regret face." I smirk at him before sticking out my tongue.

He smiles back and rolls off of me.

"Now, love," he says. "Are you gonna be a bad girl and get cheeky with me?"

"What if I am?" I tease. He looks at me with a devious smile.

"Try me and find out."

18

 ZANE

Ava is standing in the bathroom, her frame peeking through the barely open door. A strand of purple hair falls in her eyes as she stands in just my T-shirt, brushing her teeth in the mirror. I don't want her to go, but I'm not going to be clingy about it.

"You could stay here another night, love," my mouth says without my permission.

Oh Zane, you clingy little bitch.

"Zane," she scolds. "I have no clothes and—thanks to *someone*—no panties."

"If you stay, you won't be needing those anyway."

She combs through her hair with her fingers and gives me a dirty look.

"Pervert," she says.

I slip in behind her and wrap my arms around her waist, squeezing her tight.

"Ow!" she yelps.

"Shit, baby, I'm sorry. What did I do? Is it your pain thing?"

"Oh, I um," she pauses and then giggles. "I'm just a little tender is all."

"Tender?" I ask. I pull up the sides of the oversized T-shirt she's wearing to reveal purple bruises on both her hips.

"It's no big deal," she says with a smile, tugging the shirt back down.

"I…" I try to say something but nothing comes out.

I hurt her? I've had sex with humans before and, as far as I know, I've never done that. I've always been careful. I know how delicate they are.

"Don't give me that face," she says, her mouth scrunching. "It's not your fault."

"How the fuck is that not my fault, love?"

Bloody… How did this happen? I was so damn worried about my venom that I didn't even consider I might lose control of my strength and cover her in bruises.

"Are there more?" I ask.

"I dunno," she says, inspecting her arms and legs. "I don't think so."

"Fuck!" I walk back into the bedroom. I grab a pillow and whip it into the wall, causing it to explode into a cloud of cotton batting.

"Whoa," she says. "Chill, dude. Don't take it out on the pillows. I'm fine."

"You didn't tell me I was hurting you…"

"I didn't notice, honestly."

Of course she didn't. You can hardly feel pain with venom in your system.

"Hey," she says, grabbing my face with both hands and staring at me with those big grey eyes. "I am okay. I wanted that to happen. I'm fine with the way everything transpired, okay? I'm an adult. You don't have to protect me."

"But you're in pain and it's my fault," I say.

"Well," she sighs. "Not trying to be a downer or anything but… I'm literally *always* in pain. That's just a fact of my life right now. Has been for a while. But this morning, for once, with you—I wasn't."

She's *always* in pain? My heart clenches just thinking about that. *Always?*

"You weren't in pain?" I ask. "When we… And that was…"

"You helped make it go away. So don't apologize for anything. Pain is something I'm very good at handling. I'm basically a badass." She laughs.

I can't help but smile. In many ways, I've always felt that my powers were evil, brought about to manipulate and hurt people. I liked to think that maybe ridding people of their inhibitions could be good for them, but it didn't even occur to me that taking away someone's pain like this could be a gift.

———◆———

KAMI

That stupid, untamed demon is officially off the rails. This last one makes six killings that I've confirmed myself. This is turning into more than just a job I'm doing for Lola. What Kieran is doing is officially putting us all in danger.

I tap at his door.

"Kieran, open the door before I break it open myself!" I shout through the door.

The demon opens the door with one of his usual snarky faces.

"Kami," he says. "Here to finally confess your undying love for me?"

I push him inside and follow behind.

"Damn, girl," he says. "If you wanted a bit of this, all you had to do was ask."

Maggot.

"I know what you've been doing," I say.

"Oh really?" he says. "And what would that be?"

"This last girl was 20 years old, Kieran." I shove him with both hands and he falls back into his dining table. "Are you insane? Killing again? And this recklessly? You're going to draw attention and it's going to get me and Zane killed."

"Oh god, you've really got your panties in a twist this time, haven't you? Who says I'm killing anyone?"

"I saw the bodies, Kieran. They were drained! Grey skin, eyes completely white, insides of their mouths coated in black. I know an Incubus kill when I see one. And Zane's been off with his little girlfriend, but somehow you haven't been going hungry without him. You think I can't put this together? You think I've managed to live this long without knowing what I'm doing?"

"First off," he says, sitting nonchalantly in his recliner and resting an ankle across his knee, "if I kill people, it's not your business. Second off, I can handle myself without Zane fucking fine."

"Zane trusts you! You're spitting in the face of everything he does to help you. I know you don't have a soul, but I never realized how truly soulless you are."

"I don't owe you shit and I *definitely* don't need to explain myself to you."

"So you're not recklessly draining your prey all over town? Do you know another Incubus in town who's that level of stupid?"

"I'm the only Incubus in town that I know of. Port Charlotte isn't exactly primo real estate for demonkind."

"Well, murdering your prey left, right, and center isn't exactly going to help with that, is it? You'll get us run out of town, killed, or worse! I'm telling Zane exactly what you're up to."

His face turns cold and his eyes fill to the edges with black.

"Fucking tell him then," he spits. "Go run off to *Mommy*. You think I don't have things I can tell Zane, too?"

This little creep is threatening me? Sure, I haven't told Zane about everything I've been up to lately or what's going on with Lola, but I'm certainly not afraid of him. Zane and I are family. He knows I do what needs to be done. He understands.

"Is that a threat, *cretin*?" I snap, stalking toward him. He stands up, his frame instantly dwarfing me. Okay, so maybe I was a little cocky to get into a fight with a demon that I have no way of killing.

"You're kidding," he says, letting out a hearty laugh. "You think I'm threatening you? I don't do threats, sweet cakes. Besides, I would crush you."

He walks past me and pours himself a small glass of liquor, then pours another and offers it to me.

Seriously?

"No!" I snap. "I'm not going to accuse you of going on a murder spree and then sit down to have a drink with you."

"Suit yourself then." He chugs both in quick succession.

"So we all done here, or you want to finish this in the bedroom?" he asks. *Friggin creep.*

"I know you murdered those people, demon. I'm going to find a way to get you under control, whatever the cost."

19

 ZANE

I've had what you could call relationships here and there. They usually weren't official and lasted a couple of weeks, but I did try it. Getting properly involved with someone never really had much appeal to me, especially a human. You're with them for a while and then what? The problem with humans is that they all have an expiration date.

For whatever reason, this feels different. Ava is different. I want her. But knowing what you want is a curse. It means you start to notice when it's missing. There's a gap that can only be filled by one thing—one person.

Needing her means figuring out a way to keep her, and for that I'm going to need help.

Kami pours us two cups of tea as we sit at her kitchen counter.

"Spill, Z," she says between sips of tea. "You're not one for house calls, so what's on your mind?"

"I wanted to talk to you about… humans."

"Humans?" she asks, raising a brow.

"About Ava… I think this might be, I don't know… something."

"Whoa, whoa! Zane, I knew you liked this girl, but are you in love with her?"

"No!"

Yes.

What? Fuck!

I let a low growl slip out.

"Yeah, I buy it," she says with a smirk.

"I'm not fucking in love, okay?"

Liar.

Shut up, brain.

"Yeah, okay," she says. "So you're not in love, you just want to have a conversation about humans. Or rather, this human."

"Yeah, I guess."

"Okay, I'll bite. What's your question?"

"So venom makes humans less susceptible to pain, but, is there any way to just get rid of the-"

"Supernatural kiss-induced horniness?"

"Yeah."

"Hmmm," she hums, taking another sip of her tea. "Not that I know of."

"Fuck. Yeah, I guess that was a long shot."

"Why? Ava becoming an ultimate fighter or something?"

I laugh as I picture her small frame beating the shit out of a serious fighter.

"No, she's sick or something," I say, trying not to share Ava's personal details.

"She's sick? What... Is she dying?"

"No, god, no."

Ava's not dying. Right? *Fuck.* Why did she put that in my head? *Fuck.*

"Okay, well, at least there would be a solution to that," she says.

"What solution?"

"You could mark her." She takes a sip of her tea.

"The mark is a myth, Kami."

"No," she says, pulling out her phone. "I've seen it myself."

She shows me a photo of a man on her phone, zooming in on what looks like a tattoo on his wrist.

"You remember Alek?" she asks. "This is his partner, David. He's marked."

The photo shows a dark knot-shaped mark on his wrist.

"That's a tattoo," I say.

"No, it's not—he really did it! He cut off his wings. I've seen the scars where they used to be. His partner is immune to venom and he's effectively immortal."

I always thought the mark was a fairy tale. I've always heard stories but I've never known of anyone crazy enough to cut off their wings.

That really works?

"Are you thinking about it?" she asks.

"No. Of course not. Even if I wanted to, we have no idea what the effects could be. I'm not turning Ava into a guinea pig."

"Interesting," she says, taking another sip of tea in a way that I've come to recognize as dubious.

"What?" I ask.

"It's interesting that your objection wasn't 'I can't cut off my bloody wings for some bird I've only known for a couple months'." Her impersonation of me is painful to listen to, especially the English accent. Kami has always had one of those impossible-to-place accents, probably from traveling and living all over the world, but she's never firmly landed on one—and at this point I don't think she can.

"Piss off, mate," I huff. "Your impersonation needs some work."

"Piss off, mate," she mimics back. I roll my eyes and head to her couch, stretching out.

She joins me in the living room and sits down on a nearby chair.

"It's good, you know?" she adds, her tone shifting. "You've closed yourself off since everything that happened in Austria."

I shut my eyes at the mention.

I instantly flash back to visions of the poor girl's bruised, lifeless body. The color was drained from her skin, blood at the corners of her mouth.

"She's good for you." Kami's words shake me from my thoughts.

"Yeah well, you and Kieran have been good for me too."

Kami shifts in her seat and narrows her eyes. She's never been Kieran's biggest fan, but they've been getting along better lately.

"Yeah," she says with a nod.

AVA

"Oh come on you whiner, it'll be fun!" I say, tugging Zane toward the front desk.

"Anything for you, love," he chuckles.

"Shoes and a round of bowling for two, please." The man at the counter nods.

"Sizes?" he asks.

"8 for me and..." I start to respond, but it occurs to me that I don't know Zane's size.

"10... Er, uh..." Zane stammers. "10 1/2 American."

The man hands us two pairs of shoes and directs us over to our lane. We sit down and tie our shoes.

"Alright, love," Zane says, grabbing a bowling ball from the feeder. "What is the goal of this game?"

"Come on, really? You knock down the pins. You want to get as many of them as possible. You don't know how bowling works?"

"I've seen it before, but I don't usually participate in sport."

"Okay, well I'm not super good, but you can watch me and I can give you some idea of how to play."

I stand up to bowl and am suddenly very aware of his eyes watching me. I shouldn't have volunteered to be an example. I'm awkward and this ball is heavy. *Here goes nothing.*

The ball rolls down the center of the lane and knocks down most of the pins, leaving a couple standing at one edge. I'll take it.

He looks at me with somewhat inquisitive eyes.

"Is that good, then?" he asks. "Seven pins?"

"I think so."

"Why not get all of them?"

"I can't tell if you're being serious or just a smartass."

"In this one particular instance I'm not being cheeky," he says with a smirk.

"You want to hit all of them, I'm just not very good."

He walks over to the ball feeder and picks up a pretty heavy one. With a swift motion, he smoothly sends the ball down the lane and there's a loud clatter as the pins tumble and fly.

Of frickin' course he gets a strike on his first try.

I see a chunk of wood in the middle of the lane. *Did that splinter come from one of the pins?* He turns around with a smirk and lifts me up in the air, planting a kiss on my cheek.

"I knew I'd be good at this," he says with a big smile.

——·——

After Zane bowled a near-perfect game and I bowled… a game, I suggested we head on out. We unlaced our bowling shoes and headed up to the counter.

"Ava!" someone calls from behind us.

Zane and I both turn to find the source. I see a blond man waving to me from the lanes. It takes me a second to recognize the nurse from the hospital.

"Hey!" he says, jogging over. He reaches us and Zane's eyes narrow. "Web Designer Girl! Remember me? Trevor."

He gives me a quick hug to greet me.

"Hey Trevor!" I say.

"Hey," he says, turning to Zane. "I'm Trevor." He reaches out and shakes Zane's hand.

"Zane," Zane says in a low huff, cutting their handshake off quickly.

"You guys just get done bowling?" he asks.

"Yeah, we were just putting our shoes back," I say.

"Cool cool. Well I dunno if you guys have other plans tonight, but if you wanna hang out my friends and I were gonna grab a few drinks here before our next game. Care to join?"

He gestures to the in-house bar.

"Uh," I look at Zane, whose stoic face isn't giving me much feedback to work with. "Sure, that sounds nice."

Zane's face changes into one of irritation. I return his look with one of my own that says '*well you should've said something then.*'

We head to the bar where two of Trevor's friends have gathered at a high-top table. Trevor sits down and orders a couple of pitchers of beer for the table.

"So how's work, Ava?" he asks. "Still taking on bad guys, one website at a time?" He chuckles to himself as he pours himself a beer.

Oof. That was terrible.

"Yeah, pretty much. I'm still enjoying it, so I can't complain. What about you?"

"Long hours, this is my first day off in ages. But otherwise good. How about you, Zane? What do you do?"

Zane glares at him and looks like he's debating how to answer.

"I own a few properties around town," he says, looping an arm around my shoulders.

This is the first I've heard of this. *Is that true or does Zane just not want to admit he doesn't have a job?*

"Oh hey, your accent—that's British, right?" Trevor asks.

"Yeah," he says, taking a long drink of his beer. "Clever one, you are."

Trevor laughs, seemingly not minding that Zane is definitely insulting him. I sip my beer and attempt to ignore the awkwardness.

"Cool cool. What do you think of the States so far?"

"Some things are proper brilliant," he says, smiling at me. "Others not my favorite." He looks back at Trevor and takes another huge swig of his beer.

"Right on," Trevor says. "Glad you're liking it."

"How are things with you?" I ask.

"Great. I'm actually transferring to another section of the hospital, so we'll probably be seeing less of each other."

"Oh dang," I say.

"Yeah, that's alright," he says. "Now I can at least hang and grab a drink with you and not have it be unethical."

Hmm… I didn't even really think about this being something he wouldn't be allowed to do.

"Oh hey, Ava," Trevor continues, turning to me. "You know Blue Panic is gonna be in town in two weeks. I got a couple tickets if you wanted to go with me."

Zane instantly tenses and his chest puffs up.

"Oh, I uh," I stutter, trying to think of a subtle way to navigate this situation.

Zane's hand quickly slides around my waist and he effortlessly scoops me from my chair into his lap.

"She's taken, mate," he says with a smile.

Trevor is visibly embarrassed and his cheeks turn a bright red.

"Oh, sorry, I didn't mean to uh… intrude. I didn't realize you guys were a couple."

"Yep," Zane responds. Trevor's eyes shift uncomfortably around the room.

Zane pulls me in by my waist and gives me a deep kiss, resting his hand on my ass. Oh, so now he's all 'Mr. Let's Make Out'. I can't even be mad because it ignites my every nerve and all I can think about if how much I want more. Zane smirks and looks at Trevor.

"So you work at the hospital, then?" Zane asks.

Trevor explains that he works as a nurse but I'm lost in watching Zane.

Why is he so pretty? It's not even fair.

I excuse myself to the bathroom to try and get a grip.

I'm alone in the ladies' room, so I splash a bit of cold water on my neck. Nope, still just as flustered as I was when I came in here.

Come on, Ava, don't be rude and be all over Zane in front of this nice guy who likes you. He's already been rejected, don't make it worse.

I remember Zane's theory about drinking water to calm down. It has helped in the past. I try to drink a little from the faucet. If anyone comes in here, I'm going to look really weird.

I return to the table and seat myself, trying to follow where the conversation has landed. I can sense Zane's gaze on me and I'm struggling to avoid eye contact, so I focus on the TVs on the opposite wall.

Keeping away from Zane is impossible. Maybe I should just give in to temptation.

Bad brain! Bad, bad brain!

We said we would stay for drinks, so we should at least hang out a little longer.

Don't look at Zane. Don't look at Zane.

I try to focus and take another sip of beer.

"Uhhh," Trevor pauses and looks at me with concern.

Oh crap, this is not my glass. *Real smooth.*

"Oh my gosh, I'm so sorry Trevor. This is yours isn't it?" I say, frantically plopping it back onto the table and pushing it toward him.

He lets out a chuckle and waves his hand forgivingly in my direction.

"No worries, Ava, I'm sure you don't have cooties." He smirks and takes another drink.

Zane catches me by surprise as he swipes the drink from Trevor's hand. The plastic tumbler cracks into a few large shards that fall to the table as beer pours out all over Trevor.

The chaos draws the attention of Trevor's friends, whose conversation has halted as they try to make sense of what just happened.

I give Zane a hard *'what the fuck'* look and step around him to help Trevor with the mess.

The bartender offers us a roll of paper towels.

"Here, let me help with that," I say, grabbing a handful of paper towels.

I feel Zane's hand grip my upper arm, attempting to hold me back from Trevor. I send some serious side eye his way.

Maybe if you didn't go around swatting at people's drinks out of their hands like a crazy person, we wouldn't be in this situation.

He releases my arm and I try to help blot beer from Trevor's sopping shirt. As I blot, I feel Trevor looking up at me.

Shit, am I being awkward right now?

"I'm sorry," I say, lifting my eyes to meet his. "I don't mean to get all up in your space."

"No," he says softly. "Please do."

Trevor's friends seem to notice his odd comment and have gone instantly silent. My hand is frozen holding a towel to his chest.

Zane's jaw is clenched, his chest is inflated, and his eyes flicker with bright green.

That was not the right thing to say, Trevor. Are you trying to get thrown into a wall?

"Uhh, um…" I stutter, trying to find the right response.

I'm shocked silent by lips meeting my neck—Trevor's lips.

What the hell??

I push him off of me and within seconds Zane's hand is wrapped around Trevor's neck, pinning him against the wall.

"Zane, I… don't…" I stutter, trying to stop him from doing something stupid. I don't actually have a good argument prepared to finish that sentence, but I'm interrupted by Trevor.

"Shit, I'm so sorry! I have no idea why I did that." Trevor cringes with embarrassment.

"God damn it!" Zane shouts. "Fuck!"

He grabs Trevor by his collar and tosses him to the side. Trevor's friends are frozen in shock.

"I don't care what your excuse is," Zane snaps. "You try it on with my girl again and I'll kill you."

Zane stomps off, roughly tugging at his hair with both hands.

I give an apologetic look to Trevor and his friends as I follow Zane out the door.

Well that wasn't awkward at all.

20

Zane has been quiet the entire drive to my apartment. His fists are clenched so tight around the wheel that his knuckles are practically white. The car pulls in to the driveway of my apartment complex.

"Zane," I say softly as he turns the engine off. "What was that?"

"I'm not allowed to get mad when some prick tries to snog my girlfriend?" His voice is low and rough.

"No, I understand that, I'm just not sure I get why you lost it on his beer before that. What did the beer do to you?"

"I… fuck…" he stumbles. A horrendous crack rings through the car as a chunk of steering wheel snaps off into his hand. "Ah shit."

"What the hell??"

"I just got it repaired. I guess they didn't do a very good job."

What in the actual hell is going on?

"Zane, what is your deal?" I ask.

"What deal?" he asks.

"God damn it Zane, cut the crap."

He turns to me and a smile spreads across his face.

"You're sexy when you're angry, love."

Damn. Damn your intense hotness.

I see a green sparkle in his eyes and before I know it he's leading me inside.

My mind is foggy and I can't see much in the dark. It's definitely sometime between midnight and dawn but beyond that, I'm not sure. I reach for Zane but he's no longer in bed.

When I sit up, I can see him pacing back and forth in the hallway.

"Zane?" I call.

"Shit," he curses under his breath.

"Happy to see you too, babe. Am I interrupting your breakdown?"

He walks toward me and the minimal light coming through the window hits his face.

Are those… *tears?*

"Whoa, hey," I say, getting up and wrapping my arms around his neck. "What's wrong?"

"Nothing, love," he says with a reassuring smile.

Bullshit.

"Okay, care to tell me what kind of something that 'nothing' means?"

"Well you just see right through me, don't you?" He tries to smile but there's a sadness behind it.

"Pretty much," I say with a smile.

Another tear falls from his eye and he's quick to wipe it away.

"I'm not who you think I am," he says, his voice softening to almost a whisper.

"And who do I think you are?"

"Human."

"And you're a werewolf?" I say with a giggle, tracing the edge of his jaw with my fingers. A low growl rumbles in his chest. I can't tell if he's intentionally trying to sound like a werewolf right now or not.

"Love, can you not touch me right now?"

Oh… Okay. *Am I in trouble?*

"Sure," I say, pulling my hands away from his face. I sit down on the bed and he joins next to me.

"Do you know what a Siren is?"

"Uh… as in the sound from a fire engine?"

"No," he chuckles. "As in the mythological creature."

"Oh, yeah," I say. "Mermaids."

"No," he says with a heavy, frustrated sigh.

"Okay then, I'm gonna say no. I guess I don't."

"Sirens are winged creatures with the power to control and lure humans."

"Are you having some kind of sleep-walking dream right now?"

"Please listen to me," he says, distress apparent in his voice. "You asked me why my eyes change color? Well, that's because I'm not human, I'm a Siren. My eyes glow when my animalistic side takes over."

Oh yeah, he's definitely having some kind of bizarre hallucination.

"Okay, Zane. You're a Siren with magical eyes. That's fine. Come back to bed."

"Damn it, Ava," he grunts. "Why is this so hard?"

He stands up and paces across the floor.

"You know how when we kiss you always feel extremely aroused?" he asks.

"Wow, okay, Mister Full-of-Himself."

You're right, but hell if I'm going to admit it.

"I'm not being…" he mumbles before letting out a deep growl. "Okay, fine."

He faces me and pulls his T-shirt up off over his head. His body is flawless as ever, black tattoos against his tanned skin. He looks to either side of himself before thrusting his shoulders forward.

In a seamless motion, a pair of large, black wings emerge from his back.

I let out a gasp and rub my eyes. Am I having another one of those super-realistic dreams? What am I looking at right now?

What?

What?!?

"Say something," he says softly. His head hangs low and his posture his hunched. He wrings one hand in the other, refusing to make eye contact.

"Wha… What?"

I step closer to him, reaching a hand to touch his wing just above his shoulder. I rub along the rough feathers. He shivers beneath my touch and the feathers ruffle.

This is too weird. My boyfriend doesn't have wings.

But how can I feel them if they're not real?

"How are you even… I'm so confused. This is crazy."

"I can make you understand," he says softly. "If you want. If I touch you and tell you to believe me, you will."

"Just like that? I'll believe? Forever?"

"Not forever, but when it fades you'll still remember that it worked, which is in itself a rather compelling argument."

"And if it doesn't work?" I ask.

"Well, then we chalk it up to some crazy dream and go back to bed."

"Okay," I say. "Seems like a definitive answer. Let's do it."

He holds out his palms and I place my hands in his.

"Believe me, I am a Siren," he says.

He is a Siren. Shit, what??

"Holy shit!" I shout.

I rub my hand along the top edge of his wing.

"These…" I say with wide eyes, my hands still following the curves of the wings, "are real?"

He shivers again and I see his eyes glowing green through the dark.

"Baby," he says, catching my forearm with his hand. "That feels a little too good for the particular conversation we're having right now."

"Oh," I say, my cheeks suddenly feeling hot. He smirks and his feathers ruffle and shake.

"So you didn't kiss me because your kisses are magic or something?"

"Not exactly," he says with a chuckle. "It's uh, venom actually."

He opens his mouth and raises his tongue, revealing two small holes on either side.

"Whoa." My eyes widen. "That's where it comes from?"

"Yeah," he says with a shrug, rubbing a hand through his hair. His wings retract and he looks at the ground.

I walk around him to inspect his back, but the only evidence that remains is two slightly prominent ridges along his spine.

"Where do they even go?" I ask.

"They don't go anywhere really, I think my body just absorbs them."

I run my fingers over the ridges. They don't feel particularly strange, but I don't know what I expected.

"Baby…" he moans.

"Shoot, sorry, I didn't realize."

"It's okay." He smirks and his eyebrows raise suggestively, but in a split second his flirtatious mood wavers and he looks down at the ground again. "So, do you want me to go?"

"No," I say. "Why would I want you to go? It's the middle of the night. Do you want to leave?"

"No," he says. "I just thought… What do you want to do?"

"About you being a mythological creature?"

"Yeah," he says, looking at the wall. "I understand if this isn't exactly what you signed up for."

"Zane…" I bring a hand up to his face. "I don't care."

"You… you don't?" His eyes widen and a smile creeps across his face.

"I mean, I have questions. Like a lot of questions. But, I kind of get that this isn't the kind of thing you just tell anyone and—wait, you don't eat people, do you?"

He bursts into laughter.

"No, love," he says with a smile. "I don't eat people, although some others do. Not Sirens, but there are others."

When he says others, what does that mean? Werewolves? Mermaids? Bigfoot?

"Other whats?"

"Immortals…" he mumbles.

"You're immortal? Like, you can't die?"

He laughs and pulls me with him into bed.

"It just means I don't age. I can die, but it's not easy to kill a Siren."

He doesn't age? Wow… this is a lot to process for my foggy brain in the middle of the night.

"So then… how old are you?" I ask.

"199…" he mumbles, wringing his hands. "But for a Siren that's not very old, the human equivalent would be around my early thirties. Is that… okay?"

So my boyfriend is almost 200 years old and he has wings… um… I guess now that I think of it the wings are the bigger revelation at this moment.

"Ummm… yeah, I guess so," I say. He sighs, seemingly relieved. "Wow, okay. I have so many questions."

"What do you want to know, love?"

"Okay, well let's start with… what was with attacking Trevor's beer?"

His face becomes more serious and he bites his cheek.

"I caught it a little late, unfortunately. I wasn't thinking and I forgot I had kissed you. That was a rookie move, I'm sorry."

"You do know you're making no sense at all right now…"

"Shit, sorry. You uh, had my venom on your lips and shared a drink. Siren venom is extremely potent. It doesn't take much."

"Wait—why is it so bad for him but not for me?"

"Err…" he ruffles his hair with his fingers. "Because it lowers your inhibitions. Makes you overcome with lust. Which is not a problem when it makes you hot for me, but more of a problem with a handsy dick who fancies my girl."

He slips a hand around my waist and onto my ass, pulling me closer.

"So that's why Trevor kissed my neck? That explains a lot I guess. But then, why would you go after him if you knew he wasn't completely himself?"

"Venom doesn't make you do anything you don't want to do. It just stops your brain from getting in your way."

"Still, Zane…"

"I think I've made it pretty obvious I don't share well, love. Not you. Not ever."

21

"So, can you fly?" Ava asks, biting into a piece of buttered toast. "I mean like, you have wings and all, but so do penguins."

"Yes." I chuckle. "I can fly. But I hardly ever do. There aren't a lot of great opportunities to get my wings out in the modern world where no one will see me."

She's in my T-shirt and a cute pair of black cotton underwear, sitting at the dining table and chowing down on breakfast.

"Fair enough," she says through a mouthful of food. "Do you have other magical powers?"

"Sure. If I'm touching someone I can compel them to do whatever I say, kind of like hypnosis. It wears off after a little while—sometimes a couple of hours, sometimes more."

"What kinds of things do you tell people to do?"

This topic can go nowhere good.

"Erm… Usually just to get free stuff or to make sure they forget they saw something otherworldly. It depends. I try not to use it too much."

"Hmm," she pauses. "Isn't that like stealing? That seems kinda messed up."

"I mean, it can be. I try to only use it on people who have it coming or wouldn't mind."

"Like, have it coming how?"

Like a pompous wanker who tried to not-so-subtly remind me that he used to fuck my girlfriend?

"You know…" I say. "Not-so-great people."

"Ahhh, so people who don't use their blinkers?" She smiles and takes a sip of orange juice.

"Well, love, that's obviously unforgivable."

"So, anything else? Can you turn invisible?"

"I'm not Superman, love, though I understand how you might think that after that shag last night."

Her cheeks turn a deep shade of red.

"Don't flatter yourself, wing boy." She gives me a light punch on the shoulder and I chuckle.

"I don't know if it counts as a power, but I'm stronger than humans. Faster, too. And my skin can't be penetrated by mortal weapons."

"*Harder, better, faster, stronger?*" she sings with a giggle.

"Well, I *certainly* could get harder for you, baby," I tease, scooping her up from her chair and into my lap. She playfully squirms against me and smacks my arm. Her grey eyes catch mine and she bites her lower lip.

On second thought, strike that. Not sure I *could* get any harder.

"Can you lift a car?" she asks.

With my dick?

Oh, never mind, we're back on the 'superpowers' thing.

"I uh," I choke. "Ahem… Probably. I never tried. It depends."

Way to not sound like an idiot.

"Depends on what?"

"On how much of a, erm, carnal state I'm in. I guess."

"Carnal?" she asked, her eyes widening. "Like when your eyes are green?"

"Yeah. The more green they are, the more that side is in control."

"They're green now," she says with a curious expression.

"Yeah, baby, I bet they are."

———•———

"Wow…" Kami says, her face frozen in a stunned expression. She's seated on my couch, her elbows leaning on her knees.

"I had to… I practically outed myself," I say.

Maybe that's not true, but I couldn't hold it in anymore. It kept running through my mind that I would keep falling further for Ava and when she knew, she wouldn't want anything to do with me. It was making me sick.

But of course, leave it to my girl to be only temporarily phased by the idea of her man having wings. Before comparing me to a penguin, that is.

I chuckle at the thought.

"You're in love with her!" Kami exclaims, jumping up so that her feet are on the cushions and she's now in a crouched position.

"I'm not…" I start to say; the words feel like bile in my throat. Say you aren't in love with her, damn it, or Kami is never going to let this go.

Lying sack of shit.

"I'm…" I try again. "She's human. You're ridiculous, Kami, okay. We… She and I… Have you ever known me to be in love?"

Smooth.

"You loooovee herrrr," she teases.

"And what if I do?" I snap.

Oh shit.

There it is.

"That's great, Zane! You deserve to be in love! Do I finally get to meet her now?"

"I… Yeah, you can meet her I guess."

"I'm not going to come onto her, Zane, for heaven's sake."

"You do and I'll rip your wings from your body," I growl.

"Oooh touchy, touchy! Maybe you are a Siren after all!" she teases. "Speaking of wings…"

"I'm not marking her, Kam," I say with a firm voice.

"But…" she stutters. "You're crazy about her. You love her. In 200 years you've never felt that once, and now you have. You think you're gonna find another person—another human no less—that would be more worth it? Or are you just attached to your wings?"

Everything out of her mouth sounds absurd. I'm not hedging my bets on another woman or choosing my wings over a real chance with Ava.

"We've discussed this, Kam. I can't risk something like that on her right now."

"Right now?" she asked.

"I don't know, okay. Right now she's sick."

"How sick?" she asks.

"She doesn't know what's wrong right now and until I know, I'm not about to put that on her. Besides, talk about coming on too strong. 'Hey, I know we've only known each other a few months, but I love you and I'm willing to cut off my body parts for you so that you and I can be linked together for eternity.'"

"Well, when you put it like that…" she says, scrunching her face.

"When I put it like that I seem like a creepy fucking cunt."

She lets out a fit of laughter.

"Alright, well on that note, it's getting late," she says, getting up and gathering her things. "I'm gonna head out."

"Alright, night love," I say, waving from my chair.

"Night, creep," she says with a chuckle.

The door slams behind her.

———◆———

ZANE

Dreiflüssestadt, Austrian Empire · Summer of 1840

"You and your like are completely and utterly foolish," Kami says with a laugh.

"My like?" I ask.

"Your like is men," she quips. "You get endless attention from ladies, quite beautiful ones too, and you haven't any interest. But this one, she's off-limits. So naturally, the first thing you do is go straight for her. It's as though you enjoy being flogged."

"And you don't like a challenge?"

"I'm a woman. There's never been a man in creation I'd consider a challenge."

"And you think I'm the cocky one…" I mumble.

"She's not a challenge, she's cursed."

I watch Ilen glide across the street, her long skirt making her seem as though she's walking on air. Her face is round and soft, with rosy cheeks and a pale complexion. Two long ringlets of brown hair frame her face. She is beautiful. Though Kami would not be incorrect in saying that my interest is mostly because I prefer a challenge. And the girl with the two dead fiancés—and another still-living one—is quite the challenge.

Let's just hope it's a challenge I can survive.

22

I stop outside Zane's door for a minute to fix my hair. I've hardly seen him this week and I know I'm spending time with his friends tonight, so I want to make a good impression. Especially since they're… supernatural… people? What do I call them? Sirens? Crap, I suppose I haven't thought this through.

Do you think Martha Stewart has an etiquette guide for supernatural dinner parties?

The door swings open, revealing Zane in a black henley shirt and tight jeans with a wide smile on his face.

"Hey, love!" he says with a hug that lifts me off my feet.

He guides me in with a hand at my back, pulling me into the dining room.

"Love, this is Kami," he says, gesturing to a stunning brunette woman in skin-tight clothing and leather boots. Her hair is perfectly coiffed and shiny and her warm-brown skin is flawless.

"Hey, Ava!" she says with what appears to be enthusiasm. "You're a total babe! I can see why Zane is so obsessed!"

She's gorgeous *and* nice? *What a bitch.*

"Thank you!"

"Now the real question is, what could you possibly see in this asshole?" she jokes, elbowing Zane in the arm. Zane winces and takes a moment to rub his arm where she prodded. This girl must be strong if she's actually able to hurt him.

"Thanks, love," he says. "I'm *definitely not* already regretting introducing you two."

I guess I'm not the only one he calls love. It's silly, but that bugs me a little. Hey, so what if she's stunning and perfect and shiny and sculpted by God himself…

I don't even care.

Totally don't care.

"So uh, how do you two know each other?" I ask.

"We uh," Zane rubs the back of his neck with one hand, the other leaning on the counter.

This pause is awkward and I already regret asking this question. On second thought, I'd rather not know if you guys had some crazy supernatural four-winged flying sex.

Oh god, now I'm picturing it. Make it stoppp. Can I just die instead? Please?

"She's kind of my sister. I've never answered this question honestly to a human before." Zane's face twists in confusion before turning to her. "Kami, uh, how do I?"

"He makes things so complicated. Yes, we're basically siblings," she chimes in, taking a sip of what appears to be a glass of caramel-colored liquor.

"Oh… So you're… Are you both…?"

"Sirens, yep!" she says. "We don't really have siblings in the traditional sense because we don't have parents. We were both born within minutes of each other, so we grew up together. Except we didn't 'grow' really because well, we were born looking like this."

That was a lot of information and I'm pretty sure that makes no sense. They were born fully grown? Who wants to push a full-sized adult out of their… but wait, they don't have parents, so what do they even come out of?

"Volcano," Zane says, handing me a beer.

"I'm sorry, *what now?*" I ask.

"I'm just trying to explain how we're born. You seemed confused. We're born from a volcano."

Of course. Naturally. The world's hottest people were born out of molten lava. Because where else would they come from?

"You literally didn't explain anything to her, did you Zane?" Kami scoffs. "I apologize for him. He's a man and therefore an idiot."

"Yep. Soooo glad I got you two together," he says before downing his beer.

We're interrupted by a knock on the door, but it opens before anyone has a chance to answer it. Kieran appears with a bottle of vodka in one hand. He's wearing a studded denim jacket, tight white T-shirt, skinny black pants, and heeled boots.

"Hey, gang!" Kieran says with a smile, plopping the vodka down onto the counter and brushing hair behind his ear.

"Kami, good to see you," Kieran says. He gives her a sly smirk and turns to me. "Ava, you look whatever type of way I'm allowed to say that won't get me castrated by your *boyfriend* here."

"Hey Kieran!" I say, giving him a quick hug.

"I just want to make it clear *she* hugged *me*, Zane," Kieran teases before turning to Kami. "Did Zane tell you about going postal the last time Ava and I were in the same room together?"

"You were checking out her tits, mate," Zane interjects.

"Of course he was!" Kami chimes. "Girl's got great tits!"

I'm suddenly very, *very* aware of my chest. I feel like I should either cover them up or push them out more, but I don't want to be seen doing either so now I'm in this awkward middle stage of remaining totally still. *Don't look at your own boobs now, either. That would just be weird.*

"Hey," Zane snaps, a slight green appearing in his eyes. "Next person to comment on Ava's tits gets a broken neck."

"I told ya, Kami," Kieran says. He raises a finger to his head and mimes the crazy gesture before whispering, "*Pooosstaaalll.*"

"So Kieran," I say in an attempt to change the subject. "You're a Siren too then?"

He looks at me dumbfounded, choking slightly on the drink he had just poured himself.

"What now?!?" Kieran says, his eyes wide and eyebrows raised. He looks to Zane, seemingly in an attempt to understand what I've just asked.

When I asked Zane to meet his friends and he said they were all non-human, I assumed that meant Kieran too. *Did I already mess this up?*

"She knows," Zane says.

"Oh, wow!" Kieran says with a sigh. "Somebody could've mentioned something, geez. I nearly choked on my vodka."

Wait, that glass is pure vodka? That is *way* too much vodka.

"So Loverboy here finally told you about the birds and the bees and the Sirens and sex demons, did he?" Kieran says with a smile.

Sex demons? Uh, no, I think he left that part out.

"Well welcome to the other side, Ava," Kieran chuckles. "Oh but wait… you think I'm a Siren?"

"I uh… I don't know what else there is."

"Ahhh, I'm just your friendly, neighborhood Incubus."

"Incubus… that's like a little gremlin—right? Don't they eat people's souls?" Kami breaks into a fit of laughter.

"No," Kieran says, throwing some side eye at Kami. "Incubi or Succubi are just demons and we feed on people's sexual energy. Not souls."

"So Succubi are girl Incubi, right?"

"Sort of," he says. "Incubus and Succubus are terms for when we look male or female. Gender is really more of a human thing than a demon thing. Some of us are created from scratch, others of us—like myself—were turned from humans. Those of us that turned sometimes have a preference, like I prefer my original form—this form. Purebred demons rarely cling to a particular gender or form."

That makes sense. I've just glossed entirely over the fact that my life has become one where this insane conversation actually does—somehow—make sense.

He takes another long sip of his drink.

"Kieran, that's not *entirely* vodka, is it?" I ask.

"You betcha," he says. "I can handle the hard stuff, unlike humans and Sirens." He shoots a playful look to Kami who doesn't seem to return his expression.

"So wait," I ask. "Aren't you guys kind of the same thing?"

"No," Kami and Kieran chime in unison.

"Sirens don't feed on humans," Kami explains. "We aren't demons. Humans can't become Sirens. And we have real gifts."

"Please," Kieran scoffs. "I could bench press a fucking train. How is that not a 'gift'?"

"Being strong isn't a gift, it just makes you a somewhat impressive gorilla." Kami crosses her arms across her chest and shoots him a glare.

Apparently this was the wrong question to ask.

"Sirens are also much easier to kill," he says with an aggressive look toward Kami.

"You wanna give it a try?" she replies with a growl.

"Oi," Zane says to them both. "If you're both quite finished with the dick measuring, how 'bout you both zip up and move on?"

Well that went sideways real fast.

———◆———

ZANE

I close the door behind Kieran after a quick goodbye. Well, I think that went well.

Once we steered the conversation away from my girlfriend's chest.

I turn to Ava, who has curled up in one corner of the couch. She's wearing a loose sweater and her hair is tucked behind her ears, with just a strand slipping through.

In the quiet, I can hear her heartbeat, the blood rushing through her veins. It's not quite right.

"Baby?" I ask. "Are you okay?"

She shrugs and nods, but she seems to hesitate and her neck muscles look stiff. Her skin is a pale grey and her expression is weak, almost lethargic.

"I don't believe you, love," I say, sitting beside her and wrapping an arm around her shoulder.

"I… I *am* okay. For me."

"So not great, then?"

"No," she says with a shrug. "I feel kind of woozy, my head hurts, and my stomach hurts."

My instinct is to immediately rush her to the hospital, but Ava has assured me in the past that it wouldn't be helpful.

Why can't human medicine just get its bloody shit together and stop being so god-damned useless?

"Would it help if I…" I pause for a minute.

Am I really offering to make out with her as a service of some kind?

"Yeah," she says softly.

"How about…" I say. "Could I try something else instead?"

"What?"

"If you're okay with it, I was thinking I could try charming you."

"Babe, you're cute, but charm doesn't solve everything," she replies with a giggle.

"Thanks, love. But I meant more supernaturally. Sirens call it charming. I could try suggesting that you're not in pain, see if it might work."

"Oh, uh… Sure? I think? Will it hurt?"

"No, love. That's kind of the whole point. I've done it before, you know. To you."

Her expression seems concerned and her eyes narrow.

"You mean when you told me you were a Siren?" she asks.

"Well, yeah that and… when I told you it was safe to ride home with me, that night after the bar."

Shit… is that a bad thing to have done?

"Mmm…" she mumbles, her gaze still suspicious.

"I'm sorry if that was the wrong thing… I… I wanted you to be safe and you seemed like you needed help."

"Okay," she says. "I guess it's just… something you do, right? Like, a cultural thing."

"Yeah." I shrug.

"You didn't, like, make me attracted to you, right?"

"No. I mean, the kiss kind of does that. But *you* kissed *me* first. And it wears off."

"The kiss or the hypnotic… charm… stuff?"

"Both. The 'hypnotic charm stuff' can last longer, depending on what it is and how much the person might be inclined to resist it. The kiss effect wears off with time or water or… you know… exercise."

I give her a quick wink and smile.

"Okay, so… how does this work?" she asks.

"Well, I just need to touch your skin and talk to you."

"Don't you do that anyway?"

"I try not to say anything suggestive. I avoid putting things in your head."

"Okay," she says with an eyebrow raised.

I hold her hand. I've never been quite so formal about this but I've also never tried to charm someone who knew that's what I was doing.

"You aren't in pain, love. You aren't uncomfortable or dizzy or nauseous. You just feel good. You feel like someone in perfect health."

I examine her expression for signs that it's working. Her eyes soften and her shoulders relax.

"How do you feel?" I ask.

"Pretty good, I think. Does that mean… Did it work?"

"I think so, love," I say with a smile, pulling her into my chest with both arms.

23

"Ooh, ooh, let's go in!" Jen says, tugging on my sleeve as we walk past the massive book store.

"Yeah, Jen, I'm sure you just desperately need more comics," I say with a smile.

"You know, Ava, you're so right. I'm downright deprived," she says, pulling me into the store.

"Okay, just let me tell Zane I'm gonna be a little longer."

I pull out my phone to text Zane.

Me

We weave our way through the various sections until we find the comics.

"Yeeeessssss!" Jen says dramatically, hugging the shelf. "My bayyy-beeees!"

"You have an addiction, girl."

"Yes I do." She nods defiantly, continuing to hug the comic shelf.

"I'm gonna tell Shayna you're cheating on her."

"Oh, she knows," Jen says with a giggle. "We have an understanding."

"So how are things going with Shayna, anyway? Are you two officially a thing?"

Her eyes shift as she thumbs through a Spider-Man comic.

"Uh, not exactly," she says with an uneasy look. "We've been spending a lot of time together, but there's a complication."

"Complication?"

"You remember Deb?"

"Your ex, Deb?" I ask.

"Yeah well, she just moved in with me."

"What the heck?" I gasp.

"We're still good friends. It's complicated. She and I have a long history."

"Is Shayna okay with this?"

"She uh…" she mumbles.

"You moved in with your ex and you haven't told the girl you're dating??"

She is gonna be in sooooo much trouble.

My phone vibrates in my pocket. Saved by the text this time, Jen.

Zane

I can come pick you up.
The one in the mall?

Me

Yep. Not sure when we'll be
done, maybe 20 minutes?

"Another text from Dickhead McGee?" Jen asks.

"If you mean Mike, then no," I say with a laugh. "It's Zane. I'm just letting him know I'm gonna be a bit later."

"Oh, that's good. Are you still getting texts from Mike?"

"Yeah," I sigh. "They swing wildly back and forth between 'I love you, let's work this out' and 'you're a total bitch and I hate you.'"

"That, my dear, is why he's Dickhead McGee," Jen says with a laugh. "You know how to avoid this entirely?"

"Don't date men?" I ask.

"Precisely, my dear! Men are seriously the worst. You never see women pulling this crap."

"Says the woman with ex-girlfriend drama going down."

"Hey, dykes!" a man's voice interjects as he approaches us.

Oh frickin great.

The guy is significantly taller than us, muscular, and wearing a truly heinous silver puffy jacket over a branded T-shirt. He has tousled brown hair, strong stubble, and an expression that says 'I've already had a few beers today.'

"Fuck off," I say, pulling Jen away and inserting myself in between them.

"Maybe you want to keep your fucking mouths shut in public if you don't want the world knowing that you're muff munchers."

"Wasn't looking for your opinion, dickwad," Jen spits.

He steps towards her with his chest puffed up, but I remain in between them.

This douche is out of his mind if he thinks I'm going to let him pull this crap.

"Buddy," I say. "Just because women look at you and then say they prefer women, doesn't mean you have to go around being a dick to every woman you suspect is a lesbian. So you can either get fucked or we can call the cops."

Jen chokes back a laugh behind me. His eyes seem furious and his hands are tensed into fists.

So I felt pretty safe saying that because I was 90% sure this guy wasn't gonna punch me in the back of a bookstore, but in hindsight I'm a little uneasy about those odds.

Shit.

I feel his hands on my shoulders and my back collides roughly with the bookshelf behind me—hard. His face is inches from mine and I let out a small yelp.

Ow.

"Is that right, bitch?" he snaps. I can see a panicked Jen dialing 911 out of the corner of my eye.

"Maybe you just need a little more dick in your life," he says, aggressively grinding his crotch into me.

His grip on my shoulders is tight and sending waves of pain through my arms. I struggle to push him off and in a split second I watch as a thick book meets his head. He turns around but hardly seems phased, so I take the opportunity to bring my knee up between his legs.

He shudders before collapsing to the ground and Jen and I both take off running to the front of the store.

———

ZANE

I pull into a parking spot a ways away from the entrance and turn off the car as a text from Ava lights up my phone screen.

Ava

Actually I can meet you at my place.

Me

I'm already here

I step out of my car and see two police cars stopped out front. I feel an uneasy sensation in my chest, but I push it aside.

She's fine. She literally just texted me.

Ava

Okay. Don't freak out.

So much for that. Her text has had the opposite of its intended effect. My feet move faster as I hurry toward the book store.

Is she sick? Did she pass out? Did she hurt herself?

No… wait. These are not ambulances, they're police cars.

Ava

There are cops here. It's a long story. We're fine. Wait in the car and I'll be out in a sec.

Okay. Okay. She's fine—no reason to lose my shit.

The doors swing open as Ava and Jen step outside. They both look okay, but Ava's expression seems unsure and focused on me. I wrap my arms around her and pull her close.

"What the hell, you two?" I say. "Why's the cavalry outside the book-"

What is that smell? What the fuck is that?

I inhale deeply and feel every hair in my body stand on end. I pull Ava away so that I can see her eyes and I instantly register what I'm smelling.

It's a man's scent; it's all over her. And another I recognize—fear.

Someone touched her. Scared her.

I try to talk myself out of hunting this person down right here and now.

I'm going to fucking kill him.

Remember, she said she's okay. They're both okay.

"Who did this?" I manage to choke out the words. My muscles are tight with rage and I can hardly hear a thing over the pounding rhythm of my heartbeat in my ears.

"You told Zane already?" Jen asked. "I'm kind of surprised! What with you all being Mister Macho and whatnot." Jen seems to be her usual playful self, but I'm struggling to maintain an equally calm facade.

Ava opens her mouth to speak but before she can Jen continues.

"You'd be proud of her, bro. She was quite the badass. I don't think either of us expected that guy to shove her like that…"

Jen's words fade in and out as I try to comprehend their meaning. Ava's eyes are locked on me, probing for any sign that I might go find this guy and rip his head off.

I struggle to fight back my instincts, screaming at me to end this fucker.

And you can bet I bloody will.

Ava will be pissed if you go after this guy right now.

Don't care. He's a fucking dead man.

You do care. Control yourself.

"…and the creep starts grinding all up on her so I grab a big-ass book and crack him over the head like a fucking pro wrestler…"

He did what now?

What?

Fucking. Dead. Man.

Okay, kill him.

"Woah, man," Jen pauses, looking at me quizzically. "Your eyes are really crazy looking right now, like… it looks like they're glowing from the inside it's so weird."

Ava keeps her gaze focused on me.

"Yeah, uh," I mumble before grabbing Jen's wrist. "No, my eyes look normal. You were saying?"

As she continues, I can hardly maintain my composure. My brain flips through every type of torture I can imagine as I drift in and out of focus.

"…Boom! Right in the nards!" Jen's voice says, bringing my attention back into the conversation.

I can't help but smile at the thought.

"Dickhead goes down, hard," she continues, "and we take off towards the front."

I chuckle a bit at the thought of these two leaving this prick in the fetal position on the floor.

"He in there?" I ask, trying my best to sound like I'm not asking so I can go beat the shit out of him.

Ava shoots me a knowing glance.

"No," Jen sighs. "He took off before anyone could really detain him, but they have him on the security tape. The cops took our statements too. Who knows if it'll amount to anything."

I rub a hand along Ava's back.

"Well, I wouldn't worry," I say with a smirk. "Something tells me this prick is gonna get what's coming to him."

24

Our walk back to the car was surprisingly quiet. Zane closes his door and leans back in his seat with a heavy sigh. The sun has just set and his eyes are practically glowing in the dimly lit car.

"Are you okay?" he asks in a soft but tense voice.

"Yeah, I'm fine—really. You don't need to worry about me."

He pauses for a moment and turns to look at me. There's pain in his eyes and he cringes, letting out a loud sound that is a mix of a high screech and a low rumbling growl.

Every once in a while I forget he's not human, and then he'll do something like that.

How do I even respond to that?

"Um," I say. "I don't really know what that means."

"Shit, love, I'm sorry," he says, burying his head in his hands. "That was very dramatic of me. I hate this… I'm sorry. I don't know how to be with you."

"In what way?"

"In any way… You're so… fragile."

Ouch.

"I don't know if I see it that way," I say.

"No, love, I don't mean like that. I mean, you're human. You can be hurt. Things can just happen to you and there's nothing I can do. It's just… how am I supposed to deal with this? I can help with the pain, but it's not the same as healing you. And now…"

He looks both angry and terrified, his eyes still a brilliant green.

"And now… what?" I ask.

"Now it's not just you being sick. Now it's random shitheads trying to hurt you when I'm not around. I can't follow you everywhere you go."

"I'm not asking you to. You don't have to protect me."

"I can't, Ava." His head hangs low, his expression defeated.

What?

He can't… protect me? Or be with me? I can feel tears flooding my eyes.

"No one's forcing you to be with me," I say.

"Bloody… Fuck… Ava, that's not what I meant." He grips his hair tight in his fingers and tugs.

"Just that I'm a burden?" I ask.

Might have just let my insecurities do the talking for me there… oops.

"Fuck, Ava, why do you have to do that? No!" he snaps. "I don't know how to let you go. I don't know how to let you live your bloody human life with your stupid, fragile human body and know that I can't be there to beat the shit out of every cockhead who lays a finger on the woman I love."

Uh… what?

What was that?

What what what what what what what?

As my brain tries to process his words, it's clear that Zane is processing them himself. His eyes suddenly widen and instantly return to brown.

Did he mean that? That he loves me?

"I uh…" he stutters. "I didn't mean to say… I mean… bloody hell. Can I try that again, love? I swear every time I talk to you I make a right arse of myself."

"Sure," I say, the uncomfortable feeling in my stomach rising.

"I'm sorry I'm not dealing with this well," he says, pausing a moment to grab my hand in his. "You're the one who's been through something and I'm having a fit. So, Sirens are beings of passion. We're known for being primal, led by our emotions, but I've spent most of my life fighting that. For a good reason. I've seen firsthand the kind of trouble feelings can get you into."

Just the kind of romantic thing every girl wants to hear from her boyfriend.

I try to read his expression, but he continues to look down at our intertwined hands, anxiously chewing the corner of his lip. He takes in a deep breath.

"But I can't fight it with you," he says. "The thought of something happening to you—or someone hurting you—baby I can't breathe just thinking about it."

His eyes look almost teary and he seems genuinely upset. I feel like I've been someone's problem my entire life. But suddenly here I am, and someone is looking at me and telling me that they want me in their life. That the problem isn't me, but the fear of losing me.

I don't know how to process it. *Why would he even…*

"I… I…" Zane stutters. "I've never been in love before, and I guess I've gone and spoiled that bit, but uh… I'm in love with you. I love you, Ava."

My heart is pounding in my chest and I see a vulnerable, almost fearful look in his eyes that he tries to hide with a smile.

I place my hand on his cheek and lean in to kiss him but he stops me.

"You don't have to say anything back," he says. "But if you do, could you do so before you kiss me? Just… so we don't confuse things?"

I smile as our foreheads touch.

"I love you too."

———

We're frantically entwined in a blur of lips and tongues and hands as we reach Zane's apartment door. He attempts to fit his key in the lock with one hand behind his back while fumbling under my shirt with the other.

The door unlatches and I push him inside and slam the door behind us. With a seamless motion, he pushes me up against the door, grinding his hips into me as he lets out a purring moan.

I tug at the back of his shirt, but he suddenly pulls away. His eyes are wide, flickering in intensity as he pants hard, his grip still tight around me. He seems conflicted.

"I… I…" he stutters, the luminance of his green eyes rapidly shifting.

I lean in to kiss him softly. Our lips touch and I can feel his heart thumping as his chest presses up against me.

"Are you okay?" I ask.

He licks his lips and his eyes settle on a vivid green.

"Yeah baby," he says, with a devious smirk. He lifts me up and I wrap my legs around his waist. He lets out another moan as he walks me into the bedroom and throws me onto the bed. "I'll be so much better when I fuck you through this mattress, though."

I hear fabric tear and I see something fly across the room. Zane has just shredded my shirt off my body.

Well, so much for that tank top. What's with the ripping?

Another rip echoes in the air and I watch as Zane's shirt falls to the floor.

On second thought, the ripping is good. Keep ripping.

I pull my jeans down before they get donated to the cause.

He lets out a sinister moan—guttural and not entirely human.

Oh, that's right, I'm about to have sex with a Siren right now. That's normal.

He shakes his head as though he's trying to compose himself, unbuttoning his jeans and sending them to the floor at a superhuman pace.

I feel a whip of wind as he rapidly appears on top of me, grinding his hips deeper into me.

"You feel what you do to me, baby?" he moans.

He stands up and rips off his boxers.

Another check in the win column for ripping.

His eyes are practically fluorescent in the dark, providing just enough glow to see his perfectly chiseled abs and the sharp lines on his hips leading to his…

Damn.

"You checking me out, baby?" he asks, jumping back on top of me. I hear another tearing sound that I imagine is the untimely demise of my panties.

"No." I quickly reply. "Maybe."

Hells yes.

He sinks himself into me and I feel my body melting with pleasure. I let out a desperate whimper. His body stiffens as another moan radiates from his chest, this one louder, practically shaking the room. His eyes flicker brighter as he shakes his head, his eyes dimming again, almost as if he's trying to reel himself in.

"Don't do that," I say, pulling his face away from mine.

"Do what?" he asks, a glimmer of confusion on his face.

"Don't hold back on me." I lock my eyes with his.

"I… I…" he stutters. "I don't want to push too far, baby. I'm… so…"

He pants, swallowing hard, trying to get his words out.

"Fuck, baby. I can't control myself with you. I don't want to do anything that might hurt you or scare you and I'm… I'm not human. I know you know that but… I… fuck, baby, I can't think straight when I'm on top of you like this."

He's shaking and his eyes are getting brighter by the minute.

"I'm a big girl, Zane," I say, leaning in to kiss his neck. "I never asked you to hold back. I want *you*—all of you. I love you."

He moans again. The sound reverberates through our connected bodies.

"Say that again, baby," he said, his eyes hooded. "Please?"

"I love you," I say.

"Fuck," he moans, thrusting into me again, his fingers digging hard into my hips.

I reach my arms around him, running my fingers along his back until I reach the ridges where his wings tuck into his body. I lightly scratch my fingernails down them and he lets out a truly inhuman moan, wrenching his torso back as his gorgeous black wings spring forth, spreading almost the width of the room before shaking out with a deep shiver.

"You want the beast, baby?" he asks, his pupils now completely eclipsed by green. "You got him."

25

 ZANE

My eyes open to a flurry of purple hair sprawled across my chest. Her scent is intoxicating and her touch even more so.

I'm so bloody in love with this girl, she could stab me in the heart and I would still want to wrap her in my arms.

As the sunlight peeks into my room, I see scattered shreds of clothing everywhere, the bedside lamp mangled on the floor, and large chunks of cotton batting strewn throughout the room.

Oh bloody hell.

Memories of last night come flooding back to me. I completely lost control.

I turn my head slightly so as not to disturb Ava. She's wrapped inside my wing. I turn to see my other wing splayed under the covers.

Bloody fucking hell. What the fuck happened to me?

My mind flashed back to last night.

That soft moan as I buried myself into her.

"Don't hold back on me."

"I want you—all of you."

"I love you."

Ava's fingernails running along my wing ridges.

I pull myself away from the memory when I realize I'm rock solid.

Okay, enough thinking about that.

Wait… last night…

Suddenly I remember the rest of the evening: Ava was attacked. I'm not about to let that one go.

I reach for my phone to text Kami, but it's not plugged into its charger.

Who bloody knows where my trousers are…

Ava stirs ever so slightly, cozying up into my wing as a contented purr leaves her lips.

My god, she's perfect.

If I fell asleep with my wings out…

I take a second to comprehend the thought.

What does that mean? I had sex with her and then I wrapped her in my wings and held her? Still in Siren form?

I keep the beast at bay because it's just that—a beast. My carnal form is the epitome of instinct and passion: lust, anger, jealousy… sure. But this?

What does that even mean?

Does all of me—even at my worst—feel the way about Ava that I do right now?

———•———

AVA

I rub my eyes and yawn as I wake from sleep. The light is bright enough that it must be mid-morning and I'm wrapped in a soft black blanket, lying on Zane's bare chest.

This is almost aggressively comfortable.

As I open my eyes, I see the room is a bit worse for the wear from last night. Little bits of pillow fluff are strewn across the floor. Zane shifts beneath me, pulling me in with one arm around my waist.

Wait, his arm is on my waist but also on my shoulder? How does that work? Whose arm is that??

I flinch as my eyes pop open further.

"You okay, baby?" Zane asks in a soft, low voice.

I look closer and discover that the blanket isn't so much a blanket as it is a wing. *Zane's wing.*

My life is really weird.

"Yeah, sorry. I didn't realize your arm was… your arm… but, not your arm," I say.

Yeah, that made sense, Ava.

"Care to try that again, love?" he says with a smile. In a seamless move, he rolls on top of me—his arms on either side of me, his body completely naked with his wings tucked slightly but still on display, the sheet wrapped around our legs.

"Your… um…"

What was I saying?

"My arms aren't my arms," he continues with a chuckle. "You mean these, love?"

He spreads his wings behind his back and smiles.

Damn.

His expression drops for a moment, even though he's trying to hide it.

"Is that… okay? Are we okay?"

"What?" I ask. "No, no. Sorry, I'm just… this is very distracting." I smile and wink as I pull him in for a kiss.

He smiles as our lips are inches apart.

"You don't mind, baby? Everything from last night?"

"Zane, I keep telling you, I'm not being hypnotized by your Siren magic or whatever. I mean, okay I am, but you can't be hypnotized into feeling something you already feel."

His smile grows wider as he kisses my cheek.

"Okay love," he says. "But I'm not kissing you until you've at least had breakfast. We don't want you passing out, now, do we?" He laughs as I playfully push him.

"You're just afraid you'll be hypnotized by *my* magical powers, aren't you?" I joke.

"Oh definitely," he says, his eyes sparkling. "You human temptress you."

He rolls off me and walks over to his dresser, pulling out a pair of boxers and a T-shirt. I look around for my clothes and see the ripped remnants of my tank top on the floor.

Oh yeah. Right…

"Um, Zane?" I ask.

He turns around as I hold up my shredded tank top.

"Oh," he says. He looks down at the T-shirt and boxers in his hand and throws them to me.

"Thanks," I say, sitting on the edge of the bed and pulling the T-shirt on over my shoulders.

In a sudden motion, Zane has me pinned beneath him on the bed. His eyes are already a glowing green.

"Damn it," he mumbles under his breath.

"What?" I ask.

"You look so good wearing my clothes, love," he says in a low, almost growling voice as he kisses my neck. "I'm afraid I'm no match for those human powers of yours."

I smirk and kiss his neck in return. He lets out a low moan in response.

"Does that mean I get my kiss now?" I ask.

"You get a whole lot more than that, baby."

ZANE

While Ava is in the shower, I figure it's as good a time as any to clean up the mess I've made in here. I straighten the furniture and reattach the curtains to the rod, collecting pillow stuffing as I go.

A buzzing noise sounds from beneath me. Ava's jeans from last night have somehow made their way under my bed and I can see her phone lighting up inside one of the pockets.

I grab and fold the jeans, placing her phone on my nightstand. The phone vibrates again, and then again.

It's probably dying from not being plugged in all night. I walk over to where I have my charger and plug it in. As the screen lights up, I see a string of messages.

Mike

> Talk to me Ava

> You're being a bitch right now

> Ava I miss you

Okay, I should not have read those. I didn't even mean to, but I shouldn't have done that.

Especially since now all I can think of is how I'm going to fillet Mike like a fucking fish.

Do I say something and admit that I basically read her private text messages or do I just let it go? *Can I even just let it go?*

I hear the shower turn off in the master bathroom and I return to cleaning up the pillow stuffing.

"Hey Zane, can I ask you something?" she asks, emerging from the bathroom in a towel.

Fuck. She knows.

"Yeah baby, what is it?" I reply.

"What's with the weird cabinet-shelf thing in your bathroom? The one with all the odd bottles?"

My brain sighs in relief. That's a much easier question to answer.

"That's basically an old-fashioned medicine cabinet," I explain. "Most of those things are Immortal medicines. Human medicine doesn't really work on our physiology."

"But if you're immortal, why do you need medicine? Can you get sick?"

"Sort of…" I explain. "We can be injured by other Immortals. Some of those bottles are anti-venoms or counteract certain poisons. A couple are, erm, recreational. Others are more like Immortal first aid, to give you more time to be healed. In my case, that would mean getting venom from another Siren or…"

"As in like, kissing?" she asks, her expression twisting into one of discomfort.

"Why baby, you jealous?" I secretly love the idea of her being jealous over me. Since the moment I met her I've been the jealous one; it's nice to see the shoe on the other foot.

"I mean, I guess if it's life or death or something, but can't you just, I dunno, spit at each other?"

"Eww, Ava. That's disturbing. But for the record, you can just deposit venom into a vial for the other to drink."

"And that's not disturbing?" she asks.

"Okay, fair dues, love. Well, there's always my favorite option," I say with a smirk.

"What's that?"

"You and I could have sex."

"Sex can heal you?" she asks, not nearly as surprised as I expected.

"Yeah I mean, basically we need to replenish our energy to heal and our energy can be boosted by things that recharge our passions."

She stares at me for about 15 seconds, not saying a word.

Fuck. Is she mad?

Is this weird?

Should I have lied?

In an instant, she bursts into laugher and starts singing.

"Sexual healing… Oh baby!"

I roll my eyes and smile as I swoop in to pick her up over my shoulder, still wrapped in her towel.

"You think you're real funny, don't you human?" I tease.

She continues to sing the words to "Sexual Healing" as I walk her to the bed. I playfully smack her arse as she lets out a yelp before setting her on the mattress.

I lay beside her and she reaches to stroke my hair, those grey eyes piercing through my every layer.

"Missed a spot!" she says with a smile, pulling a clump of pillow stuffing from my hair. I laugh and blow the cotton batting away with a puff of air.

"They're everywhere," I say with an eye roll. "This apartment will be haunted by the specter of those pillows until the end of time."

"Can I ask you a personal question?"

"Only if you stop singing."

"Deal," she says. "So… Are you… There's no right way to say this, is there?"

This can't possibly be a good question.

"You're scaring me, love," I say with an uneasy chuckle.

"Sorry, it's nothing bad. I'm just trying not to be offensive."

"Okaayyy…"

"Are you like… a bird?"

A burst of laughter leaves my lips.

"Did you just ask me if I'm a bird, love?"

"I'm sorry I mean like… shoot, is that offensive? I'm sorry."

I continue to laugh.

"I'm assuming you don't mean bird in the English way as in, *a lady*, because, well…" I tease with a smile. "I'm pretty sure I've shown you quite recently that I'm all man. But I'd be glad to show you again."

"No!" she says, smacking my chest.

"I figured. So you're back to asking if I'm a bloody penguin again?"

"No! I just… I noticed your pillows are cotton and not feathers and I was wondering if that's because you… I dunno… if you're a bird-person maybe you feel weird sleeping on other birds' feathers?"

Fuck she's adorable.

I can't help but laugh again.

"Baby," I say with a grin. "I just bought pillows. I'm a guy. I didn't put that much thought into it. They're pillows. I'm not part bird just because I have wings."

"Oh." Her cheeks flush and she tilts her head down. "I dunno. I don't really know that much about wings or people with wings. I wouldn't know if someone, like, made pillows out of Sirens or something and it was a horrible tragedy."

"Baby," I say through a stifled laugh. "You're lovely to be considerate of that—and very weird—but that would be the least comfortable pillow known to man."

"Why's that?"

"Here, I'll show you." I step off the bed and extend my wings from my body, bending one forward so the tips of the feathers are next to her. "Feel."

"Oh!" she says as she runs her fingers over the edges. "They're soft but then they're also kind of… hard? Like a toothbrush or something."

"Yeah, the closer you get to the shaft, the tougher they are. My skin is impenetrable to human weapons and my feathers are made of the same stuff."

"Do they fall out?" she asks.

"No. The only way I can lose them is if they're cut or damaged by certain things."

"What things?"

"It's pretty rare to come by anything that can harm a Siren. Few other Immortals have the strength to do it, not even other Sirens. We can be cut by a demon's claws or a very special type of knife. Sirens' feathers are not something that you really can just separate from the Siren. Unless we pull them out ourselves."

"What? Why would you do that?"

"I mean you wouldn't, unless you had to for some reason. But we can remove our own."

There's really only one reason, but it's one I rather not scare her with.

"Do they grow back?" she asks as she strokes a feather, both concerned and fascinated.

"Yeah. Why?"

"No reason." Her eyes dart away and she bites her lip slightly.

"If you were trying not to be suspicious, you failed gloriously."

"Sorry, this is silly. I just like your wings and they remind me of you and I was thinking it would be nice… if you had feathers and all… if I could have one. That's really weird, isn't it? I'm sorry."

No one has ever asked that of me. Mostly because Immortals understand exactly what it means. But her innocent grey eyes staring at me make me want to give her anything.

This girl will definitely be the death of me.

I bend a wing around my body so I can reach a feather with my arms, slowly plucking it from my wing. There's a tiny surge of pain as I do, but it's brief.

"Only for you, baby," I say, handing her the black feather.

She looks at the feather in her hand with shock and a huge smile stretches across her face. She pulls me in with the other hand and kisses me on the cheek.

"Thank you," she says, her eyes meeting mine. "I love it."

"Be careful with that, okay?" I say. "The quill end is a lot sharper than it looks."

There are two known objects that can kill a Siren… and I just handed one to the love of my life.

26

If someone had told me four months ago that my future would involve dinner at Table, one of the fanciest restaurants in town, with my incredibly gorgeous Siren boyfriend, I would have laughed in their face.

If they had said I'd be wrapped in a comforter on my couch watching my eighth straight hour of Netflix, *that* I would believe.

Yet here I am, dressed up with Zane, enjoying the best seats in the house yet again.

"So do you use your superpowers to get this table every time or is it just because you know the owner?" I ask.

He smiles and shakes his head. "I know the owner? Is that what I told you?"

"Yesss…?" I say. "That's not true?"

Why would he lie about that?

"Oh it's true. But to be honest love, I'm pretty sure you have more pull with the owner than anyone else."

I have pull with the owner? I don't know the owner… What is he talking about?

"Well, you *are* fucking him," he says with a smirk.

Wait… What? Either he's accusing me of cheating on him or… Zane owns this place?!?

"Not sure why I didn't tell you the first time 'round," he continues. "I guess I tend to keep my private life to myself."

"You told me you owned some properties around the city, but I didn't realize you owned Table!"

"Well, I had a lot of money and only recently moved to the States. I had to find something to do."

"So you decided to become a professional rich person?"

He bursts into laughter.

"I suppose you could think of it that way," he says, taking a sip of his wine.

"So what did you do in London then?"

"Well uh…" he says, his eyes shifting as he fiddles with the cloth napkin on his lap.

What's with this reaction? He wasn't actually in the mob, was he?

"It's a long story. In London there's a larger, more formal Immortal community and my job was to uh… use my powers on people."

Oh. *Oh.*

"So, you were a sex worker?" I ask.

Is he worried I'll judge him?

"No, love," he says with a bit of a chuckle. "Feeling jealous?"

"No, butthead," I say with a scowl.

"I worked for our kind of law enforcement. There's not really a human equivalent, but I was a compeller."

He takes another sip of his drink. I don't understand what that means, but he's being so weird about it.

"Okay, shifty," I say. "Spill. What does a compeller do?"

"I would touch people and charm them into giving us information or doing things we wanted. Sometimes it felt like the right thing to do but, sometimes they had me do more questionable things. In hindsight, I shouldn't have gone along with everything, but the Immortals I worked for were pretty powerful and I thought I needed to be on the right side of that power."

"Wow, that sucks." I reach for his hand and grasp it in mine. "I'm sorry about that, but I'm glad you got out of there. Why did you move, anyway?"

"Kami caught some heat with the police around there. She may or may not have used her powers on a prominent judge. We decided to move away until everything calmed down a bit."

"Do you guys have any other family there?" I ask.

"We don't have other family," he says. "It's just me and Kami. What about you? You always talk about your mom, but you never talk about anyone else."

Oh crap. I didn't mean to lead the conversation this way. I'm usually working to push it in the opposite direction and here I am steering right into it.

"Uh well, you know my mom died a few years ago…"

He specifically asked about family besides your mom, genius. Nailed it.

"And um… I have a dad…"

I have no idea where to go from here.

Where is he? *Probably passed out at home about a half an hour's drive from here, likely after some ill-advised combination of alcohol and painkillers. It's no big deal, he's just the source of all my self-esteem issues from a lifetime of emotional abuse.*

Yeah, that will make me sound super well-adjusted.

"And I have a half brother on my dad's side."

Who, much like my dad, is an alcoholic and a total ass.

"Wow," he laughs. "Your stories are so detailed!"

"Oh shut up," I say, lightly smacking his arm.

"Ooh, kinky! Do it again!" he says with a wink as he reaches out to hold my hand again.

"Shush, mister! Someone's going to hear you!"

"Who?" he says, looking around in our isolated corner of the restaurant.

Okay, good point.

"The waiter? I dunno…"

"Well, so what if he has a problem—fuck him. It's my restaurant." He lets out another laugh.

Suddenly I'm feeling very strange, and I find my eyes scanning around the room for the waiter.

What am I doing?

I stand up from my seat to go find the waiter, but I feel Zane's hand around my wrist, holding me back.

"Where are you going, baby?" he asks, tilting his head in confusion.

"I'm going to go have sex with the waiter," I say.

I am? Wait… what am I doing?

His expression shifts and his eyes go green instantly.

"The hell you are," he says gruffly. "Are you having a laugh? 'Cause this really isn't my kind of joke, love."

"Nope."

Wait, why am I doing this?

"Seriously. Not fucking funny."

"I'm not joking. I just… I *need to.*"

His eyes scan my face as his hand stays firmly grasped around my wrist.

"Sit down," he says.

I take my seat and his face falls into his palms.

"Oh bloody hell. Did I just say… fuck…" he says, tugging his hair in his hands.

He reaches out and grabs my hand again.

"Do not fuck the waiter. Under no circumstances are you to fuck the waiter."

"Okay," I say. "Wait, why was I saying I was…"

"I'm sorry, baby, that was a bit of a cock-up on my part. I charmed you."

Oh. *Oh.*

"I'll be more careful with what I say." He looks up at me through apologetic eyes. "It won't happen again, okay?"

"So that's how that power works, huh? Wow, that's dangerous…"

"Yeah, you can see why I'm usually so careful."

I start feeling extremely nauseous and I bend forward slightly to ease the sharp pain in my stomach. I don't want to interrupt our dinner with this.

Maybe he won't notice…

"What's wrong?"

Orrr maybe he will.

"It's uh, my stomach. It's fine."

"Baby, I can fix that for you. Do you want me to?"

"Would you mind?" I ask.

"Never," he says, resting his hand on my cheek. "Your stomach is feeling much better now."

As he says it, the pain eases and I no longer feel like I'm going to throw up.

"Wow," I say. "That's nifty!"

"Yeah, when I'm not accidentally sending you off to shag the waiter."

I giggle. "Yeah, besides that part."

"I don't find this nearly as humorous as you do."

ZANE

Dreiflüssestadt, Austrian Empire - Summer of 1840

"We shouldn't," Ilen whispers with a slight giggle as I roll on top of her.

"And why?" I ask.

She blushes and squirms bashfully as I stare into her eyes, licking my lips.

"Because I am an engaged woman," she says playfully. "In a week, I will be married."

"A week is not today," I say with a grin. "And today, my Ilen, you and I are together."

She bats her eyelashes at me.

"We will be discovered," she says, wide-eyed. "The Count has been gracious in allowing me to stay here at his estate. It would be a betrayal to his kindness…"

"He'll have you for all eternity," I say, planting kisses on her neck. "I only ask for this moment."

She holds my face in her delicate hands before pulling me in for a kiss.

<hr>

AVA

I take my earrings off and set them down on Zane's bathroom counter in the bathroom beside my overnight bag.

"Your phone is ringing," Zane says from the bedroom.

I walk in to see Zane sitting on the bed with a devious smile slowly stretching across his face.

What is he smirking about?

I catch a glimpse of my phone's screen and see the name on caller ID: Mike.

Oh no.

My eyes widen as I grab for the phone, but Zane has already answered it.

"Hello, Michael."

27

 ZANE

"Hello, Michael," I say into the phone.

Ava stares at me with wide eyes, gesturing to me to hang up as she mouths the word *NO* over and over.

"Give me the phone!" she whispers. She makes a quick reach for the phone, forgetting that my reflexes are substantially faster than hers.

"I… I… Who… Who is this?" Mike stammers on the other end of the line.

"Oh, Michael, you don't remember me? I'm hurt!" I say as I turn my body so that Ava can't grab the phone from my hand.

"What the fuck are you doing answering Ava's phone?" he spits. His voice is rough and he seems to be putting on his best 'intimidating' tone.

"Oh, so you do remember me! Here's a better question for you, mate: why the fuck are you *calling* Ava's phone?"

"None of your business. Let me talk to Ava."

That's not happening. I look at Ava who's glaring at me with her lips pursed.

"Sorry, Michael," I say with a wink to Ava. "She's otherwise *occupied* at the moment."

Ava's eyes go wide and her mouth falls open. She reaches over and smacks me hard on the arm.

"You son of a bitch," Mike growls in response. "You're disgusting."

This is fun.

"I knew you two were lying about fucking around behind my back," he spits.

"Funny thing about that—I wasn't lying," I say, "but I figured if I was already doing the time, might as well be doing the crime, eh?"

"I guess you have a thing for whores then."

This prick has a death wish.

"Your best insult is insinuating she has sex at a professional level?" I say with a laugh. "Do you think I'm the Virgin fucking Mary?"

Ava crosses her arms and narrows her eyes at me, hopefully in response to what Mike said and not at me.

"You two deserve each other," Mike snaps. "You can have her."

"But the point here, Michael, is that I do *have* her. But you don't quite seem to get that, because I keep seeing your name *on her bloody mobile.*"

My voice gets louder as my ability to mask my anger begins to falter.

"So you're not going to contact her again," I say. "You're not going to so much as look at her if you see her on the street. Do you understand me?"

There's silence on the other end, but the faint sound of his breathing tells me he's still there.

"I'll take that as a yes," I say. "And if I hear you've said even one word to my girl, the next thing to come out of that mouth will be your fucking tongue."

I end the call and pass the phone back to Ava.

"Really, Zane?" she says with one eyebrow raised.

Okay, I might be in a little bit of trouble.

"I was perfectly fine ignoring his calls and messages," she continued. "But you had to get all alpha male on him?"

"You honestly think I was going to let that shit go, baby? You do realize who I am, don't you?"

She rolls her eyes and sighs.

"You're an idiot," she says, cracking a slight smile. "Wait… Did you say you've seen his name on my phone before?"

"I uh," I mumble. "What?"

Did I let that slip? Shit.

"I wasn't spying," I say. "I just happened to see some texts once."

She seems to be mulling it all over in her mind.

"You're right," she says, narrowing her eyes.

Why does that seem like a very bad thing right now?

"I *do* know you," she continues.

What is she getting at?

"You wouldn't let this go, just like there's no way in hell you let Mike get away with saying whatever sexual things about me he said when you had that run-in at Pike's."

Oh.

"I uh," I try to explain, but I don't know where to begin.

"Did you beat him up?" she asks.

"No… but I may have been involved in that a bit more than I told you at the time."

She crosses her arms and purses her lips.

"*Involved?*" she asks. "You told me he got into a fight with anoth-… Oh my god, you didn't!"

I'm so busted right now.

"I may have," I mutter with a shrug.

"You charmed him?"

"Yeah."

She smacks me on the arm with a high-pitched squeak.

"Zane!" she exclaims. "He had to get surgery to fix his face! Yes, Mike can be a douche, but you could have gotten him killed!"

"I…" I sigh and my shoulders drop. "I'm sorry, baby. I don't always get this human shit. And with you, it's like my brain gets bypassed and I just go full animal."

The tension in her face seems to calm.

"I shouldn't have done what I did at the bar," I say with another sigh. "But you should know that I only think that because it could have hurt you. I would kill him if it came to it and I wouldn't have remorse. I have no problem killing anyone who puts you in danger and I've killed before, when I had to."

Her expression shifts to one of shock, and maybe sadness.

The look in her eyes shatters my heart. I worry that I've just watched her fall out of love with me.

"Okay," she says, her expression surprisingly stoic.

"Okay?" I ask, the shock clear in my voice. "You're okay with me killing people?"

"You kill bad people, right?" she asks. "You kill for a reason?"

"Yes." I can't believe what she's saying.

"Zane, I'm not perfect. A lot of parts of my life that you don't know about have been fucked up. And some of those fucked-up things have made me think that, yeah, there are some people that the world would be better off without. It's not all black and white."

She's not leaving? My chest finally relaxes as I release my breath.

"I trust you," she says, walking over to me and resting her head on my chest.

I never want to let her go.

28

28

ZANE

"I don't understand how I can't find one bloody human," I say with a sigh.

The man who attacked Ava and Jen is somehow still evading me and I'm bloody sick of it.

"I know you're worked up about this, Z," Kami says in a calm tone. "But Ava is fine. Maybe this is just a human issue. This guy is bound to get himself arrested soon, right?"

"And that's good enough for you? That someone attacked Ava and Jen and we're just gonna let it go?"

"I don't know, Z. I understand, but it's been months. Maybe this creep doesn't even live here."

"I know you don't trust Kieran, but I'm going to talk to him. His senses are much stronger than ours. He can help."

Kami sighs and sets her drink on the table, opening her mouth to say something.

We're interrupted by a ring at Kami's front door.

"Expecting company?" I ask.

"Not that I know of," she says. "Wait here."

"Hey, hon!" a voice says from the other room. "Wanted to check in with you on our little predicament."

Who is this now?

"I've got company, Lols, but you probably already know that," Kami says.

Kami rounds the corner with a petite, bronze-skinned woman who looks about the same age as we do. The woman is wearing a long flowing dress with a vibrant green floral pattern and her hair is in a very long braid over her shoulder.

"Lola, this is…" Kami says.

"Zane," Lola interjects. "Nice to meet you. Lola."

How does she know my name?

"Because I'm a Seer. I can see things most people can't, although I can't always choose what I see. That's why I'm here. Kami is helping me bring light to some of the shadows in my visions."

"What visions?" I ask, turning to Kami.

"Uh," Kami pauses.

"I take it she hasn't told you," Lola interjects. "Your demon has been creating problems for us all, and you're just enabling him."

I squint my eyes at her in a mix of confusion and irritation. I've just met the woman and I'm already being accused of something.

"Your Incubus is murdering half the city," she continues.

I can hardly comprehend what's going on. *What the fuck is happening with Kieran?*

"What are you talking about?" I ask.

"He's dropping bodies and not cleaning up after himself. The police are starting to notice a pattern and we're all in danger of being discovered."

Kieran? No way. That doesn't make any sense.

"Where's your proof?" I ask.

"I don't have it yet," she says. "But I will."

"Lola," Kami interjects. "This is not the time or place for this conversation."

"I'm just being honest," Lola says, turning to me. "I'm sorry. I know Kami speaks very highly of you and I trust that you wouldn't be involved with the demon if you honestly thought he was hurting people. I'm sorry for getting off on the wrong foot."

"I…" I try to respond but nothing I can think of seems appropriate. "Okay."

"Lola," Kami interjects. "Maybe you can help us with a problem we're having. We've been looking for someone that attacked our friend—a human."

"A human attacked an Immortal?" she asks.

"No," Kami explains. "Our friend is also a human. She's… Zane's lover."

Oh bloody hell, I hate that word.

"Really, Kam? Lover?" I ask.

"Mate… Girlfriend… Thing…" she adds. "Whatever you wanna call it."

Thing? I can't decide if that's better or worse than lover.

"Oh, hmm… Interesting," she says. "Okay, I can tell you what I see. But I can't guarantee it'll be what you need. Is your '*whatever*' here?"

"I uh… no," I reply.

"Okay, then I'll try you," she says, holding out her hand with her palm facing upward.

I give Kami a skeptical look but she nods, encouraging me to play along. I reluctantly put my hand in Lola's and she closes her eyes.

"Oh," Lola says, her eyes still closed. "Interesting,"

What does that mean?

"Do you know the lore on twin souls?" she asks, her eyes still closed.

"That's not real though, is it?" Kami asks.

"Oh, it's real," Lola says. "Just incredibly rare. Very interesting."

Her face scrunches up slightly as she continues to read me.

"Someone gonna clue me in here?" I ask.

"Twin souls. Your other half." Lola says. "True love, soulmates, all that jazz?"

Wait… What??

"Your whatever…" Lola says, closing her eyes again, "is your soulmate."

I don't even know what to feel. Part of me feels like I've always known Ava was the one for me, but another part is terrified of what that might mean.

Kami gives me an overzealous punch to the arm.

"Oh my god, Zane!" Kami shouts. "I knew it!"

"Five seconds ago you thought soulmates weren't real!" I say, rubbing my arm where she slugged it.

"Oh shut up, Z, you know what I mean!"

"Hmm," Lola says, grasping my hand as her brows furrow.

"What?" I ask. Her face looks stern and her attitude seems to have shifted.

"I told you, I never know what I'm going to see," she says with a stern voice.

Yeah, just what I want to hear from a Seer who's looking at my future.

She rips her hand back and steps away, her body language stiff and her eyes glaring in my direction.

"Did you see the guy who attacked Ava?" I ask. "What did you see? Tell me."

"I'm 847 years old, child," she snaps. "I don't take orders from baby Sirens, especially not you."

"Especially not me?" I ask. "Excuse me? Do we have a fucking problem, love?"

"Considering how few people ever encounter their other half, it seems a complete and utter shame that you are the one who got to claim yours."

Lola jumps suddenly to the side as Kami lunges at her, just nearly missing.

"Lola," Kami snarls. "You are my friend, but Zane is my brother and you're out of line."

I can hardly comprehend what's going on. *What the fuck did she see?*

"Kami, darling," Lola said. "I'm sorry, I know he's like a brother to you, but I'm just being honest."

"How could you say that?" Kami asks. "You don't even know him."

She's right. This woman doesn't know me. *Why the fuck is she holding a grudge against me all of a sudden?*

"I can see I have overstayed my welcome," Lola says, gathering her things. "The truth is hard for a lot of people to take."

What could she possibly have seen?

Part of me doesn't want to ask, but another part has to know.

"Do I hurt Ava?" I ask. "Will something happen to her because of me?"

"Ava deserves better than you. But she will be fine…" Lola replies as she walks down the hall towards the door. I feel a weight lift off my chest, but she continues. "…*in spite* of you."

—⋅—

I launch a chair across the room and it shatters into wood chips, taking a vase and a painting down with it.

"Zane, okay, I like her and she's my friend, but forget Lola's nonsense okay?" Kami says. "Whatever she saw, or thought she saw, is wrong. It's obvious that she's not seeing the whole picture."

I scream in frustration as I grab anything I can find and send it flying across the room.

"She said Ava will be fine. So whether we believe her or not—and to be clear, we do not—Ava is going to be okay. You love her, you would never hurt her. You're soulmates, remember?"

"In bloody *spite of me*, Kam?!"

"Well, I call bullshit on that."

I sink to the floor, my knees falling to the ground as I rest my head in my hands.

"What do I do with any of this? Ava is my soulmate and I'm apparently about to do something that's bad enough to make someone who doesn't know me despise me."

"She's a pretentious bitch anyways."

"Really? Because she was your friend an hour ago."

"Yeah, well," she says, sitting next to me on the floor, "my real friends aren't bitches to my brother."

"And what the fuck is going on with Kieran?"

She sighed and her eyes shifted away.

"Let's not worry about Kieran right now."

Yeah, that seems totally innocent.

"What aren't you telling me Kami?" I ask.

"We don't know anything. There may be an Incubus problem, but we don't know for sure it's Kieran."

"Incubus problem?"

I can't bloody believe this right now.

"Somebody—an Incubus—is overfeeding and… killing people."

"That's why he's not asking for my help as much?" I ask.

She sighs and doesn't respond.

No way. No fucking way.

Kieran isn't killing people. I would know.

Wouldn't I?

"Bullshit!" I snap. "It's not him."

"Okay," Kami says, rubbing my back. "I trust you. If you think it's not him, then it's not him."

It can't be.

Can it?

ZANE

Dreiflüssestadt, Austrian Empire - Autumn of 1840

This can't be happening.

"No, no, no," I say, cradling Ilen's cold, naked body in my hands.

Tears pour uncontrollably from my eyes as I shake her.

"Ilen, please darling. Wake up!"

My own voice sounds unfamiliar through my sobs.

This doesn't feel real. It can't be that this lifeless, bruised, and bloodied body is the girl I know. No twinkle in her eye. No bashful smile. No contagious laugh. My Ilen is so full of life—or, was.

But I took that from her.

29

Jen hands me a cup of tea as she slumps next to me on my couch. I'm wrapped in a blanket because I'm feeling shitty, as usual. My head is pounding and it feels like bugs are crawling under my skin.

"Have you finally talked to Shayna?" I ask, taking a sip of my tea.

Almost instantly, I burn my tongue and pant like a maniac trying to cool it.

Hot. Hot. Hot.

"I did actually!" she proclaims proudly.

"Really?? It only took like… a month and a half of hiding your ex-girlfriend in your own home." I smirk as she slugs me in the shoulder with a pillow.

"I see how it is, hater," she says with a playful glare.

"I'm mostly kidding," I say. "How'd it go?"

"She said she's okay with it! So I guess I worried for nothing."

"Well, that's a relief at least."

I take another sip of my tea and immediately regret it, burning my tongue again.

Why do I literally always do this?

"Yeah," she says, reaching into her purse and handing me a white bag. "Here's your prescription, girlie."

"Oh thank you for picking this up, you're my hero."

"No problem. What is it, though? The pharmacist insisted on telling me all of these scary side effects: seizures, face swelling, paranoia… and I swear she said dizziness, but isn't that one of the symptoms you're trying to treat?"

I laugh. "Yeah, that's pretty much common for everything they give me. Helps with one thing, messes up another thing."

She grabs the information sheet and reads it over.

"'Not breathing'??" Jen gasps. "How is that a side effect?? And how is that not just called 'death'?"

I giggle as she continues reading.

"'Pale lips'?" she continues. "Well yeah, no shit if you're not breathing!"

"So basically, I'm going to be a zombie."

"'Experiencing things that are not real'? What the heck is this nightmare drug?"

"They want me to try it for the pain and headaches. They said if it works then we'll know it's a neurological problem. So it's like a test run for a few weeks."

"A test run that could end in death?" Jen scrunches her face. "Heck, every time I talk to you, I remember how totally insane the medical industry is."

"Glad I can be your education," I say sarcastically.

———·———

ZANE

After my conversation with Kami, I drove straight over to Pike's. I'm getting to the bottom of this right now.

The door swings open to reveal a mostly empty bar, which I would expect for midday.

"We're not open yet," Kieran's voice shouts from the back room.

"Well, look who it is! He lives!" he says as he emerges.

I'm not really in the mood for his usual rubbish right now.

"After last Thursday, I assumed Ava had fucked you into a coma or something!" he says, adjusting things behind the bar as I approach.

"Wait… what? How do you know about Thursday?" I ask.

"I was getting a midnight snack of my own a few blocks away and I couldn't help but overhear some dirty Siren sounds coming from your place. You get yours, Z-Man!"

This is not how I saw this conversation starting.

"I've gotta know, what did she do that made you so loud?!" he says with a laugh. "Are you sure you're a Siren and not a Banshee because I'm-"

"Kieran," I say, cutting him off as I push him from across the bar. "Keep your bloody ears to yourself."

"Damn, dude," he says, grimacing as he rubs his shoulder. "You've gotten a lot stronger lately, haven't you?"

"I don't have time for this conversation."

"Wow, okay pouty face," he grumbles. "Somebody's got their panties in a twist!"

"We need to talk."

"Are you breaking up with me, Z-Man?" Kieran smirks and turns his back to me to dry a stack of empty glasses with a towel. "Is it because I'm fucking other men? …and women?"

"The fucking is one thing, sucking them dry is another."

"Well, sorry to break it to you, but I'm definitely doing quite a bit of sucking, too," he says with a laugh. When he turns around, his expression drops as he sees that I'm not laughing.

"You know what I mean, Kieran."

"It's *Kieran* now, is it? Not mate?" he asks, his brows furrowed. "So I guess you've been talking to Kami."

"So it's true?" I ask.

"No," he spits. "It's not fucking *true*. Just because your crazy-ass sister is convinced I'm a mindless animal doesn't mean I am!"

"Then how are you feeding? Because I haven't been helping you nearly as much since I started seeing Ava, but you don't seem to be starving."

He sets down the towel and glass he was holding.

"Wow," he says. "So that's what you think, then? You agree with her? You think I'm spiraling out of control?"

"Why don't you answer me, then?"

"You wanna know how I'm feeding? It's pretty fucking ironic, Zane, because I took a page out of your book."

"How's that?"

"I decided to try the relationship thing," he sighed. "I didn't wanna keep relying on your help, and what you were doing made a lot of sense. Rather than having to constantly convince new people to sleep with me, I figured I'd just convince someone to keep sleeping with me."

How romantic.

Wait… Kieran is in a relationship? With who?

"Wha-… What?" I stutter. "That doesn't make any sense. You can't survive off the energy of just one person. Not without the boost from my venom."

"Whoa, whoa! I never said it was just one!" Kieran says, bringing his hand to his chest as if he's deeply offended. "I'm a demon, Zane, not an idiot. I got, like, eight of them."

"Eight?" I ask, a bit of a chuckle escaping with it.

Okay, that makes a lot more sense.

Kieran pauses a moment, clearly doing some mental math and counting his fingers.

"Eight currently," he says. "No, wait… nine?"

I burst into laughter, partly from the humor of the situation and partly in relief.

"So you're not draining humans all around town? Then who is?" I ask.

"Fuck if I know, dude. I don't know any other Incubi or Succubi in town, but it's not like we have a newsletter."

I sigh for a minute. He seems genuine and his explanation makes sense.

"So the other night—your midnight snack—that was…"

"Kyle," he says.

Wow, Kieran just remembered a partner's name for once. *This has to be a miracle.*

"He's pretty fucking hot and he does this thing whe-" he continues.

"Okay, okay!" I interrupt. "Too much information. I believe you."

Kieran smirks, the usual snarky glint returning to his eye.

"You sure you don't want to hear? Because I sure got an earful of your sex life that I didn't ask for, so I feel like it's only fair that I return the favor."

"I won't hesitate to rip that tongue out, mate."

"Touchy touchy!"

"You know what, I believe you, okay. I don't need the details."

"Aww, I'm touched," he says sarcastically. "Speaking of touched…"

"Okay, change of subject!" I say, cutting him off before I have to hear more details about Kieran's sex life. "I have something else to talk to you about."

"Oh yeah?" he asks. "Finally decided to share Ava?"

This prick is seriously asking for it.

"What did I just say about that tongue?" I snap. I take a swing at him but he dodges it.

"Oh fine, dude. You can accuse me of murder but I can't joke about sleeping with your girlfriend? You're no fun!"

I decide to ignore his comment and continue.

"I need you to track someone down for me," I say, pulling Ava's balled up shirt from my pocket.

He squints before grabbing the shirt, picking it up, and sniffing it.

"Ava?" he asks. "Dude, if she's hiding from you, that's a pretty clear indicator that you've done something wrong."

"Not Ava, you arse."

"Uhh," he says, taking another sniff. His eyes furrow and his expression falls. "Wait… what happened? Did someone hurt Ava?"

"Some prick went after her and Jen. She's fine, but you can bet I'm not about to let it go. That's why I need your help."

"He attacked her?" he asks, holding the fabric up to examine it. "Enough to rip her shirt apart?"

"Uh," I stumble, remembering that I had torn the shirt off her later that night. "No, that wasn't him."

Kieran looks particularly smug and laughs.

"You dirty fucking bastard," he jokes. "I've had an excellent influence on you."

"Can we not have this conversation?" I ask.

"Alright," he says. "Well, I've got the scent now. Whoever this guy is, he's as good as dead."

30

The cab drops us off in front of a local nightclub called Tempt, a grand building with columns lit in purple and blue lights. The word "Tempt" is written in dozens of tiny white bulbs above the entrance. There's a line of people waiting practically around the block, flanked by velvet ropes. It's freezing cold tonight and everyone is huddled in their coats.

Everyone in line looks like a supermodel and is wearing what I imagine is designer clothing, that is, if I were fancy enough of a person to recognize what designer stuff looks like.

I'm glad Kami talked me into wearing one of my nicer going-out dresses. Under my wool coat I've got on my favorite piece of clothing—a red bandage dress that is so tight it's almost suffocating, but it makes my boobs look fantastic.

I haven't gone to a club in years, mostly because of the body-unfriendly combination of painful heels hurting my feet, dancing draining my energy, and alcohol upsetting my stomach. But, using Zane's charm power, I've managed to put that discomfort off for one night of feeling like a twenty-something again.

"I can't believe I let you three talk me into this," Zane huffs, stuffing his hands in the pockets of his blazer. "Nightclubs are the absolute bloody worst."

"I think it's a testament to how whipped you are that Ava was able to talk you into coming along," Kieran says with a laugh. "He never does this."

Zane rolls his eyes and we follow Kami as she charms our way past the bouncer. The hallway is mirrored and lined with neon lights.

"Go get us a booth while we drop off our coats," Kami says to Zane and Kieran as we stop at the coat check.

"Oh? Am I your errand boy, now?" Zane teases.

"Go, errand boy!" she jokes, pointing toward the main area of the club. Zane laughs and flips her off as he and Kieran walk away.

I pull my coat off as we reach the coat check.

"Oh damn," Kami says, looking me up and down, her eyes flickering a slight gold. "This is… wow girl, you brought it tonight! Has Zane seen this little number yet?"

"No, I don't think so. I've had my coat on so far."

"Well this ought to be entertaining, then," she says with a smirk. "That boy is gonna pass out."

"Well, thanks," I say awkwardly.

The main area has two levels and a high ceiling, decked in blue lights. Overhead lights are flashing and spinning to the beat of the music and a sweaty crowd of good-looking people fills the dance floor.

We spot the boys across the club at a big velvet booth and head in their direction.

Kieran sees us and his eyes go wide. Zane turns around and his eyes widen too, before quickly shifting to a glowing green.

"Tha… Wha… This is a… uh… That is…" Zane stutters.

"Nailing it, Z," Kami jokes as we both take a seat.

Kieran is holding a cocktail, biting his lower lip and swallowing hard. Before my eyes, tattoos appear down his arm.

"Wait, what the heck? You *do* have tattoos!" I say. "They're, like, magical tattoos? They just appeared on your arm out of nowhere!"

Zane's expression shifts and his jaw clenches.

"They better bloody disappear as fast as they appeared," Zane says with a scowl.

I think there's something I'm not understanding here, but I can't quite tell what. Kieran looks down at them and they slowly fade away.

"There, Cranky Britches," Kieran says. "Happy?"

Zane gives him side eye but then leans toward me with a smile, his eyes still glowing green.

"So love," he says, placing his hands on my hips. "Was this dress part of an attempt to kill me? Because it might work."

"Well I had to see how immortal you really are," I say with a smirk.

He leans over and plants a kiss on my neck, then moves upward to whisper into my ear. "You sure you want to do this whole club thing? Because if we left now I could be fucking you senseless in about 15 minutes."

Aaaand my legs are jelly. Do I even have legs? What are legs?

My cheeks suddenly feel hot and I consider bailing on this whole night out.

"No, I want to stay," I say. "The whole reason we're doing this is because I can finally feel good and do normal young person things again. We can control ourselves."

"Speak for yourself, love," he says, his eyes still glowing green.

"I thought you were well known for your self-control."

"Yeah, but you know you're my weakness baby." His fingers brush along my cheek. His jaw clenches and he shakes his head, the glow in his eyes fading slightly.

"Okay," he says, taking a long breath in. "A night out it is. Whatever my girl wants, she gets."

He pulls away from me as the glow in his eyes fades further and he turns to watch the crowd on the dance floor.

"Okay, first thing: I'm ordering a round of drinks!" Kami declares as she stands up. "This is gonna be awesome! And we might even run into a surprise guest!" She winks at Zane as she steps out of the booth. Zane squints his eyes in confusion.

"Surprise guest?" Kieran asks.

"No idea," Zane says, rolling his eyes. "Kami does enjoy her surprises."

"You wanna dance?" I ask Zane.

"Not right now, love," he says. "Maybe in a bit."

"I'll dance with you Ava," Kieran says.

Zane shoots Kieran a harsh look.

"Hey, you're the one who said no!" Kieran says. "Fiiine. Sorry Ava, your pussy of a boyfriend won't let me."

Zane crosses his arms and sighs. Kami returns to the table with a server carrying a huge platter of drinks and a pretty blond girl following closely behind

"Look who I found!" she says in an excited voice.

She steps to the side to reveal a gorgeous woman with tanned skin and long blond curls down to her waist. She's wearing a black leather dress that seems more like a long tank top than a full-size garment.

"And who's this?" Kieran asks, flashing her a flirtatious smile as he stands up from his seat

"This is my friend Gabby," Kami says. "Gabby, this is Kieran. He's a demon and he's definitely going to try and get in your pants, so feel free to stab him if he gets handsy."

"Whoaahh," Kieran says. "How rude! I thought we were friends!" He holds a hand to his chest, pretending to be wounded.

"Uh, hi Kieran," Gabby says with a bit of trepidation.

"Hellooooo beautiful," Kieran says, pulling her hand to his lips to plant a kiss on it.

"Annnnyyyywaaayyy," Kami interjects. "Gabby, you remember Zane."

"Yeah hey," Zane says, barely making eye contact with the woman.

"Hey, Z!" she says, throwing her arms around his shoulder and hugging him a bit too aggressively for my liking. "And who's this?"

She gestures toward me and then looks back at Zane.

"Uh this is… um…" he stutters, refusing to look directly at me. "This is Ava."

Oh wow, okay. I'm just Ava then?

31

"Hey Ava!" Gabby says in a high, excited voice, leaning in to give me an equally enthusiastic hug. "So nice to meet you!"

"Hi," I say.

Everyone steps around the booth to make space for her as I sit down on Zane's lap. Zane's eyes go wide and his body jolts as he abruptly pulls away and lifts me off of his lap to place me in the seat next to him.

What. The. Hell.

First, he avoids calling me his girlfriend, then all of a sudden I can't sit on his lap? *Is it really that much of a burden to be seen with me?*

"Just not right now, love," he whispers into my ear.

Oh wow. Yeah, by *right now* he means *while the sexy blonde is here.*

"Are you two together?" Gabby asks, gesturing between Kieran and me.

Kieran nearly chokes on his drink with laughter, undoubtedly expecting a reaction from Zane.

"No," Zane says sharply. "She's with me."

He gives me a quick glance and I can see a green glint before his eyes rapidly dodge away.

"Oh my gosh, Zane! You have a girlfriend? I didn't know that!" she squeaks.

Of course you didn't. He clearly wasn't too enthusiastic about telling you.

"She's gorgeous!" she says. "Oh my god, girl, look at you! You're *stunning*!"

I want to hate her but she just keeps complimenting me. *Damn it.*

"Has someone finally won over the Iron Siren?" she says with a giggle.

What does that mean?

"Oh you have no idea," Kami chimes in.

"I'm gonna go grab a pint," Zane says, quickly jumping out of his seat and walking toward the bar.

Is there something going on between Zane and this girl or am I just letting my imagination get the better of me?

"He's caving," Kieran says, taking a sip of his drink. "Ten bucks says he comes back here with a bottle of Jäger."

"Absinthe or Sambuca work too," Kami chimes in.

"What are we talking about?" I ask.

Kieran chuckles and opens his mouth to speak, but Gabby interjects.

"So what's your deal, girl? Are you a Siren?" Gabby asks me.

"Oh my god, Gabby, rude!" Kami says.

"Oh come on, we're all friends here. What's the point of all the pomp and circumstance? It's like, obviously this girl isn't human and I know you and Zane are Sirens, so what's the big deal? I'll go first—I'm a nymph."

"Why do you say it's obvious that I'm not human?" I ask.

"Well Zane's big 'no humans' policy, you know. He's always been intent on not getting involved with humans, right?"

Ouch.

"Hey," Kami says as Zane returns to his seat. "Where's your pint?"

"Oh uh," he mumbles. "Line was too long. Gave up."

"What?" Kami asks. "Z, you didn't seriously wait in line, did you? What is wrong with you? Did you forget you had powers?"

"Let it go, Kam," he mumbles. He seems to think I didn't hear him, but I did.

This whole evening is not turning out the way I planned.

"Hey guys, I'm gonna go to the bathroom. I'll be right back," I say, making my way out of our booth.

"Hey," Zane says as he taps my shoulder, having followed behind me. "You okay, love?"

"Oh yeah, don't let me interrupt your quality time with Gabby," I snap.

His eyes narrow and I can't tell if he's confused or guilty.

Before he has a chance to respond, I push through a sea of clubgoers to make my way to the bathroom and lock myself in a stall.

I let out a heavy sigh.

What am I doing? Why am I letting whatever is going on between this girl and

Zane upset me so much? I take a moment to compose myself and touch up my makeup.

Maybe I just need a drink to calm myself down.

As soon as I open the door, the club music blares and I try to push past the hoard of sweaty, beautiful people grinding up on each other and make my way to the bar. There's a long line to the front, so I find myself a spot behind two very intoxicated girls who most-certainly do not need another drink.

Is it just me or does every club have the same two intoxicated ladies, each laughing hysterically directly into the other's face?

"Hello, love," a voice says over my shoulder.

The voice and accent are similar to Zane's, yet different.

"Um, hello," I say, as I briefly look over my shoulder to see the man. He's taller than me, but not by much, with a sturdy build. He has light, freckled skin, red hair, and a short beard. The sleeves of his plaid shirt are rolled up and it's unbuttoned one or two buttons further than most men would do.

"Sorry to bother you, just wonderin' how you know my friend Zane over there," he says in an accent I now recognize as Irish.

He knows Zane? How does he even know *I* know Zane?

"I just noticed he's been rather, well… *obsessed* with you since you walked over here. He's watching your every move." He gestures over to Zane, who is of course sitting next to Gabby. The group seems to be enjoying themselves but all I can make out are everyone's general shapes in the low club lighting.

"Oh uh, yeah we're um…" I say, pausing for a minute.

Should I tell him we're dating? Zane certainly wasn't particularly forthright with that information earlier. And I don't even know who this guy is…

You know what, fuck it.

"He's my boyfriend," I reply.

"Zane has a girlfriend?" the man asks. "Wow! Who'd have thought? Oh and I'm Finn, by the way."

"Um, yeah, I'm Ava," I say, looking back at Zane.

Gabby has maneuvered herself onto Zane's lap.

I feel immediately sick to my stomach as I see his eyes glowing green.

How could I be so stupid? It's clear that he's interested in this woman and now he has just pushed me aside. He's a Siren. Everyone has told me he's not the relationship type, and I've just ignored it.

I feel a tear fall down my cheek as the Irish man looks back and forth from me to Zane at the other end of the room.

"Ignore that, it's nothing," he says. "What you're looking at there is Zane being an eejit. I promise you he's not interested in her. Don't upset yourself over it."

Yeah… sure.

This guy must not know that Zane's eyes are basically big flashing indicator lights that show he's interested.

"No, really, love. He saw that you were jealous, so he didn't immediately move her off when she sat down. It's an ego trip. Honestly, Zane isn't usually so needy. I think you've got him going out of his way to get your attention; that's something I've never seen from him."

Sure, that's why his eyes are glowing.

Finn turns back to look at Zane again and sighs.

"No, love. The eyes aren't for her," he says.

Wait… what?

I didn't say that out loud, did I?

What the heck is happening?

"I tend not to lead with this when I meet someone, but uh, I'm telepathic," he says.

Telepathic? As in, he reads minds? Oh my god is he reading my mind right now? Oh crap… don't think something awkward. It would be so embarrassing if I were thinking 'I wonder how big his penis is?' or something.

Oh god, now that's all I can think about.

Penis.

Stop thinking about this random guy's penis.

Penis.

Noooo! Stop it!

Finn chuckles and smiles. "It's okay, that's actually a pretty common response. I mean not specifically thinking about my penis, but I've certainly heard worse."

Oh my god, someone kill me please.

"It's alright, really. My people communicate telepathically, so we're used to hearing everyone's thoughts."

That sounds like a nightmare.

"Wait, the eyes aren't for her? What do you mean?" I ask. "They're not for me. He can hardly see me this far away in the dark."

Why am I talking about this with some guy I've just met?

"Well technically they're for me," he says with a smirk.

I turn back to see Zane's eyes glowing intensely, staring right at us. Gabby is now sitting on Kami's lap instead.

"He's about ready to kill me, actually," he says through another chuckle. "Well not me, exactly, because he can't tell who I am from that far away. He's thinking about doing some rather unsettling things to my testicles. Your boyfriend is a rather twisted fellow."

His eyes are glowing because he's jealous?

"Serves him right, really," he adds. "It's rather poetic, since he was enjoying making you jealous. I'd say that backfired rather splendidly. Of course he doesn't know that it's me you're talking to."

"How do you know Za-" I start to ask, but as I look back I see that Zane has vanished from his spot at the booth. *Where did he go?*

In a split second, Zane appears between me and Finn, pinning me against the wall with his hand cradling the nape of my neck, leaning in for a kiss but just shy of actually kissing me.

"Hey there, gorgeous," he says in a low voice, his lips inches from mine. "I missed you."

His eyes are green and have an especially bright glow in the dim club light. His body presses up against me and I'm suddenly forgetting why I was mad.

"Oi! I don't recommend in-the-middle-of-the-club sex. Not hygienic," Finn says from over his shoulder.

A low, roar-like sound rumbles from Zane's chest as he snaps around in a fraction of a second and grabs Finn by the collar.

"Take a hint, mate!" Zane says through his teeth, but his expression suddenly shifts into one of confusion.

His mouth parts and his eyes widen.

"Finn?"

32

"What the hell are you doing here?" I ask. I can feel my heartbeat slowing and I release his shirt from my balled fist.

"Kami told me you'd all be here and we thought I'd surprise you," Finn says.

My heart is still beating heavily.

Okay, the guy talking to Ava was Finn. So he wasn't hitting on her.

Someone isn't trying to take her from me.

She's not going to leave me.

It was just Finn.

Damn it. I'm a Siren. I'm supposed to be the one that others yearn for, obsess over, get jealous of. But with Ava, even when I try and turn the tables, I can't.

I'm acting like a desperate idiot.

"Mate, that's what love is," Finn's voice says in my head. *"It's another person making you completely helpless."*

"We already getting sappy?" I think.

"Well, you did just imagine some aggressive things about my balls, so I feel like we're at that level in our relationship."

I chuckle as he brings me in for a hug.

"What the heck?" Ava asks, staring blankly at us. "You were trying to kill him a second ago and now you're hugging?"

"My apologies," Finn says with a smile. "Forgot to use my outside voice."

"Finn can communicate telepathically," I explain to Ava.

"Yeah uh, I know," she says, blushing slightly.

He told her he was telepathic already? That's unusual.

"While you were obsessing over my balls, Ava here was…" he looks to her with a smirk then back at me. "Well, let's just say you have similar interests."

What's this now?

Ava lightly smacks Finn in the chest.

"First rule of thought club!" she says. "Geez!"

They're probably talking about something she was thinking about me, right?

Right?

The bartender makes his way to our end of the bar; we seem to be up next.

"Anything for you three?" he says, turning to me. "You already back for another? Gotta go easy on that absinthe, dude, it's heavy stuff."

Finn explodes with laughter.

Oh shut up, mate.

"I am so confused," Ava says.

"A Guinness, a cider…" Finn says to the bartender, pausing to turn to me and struggling to hold back his laughter. "Another absinthe for the Iron Siren?"

I might need it to prevent me from killing you.

"Okay, no absinthe then," he says with a smile.

———•———

As we make our way back to the booth, I pull Ava in to my side.

With her in that dress, I can't believe I let her walk to the bathroom without a bodyguard.

I look down at her as we walk and my eyes can't help but stop at her breasts.

Fuck.

This dress is going to kill me. I've hardly been able to look at her all night.

I could take her to the coatroom, charm the attendant into letting us back there, take her against the wall…

"What's the deal with absinthe, anyway?" Ava asks, shaking me from my thoughts.

This is embarrassing.

"It contains a particular spice that, erm… has a calming effect in Sirens."

"Calming?" she asks, nearly shouting trying to speak over the music.

"I had some because I haven't been able to get you off my mind all night. It's driving me mad. There's a reason I couldn't have you sitting on my lap, love. It's a miracle I've kept my hands to myself this long."

She blushes and looks up at me with those grey eyes.

"I couldn't help but notice it was fine when Gabby sat on your lap." Her expression is playfully pouty.

"As much as I love seeing you jealous over me," I say into her ear, "I can't fucking stand Gabby. Not that any woman could possibly be competition for you. She sat on me for a couple seconds and I hardly noticed. I was more focused on you getting chatted up by… well, Finn, apparently."

"How would you feel if I sat down on another man's lap?"

Well fuck. My blood starts to boil just thinking about it.

"You're right. It won't happen again."

She smiles and seems to be satisfied with my answer. Lucky for me, the alcohol seems to have her in a forgiving mood.

"Finn, you gorgeous motherfucker!" Kieran shouts as we approach the booth.

"Heeyyyy!" Finn says, pulling Kieran in for a hug. Finn gives Kami a quick hug as well and introduces himself to Gabby.

I take a seat between Ava and Finn. Ava leans into me and rests her head on my shoulder.

Damn it, even this is distracting.

So much for the old absinthe trick.

Maybe I *should* have another. Or maybe I should just carry some aster on me whenever I'm with Ava. Loads of Sirens keep some on hand just in case.

"You got it that bad?" Finn asks through my thoughts.

Oh piss off. Get outta my head.

"Ava, I love what you've done with our boy, here," he says aloud with a smile and a pat on my back. "The 'Iron Siren' thing was so boring!"

That nickname just won't die, will it?

"I know, right?" Kieran says. "Where was the fire? The intensity? I was beginning to think he wasn't a Siren at all."

"Iron Siren?" Ava asks. I turn toward her but find my eyes dodging the moment we make eye contact. Every time I properly look at her, I just want to jump her.

The irony of this conversation is not lost on me.

"For a while, Zane was known for being very controlled, very unshakeable," Kami explains. "Most Sirens are the opposite—feisty, quick-tempered, possessive, sexual…"

"That sounds like you to me," Ava says, giving me a wink.

Keep it together, Zane.

"Yeah well, it is now," Kami says. "Thanks to you."

"I didn't even know the color of your Siren eyes 'til tonight!" Finn says with a laugh. "I can't believe I got to see it all first hand!"

"Oh get used to it, Finny," Keiran chimes in. "The eyes are flashing on and off nonstop these days."

"Can we talk about a subject that's not me, please?" I ask. "How have you been, Finn? How's Marella?"

"She's great," Finn says. "We just got done visiting her family so I'm looking forward to some land time."

Ava looks at him with an odd expression.

"My wife is mostly confined to the water," Finn says. "She's a water spirit, so she can only come on land at certain times. We live in the Pacific most of the time, then I come on land to manage our affairs for a few months every year."

Ava nods but I can tell she's very confused.

"Yeah, well I'm a Selkie," he says, presumably answering a question in her thoughts.

Of course, she probably doesn't know what that means.

"He's a lovely little mermaid!" Kieran says with a giggle. A slight slur in his voice makes it clear that the alcohol has kicked in.

"Something like that," Finn says, taking a sip of his drink.

It's more or less correct. Part seal, part human, that's basically a mermaid. (Although, you might hear a very different opinion from actual Merpeople.)

"So I'm back for a while to keep everything in order," Finn continues, "and hang out with a couple of my favorite Sirens."

He laughs and squeezes my and Kami's knees.

"So you're married?" Gabby asks. She's just met Finn, so I imagine she's feeling left out.

"Oh yeah, coming up on a hundred years or so."

Selkies are hardcore monogamists once they find their partner. Since they live for thousands of years, it takes 'mating for life' to a whole new level.

Kieran's eyes go wide. "Jesus, Finn, you've been married for almost a hundred years? That's literally my worst nightmare."

Finn chuckles and takes a gulp of his Guinness. "I'm pretty sure being married to you for a hundred years would be anyone's worst nightmare."

"Ohhhhh!" Kieran yells, holding his hand up to Finn for a high five. "Nice one."

"What about you two?" Finn asks, gesturing toward me and Ava. He points to the rose tattoo on Ava's wrist. "Is that just a tattoo or is it covering…"

Shut up, Finn.

"*Shit, sorry… sore subject?*" Finn's voice echoes in my head.

"Uhh," he continues, stumbling over his words. "I mean, you guys both have tattoos so you've committed to having those for a long time."

He gives up on his clumsy save and opts for chugging the remainder of his beer instead.

"*Okay, that wasn't my finest. And from her thoughts it sounds like she's not buying it. I'm thick. I just thought…*" Finn says telepathically. "*You're so wild about her and she has a tattoo on her wrist.*"

She doesn't know about the mark, Finn.

I look over at Ava who's squinting in my direction, confusion evident in her expression.

"I've always wanted to get a tattoo," Gabby interrupts.

Thank fuck for Gabby right now.

"I think I would look super good with one," Gabby adds. "Like on my chest, so it would only show when I wear low-cut stuff."

It's no surprise that Gabby's remark has caught Kieran's attention.

"I think that would be a great idea," Kieran says, staring shamelessly at Gabby's cleavage. "But like, where exactly?"

"Don't answer that, Gabby," Kami snaps, glaring at Kieran.

Aaaand we've lost Kieran.

"If you get it on the sternum area it's supposed to be really painful," Ava says. "I looked into it a while ago, but I've heard it's not worth it."

Uhhh…

My eyes migrate back to Ava's chest.

Damn it.

Her eyes catch mine and I can no longer think straight. Her eyes and smile have an effect on me that her body can't even touch.

I've completely lost track of the conversation.

Ava takes a drink of her cider and wraps her lips around the tip of the bottle.

Fuck.

My mind floods with a series of vivid thoughts.

"You dirty slut," Finn's voice says in my head.

Get out of my head, Finn.

"See! There they go again!" Kieran says, pointing at me.

There what go again?

"I don't know why you'd be triggered now," Kieran says. "I didn't even say anything about Ava's tits yet."

Yet? I'm seriously going to kill him.

"Haha, there we go, they're even brighter now," Kieran says. "Oh oh, Finn! This is perfect. You can tell us, what's he thinking? Does he want to kill me or does the thought of a threesome with me just turn him on?"

Gotta admit, thinking about sex with Kieran is a great way to kill my libido. Now I just want to smash Kieran's face into the wall.

"I never kiss and tell," Finn says, giving me a wink.

Thankfully I know Finn keeps other people's thoughts to himself. That's especially helpful now since my mind has been on sex since the minute Ava revealed that damn dress.

She thinks I can handle dancing with her when she's looking this good? I'm nearly dying just looking at her, let alone touching her. Or having her touching me.

Fucking evil dress is what it is.

Bloody hell.

I lean in to whisper into Ava's ear.

"Follow me. *Now.*"

I pull Ava through the crowd toward the entrance.

She giggles and asks, "Where are we going?"

I have a bit of tunnel vision as we make our way to the coat check.

"Are we leaving?" she asks.

"Nope."

"Excuse me," I say, lightly touching the wrist of the woman behind the counter. "Quietly let us back to the coatroom, then give us some privacy. When we leave, you're going to forget we were ever here."

The woman quietly nods as she opens the door to let us back.

"Zane," Ava says, playfully admonishing me. "You're not serious."

We enter the larger closet section. It's dimly lit and lined wall-to-wall with coats. I close the door behind us and pin Ava against a rack of coats. I can see her face is slightly illuminated by the glow of my own eyes.

"Dead serious, baby," I say.

She smiles slightly and her lips part. She pulls me in by the front of my shirt and brings her lips to mine; softly at first, then faster. The taste of apples and alcohol from the cider lingers on her lips.

I slip my arms around her hips and lift her up, knocking coats off their hangers as she wraps her legs around me.

Her eyes remind me of the first time we kissed, or rather—when she kissed me. They're a beautiful, soft grey with wide pupils and a look of lust. It was the only time I had ever let someone catch me off guard. The first moment of many when this woman captivated me; took me by surprise.

Is it possible she's gotten more beautiful? More entrancing?

Those wide pupils hold my greatest fear: that her love is nothing more than an effect of my powers. But in this moment, I see a true intensity of emotion behind them. Maybe even nearing my own.

I find myself unable to hold back my own increasingly frantic touches, as though I need to take in all of her at once, by feel alone.

This dress hugs her every curve and her chest is gloriously on display.

Evil. Evil. Evil dress.

My trousers feel unreasonably tight. Her fingers fumble at my shirt's buttons and I rip it open in one quick motion.

She giggles as I lightly bite her neck. It's taking more restraint than I'd like to admit not to bite harder.

The dress has ridden up her thighs, and I pull it further up to her hips.

Evil. Evil. Bloody genius dress.

She's managed to unbuckle my belt already and pulls my zipper down. I shiver under her touch, letting out a bit of a growl. She strokes me through my pants and I swear I'm seeing stars.

"What are you doing to me?" I moan, aching for more of her touch.

The club music is booming on the other side of the walls, making the room vibrate. My subconscious has taken over my body and every move of my hands and hips is out of my control. We both pant and grope until I sink into her, both of us groaning in relief.

Soft moans escape her lips as I thrust at a desperate pace. I've knocked over roughly eighty percent of the coats in this room, but damn it if I won't get to a hundred.

My eyes trace the lines of the red dress from her shoulder across her chest and down as it wraps around her hips. Her nails dig into my back and down the ridges where my wings would emerge. I grab hold of the wall to steady myself as my legs start to shake beneath me.

A loud, thick growl emerges from my throat.

"Shhh," Ava whispers in my ear.

With one more thrust we both come undone and I collapse to my knees.

"Alright love," I say between heavy breaths. "You want to go dance?"

33

"Why is Kami so big on Halloween?" Ava asks, sifting through the racks of costumes.

"I think a lot of Sirens are," I say. "It's a pretty sexed-up holiday. But honestly, I think Kami loves any excuse to throw a party."

"So are you big on Halloween, then?" she asks.

I've never been as interested in debauchery as others of my kind. Probably because I've made an effort to remain controlled and these celebrations are notoriously *out* of control.

"Eh," I say. "It's always been more of a human thing to me."

"Hmm," Ava says, her expression falling.

"What was that, love?" I ask, bringing my hand to the small of her back.

"Oh just… I guess you aren't much for humans usually."

I step behind her and nuzzle my face into her neck.

"I'm awfully fond of this one," I say.

"Mmm-hmm."

"Something on your mind, love?"

"It's just," she says with a sigh. "Last night, Gabby asked me what kind of Immortal I was."

Of course, that's an incredibly inappropriate question to ask amongst Immortals, but Gabby has never had much of a filter—one of many reasons I can't stand her. I only tolerate her since she and Kami are close.

"I'm sorry," I say. "Gabby has no tact. She didn't mean to offend; that's just how she is."

"I mean, I don't have a problem with it, I just… she said she knew I wasn't human because you're so anti-human."

Of bloody course she did. Fucking Gabrielle and her giant mouth.

"Love," I say. "I've never been anti-human, that's wrong. And human or Immortal, you're the most important being in the world to me. Never question that."

She looks up from the costume rack with wide eyes and a look that practically melts me.

Did she seriously doubt any of that for a moment?

If she only knew…

"I used to avoid getting involved with humans," I explain. "That part is true. But that's because of the complications that go along with that, the same ones you and I have discussed."

"Like trying to get your girlfriend to go bone the waiter?" she says with a smirk.

I let out a low growl and spin her toward me so my hands are now wrapped around her arse.

"Not funny, love," I say, giving her a small, playful spank.

"Public, you perv," she scolds under her breath, pushing on my chest. "Behave."

"Whatever you say, mistress," I tease and she shoots me a glare.

She pulls a costume from the rack and shows it to me.

"Speaking of mistress…" she says.

The costume is a black catsuit with red tassels and a whip labeled 'Sexy Ringleader.'

"As ridiculous as that costume is," I say, "I wouldn't mind seeing you in it."

I wink and she blushes as she returns the costume to the rack.

"How *sexy* is this party supposed to be?" she asks.

"I mean, it's Kami." I shrug.

"So pretty sexy, then."

"You can wear whatever you want, love. Just because she likes to host a brothel doesn't mean you have to participate."

"So not like this, then?" she asks with a giggle, holding up a costume labeled 'Naughty Nurse Nancy.'

What is with these bloody names?

Humans are weird.

The costume consists of a thin strip of red and white fabric covering just the nipples and extending downward into a thong with a tutu over it. The woman in the photo on the package has a pair of knee-high white stockings on, presumably so she won't get cold?

"Oh hell no," I say, pulling it out of her hands and putting it back on the rack. "Trying not to tell you what to wear, love, but unless you want to see a bloodbath, that one is out."

"Ohhh so you don't want me making you jealous, huh?" she asks with an unmistakable glint in her eye.

Oh shit. I'm in trouble.

"Uh," I say, but I'm not sure where to go with it.

I should've known I wasn't going to get away with provoking her jealousy last night.

"You don't want me to try this on here then?" she asks, pulling the nurse outfit back out and pointing to the two small dressing rooms with a shared mirror out in the main area.

"Wha-… what are you doing?"

"Nothing," she says with a smirk. "Just asking a question."

"You…" I stutter. I look around and see several people in the store, including one well-built frat boy whose ass I already want to kick. "You wouldn't… You know how I… Love, why are you…"

She mischievously smacks me over the head with the costume bag.

"Then I guess it's not nice to try and make someone jealous, is it?" she asks, furrowing her brows and returning the costume to the rack.

Alright, she's got me there.

"I'm sorry, love," I say with a sigh.

Then again, that whole thing didn't go too well for me anyway. I just ended up in a jealous rage over her anyway—like always.

"I'm just…" I continue. "I'm used to being the object of everyone's desire. My whole life I've been wanted—by everyone. And then you come along and all I want is for you to want me like that. It's stupid and I'm sorry for being immature, but what they said last night was true. You bring out the Siren in me."

"Uh, okay well," she says, stuttering slightly. "Damn it, Zane, I didn't expect your response to be all sweet and sexy."

I smirk and a laugh sneaks out my lips.

"So sorry love," I say jokingly.

"You need one too, you know," she says, pointing over to the men's costumes.

I chuckle to myself.

"You mean like wings?" I ask.

"Oh," she says, her face contorting. "Do you do that? Just bring your wings out and people think it's a costume?"

"Sometimes," I say. "Sometimes I dress up. I haven't done the Halloween thing in the last few years. Got boring for me."

"What about this year?" she asks. "I'm telling you right now I do *not* do couples costumes."

"No promises," I say with a laugh, "but I'll take a look."

I walk toward the men's section as she scoops up a few costumes in her hands and heads toward the dressing rooms.

"No nurse!" I say, looking back in her direction.

"No couple's costumes!" she replies with a smirk.

I look at the selections for the men. They seem to be on either end of a very confusing spectrum between aggressively lame and disturbingly sexual.

It's either 'man riding an inflatable ostrich' or the 'fireman and his hose.'

Humans are really weird.

A lot of these are just things I or other Immortals have worn at some point in time—lederhosen, togas, bellbottoms. These aren't costumes, they're just clothing styles that have fallen out of fashion.

"What do you think?" Ava's voice asks behind me.

I turn around to see Ava in a short black dress and a little pair of black wings. She smiles at me with a hint of insecurity.

I step towards her, rubbing my thumb across her jawline.

"Love, you look…" I pause to find my words.

"I'm sorry," she says, her eyes falling to her feet. "I didn't even consider… is this offensive?"

I chuckle. "I keep telling you, love, I'm not a penguin."

"No I mean…" she mutters. "I dunno."

"I'm not offended. You look beautiful."

She does look beautiful, but she always does. Is she still stuck on the whole human thing? Does she think I want her to be a Siren?

"You like it?" she asks with a smile.

I put a hand around her waist.

"I like you in anything," I say, stroking the small of her back as our foreheads touch. "Just one small thing."

Her eyes hold a look of confusion. I reach around to the straps holding the wings to her back and slowly slip them off her shoulders.

"I… what…" she mutters.

The wings fall to the floor and I kiss her shoulder.

"There," I say. "Perfect."

"But, I thought…"

"You thought that I might prefer you as a Siren?" I ask, my expression scolding her for the very idea.

"I dunno," she says shyly.

"I prefer you as you are, love. Beautifully human."

I kiss her neck and she giggles as a deep pink blush appears on her cheeks.

"Public…" she whispers.

"What can I say? I'm a naughty boy," I say with a smirk, kissing her neck again.

"I'm going to try something else on," she says, pulling away and smiling.

I continue to peruse the racks of costumes. After a moment, she comes out in a blue-green toga with leather straps around it and leather cuffs, complete with a heeled version of a gladiator sandal.

Bloody hell. I like this one.

"I…" I stutter. "I'm a fan."

She giggles.

"Very Xena Warrior Princess, huh?" she asks.

"Who?" I ask.

She giggles again.

"You really *are* old aren't you?" she teases.

"Want me to take you back into that dressing room and show you how young I am, gorgeous?" I say flirtatiously, raising an eyebrow.

"You think you're funny, old man?" she jokes.

I grab my arms around her waist and tug her towards me.

"Call me old man again, love. I dare you…" The warmth of her body against mine is testing my control.

"Next costume," she says in an almost-yelp.

"Good choice," I tease.

She walks back to the dressing room.

What was I doing again?

Ahh, yes—looking at really terrible Halloween costumes.

After a few minutes, I decide that, once again, I'm going as a Siren for Kami's Halloween party. These choices are dreadful.

"Okay, this is a big ol' nope," Ava says behind me.

I turn around to see her in an incredibly revealing school uniform that schoolgirls certainly do not wear in England. Her blouse is tied just below her breasts and is entirely unbuttoned to reveal her cleavage. She's wearing a red plaid skirt with white knee-high stockings.

I clench my teeth so tightly, I'm surprised they don't shatter.

Bloody hell this woman is trying to kill me.

"Why… do… uh… you said… why nope?" I manage to say.

"Eloquent," she teases.

"Sorry, miss," I say, wrapping my arms around her waist. "Perhaps I need an English tutor. Can you come to my house after school?

"Guess you should've paid more attention in class!" she says with a giggle.

"This one is not for the party," I say.

"Yeah I agree," she says. "My stomach is super cold in this."

She turns to walk back to the dressing room.

"On second thought, Ava," I say. She stops and turns back to me.

"Yeah?"

"You should get that one, just not for the party."

"Ava?!?" I hear a man's voice call.

I flip around to see a man with spiky bleach blonde hair and chiseled features approaching Ava. He has a huge fit frame, probably even an inch or two taller than me. He's wearing a blue leather jacket, tight jeans, and short leather boots.

"Lucas!" Ava says enthusiastically, opening her arms as they both go in for a hug.

Nope. Nope. Nope.

I walk over to them at a speed slightly faster than one might consider human.

"Whoa, uh… hi?" the blonde says to me.

"Hi," I reply.

Ava looks at me scoldingly.

"Zane, this is Lucas. Lucas is an old friend," she says.

"Zane," I say, reaching out for a firm handshake. "Ava's boyfriend."

"Oh hey," he says. "British, huh?"

"Yep."

He turns back to Ava.

"Look at you, damn!" he says. "You were hot in high school but you look like a fuckin' sex kitten."

That's it. Let's see what he thinks without his eyeballs.

I wrap an arm around her waist.

Take a bloody hint, mate.

"Uh thanks," Ava says with a laugh. "This isn't exactly my everyday look."

"Yeah I figured," he replies with a chuckle.

"So how are you?" she asks him. "Are you back in Port Charlotte?"

"No, just visiting family. Are you?"

"Yeah," she says.

"That's crazy! I visit all the time and I never see you around."

"Well, I'm downtown. I usually don't hang out in the old neighborhood, but this was the only costume place I knew of."

I'm trying so hard not to kill this guy that their conversation hardly registers. Apparently Ava used to live in this neighborhood?

"Well this look is certainly a winner," he says. "I'd do you."

I find myself between him and Ava before I've even thought through the action.

"You have the bloody nerve to say that in front of me?" I say.

I hear Ava's quiet pleas of "Zane" but I'm seeing red now and can hardly focus. She tugs at the back of my shirt.

"Oh my god," he says. "So goals! We fucking love a jealous queen!"

I… what?

I think I'm going to have to google at least half of the words in that sentence, but the way he said it has me a bit taken aback.

A giggle escapes Ava's mouth and both she and her friend begin laughing.

"For the record, I'm super gay," he says to me.

Gay.

Oh.

This is awkward.

"Oh uh, yeah," I say. "Sorry, mate. I er… I thought you were just being… inappropriate."

"Oh yeah, I'm totally inappropriate, but not in that way!" he says with a laugh. "Anyways, I gotta get going but good seeing you Ava and Ava's sexy British boyfriend."

He hugs us both goodbye and we walk back to the dressing rooms. When we're out of earshot, Ava busts up laughing.

"That was amazing," she says through stifled laughter.

"Not funny," I say.

———

Ava settled on the green toga and, after a bit of convincing, I talked her into letting me buy the schoolgirl outfit too. We purchased them and started heading back to the parking structure.

The sun has just set and streetlights are starting to turn on, lighting up the dilapidated buildings that look even more broken-down as night falls.

"So you used to live around here?" I ask.

"Yeah," she says shortly.

Okay then. I guess that's a touchy subject.

"So were…" I start to say, but we're interrupted by a male voice.

"Oh look who it iiiissssss!"

Ava looks concerned but keeps looking forward, walking faster. Her heartbeat quickens as she looks at her feet.

I turn to look and see a scrawny man across the street, covered in tattoos and staggering drunk. He's got a scruffy goatee and gauges in his ears, is wearing an oversized black hoodie and a baseball cap, and is taking puffs of a cigarette. The man is staring right at us. Ava continues to pull me forward by my hand.

"Aaaavvvaaa," he calls teasingly.

My neck snaps toward him, then back to her.

"Who is this guy?" I ask.

"Nobody," she says, pulling me faster down the street. "Let's just go."

Is this another ex-boyfriend? If he's anything like Mike, I'm sure he's just bloody delightful.

"Stuck-up bitch!" he screams. "I'm fucking talking to you!"

My body is shaking with rage and stiffens with his words.

"Ava, I'm about to kill this guy right now. I'm not even joking," I say, my voice thick with anger.

"Please, let's go," she says, pleading with those grey eyes.

Fuck.

Okay, I can do this.

I take another step forward when a bottle whizzes past us. I catch it by the neck before it comes anywhere close to Ava. My muscles tense and the bottle shatters in my fist.

"Zane," she cautions.

I dust the glass shards off of my palms and I slowly turn toward the man.

"Who the fuck is this?" the guy asks in a slurred voice, gesturing toward me as he stumbles closer.

"The last bloody thing you're ever going to see, mate," I spit, rushing toward him and pinning him against a nearby brick wall.

"Fucking around on your boyfriend?" he asks Ava. "Why am I not surprised?"

"Ava, who *the bloody fuck* is this guy?" I ask, ready to crush his larynx. She looks genuinely frightened and at the moment I can't tell if it's of him or me.

"He's…" she says softly. "He's my brother."

34

Zane's eyes look in my direction while his body stays rigid, pinning Dylan to the wall.

A few men on the other side of the street are smoking and drinking outside the Ale House. Judging by their laughter, they're probably some of my brother's drinking buddies.

I knew I shouldn't have come back here.

"Your brother?" Zane asks in a shaky, low voice.

"Awww…" Dylan slurs with a wicked smile. "You didn't tell your side chick about me? I'm hurt."

"Shut up Dylan," I snap. "Zane, let's go."

I step close enough to put my hand on Zane's shoulder. His eyes are an unusually bright, almost terrifying shade of green. He's shivering with rage and I can tell he's struggling to maintain control, but he doesn't move an inch.

"You threw a bottle at your sister's head?" Zane snarls through his teeth.

"That's between her and me," Dylan says with the same kind of smart-ass attitude that has lost him a few teeth over the years.

A low growl rumbles from Zane's chest as he tightens his grip around Dylan's neck. Dylan's face starts to turn a purplish-red as he struggles against Zane's hold.

"Zane," I say, pulling at his arm. "It's okay. I can handle Dylan."

He manages to pull his hand off and drop Dylan to the ground.

"Shit man, is this fucker on PCP or something?" Dylan asks, rubbing his neck. "His eyes are nuts and he's really strong. And he's having some major shakes."

Zane continues to tremble with anger as I rub my hand across his back to calm him down.

"This guy seems like a real winner," Dylan says.

"What do you want?" I ask, ignoring his usual bullshit.

"What do you mean, what do I want? I've been calling you for fucking ever; you know what I want."

It's true. He wants me to start talking to Dad again. That's a hard pass.

"Not gonna happen," I say.

I try to pull Zane in the direction of the parking lot, but he manages to take just a single step back toward me.

"Then I guess I'll just tell your boyfriend about this then?" Dylan says with a sneer.

"Tell Mike whatever you want," I say. "He and I have been done for a long time."

"Of course," he says. "You never could keep 'em around long."

"Ava," Zane says in a low, quiet voice. His tone lets me know that Dylan is very close to becoming mincemeat.

"We're done here," I say, pulling Zane again. He reluctantly begins to follow.

"We can't talk?" Dylan says, following behind.

"About what?" I stop and whip around.

"I just want to see how life is on the other side. What made Princess abandon her fucking family."

"I don't owe you an explanation, Dylan."

He knows exactly why I don't speak to him or Dad. Being nine years apart, he and I were never particularly close, and he turned out exactly like our father: violent, substance-addicted, and pissed off at the world.

The best thing I ever did was cut them both out of my life.

"I don't care if you take my calls, but you need to make up with Dad," Dylan says. "He has a heart condition. You're so selfish that you're just going to let him die and never let this go?"

I want to tell him that I'm not about to invite an abusive asshole back into my life. I want to tell him that the only time Dad cares about me is when he needs money, but I'm pretty sure saying any of these things would escalate this situation when we desperately need to *de*-escalate.

"I'm sick too, Dylan, and I've done plenty fine on my own. He will too."

"Oh, how could I forget," he says sarcastically. "There's always something wrong with poor Ava!"

My hand is around Zane's arm and I can feel his muscles tense. Dylan is being the particular kind of asshole that he always is—the kind that you almost certainly do not want to be toward a mythological creature that can crush your skull.

"You wanna try that again?" Zane says. His voice is hoarse and deep and downright chilling.

"Is your boyfriend here to save you? What happened to Mike, anyway? He get tired of your bullshit?" He slurs over each word and stumbles in place. As usual, Dylan is wasted off his ass.

Zane inflates his chest and lets out a truly animalistic sound that I would imagine might come out of a tiger-pterodactyl hybrid.

It seems to be enough to shut Dylan up, because he staggers backward and his expression drops. Zane smiles, his eyes glowing and a seriously sinister look is plastered on his face.

I tug firmly on his arm.

"Let's. Go."

He looks down at me and his eyes dim a little, but I can tell he's still ready for a fight. I tug him hard in the direction of the parking lot and he relaxes a bit further, but his feet are still firmly planted.

"Just one thing," he says.

In the blink of an eye, Zane swings and Dylan is on the ground with a hand cradling his bleeding nose.

"Okay," Zane says. "Let's go."

———·———

The drive back to my apartment has been eerily quiet. Zane hasn't said a word since we got back to my car. For the past ten minutes, it has been nothing but the low hum of music on the radio and the repetitive drone of wheels on pavement.

"Are you okay?" I finally ask.

"Am *I* okay?"

"Yeah, I know you got pretty worked up back there."

"I just nearly killed your brother and you're worried about me?"

"Half brother," I correct.

He lets out a short laugh.

"That's the part of that you had a problem with?" he asks. "What went on between you two? Is that what he's usually like?"

I had hoped we would never have to have this conversation.

"It's not any one thing," I say. "He's an asshole. My dad's an asshole. I don't waste my time with assholes. End of story."

"You never talk about them."

"Yeah." I shrug, my eyes still focused on the road. "There's not much more to say about it than that."

Okay, so there's a bit more, but no more that I feel like sharing.

"So you're really not going to tell me?" he asks. "Why is your family such a big secret?"

I reach my apartment and pull into my parking space, shutting off the car.

"You don't tell me all of your secrets," I say. We both grab our bags and head inside.

"What secrets?" he asks.

I'm not sure if it's fair to call them secrets, because I've never asked. But there are certainly a lot of topics he seems to be uncomfortable about.

"Nevermind," I say.

I don't want to get into this because he might just tell me the truth, and if he does, I know he'll want to know more about my brother and my family.

I unlock my door and we make our way inside.

"Go ahead, love," he says. "What do you want to know?"

This is definitely a trap.

I struggle to think of a question he has dodged in the past. Come to think of it, last night it seemed like there were a few.

"Okay," I say. "Why did Finn ask about my tattoo last night?"

His eyes are suddenly wide and his jaw clenches.

Bullseye!

Now I won't have to answer his questions.

"Uh… erm… um… what?" he stutters. "I'm not sure what you mean."

Yeah, you don't know what I mean, that's why you just tripped over your tongue.

"Hey, it's fine if you don't want to answer. All I'm saying is we all have our secrets."

"Mmm-hmm," he says with a scowl. "Alright, cheeky girl."

Perfect. Successfully avoided that question.

"I'll tell you," he adds.

Oh crap.

"So he was wondering if we were… um… sort of married in a sense," he says.

"Married??" I ask.

That is not what I expected him to say. I didn't know what I did expect but it wasn't that.

"What does that have to do with my tattoo?"

"The um," he says. "The thing is… with Sirens, when we bond with a human partner we sometimes… um…"

"Is this a weird sex thing?"

"No!" He narrows his eyes at me. "It's… The thing is… It's called a mark. It looks like a tattoo but it's not. It's a symbol that appears on a human that has been marked by a Siren. Always on the inner wrist."

"Ermm, marked? Like a dog peeing on a tree?"

No thanks, I don't want to get peed on.

"No," he says with a grumpy look and a sigh. "It's a literal mark but it represents a particular connection. The human is marked as the mate of a Siren and it's kind of like a claim, warning other Immortals to leave them alone, but it also shows that they are connected."

"Connected like married?" I ask.

"Ermm, kind of."

"Kind of?"

"They are connected by Immortal blood, so they share a life thread. The human becomes immortal so long as their Immortal partner lives. The human doesn't gain any Siren gifts or anything like that, but they share immortality."

That's a little more intense than I was expecting.

"So if the Immortal dies, the human dies?" I ask.

"No, if the Immortal dies, the bond is broken. The human returns to their mortal life."

"Oh, okay," I say.

Honestly, I'm not sure where to go with that. I guess he doesn't want to do this with me and that's why he was so awkward about it the other night.

"Don't worry. You don't have to do that, love," he says.

He seems to think I'm the reluctant one. *Does that mean he does want to do this mark thing?*

"What do you mean?" I ask.

"Well I mean, there's no pressure. I wouldn't want to risk anything going wrong or something happening to you. We're already soulmates, we have nothing to prove, right?"

Wait… *we're what?*

"Soulmates?"

"Er, I mean… I love you and… I mean, whatever." He runs his hands anxiously through his hair, his eyes widening in panic.

Hearing him call us soulmates makes my heart jump.

Does he really think I'm his soulmate?

"So your turn, love," he says in a rather transparent attempt to change the subject.

Ah crap, I was kind of hoping he would forget.

"My turn to what?" I ask innocently.

"What happened between you and your brother and your dad?"

Damn it.

"I mean, a lot," I say with a sigh.

Where do I even start?

"My parents got married when my brother was around eight years old. They had me. My dad never really wanted to be a dad. My brother certainly didn't want to be a brother. My mom and dad got divorced. Then a few years ago my mom died."

"Is that all the detail you're going to give me?" he says, one eyebrow raised.

"What detail do you want?"

"Did they hurt you?" he asks, clenching his jaw.

I feel the uncomfortable out-in-the-cold sensation of being vulnerable and my instincts tell me to burrow into the ground and hide.

"Not really. When my dad would mix alcohol and painkillers, he might smack me or Dylan, but that only happened a few times. He and Dylan both have a habit of throwing things too, but they wouldn't really try to hit you—it was just about throwing a fit."

I see Zane's eyes glow slightly green and his expression seems serious.

"It's not a big deal," I say.

"Okay," Zane says through clenched teeth. "When did you stop talking to them?"

"I stopped talking to my dad when my mom died. I didn't technically stop talking to Dylan as much as we never talked in the first place. He only started talking to me when I stopped talking to Dad—just trying to get me to forgive him."

My father was always really shitty to my mom, tearing her down and wrecking her self-esteem. Even though she left, she was never really free of him.

When she died, he just had to say something heartless. I don't even remember the words he used. After years of abusive behavior and nasty comments, I stopped keeping track. I just remember the spite in his words and his cold, uncaring demeanor.

In that moment, I was done.

Zane's expression is torn between fury and sadness, and I can tell he's struggling between wanting to know more and wanting to respect my privacy.

"I'm glad I punched him," Zane says with a bit of a smirk.

He pulls me in for a hug and runs his hand through my hair in a comforting way. It's the most Zane way of reassuring me and exactly what I need right now.

35

 ZANE

I pull up outside of Pike's with Ava in the passenger seat. Kieran was supposed to meet us outside but, as usual, he's not ready on time.

"I'll give him a call," I say to Ava. She nods.

The call rings a few times before going to voicemail. I guess I should've expected that.

"Alright, I'm gonna go get him," I say.

Ava looks great in her costume and I'm second-guessing why I encouraged Kami to invite Kieran to the party.

I give her a quick kiss and jump out of the car.

It must not be too busy as there's no one inside, but it's also a bit early for their usual patrons.

"Kieran!" I call. "We're here to pick you up for Kami's Halloween do. Get your arse out here!"

I wait but I don't get a response.

Damn it, Kieran.

A few shuffling sounds echo from the back kitchen area, so I walk back through the 'Employees Only' door.

As I turn the corner, I see Kieran with some woman's legs wrapped around him and his pants around his ankles. The woman is busty with wide hips and shoulder-length brown hair. I see a light white smoke passing from her mouth into his.

"Oh fuck," I curse, covering my eyes.

"Shit!" Kieran says under his breath.

I do my best to look at the floor.

"Oh my god!" the woman shouts as they both scramble to re-clothe themselves. Her voice seems somewhat familiar, but I can't place it.

"This is… I know this looks bad… Oh my god I'm so embarrassed… Please don't tell Ava about this," the voice says.

I look up at the woman again and recognize a familiar face. It's Shayna—Jen's girlfriend.

Bloody hell.

———

"Relax, Z-Man," Kieran huffs as we make our way out into the main bar.

"Really?? Shayna??" I ask.

"She's a big girl who can make her own decisions."

"She's dating Jen."

"Yeah but not like, exclusively… right?" His brow pinches slightly with his question, like he hadn't even considered it until now.

I'm not ready to weigh the implications of what I just saw between Kieran and Shayna, let alone whether I should tell Ava.

"You know what—no—we're not talking about this right now," I say. "Ava's waiting in the car and she's excited for this party. We're not ruining it with whatever the hell I just saw."

"Great. Cool," Kieran says. "Not talking is good."

I hear him shuffling behind me.

"What are you doing?" I ask as I turn around to see him taking off his shirt.

"I'm changing into my costume," he says.

He's wearing bright red suit pants and swings a matching blazer on over his shoulders.

"No shirt?" I ask, immediately wondering why I've bothered. It's Kieran I'm talking to.

"If you've got it, flaunt it," he says with a smirk.

"What are you supposed to be, anyway?"

"One sec," he says. Two horns emerge atop his head.

His real horns are black and curve around his head, but these are red and pointed. I guess he's taking the literal approach tonight.

"Really?" I ask.

"Get it? I'm a demon!" he says with a smirk.

I roll my eyes and gesture to him to move along.

"You're no fun!" he says. "What are you, then? English guy with a stick up his ass?"

I'm currently wearing only part of my costume: a white T-shirt and jeans with the cuffs rolled up over short black boots.

"Well, I figured I'd finish getting ready once we get there. I had a feeling if I didn't leave early some dickhead was going to make us late."

"Awww, you and your pet names are so sweet," he says with a cheeky grin.

We walk over to the driver's side of my Challenger and I let Kieran in the back. Ava is already seated in the passenger seat in her blue-green toga costume.

"Hey Ava," Kieran says. "You're looking… whatever kind of word I can say that won't sic your boyfriend on me."

"Try no words," I say as I push my chair back hard into his knees.

"Hey Kieran," she says. "So you're a…"

"I'm a horny devil, of course," he says with a cheeky tone.

I resist the urge to turn around and smack him on the head.

We drive to Kami's place as Kieran jabbers on, having completely bypassed the incident in the bar. But really… of course he did. Kieran has never given much thought to things like who he sleeps with and who that might affect.

We pull into the long driveway and it's already lined with cars and people. Kami's place is packed to the roof with purple and orange lights, with orange lanterns lining the front path. A slew of half-naked men and women are gathered in the entryway.

I grab a tub of hair gel from my car's glove box and slick back my hair in the mirror.

"Is this part of the costume?" Kieran asks.

"Yep," I reply, not giving him the satisfaction of any clue because I know it's driving him mad.

"Dang, should I have gone sexier?" Ava asks. "Everyone looks like they're dressed for a costumed orgy."

"Not unless you wanna give our boy here an aneurism," Kieran says with a pat to my back.

"You're plenty sexy, love," I say, ignoring Kieran's comments.

She looks down at her breasts, grabs them, and does a little shimmy to adjust her cleavage.

Damn.

What were we talking about?

"You gonna be alright there or are we gonna need to get you a change of pants, Z?" Kieran says.

"Oh fuck off, Kieran," I say as I hop out of the car and step around to help Ava out.

I offer her my hand as she steps out in her high-heeled gladiator sandals and I see just how far the slit in this dress climbs up her thigh.

Bloody hell.

Before I get too distracted, I pop the trunk of my car and pull out my leather jacket and slip it on.

"Oh dang!" Kieran says. "Going for the Fifties greaser look, eh?"

Technically these are just my leftover clothes from that era, but I figure better the real thing than all the lame knock-offs I was encountering.

"Wow," Ava says with a bit of a stunned look.

With that reaction, maybe I ought to wear this every day.

"I do love me a bad boy," Kieran says with a wink.

I ignore his comment and take Ava's hand, leading her inside as Kieran follows behind. Several party guests have spilled out into the front patio. One woman is wearing a bondage-esque Catwoman outfit. The man next to her is wearing just a gold thong. A woman in a white bra and panties with angel wings is snogging a man in a Phantom of the Opera mask.

"Have I told you how much I love you for talking Kami into inviting me?" Kieran says as he takes in the scene.

"Don't make me regret it," I say.

We walk through until we find Kami on her open back patio overlooking the pool. She's wearing a tight black leather leotard with a tiny red tutu, fishnet stockings, and black platform stilettos. Her face is painted like a sugar skull and she's wearing a crown of roses. She's stretched out on a long chair, flanked by two attractive men fawning over her. It's a bit on-the-nose, really.

"Zane! Ava! You made it!" she says, jumping up to give us both a hug. "Look at you, Z! I remember this outfit! Bringing back a classic, I see!"

She turns to Ava and continues. "And Ava! Talk about a classic! I love it!"

"Aww," Kieran says. "No love for your favorite demon?"

"Oh, is Azazel here?" she asks.

Kieran lets out a gasp and put a hand to his chest.

"You wound me!" he says jokingly.

She shoots him a glare, but turns her attention back to Ava and me.

"You guys like the decorations? It took like, 12 people to set up all these lights," she says.

"Did you compel 12 people to do your party decorations?" I ask.

"You know, Z," she says, placing one hand on her hip, "there are other ways to get people to do things for you."

I squint my eyes skeptically.

"Money," she says. "I paid them."

"Oh," I say, feeling kind of bad that I assumed otherwise.

"You can make it up to me by grabbing me a drink," she says, gesturing to the poolside bar, complete with a shirtless male bartender with a black bow tie.

"Alright, love," I say, turning to Ava. "Would you like anything, gorgeous?"

"A cider please," she says.

"What about me?" Kieran asks. "Aren't I gorgeous?"

I throw a scowl in his direction.

"Alright, I'll come with," he says. "Besides, there's a cheerleader over there that looks like she could use a little devil in her, if you know what I mean."

"I always know what you mean." I say as we work our way toward the bar. "Always."

We get to the bar and the bartender pours our drinks as Kieran chats up the cheerleader.

I overhear the tail end of a conversation between two men a few feet away from me.

"…shoot my shot with that Greek goddess over there."

My attention instantly focuses on their conversation, and judging by Kieran's wide eyes and the slow smile appearing on his face, he heard it too.

I turn to see the man. He's about six feet tall and wearing an elaborate pirate costume. The man he's talking to is wearing a red smoking jacket and pajama pants.

"Niiiccee," his mate says, looking over at Ava. "Girls with colored hair are always crazy in bed."

I'm going to skin them both alive.

Kieran instantly pops up next to me with a big grin on his face.

"Hey buddy," he says with a pat to my back. "Wanted to get a front-row seat to the carnage."

I ignore his comment and approach the men.

"You're gonna have to set your sights elsewhere, mate," I say.

"Excuse me?" the pirate says with a level of confidence that tells me he has no idea who he's dealing with.

Kieran lets out a hard laugh.

I take a moment to gather my composure. I'm not going to lose my cool at Kami's big party. I can do this.

I grab the man's wrist hard and look him in the eyes.

"You're going to leave her alone," I say.

"Oh yeah?" he asks with a smirk. "How do you figure?"

My expression drops and I squint in confusion as my brain searches for an answer.

Why didn't that work?

In my periphery, I see Kieran's eyes widen as he comes to the same conclusion I have: *This guy isn't human.*

36

 ZANE

"Okay, that's unexpected," Kieran says.

He's not wrong. This creep in the pirate outfit certainly took me by surprise by resisting my attempt at charming him.

"Who are you?" I ask. "How do you know Kami?"

"Excuse me?" he asks. "You butt in to my conversation and then you ask me who *I* am? Who the hell are *you*?"

"Don't," I say, my tone getting harsher. "I'm Zane. All you need to know about me is that the 'Greek goddess' over there is my bloody girlfriend."

"Oh come on," the guy says. "So I think your girlfriend is hot, so what? It's not like there's a taken sign on her. You afraid she'd take me up on the offer?"

"Okay, pal," Kieran says, stepping between us. "You need to back off. As much as I'd love to see Zane paint the pavement with your intestines, you're disrespecting my bro and you're disrespecting his girl, who is also my friend. You need to cut your shit and get over that Immortal holier-than-thou bullshit and move along."

The guy squints his eyes as if he's sizing us up, clearly taking note of Kieran's comment.

"Okay, whatever," he says, taking a step back. "Just don't call me an *Immortal.*"

The two men turn to leave and now I'm more confused than I am irritated.

"What does that even mean?" I ask. "He's immune to my charms and knows what Immortals are, but isn't one? What else is there?"

"Does that mean he's marked?" Kieran asks.

We head quickly back to Kami and Ava.

"Hey Kam," I ask. "Is one of your guests a marked human?"

"Uh… What?" she asks, looking perplexed. "No, not that I know of."

"We just ran into some guy in a pirate outfit who was immune to my charms and he told us he wasn't an Immortal," I explain.

"I mean, there are a few Immortals here but I didn't even invite any Sirens. I don't know who everyone brought as their guests…" Her face twists into a concerned expression. "But not being Immortal doesn't necessarily mean he's a marked human. Those are pretty rare."

"What else could he be?" I ask.

"He could be a demon," Kieran says with a serious expression.

Oh.

Shit.

I don't know why the thought didn't occur to me.

"Could you sense that? If he was a demon?" I ask Kieran.

"No," Kieran says. "If a demon doesn't want to reveal themselves then they'd just appear to be like anyone else."

Ava looks concerned, so I swing an arm around her and pull her close.

"A demon?" she asks.

"It's fine, love," I say. "Kieran's a demon. Every demon is different."

"Then why does everyone look so nervous?" she asks.

"Just…" I pause, deciding how much is right to reveal in this moment. It's a lot to process and I don't want to scare her. I settle on a somewhat simple version of the truth. "Kami didn't invite any demons to her party. So if there is one here, he might be an uninvited guest, which is concerning because we weren't aware of any demons in town."

"Besides me," Kieran says.

"Naturally," Ava says. She looks uneasy and takes several gulps of her cider.

Kieran and I agree to go look for the guy while Kami stays with Ava. It's not particularly concerning to encounter a demon at a party with Immortals, albeit there's usually some tension between the two groups, but when we know there's a demon in town killing humans it's a bit of a different story.

After a quick sweep of the property, it looks like the man is nowhere to be found.

"It's possible he shifted," says Kieran. "But even if he changed his face, he'd have to find a new set of clothes. My guess is he just bailed."

"I think you're right," I say, the heavy feeling in my chest relaxing a little.

As long as he's gone, there's no immediate threat to Ava's safety tonight.

We return to Ava and Kami who are now chatting to a blond woman and three men, one of whom appears to have a costume made entirely of body paint.

I casually slip between him and Ava.

"Hey gorgeous," I say. "Having fun?"

"Yeaaah," she says, slightly drunkenly. It looks like she has finished off her cider.

"Good," I say, turning to Kami. "Our friend appears to have left."

"Well that's good," she says. "Although, I would like to learn more about this party crasher. But tonight, we can get back to enjoying the party!"

"Hey, Zaaannee!" The voice is Gabby's, but it takes me a second to recognize her in her costume. She's wearing black shorts and stockings and a white shirt with black fuzzy ears on her head.

I have no idea what this is supposed to be.

"Hey Gabby," I say.

"Loving the James Dean look on you!"

"Thanks," I say, hoping she doesn't expect me to comment on her outfit because I have no bloody idea what it is.

"Guess what I am!" she says.

Bloody hell.

"Um, I don't know, love," I say. "I'm not very good at these pop culture things."

Ava gives me an irritated look and pulls away from me.

Wait, what did I do?

"Oh, come on!" Gabby says. "It's not a pop culture thing! I'm a panda!"

She gives my arm a playful smack.

I hate this game.

"Oh my god," Ava says, her voice dripping in irritation. "Why don't you two get a fucking room?"

All of us freeze in shock at her comment.

What is she talking about? She knows I don't like Gabby. Literally—I don't even *like* her.

"Love, are you okay?" I ask.

"Love?" Ava asks with a scoff. She's wobbling a little and her speech is slightly slurred. She must've had more to drink than I had realized. "Oh so now I'm *looovve?* A second ago Gabby was your *looooovvve…*"

Is that what upset her?

"Baby, I just call everyone love. You know that."

I reach an arm around her but she stumbles back.

"No!" she says, pushing me away. "You don't even… You doonnn't…"

"Ava," Kami says. "Honey, it's alright, he really doesn't mean anything by it."

"Yeah," Gabby adds. "I promise nothing is going on with me and Zane. He's completely head over heels for you."

"Ohh shuuttt uppp! Yooouu think I don't see what you're doing?" Ava yells, grabbing Gabby's drink from her hand and throwing it at her. "And you don't even look like a panda!"

Gabby just stands there in shock, without a word, as Kami tries to step in.

"Ava, what's going on?" Kami asks. "This isn't like you. Are you oka-"

"Get away from me!" Ava yells, staggering away. I reach to grab her arm but she backs up further.

The way she recoils from me shatters my heart. I don't understand what's happening, but I just want to make it better.

She takes another few clumsy steps, way too close to the edge of the pool.

"Ava!" Kieran shouts, clearly coming to the same conclusion. "Watch the edge!"

In a split second she has stepped one inch too far and her heel hooks over the edge of the pool. I see Kieran speed in her direction, which is good because he's much faster than me. He grabs her arm but their momentum sends them both tumbling into the pool.

Kieran emerges with an arm around Ava, probably the first time I've ever been grateful to see such a sight. She's punching his arm and yelling curse words at him.

At least she's still Ava.

I run to the edge of the pool and help them out of the water.

"Well, that was fun," Kieran says, lifting her up to me.

Her makeup is running, her skin is covered in tiny beads of water, and the loose toga is sopping and stuck tightly to her skin.

"Take my hand, love," I say to her as she begrudgingly does. As I catch her eyes, I see that her pupils are so wide that the usual grey is almost completely eclipsed by black.

Kami meets us at the edge of the pool and talks Ava into coming with her back to her bedroom. After a minute or so, Kami comes back out to talk to us.

"What is going on?" I ask her in a panic. "What's wrong with her?"

"I…" she says with a pause. "I have no idea."

37

My sopping wet dress is stuck to the leather passenger seat of Zane's Challenger. I'm wrapped in a tan, monogrammed towel I borrowed from Kami's. Zane has the heater on high in an attempt to keep me warm. He pats my knee and gives me a soft smile.

This may be the most embarrassing moment of my entire life.

"I'm sorry," I say. "I have no idea why I acted that way. I think the alcohol really got to me tonight."

Aka I have no explanation for why I just acted full-on psycho about you talking to a girl and then gracefully tumbled my way into the pool during your friend's Halloween party.

"It's alright, love," he says in a soft, concerned voice. "I did try to make you jealous of Gabby when you first met her. I shouldn't have done that. You never have anything to worry about with me, baby."

There's an undertone of sadness in his voice that makes me feel even worse—as if that were possible.

"I shouldn't have reacted that way," I say. "I don't know what came over me; I just kind of lost my marbles for a second. I have no excuse."

There's a flicker of concern in his eyes as he glances at me for a moment before looking back at the road. His jaw is tense as he stares ahead.

"Are you upset with me?" I ask. I'm almost dreading his answer. His whole demeanor has been cold and distant since the incident, even though he's tried to hide it behind smiles.

"No, love," he says with a bit of a sigh. "I'm not upset with you."

Really? Because that sounds a whole lot like how someone would say that if they were definitely, big-time upset with me.

We pull up to my apartment complex and walk to my door. Zane gives me a hug and a kiss on the forehead.

"Goodnight, love," he says.

Wait… he's leaving?

"You're not coming in?"

"Oh uh… not tonight, love. I've got to get up early tomorrow."

You don't even have a job, Zane.

"You can stay here and still get up early," I say.

"Yeah, but I left my stuff at home," he says, slowly stepping back toward his car. "I'll see you later, okay?"

"Okay."

I close my door behind me and slump onto the floor.

Damn it.

Have I just ruined everything?

ZANE

"What the *bloody fucking fuck* happened tonight?" I yell, hurling a lamp across the kitchen.

"Jesus Christ, Z," Kami says. "There are still guests around and you're really becoming a danger to my décor."

"How's Ava?" Kieran asks, sitting on the counter. Kami glares at him, but doesn't scold him for once.

"She's okay," I say. "She has no idea what happened."

"You say that like we do," Kami says. "You're making assumptions. We don't know for sure tha-"

"Sure we do. Come on, you know you're thinking it. We're all thinking it. Madness? Obsession? Delusion?"

"I've never heard of a single case," she says. "There's no reason to suspect it's real, Z."

"Have you ever known of a Siren to carry on this long with a human without marking them?" I ask.

"I… Well I…"

"Exactly."

"I don't understand," Kieran says. "All that stuff about Sirens driving humans insane—that's what we're talking about here?"

Kami gives Kieran a knowing look as I feel a sharp pain in my chest. I fall to my knees on the kitchen floor and struggle to breathe as the panic sets in.

"My venom is killing her."

KAMI

I rub along Zane's back as he chokes back tears. I've never seen him this devastated.

Not ever.

"She knew," he says through stifled sobs.

"Who knew? What did someone know?" I ask.

"Lo… la…" he manages to say between staggered breaths.

What if this is what Lola meant? That Zane was putting Ava in danger somehow? Maybe she thought he knew and was doing it intentionally.

That is, if this 'venom madness' even exists.

"Lola?" Kieran asks.

"She's m-… she was my friend," I explain. "She's a Seer."

"What did she see?" Kieran asks.

"She saw something happening to Ava because of something I did," Zane says.

"What?" he asks. "No way. You wouldn't hurt Ava."

"Unless I didn't know I was doing it."

"Why don't you just ask this Lola chick?"

Honestly, it's not a bad idea. Seers are pretty careful about how much of the future they'll share, but now that I have a specific question, maybe she'll give me an answer.

Zane looks at me with slightly hopeful eyes.

"Could you?" he says in the most heartbreaking voice.

I can see in his eyes now that if something happens to Ava, he'll never recover. He will be broken.

I agree on two conditions: First—that Kieran leave with the rest of the lingering party guests. Second—that I talk to Lola on my own, without Zane present.

I know that Zane is panicked right now, so the last thing I need is Lola and her big mouth saying something that will devastate him. Zane can stay, but I'm going down the hall to make the phone call.

If she does have bad news, I don't know if I'll have the heart to tell him, but I know that I'll want to control what he hears. Right now, as fragile as he is, he's moments away from any number of bad decisions.

———•———

I close the door behind me and flip the lock for good measure before dialing Lola's number. It can be a challenge to evade a Siren's hearing, so I've chosen the farthest room from the bedroom where I left Zane.

"Kami?" Lola's voice says from the other end of the line. She's surprised to hear from me, so I guess there *are* things she can't see coming.

"Hey," I say. "I need a favor."

"A favor? Are we on speaking terms again?"

"It's serious. It's about Ava—my friend, Zane's soulmate. She's in trouble."

"Mmm-hmm…"

"I need to know what you know," I say.

"Kami, doll," she says with a sigh. "Some things I can share, some things I can't."

"Well make this one that you can."

"It's not that easy. The consequences of revealing too much of someone's future can make things go much much worse. Or I can end up causing the very thing I'm trying to warn someone about."

"Then what can you tell me?" I ask.

"If you ask a specific question, I might be able to answer it. I have to be careful, though."

"Okay," I say, pondering for a moment. "Is the Siren's curse—making humans go mad—is that real?"

"Unfortunately, I don't know that. It wasn't part of what I saw."

"Okay," I say with a frustrated sigh. "Is Zane hurting Ava in some way?"

She clears her throat on the other end of the line but says nothing.

"Kami, I…" she says in a soft voice. "I'm not comfortable answering that."

I don't know any other way to interpret that but yes.

What does this mean?

My heart is breaking for Zane and Ava right now.

"Can I fix it?" I ask. "How can I help them?"

"Hmm…" she says, pausing for a moment. "I don't know that you can."

"Lola, you have to help me out here. We can't just let something bad happen, and I can't just tell Zane and Ava to never see each other again. They're soulmates—you said it yourself!"

I try to compose myself before my voice reaches a volume Zane might be able to hear down the hall.

Lola remains silent on the other end of the line.

"Jesus, do Seers have to be this cryptic?!" I say in a harsh but muted way.

"You have no idea the complicated position I'm in," she says with a frustrated sigh. "I don't want bad things to happen, but knowing something might happen and being able to stop it are two very different things. I don't know if what I say will make things that much worse."

"So what do I do here, Lola? What would you do? Two people you care about are meant to be together, but being together is hurting them. What do you do? Just say tough shit, you're soulmates, but you can't be together? I see it on his face, Lola, just thinking about leaving her is tearing him up inside. He's ready to do it because he thinks he has to—to protect her. Because, despite what you think of him, he's a good person and he loves her. He'll sacrifice her happiness if he thinks he needs to in order to keep her safe."

"Then he should," Lola says in a somber voice.

My heart sinks to my stomach.

"Seriously, Lola?" I ask in a hushed tone. "I'm not about to tell him to leave her. That will kill him."

"You wanted my advice, that's it."

"No, Lola, I wanted your help," I say, slamming the phone to the floor and smashing it to pieces.

What the freakin' hell am I going to tell Zane?

I collect myself and take a few deep breaths before opening the door to the hallway.

I'm met instantly with Zane's glossy, reddened eyes and an expression that lets me know he just heard everything I said.

38

AVA

My phone buzzes on the nightstand and I struggle to force my eyes open. There's a pounding in my ears and every muscle in my body is aching—undoubtedly thanks to my gymnastic plunge into the pool last night.

Oh god—tell me that didn't actually happen.

My phone vibrates again and I see the time on the screen: 10:30 am.

Ahh crap.

I'm soooo not ready to deal with everything that happened last night. Then I see the name of the caller: **Zane**.

Double crap.

The call goes to voicemail before I have the strength to force myself out of bed. I guess the latest medication isn't doing whatever it's supposed to do because I feel like hot garbage. I attempt to drag myself toward the phone, each muscle frozen and fighting me along the way.

The screen reads: **8 Missed Calls**.

Super crap.

Sure enough, they're all from Zane.

My mind immediately expects the worst. I acted so crazy, and he already seemed put off by the encounter with my brother the other day.

Is he giving up on me? Has he decided I'm super crazy and all my baggage is not worth dealing with?

I stare at the screen, completely paralyzed as my heart sinks.

Maybe he's just checking up on you. Maybe you're making a mountain out of a molehill. He could just be worried about you.

If he was worried about you, why didn't he stay over last night?

Damn brain.

I'm startled by the phone vibrating in my hand. It's Zane again. I hit the answer button before I lose my nerve.

"Hey," I say into the phone.

"Hey," Zane's voice echoes softly.

That's not a good voice.

There's an uncomfortable silence on the other end of the line.

"Everything okay?" I ask.

"Uh," Zane's voice says softly after a pause. "We need to talk."

No.

No.

No.

This can't be happening.

No, calm down. Zane wouldn't break up with you over the phone.

"Uh, okay," I say, fighting back the lump in my throat. "That sounds really ominous."

Once again, his end of the line is silent.

"Do you wanna come over?" I ask.

"No," he replies quickly. "I... we... this isn't working out."

My heart feels like it's being crushed inside a trash compactor.

The other day we were soulmates. Now it *'isn't working out'*?

Suddenly the ache in my muscles feels like nothing in comparison to the stabbing pain in my chest.

"You're... you're breaking up with me?" I ask.

"Yeah," he says roughly, almost as if he's choking back a cough.

"Wh-... Why? I mean, I know I went a little crazy last night, but I think that the alcohol just really got to me more than usual. I don't know if-"

"No, it's not about last night," he says. "I just can't."

"I don't understand." My voice wavers as tears begin to spill onto my cheeks. "Can we talk about this in person?"

"No. I'm not changing my mind."

Zane's voice is hard and restrained.

"If you're going to break up with me over the phone, I at least deserve to know why," I say.

"Because, I…" he begins to say, but then doesn't finish.

"Can I just come over and we can talk? This doesn't make any se-"

"Because I don't want to be with you anymore."

His words feel like they've sliced right through my throat and I struggle to speak or breathe. The line disconnects and the silent hum of the phone fades into complete silence.

He's gone.

———•———

ZANE

Bile creeps up my throat and, in a violent lurch, I collapse to the ground and empty my stomach into the bin as the room spins around me.

In my almost 200 years, I've never thrown up before. Apparently being immune to illness does not make me immune to the overwhelming disgust I have with myself for telling Ava I don't want to be with her.

I can't imagine a more despicable thing I could do than to make her cry like that. Hearing her tears on the phone shattered me.

How am I ever going to let her go?

My lungs sting with every breath and my chest grows tighter still.

FUCK.

How much fucking alcohol am I going to have to drink to make this stop hurting?

I stagger toward the kitchen and rifle through the cupboards until I've gathered about 11 bottles of various alcohol varieties—a few whiskeys, several bottles of vodka that I keep on hand for Kieran, and a few unopened bottles of rum, tequila, and gin.

I line them up and start to down them, one bottle at a time.

I drink the first bottle in under a minute. After 20 minutes I've cleared every last one and am laying on the rug, surrounded by empty bottles while the room rotates and tilts around me.

My vision is blurred and before I know it, I black out.

When I come to, I have several missed calls from Kami and the room is dark. The clock reads 2:00 am.

Fuck.

I'm going to need a lot more alcohol.

I stagger into my bathroom and find my hands rummaging through the apothecary cabinet. I pull out a cloudy black glass bottle with a yellowed paper label that's almost entirely worn off, closed with a cork coated in wax.

I make my way over to the living room and slump onto the couch.

What am I thinking?

Ava's face enters my mind. Flashes of grey eyes and strands of purple hair. The sound of her voice as she cried.

My eyes focus on the bottle again.

I can't do this.

I can't hear her voice as she cries again, knowing that I'm the one that caused those tears.

This is the worst idea I've ever had.

My phone rings and I grope around the sofa cushions until I find it, answering in a fumble.

"Hello," I say. My voice comes out hoarse and cracked.

"Jesus, Z, where the hell have you been?!" Kami's voice shouts on the phone.

"I'm home," I attempt to say, though it comes out as more of a drunken slur.

"Oh, god… Tell me you didn't."

I say nothing in response, still watching the room spin and rolling the bottle in my palm.

Am I really this desperate?

"Zane, are you okay?" she asks.

"No."

"We can fix this, okay? We can find an answer."

"I know," I say. My thumb hovers over the 'End Call' button and I press it.

I've found an answer and I'm looking right at it.

I pop the cork of the bottle and take a drink.

39

 ZANE

I walk into the pub and see Kieran behind the bar, serving an older gentleman with a beard.

"Hey, mate," I say, grabbing a seat at the other end of the bar. "You know where I could get a beer around here?"

"Nope," he says with a smile. "We don't serve dickheads here."

He smiles and pours me a Guinness from the tap.

"So you wanna tell me what the heck you did?" he asks.

"What do you mean?"

"Kami has called me like, eight times since yesterday asking if I've talked to you. She wouldn't tell me what was going on."

"Oh yeah?" I ask. "I'm not sure what that would be about."

"Something went down once you guys called Lola, right?"

"Mmm," I mumble, diving into my beer.

"Well, I also got a call earlier from a certain purple-haired vixen looking for you too," he adds, leaning his elbows on the bar. "You want me to let her know you're here?"

"Ahh no thanks," I say, taking another sip.

"Ooh, trouble in paradise?" he asks. "Well, if she's on the market just let me know."

He smiles and winks at me.

"Go ahead," I say. "All yours."

Kieran squints his eyes and leans on the bar again, looking me over like he's sizing me up.

In a flash, he has his hand laid on the bar holding a knife, its tip pointed at my chest. It's probably not capable of doing any damage to me, but it's hard to tell what kind of blade it is just by looking.

Shit.

"Who the fuck are you?" Kieran asks.

"Whoa—hold on," I say, making eye contact in an attempt to calm him.

This is not how I expected an outing to the pub would go.

Kieran's eyes go black from edge to edge.

"Who… the fuck… are you?" he asks again, a vicious tone in his voice.

"It's me," I say. "It's Zane. I swear."

"Well, you're stupid but you're ballsy as shit, I'll give you that. What are you—A demon? A shifter?"

"I'm not a demon."

"You're sure as fuck not fooling me wearing Zane's skin, I'll tell you that much."

He moves the knife closer to my chest, just touching the fabric of my shirt. Even if this knife couldn't pierce my skin, Kieran could still annihilate me if he wanted to.

"Okay, okay," I say. "It's me but uh, not entirely."

I reach slowly for my inner jacket pocket and delicately pull out the bottle with my fingertips, placing it on the bar.

"I may or may not have woken up with this," I say, pushing the bottle toward him.

"You," Kieran says with a pause, investigating the label. "…stupid fuck. What the hell did you do?"

"I don't know. I mean, that's kind of the point."

His jaw goes slack as he looks closer at the bottle. You can still just make out the word "Λήθη" on the faded and yellowed label.

"Tell me this isn't what I think it is…" he says with a shake of his head.

I nod.

"I guess I was desperate," I say.

"Desperate? No shit!" he says. "Desperate enough for lethe? That is what this is—isn't it?"

I nod again.

"Weren't you the one who warned me against using lethe? What happened to 'only idiots use lethe to forget their problems'? What happened to 'it's the worst comedown of your life'?"

He's not wrong. Lethe will make you forget for a while, but when those memories come back, they hit you like a sledgehammer to the skull. Whatever I wanted to forget, it must have been bad. But the last thing I want to do is waste whatever time I have focusing on what I clearly didn't want to remember.

In a swift motion, he grabs a small pronged knife from behind the bar and stabs it hard down into the flesh between my thumb and forefinger.

"Bloody hell!" I say, flinching as the tip of the knife contorts and snaps off as it contacts my hand.

"Just making sure," he says with a smile. "Plus, it's fun to scare the shit out of you."

I lower my eyebrows and glare at him.

"You're hilarious," I grumble.

"I've always thought so," he says with a smirk. "So how much did you forget?"

"Well, based on the date on my phone, about five years."

"Shit, Z-Man."

"I told you not to call me that."

"Yeah, well now you've learned to love it," he says with a smile.

I doubt that.

"Does Kami know?" he asks.

"About the lethe? I'm not sure," I say. "I just woke up, found the bottle and this…"

I hold up my phone. It's a few years nicer than the one I'm used to. Turns out wiping your memory is a lot more convenient in the era of cell phones.

"I saw the date and did the math. Saw on my phone that your number was listed as 'Kieran/The Pike' so I was curious and found the place. You're a bartender now? How fitting."

"Beer and drunk hotties—my favorite things," he says with a smirk.

"I had a bunch of missed calls from Kami too, but I don't particularly feel like getting scolded right now," I say.

"Oh yeah, she's gonna kill you." He has a bit of a smile that says he's finally enjoying me being the fuckup for a change.

Another customer down the bar waves to get Kieran's attention and he steps over to help him.

I take another drink of my beer and I hear a woman's footsteps approaching me from behind. A woman in a red button-up blouse and tight jeans takes the seat beside me at the bar.

Of course I've lured in a human without even trying. With everything I've got going on right now, I'm not interested in another meaningless conquest.

"Hey," she says with a soft voice.

"Hi," I say without turning to make eye contact.

Take a hint, lady.

"Have I seen you here before?" she asks.

Really? It seems there hasn't been a lot of innovation in pickup lines over the last five years.

"You know, I'm not sure, love," I say. "My memory's not so great these days."

I chuckle to myself at the bad inside joke.

"Can I buy you a drink?" she asks.

"Sure," I say. Now that I think about it, I don't know what else I'm supposed to do with my time.

Taking lethe is a short reprieve followed by a sharp plummet back into reality. Now I'm just biding my time, waiting for the other shoe to drop. It's a bit torturous, really. What could have possibly happened to me that could have made this seem like a good idea? I'm curious, but then again, I guess I don't want to know.

Kieran walks back over to us and asks the woman if she'd like a drink.

"A whiskey sour for me and whatever he'd like," she says, gesturing to me with her head.

"Erm, okay," Kieran says with narrowed eyes. "Another Guinness?"

"Sure," I say, drinking down most of my current one.

He pours our drinks and passes them to us.

"You uh," Kieran says to me. "You have to get going soon, right bud?"

He raises his eyebrows as if he's trying to hint something to me. Whatever he's referencing is lost on me right now.

Do I know this woman? Or does he just want her for himself?

I turn to the woman in an attempt to discover any clues as to who she might be. She's about 30 with long brown hair and a dark tan. She has long, ivory painted fingernails and no noticeable wedding ring.

"Um…" I say, trying to figure out what he's getting at. "Probably soon, yeah."

"Oh, really?" she asks, lightly touching my arm with her hand. "That's a shame."

"Don't worry, doll," Kieran says. "I'll be here to keep you company."

Ahh okay, he's just trying to get this one.

Fine. I honestly don't care.

———·———

The pub door jingles behind us as another patron enters the bar.

Kieran's eyes go wide and his skin turns pale.

"Fuck," he says under his breath.

I turn around to see a cute 20-something-year-old woman with vivid purple hair wearing a black-and-white striped shirt, ripped black jeans, and combat boots. She looks tired and there's something slightly off about her posture, like she's just lost a fight. A small tattoo peeks out from under her T-shirt sleeve, with another on her wrist.

This must be the purple-haired girl we were talking about when Kieran flipped out on me. Based on that reaction, it's safe to assume that this is going to be a delicate situation.

Her eyes connect with mine and I feel a deep sadness in them. I must have done something terrible to this woman.

Great.

Her eyes bounce back and forth between me and the woman next to me and her expression drops, then she tenses and walks toward us. She marches up in a forceful way that tells me she's not here because she wants to grab a bite and play some pool with us.

"Hey Ava," Kieran says with a smile, poorly masking an obvious discomfort. "Can I get you a drink?"

Who is this girl? And why does Kieran look like he's going to shit himself?

The girl's grey eyes stay firmly locked on me, her lips pursed and brows furrowed. There's something unique about her, but I'm not sure what. *Ava.* She's not familiar, per se, but there's something still drawing my focus to her.

"Who's your friend?" she asks.

"Oh, is this your girlfriend?" the woman asks, looking at Ava.

I'm pretty sure the answer to that question is no, since the only thing I can truly discern about this girl Ava is that she really—*really*—hates my guts.

"Ava, he's not himself right now," Kieran says apologetically. "He's ju-"

"Kieran, I'm sorry," she says, holding up a flat palm toward him to cut him off. "This is between me and Zane right now."

"Okay," I say with my best calming voice. "Let's go grab a table and talk, alright?"

"Mmkay." Her crossed arms let me know she's barely humoring my request.

"Human?" I mouth to Kieran as she turns around.

He nods but his wide eyes tell me there's more to the story. We find a booth about ten feet away and settle in.

"What would you like to talk about, love?" I ask, laying on my best charming smile.

"Really?" she asks. "I don't know, maybe how some dickhead broke up with me over the frigging phone and didn't even have the decency to tell me why??"

I hear glass shatter and we both turn to see a stunned Kieran with a tipped broken beer glass on the counter. With their lightning-fast reflexes, you rarely see a demon fall victim to clumsiness. He has definitely been caught off guard.

By her tone, I would assume that she was talking about me, but I can't see a situation in which I would date a human in the first place, let alone break up with anyone over the phone.

Is she talking about Kieran?

He certainly seemed to react strongly to her. But then why would she be so angry at me?

"Mmm, well," I say. "I'm sorry about that, love."

"You're sorry?" she asks. "Well geez, Zane, that's really friggin' great and all but I'm looking for a little more than just *sorry*."

She's not exactly making this easy, but I can't help but love how forthright this girl is. For a human, she's quite feisty.

Something about the look of betrayal on her face makes me angry at the wanker who hurt her, even if that wanker may have been me.

I'm kind of hoping it was Kieran. It would be much easier to kick Kieran's ass than my own.

Rather than try my hand at solving this particular puzzle right now, I decide to grasp her hand.

"Love," I say. "You're going to go ho-"

She rips her hand from mine in a swift motion.

"Were you just trying to *charm me* into leaving and letting this go?" she says, her volume rising with every syllable.

Oh, shit.

I guess when I asked Kieran if she was human, I should have added a few more questions.

"I'm sorry, love," I say with a sigh. "To be honest, I don't really know what you want from me and yes—I was hoping that would settle you."

"Settle me?" she says.

Her soft hand collides with my face and a loud cracking sound radiates through my ear.

I can't help but crack a bit of a smile knowing that this tiny woman just smacked me, but my reaction doesn't go unnoticed by her.

"That's it," she says, grabbing her purse and standing up to leave. "Fuck you."

Kieran appears at our table in a frantic state.

"Ava," he says, placing a calming hand on her shoulder. "Please don't take him seriously right now, he's had a shit ton to drink. You really don't even know the half of it."

"Oh, he seems very clear on what he wants," she says. "You want this settled, Zane? Fine. We're settled."

Her combat boots drum rapidly across the floor as she leaves the pub.

"Fuck," Kieran says, slumping into the booth across from me and dropping his head into his hands. "When you get your memory back, you're gonna hate yourself for that."

40

I didn't even make a conscious decision to show up at Jen's but, through a teary haze, I find myself pulling into her driveway and walking up to the door. The door is frosted glass and I can just make out two silhouettes through the warm light emanating from the house.

My fist taps at the door before I have a chance to pull it back out of embarrassment.

What am I even going to say?

As I try to think about it, tears start streaming out of my eyes and down my cheeks and I quickly descend into a blubbering mess. The door swings open and I'm met by the very confused but concerned face of Deb, Jen's ex and roommate.

Now I'm crying on Jen's doorstep in front of her ex-girlfriend like a crazy person.

This is great. I'm great. Things are going great right now.

"Ava," she says with a soft, sympathetic voice. "Oh my gosh, come in honey!"

She pulls me in with a reassuring arm around my shoulders and guides me inside. My eyes continue to gush tears as I breathe in gasps and stutters, attempting—unsuccessfully—to sound the least bit coherent.

Deb sits down in an armchair as Jen rushes to me and sits me down on their big, plush brown couch, giving me a big bear hug.

"Who are we killing?" Jen asks, her lips in a tight, straight line.

"Z-... Za-..." I stutter.

"Zane, that son of a bitch!" she exclaims, instantly launching up from her seat. Jen's fury in my defense is palpable. "What did he do? Did he cheat on you?

That motherfucker cheated on my girl? That's it, he's getting a swift kick to the chicken tenders!"

"No," I manage to eke out. "He… bro… ke up… wi-ith… m-me…"

She bites her lip and scrunches her face. "I'm sorry hon, I have no idea what you just said. It sounded like something about Hebrew Butterfree?"

"I think she said homo coffee," Deb chimes in.

"What the heck is homo coffee, Deb?" Jen snaps.

"Well, I'm sorry *Jennifer*," Deb says with sarcasm. "Clearly Hebrew Butterfree makes way more sense!"

As I watch the two, I hear a burst of laughter. It takes me a moment to realize it's coming from me. The reality of the whole situation is overwhelming and I find myself laughing at the notion that I got dumped by a mythical creature over the phone and now I'm here covered in gross crying-goo having an epic meltdown in front of Jen and her ex-girlfriend, while they both try to translate my nonsense wailing.

What is my life right now?

"Well, we broke Ava," Jen says to Deb in a flat voice.

I continue to laugh and cry simultaneously.

With a few deep breaths, I manage to compose myself and say, "He broke up with me."

Jen places a reassuring hand on my shoulder.

"Well yeah, hon, I kinda assumed that, but why? What happened?"

"He just said he doesn't want to be with me," I say with a sniffle. "He did it over the phone. He wouldn't even explain in person."

"Over the phone?" she asks with wide eyes. "What a fucking douche donut!"

"Did something happen before this?" Deb asks.

My eyes fall to my lap as I remember my crazy behavior at the party. And before that, our encounter with my jerk of a half brother. I told him a bunch of the details of my stupid, messed-up life.

Why wouldn't he run away from the mountain of baggage I unloaded on him?

I explain everything as Jen shifts between concern for me and a poorly masked desire to murder Zane.

"I mean," she says. "That's not like you, he knows that. And your brother is not your fault. If those are his reasons for breaking up with you, he's stupid."

Deb returns from the kitchen with a glass of ice water for me and places it on a coaster before excusing herself for the evening so we can talk.

"I don't know, Jen," I say. "You didn't see it. I was totally paranoid and he probably thinks I'm a drunk like my brother and dad."

"Wait," she says with a furrowed brow. "Wasn't that one of the side effects for your medication? Paranoia?"

"Oh, I'm not sure."

"Hold on, what's it called?" she asks. "Loranizapran? Lernapralozem? Okay screw it you type it…"

She passes the phone to me and I type it in.

"Bingo!" she says. "Paranoia and erratic behavior—common. It also says 'may enhance the effects of alcohol.'"

"Oh."

"I mean, Zane is still a dick and doesn't deserve you but I just want to be clear that what happened wasn't you. I know that, and quite honestly he should've known that too."

"It doesn't change anything."

"That's okay, I just don't want you beating yourself up thinking that you deserved to be broken up with. Because A: You didn't. And B: Even if you went all wild jealous, you're still worth sticking it out for. You're kick-ass and him not getting that just shows what a total idiot he is."

Part of me wants to argue with her.

I don't feel kick-ass—I feel like a total train wreck.

At the same time, I'm mad that he insisted on getting to know me, on asking about my family and my life, and then judged me for it.

This is why I feel like I can't ever reveal too much. There will always be those little landmines in a relationship that, once you stumble upon them, blow everything to hell. That person will never look at you the same way. It's too late— the damage is done.

"Do you want me to ask Shayna to spike his drinks with laxatives?" she asks, in a sweet tone that only works coming out of Jen's mouth.

"Things still going well between you two?" I ask, desperate to change the subject after one too many hours of crying.

"Yeah, it's great. I was worried at first because she got kind of upset over the whole living situation thing, but now we're great."

Jen smiles and pulls me in for a hug, adding, "I'm pretty confident I could get her to poison someone for me. Just sayin'."

———•———

Jen talked me into swinging by my place to grab some of my things so that I can stay with her for a few days.

"Okay, tomorrow I'm taking you into the doctor and we're getting you off this creepy medicine," she says, pulling her car into my empty spot. I recognize a familiar but unexpected car in the lot: a red seventies-era pickup truck.

Kieran is here.

"Oh," Jen says, eyeing Kieran's truck. "Listen, if he brought that British asshat I'm happy to handle it."

It didn't occur to me that Zane might be with him, but I see Kieran standing alone at my door. He gives me a small, almost apologetic wave.

I tell Jen I can handle it and ask her to wait in the car. With a little pushing, she finally agrees.

"What, Kieran?" I ask, not intending to sound as harsh as I actually do.

"Are you okay?" he asks in a soft, serious tone that I've never heard from him before.

"Not really," I say with a sigh.

"I'm sorry. I know I'm Zane's friend and all, but you're my friend too. At least, *I* consider *you* a friend. I just want to help. Zane can be a great guy, but he can also be a total idiot."

We both chuckle a little as I let myself into the apartment and invite him to follow.

"I'm just stopping by to grab some things," I explain.

"You gonna stay with Jen?" he asks.

"Yeah, for a bit."

"If you want me to beat him up for you, I'm happy to," he says with a smirk. "It's one of my favorite pastimes anyway."

"Thanks, but uh, Jen has already pretty aggressively volunteered for the job."

"Jen is a legend." He smiles.

I turn to grab a hairbrush from the bathroom.

"You know I'm not good at this—like, understatement of the century—but he loves you. This, what he's doing, it's all bullshit. He's lying. He wants to be with you."

"Stop!" I say, chucking the hairbrush at him. "If he wanted to be with me, he wouldn't have broken up with me!"

I gasp and cover my mouth in shock. I can't believe I've escalated to throwing things at Kieran. He pauses for a moment with the hairbrush in his hand, his eyes wide and his mouth agape.

"I'm so sorry, Kieran," I say, feeling really guilty.

"You suck at throwing," he says with a smile. "Is this one of those ionizing brushes? How do you like it?"

I chuckle as he inspects the hairbrush.

"This hair isn't as effortless as I make it seem," he says with a hair toss. "Even demons aren't immune to frizz."

I smile and gather up my last few things before we walk out together.

"Just so you know, what Zane does and what he wants are often two different things," he says before he returns to his car. "Everyone calls him the Iron Siren because he's always been very good at resisting what he really wants. He'll do what he thinks is right, even if it hurts him."

41

 ZANE

Kami sits across from me in a dark grey armchair next to a slate coffee table. The table, much like the rest of the apartment, is covered in empty liquor bottles and debris. Shards of wood and glass coat every surface, making the whole place look more like an extreme obstacle course than a place someone might live. Multiple large chunks are missing from the drywall, including a couple of rather telling fist-sized holes.

"Glad to see your problem isn't just with *my* furniture," Kami says with her brows furrowed.

"Er, yeah," I say. "I'm assuming this isn't just my new, futuristic decorating style."

"Now if only you could've used those brilliant deductive skills to not get yourself into this mess in the first place."

"I can always count on you for an 'I told you so,'" I say, narrowing my eyes.

"Then stop doing shit I tell you not to do, Z."

I drop my head into my hands, my elbows resting on my knees.

She's not wrong.

"You know, love, you're really preaching to the choir. I never once thought this was a good idea. Future me must be an idiot."

"You're half right," she says. She leans back in her chair and sighs. "Future you *is* an idiot. The only problem is that you're already becoming that idiot again."

"I fucking better not be. I should have more time than that. Why d-"

"Since I've gotten here, you've downed two beers," she says. "Your hands are shaking and you're sweating."

"I haven't remembered anything."

"I think your body is remembering," she says. "That's the first sign. It's gonna come back and it's going to be fast."

There's a rapping of knuckles at the door followed by the door swinging open. Kieran pops in and closes it behind him.

"How's it going?" he asks. I can't tell if he's asking me or Kami.

"He says he doesn't remember anything yet," Kami says.

She pulls up a chair for Kieran, brushing off what appear to be fragments of dark green glass.

Kieran sits down and his scent catches my attention. I can't tell if part of me is recognizing it or if it's drawing my attention for another reason, but it's stirring something in me that I can't shake.

"What is that?" I ask. "What is that smell?"

"Oh, I uh," Kieran stammers, looking to Kami as if he needed guidance.

She pinches the bridge of her nose and sighs.

"Told you," she says to Kieran. "It's wearing off."

"Anybody want to let me in on the secret?" I ask.

They exchange looks and both glance down at my hands. My hand is wet and sticky, holding a few shards of brown glass.

Bloody hell, why did I crush my beer?

I jump up with my chest inflated and my fists balled tight.

"Seriously, what the fuck is that, Kieran?" I ask in a low growl. "I don't like it."

"Calm down, bro," Kieran says, holding up his hands in a surrender gesture.

In a blur, I rip him from his chair and pin him to the opposite wall. He chuckles and coughs despite having the wind knocked out of him.

Bloody hell, what is wrong with me? I'm losing my cool over nothing.

I can't help it. My body seems as if it's operating entirely on autopilot.

This is exactly why you don't fuck with lethe, you ignorant wanker.

I lean closer to take in more of the scent. I can feel it as it hits every single cell in my system, burning like saltwater in a wound.

A series of images flash in my mind: Gas station. My apartment. Kieran. The Pike. Random street. Kami. Kieran's truck. Hospital. Purple hair. Grey eyes.

"Just follow the arrows to B Campus..." the girl's voice rings in my head.

Grey eyes.

"Fuck!" I say, releasing Kieran's shoulder.

"You okay?" he asks.

"What are the odds that was it and I'm all caught up?" I ask.

"Yeah uh," Kami says, "I think you'll know."

I feel a sharp pain in my temple, like an ice pick to the head.

The Pike. My car. Ava's flat. Grey eyes. A kiss.

"Fuck," I say, falling to my knees and gripping my head.

I look at Kieran, whose eyes are inspecting me carefully.

It's Ava. The scent on him is Ava.

"Where did you go?" I ask through my clenched jaw. "After the Pike, I came here. Where did you go?"

"Okay, okay," Kieran says with a defensive posture. "I went to go see Ava."

I stand and swing for him but he dodges.

"Of fucking course you did," I sneer. "I blow it and you try to swoop in and play the hero. You're trying to manipulate her because you think you have a shot."

"Wow, Z-Man, glad to finally hear what you really think of me," he snaps.

I swing at him again but he grabs my arm and extends his claws, digging them into my skin.

"I was making sure she was okay," he says with a tight jaw. "And trying to fucking undo some of the damage you've done with this little bullshit breakdown you've been having."

I want to tear him apart, but it occurs to me that the one who really deserves my fury is me.

"Fuck," I say, pulling out of his grip and resting my forehead on the nearby wall.

More images flash across my vision; memories of voices, places, touches… and grey eyes.

"You helped make it go away."

An inhuman scream claws its way out of my throat.

"I mean like, you have wings and all, but so do penguins."

My eyes sting and I grip desperately at my head in a futile attempt to make it stop.

"I love you too."

My skull pounds and I feel tears run down my cheeks.

Fuck.

"Wh-… Why?… I don't understand."

Stop.

"You want this settled, Zane? Fine. We're settled."

———◆———

I open my eyes to my white ceiling in the mid-day sun, squinting and pulling a hand up to shield myself from the brightness. My eyes are dry, my throat is raw, and there's a high-pitched ringing in my ears.

"Hey there, Sleeping Beauty," Kieran's voice says, making me flinch at the unexpected visitor.

"Bloody hell," I say, my voice course and gravely. "What are you doing, stalking me in my sleep?"

I look over to see Kieran perched atop my dresser cross-legged, with a comically-large baguette in his hand as he bites a chunk off the tip.

"Yehmpp," he says through a mouthful of starch.

I sit up and rub my eyes.

"Seriously, what are you doing here?" I ask.

"Babysitting you," he says, ripping another piece of bread off with his teeth.

Fuck. If you could be hung over after dying, I imagine this is what it would feel like.

"And I need babysitting why?" I ask.

"Because you've been unconscious for," he pauses for a moment to look at his phone, "well over 48 hours."

"What??"

"Yeah your memories started coming back—seemed like that was going well— and you were all 'AARRGHHH! FUCK! FUCK! FUCK! MEEERRRGGHHH!'" Kieran mimes grabbing his head with his hands and rocking back and forth. "Then you went headfirst into the carpet like a big, buff toddler."

I rub my forehead as I struggle to remember how I found myself here.

Oh yeah, that's right—I ruined my whole fucking life.

"Where's Kami?" I ask.

"Out on a job. It's my turn to watch the little guy," he says with a smug grin.

Suddenly, a realization hits me.

"You saw Ava. Is she okay?" I ask.

Kieran stops mid-chew with a demon-in-the-headlights look.

"Mmm," he hums as he finishes his bite. "She's uh, not great. She's been staying with Jen. You fucked up pretty bad."

Obviously.

"You don't think I know that?" I ask. "What choice did I have? Lola pretty much admitted my staying with Ava was killing her."

"Well, then she's full of crap."

"How do you figure?"

"Ava freaked out on you because she was on some new medicine that messed with her hormones, not Siren madness," he says, using the baguette to gesture around. "She and Jen were talking about it."

His words hit me like a crowbar to the gut.

What does that even mean?

Lola was wrong? My venom isn't killing Ava?

But then why did she tell Kami I should leave?

"But," I say. "She said Ava would be better off without me. She said I should leave. She basically confirmed everything with Kami."

"Seers are annoyingly-vague little hustlers, I wouldn't trust a fuckin' word she says. What did Ava say about all this anyway?"

I awkwardly choke on my own saliva.

"I uh," I say. "I didn't tell her."

Kieran does a spit take with a mouth full of bread.

Yeah. Fuck. I'm such a wanker.

"It doesn't matter now. I did it, it's done, she's free of me and however I'm going to hurt her. I can move to bloody Iceland or something and drink myself into oblivion."

"Yeah, can't see anything wrong with that plan," he says. "Or you could nut up and *talk to her*."

I let her go, but I don't have the strength to do it again. It's better to keep her out of all of my life-ruining bullshit before it's too late.

"She's coming to Pike's tonight," he says.

"Fuck! Don't tell me that! Why the bloody hell do you even know that?"

"Jen called to threaten me into making sure you stayed away."

"Then I'm literally the last person who should be there."

"I'm pretty sure I could take Jen," he says with a chuckle. "She's like 5'2" and—you know—not a demon."

"Kind of not the point. I'm not showing up somewhere I'm not wanted."

I look around and spot a bottle of vodka that Kieran must have brought out at some point. I walk over to it and grab it by the neck.

"Here we go," I say. "Oblivion, here I come."

The driver pulls into the car park outside Pike's at an unbearably slow crawl. I'm desperately regretting getting drunk, but I did not expect to find myself here tonight, relying on Uber-driver Todd to get me somewhere in an emergency. I jump out the door as we arrive and jog up to the bar, my heart racing.

Fuck. This better not be a trap.

I open the door and scan through the crowd of lively, chatting people until I locate Jen and Ava in the back room with a few other people I don't recognize. Before they see me, I find Kieran at the bar.

"What's the emergency?" I ask in a huff. "I swear to god if you faked an emergency to Parent Trap me into talking to Ava I will personally disembowel you."

"Yikes," he says. "A bit graphic."

"Kieran, you texted me saying something was wrong and Ava was in danger. If she's not in danger, I'm leaving."

"Errrmm," he mumbles with wide eyes looking just past my shoulder.

I turn and my eyes are met by Ava's. It's been far too long since I've seen her, and it's both excruciating and soothing to see her in person. Her expression isn't the angry one I expected, but rather a soft, almost flirtatious one.

"Oh hey," she says quietly. She looks up at me through her lashes and bats her eyes at me a few times.

This is an unexpected response.

She brushes a piece of hair behind her ear and bites her lip.

I'm fucked.

I look back to Kieran, who raises his eyebrows slightly and subtly gestures back at Ava.

Is this a ploy or is something really wrong with her?

I inspect a little closer. She's wearing a delicate black tank top and a burgundy leather skirt with black flats. Her cheeks and chest are flushed and her skin is dewy. Her eyes are shy and seem to be mostly avoiding mine. I catch them for a moment and see notably dilated pupils.

Wait… What? That can't be right.

I quickly scan around the bar to see if I recognize any of the patrons, but no one looks familiar beside Jen, who is giving me a very unfriendly look.

Kieran nods silently, seeming to agree with my conclusion.

There's another Siren here—and they're after Ava.

42

Zane's eyes search frantically around us and he looks particularly on edge.

Part of me feels anxious about seeing him but I can't stop thinking about how attractive he looks. He's wearing a jean jacket and a grey T-shirt with black jeans and his go-to black boots. His hair is tousled and a bit messier than usual, his eyes are sunken with dark bags beneath them, and his skin is pale and lifeless. He still looks amazing, but not quite his usual self.

I wonder if he's been crying.

"Who are you with?" he asks in a low, serious tone as his eyes scan the room.

"Hey Ava," Jen's voice says from behind me. "So Dave is totally game for body shots…"

She turns toward Zane with a slight glare. "Oh hi, Zach," she says. "I didn't see you there."

Subtle, Jen.

"Hi Jen," Zane says with a grumble, his jaw tight. "Which one is Dave?"

"Why would you need to know that?" Jen asks. "You don't have any right to butt into Ava's personal business as her *EX*-boyfriend."

Zane visibly shudders at the word and his eyes pinch shut.

"Jen," he says with a sigh. His voice is tight and strained. "You're right. I just need to talk to Ava alone for a second."

"Oh, so you *can* talk in person? I thought you were more of an over-the-phone kind of guy," she says with a spiteful tone, stepping in between me and Zane. "I'm sorry, but as you can see, Ava has company for the evening."

Jen gestures to the men we've been talking to: Dave, a 6-and-a-half-foot tall, muscular construction foreman with tan skin and medium-long brown hair, and Alex, a model-type, shorter than Dave but still relatively tall, with sharp features and spiky short hair.

If you were ever going to run into an ex, these are the men you'd want to be with.

Jen thought I needed a night of frivolity and—her words, not mine—stranger-boning. I didn't really intend on the stranger-boning bit, although I'm starting to rethink that plan. Dave is *really cute* and definitely interested. But having Zane here is bringing up all these feelings that I wasn't counting on dealing with.

"Ava," Zane says through gritted teeth. "I need to talk to you. Now."

As his eyes meet mine, I see that they're beginning to turn green.

A little late to be jealous, buddy.

"She doesn't owe you a conversation, Benedict Arnold," Jen spits.

Zane lets out a little growl while his jaw remains tightly clenched. I let my eyes fall to the floor. I can't help but find him captivating, even though he broke my heart a few days ago.

What is wrong with me?

"Get over yourself," Jen says to Zane. "You gave up the right to have an opinion here."

"Jen," he says with a low grumble. "I know you're trying to protect her and I appreciate that, but this is not the time."

"You're right," she replies. "It's not the time—you should leave. You're not welcome here."

He lets out another low growl as she puts her arm around me.

"Come on, Ava," she says. "It turns out there's one kind of pussy even I don't like."

Kieran lets out a burst of laughter at her comment.

"Oh you are so not off the hook," she says to Kieran with a glare. "You were supposed to keep the riffraff out."

Kieran's eyes widen with guilt.

As we turn to leave, Zane reaches out and grabs Jen's arm.

"Excuse me!" she yells.

"You're going to go back to your group now and you're going to let me talk to Ava," Zane says.

Her expression softens and she turns to me.

"Holler if you need me, hon," she says, before giving Zane the 'I'm watching you' gesture as she walks back to the pool table area with the boys.

"Using your powers on Jen?" I ask. "Really??"

I try to avoid looking directly at his face because it's hard to be mad when he's looking this attractive.

Stop it.

Bad brain.

"Ava, what have you had to drink tonight?" Zane asks.

"I'm not drunk, you ass," I say.

I'm not drunk, *right?*

I only had one beer, and I drank it pretty slowly. Since I'm off of that medication there's no reason it should affect me this strongly, though I can't help but feel a little intoxicated.

Actually, it's less intoxicated and more like it would feel when I would kiss Zane. But obviously that hasn't happened in a while.

"I'm not saying you're drunk, love," he says with a sigh. "Please just…"

His eyes look glossy and when he blinks a few tears fall out.

"Are you crying?" I ask.

"I… Fuck," he says, wiping his eyes with the sleeve of his jacket. "Can we talk outside?"

I nod and we make our way out of the bar in silence. The air is crisp and cold, but it's a welcome change from the hot, stuffy pub.

"Are you okay?" I ask. My breath makes fog in the air.

"No, Ava, I'm not fucking okay," he says, resting his forehead on the brick exterior wall of the pub. "I ruin every bloody thing I come into contact with."

Does he really believe that?

"I was trying to keep you safe," he adds. A few more tears roll down his cheek. "I thought it was the right thing. I thought you were in danger from me but now, I don't even know. Nothing I do works. I just had to know you, had to spend time with you, and now you're paying the price for my lack of self-control."

He rakes his hands through his hair in a panic. I've never seen him look so distraught. I can't help but feel a little bad for him.

"What are you talking about?" I ask. "Why do you think I'm in danger?"

"You've been dosed with Siren venom," he says, looking up at me through strands of hair that have fallen into his face. His eyes are teary and he looks ragged and broken.

"I…" I start to deny it, but what he's saying makes a lot of sense.

That's exactly what I've been feeling. It's not the alcohol, it's the venom.

"How do you know?" I ask.

"Your fast pulse, your blown pupils. You're sweating, your skin is flushed. The way you reacted to me, like you didn't hate me."

"Oh."

"Did anyone have access to your drink?" he asks.

"No, I-" I pause to think for a minute.

I got my beer directly from Kieran at the bar, and it had been in my hand the whole time. When we were playing pool, I sat the drink down in front of me.

"You," Zane says with a strained voice. "You didn't… Did you…"

He grimaces and grabs the fabric of his T-shirt at his chest, twisting it in his fist.

"Did you kiss someone?" he asks with his chin down, not able to lift his eyes to meet mine. His fist hits the wall and sends a crack splitting through a few bricks.

I can't help but feel a bit of joy in his jealousy, if only because it proves he's regretting breaking up with me.

Good.

It's hard to take comfort in his misery when he looks so completely devastated.

Damn it.

"No," I say. "I haven't kissed anyone."

He releases a hard, shaky breath and leans back against the wall.

"I must've taken my eyes off my drink and just not remembered," I say. "You guys are also like, super-fast, so maybe they were just faster than I could see."

"How do you know those guys you were with?"

"Well, Alex went to middle school with us, so I'm pretty certain he's not a Siren," I say.

"Alex," Zane grumbles, his eyes flashing green.

"Dave is Alex's friend, so I guess he could be a Siren," I say. "He does have that supernaturally-good-looking thing going on."

Did I say that just to be petty? Maybe.

Zane lets out another rumbling growl.

"Did h-" Zane begins to say, as the door swings open next to us.

It's Dave, of course. *Perfect timing.*

"Hey, gorgeous!" he says with a smile. "We were wondering where you disappeared to."

Dave gives Zane a brief nod hello before turning back to me.

Zane ducks his head slightly, probably trying to hide the fact that he's been crying.

"Brrr," Dave says with a shiver. "You must be freezing out here."

He pulls off his leather jacket.

"Here," he says, wrapping it around my shoulders. "Wouldn't want you to get hypothermia."

Zane lets out a growl that sounds more like it came from a tiger than a man. His eyes are glowing green in the dim lighting outside Pike's.

Dave seems caught off guard by Zane's reaction, but is stumped on how to react.

"She's fine," Zane says, his voice gravelly and deeper than usual.

"I uh," Dave says, raising an eyebrow. "Maybe we should go back inside."

Zane looks up at him, likely contemplating his options. I'm not sure what these options are, but I doubt they're good. Before I can think of a way to deescalate the situation, a blur zooms past my face—it's Zane's fist, and I watch in shock as it connects with Dave's jaw.

Dave stumbles back, his nose bleeding. As a practical giant, this guy probably doesn't get punched a lot, and he looks almost shocked that someone had the guts to hit him.

"The hell was that for?" Dave asks, pushing out his chest and stomping toward Zane.

Zane rolls his eyes and grabs both of Dave's wrists.

"Stop," he says. "Go clean yourself up and then go back to your mates and forget you ever met me."

"Zane!" I scold.

Dave turns around and complies with Zane's command.

"What the hell, Zane?" I say, pushing his chest. "You can't just go punching people because they're interested in me! You broke up with me, remember?"

"I was trying to figure out if he was a Siren," he says, narrowing his eyes.

"How does punching him do that?" I ask.

"He bled," he says. "Sirens don't bleed that easy."

"Oh."

I guess that does kind of make sense.

"Why couldn't you just charm him?" I ask.

"Well, you can fake being susceptible to charms," he says. "Plus, I really wanted to punch him."

I roll my eyes and scoff.

"Can you come stay with me tonight?" he asks. "I'll sleep on the couch, I swear. I just want to make sure you're safe."

"I'm not staying at your house, Zane," I say.

"Would you prefer I stay at yours?" Zane asks.

"No. I can stay with Jen."

"Jen can't protect you from a Siren. I can."

"So can Kami," I say. "Or Kieran."

"Fine, can I take you to Kami's then?" he asks. "Please?"

This may or may not be a really bad decision.

43

When Jen suggested a night of 'drinking and stranger-boning' to help me get over my ex, ending up in the back of a private car *with the aforementioned ex* was pretty much the last possible result I had in mind.

But here I am, sitting in the back of a black SUV in awkward silence.

Someone kill me.

"So where's the Challenger?" I ask, if only to interrupt the uncomfortable moment.

"At my place," he said. "I got a ride here."

"You left your car at home?"

"Yeah, I was drunk."

That's odd. Zane's not much of a heavy drinker; I've only seen him drunk a handful of times.

"You were drunk and you got a ride to a bar?" I ask. "Doesn't that seem a little redundant?"

"Yeah, well I've been drunk a lot lately," he says. "Kind of comes with the whole fuckup territory."

He leans on the window and his breath clouds the glass. Even with the sadness behind his eyes, he's still incredibly beautiful.

Shut up, brain.

"So earlier, why did you say you thought I was in danger from you?" I ask, mostly in an attempt to distract myself.

"I uh," he pauses and his eyes fall to his lap. "There's this old wives' tale of sorts in the Immortal community, that long-term exposure to Siren venom can drive humans insane. That eventually, they either lose their minds or die."

"Oh."

It's never good to have an ex tell you they thought you were *literally* going insane.

"I didn't know," he says. "About your medication side effects. I thought... I thought I was killing you. I thought I had to…"

"Had to break up with me over the phone?"

I try to sound playful and not bitter but my tone definitely gives me away.

"Fuck," he says, dropping his head into his hand. "I'm so sorry about that, Ava. I couldn't risk seeing you… I knew if I could see your face, touch you, I'd never be able to do it. I was sobbing; I could barely hold it together. But I wanted you to be able to move on and just think I was a tosser and go have the kind of life you deserve."

Bullshit.

"Bullshit," I say. "If you were so broken up about me, then why were you laughing at the bar with Kieran and some girl the next day? You didn't look real devastated to me."

"Kieran didn't tell you?" he asks.

"Tell me what?" I ask.

"I er," he sighs and looks out the window again. "I took something. It's called lethe. It's kind of a magical drug of sorts. It makes you forget."

"Forget what?"

"It depends how much you take. For mortals, how much you drink determines how much you forget, and the effect is permanent."

"As in, you never get those memories back?"

"Yeah…" he says with a sigh. "But for Immortals, drinking more can make you forget more or it can make the effects last longer before they wear off."

"So you took this stuff to forget me?" I ask.

"I…" he says, then pauses a moment. "Fuck, I don't even know. I took it because I was in pain. I couldn't bear the thought of having hurt you like that, it was miserable. I just kept hearing your voice, seeing your face. I just kept picturing a future without you and it seemed unbearable. It felt like a snake eating a hole in my chest. I just couldn't handle it. I was desperate."

"So when I found you at Pike's…" I say.

"I had no memory of the last five years."

That explains a lot.

"So that's why Kieran said you weren't yourself. I thought he was just defending you being a dick."

"Yeah," he says. "I'm still a dick, but not in the way you thought."

I don't know what to do with this information. Deep down, I was hoping that we could still work things out, but I didn't expect any of this and it's overwhelming.

"I'm so sorry, love," he says.

I melt hearing him say that, but I wish I didn't.

"Don't call me that."

He cringes and pulls his lips tightly closed.

"Why didn't you talk to me?" I ask. "Why didn't you tell me what was going on?"

"I was worried you weren't in your right mind and couldn't reasonably make the choice. I thought you'd want to stay with me and I wouldn't be able to say no. I was trying to protect you and it was the only way I could think of."

I feel a wave of anger rising in my chest.

"So rather than try to talk to me about it or work it out *with me*, you decided *without me*. You decided my choice didn't matter. You can wrap that up in the excuse that you were doing it to protect me, but I never asked for that. I never asked to have my feelings taken out of the equation. You made the choice for me—and you made it without me. Did you ever think that maybe the person who would know what's best for me might be *me*?"

He stares at me wide-eyed and slack-jawed, like the thought hadn't even occurred to him.

"I... I..." he stutters. "You're right."

He sighs as tears fall down his cheek. I don't think I've ever really seen him properly cry like this.

"I panicked," he says. "I want so badly to be able to protect you, but you're right. You need a partner, not a martyr. I... I'm a bloody idiot."

We both sit in silence for a minute as the car pulls up to Kami's house. We walk up to the front door without saying a word to each other.

"So what would you have said?" he asks when we get to the door. "If I had told you everything?"

"I would've tried to figure it out and probably would've figured out it was my medication, like I eventually did. And then there would be nothing to work out."

"Then what about now?" he asks. "What if I said to you that I'm a complete wanker who got everything wrong and breaking up with you was the biggest mistake of my 200 years of life? I would do anything possible to make things right with you if you'd give me a chance to prove it. I am so sorry. I won't take away your choice again. I'll trust you to make decisions with me. I can learn—I can."

I look at Zane dumbfounded, unsure what to say. All I can think is how much I want to kiss him, but I'm pretty sure that's the Siren venom talking. But how can I trust someone who doesn't show me that same trust?

"You broke my heart, Zane," I say. "I don't trust you anymore. You just threw me away."

"I didn-"

"You did! How do I know that you won't do it again?"

The large wooden door swings open to reveal Kami.

"Hey sleepover pals!" she says with a smile, but her expression quickly falls as she sees she's interrupting a serious conversation. "I… uh… I can come back."

"No, we're good," I say, avoiding eye contact with Zane.

If being in the middle of a really awkward relationship conversation is good.

———·———

Kami set me up in a guest bedroom larger than my entire apartment. The room has a seating area next to a fireplace and panel windows overlooking the back yard and pool. I put on the pajamas she set aside for me, a beige silk set that probably cost more than my car. I look like I'm dressed to match the rest of the home: sleek, neutral-toned, and unreasonably expensive.

There's a light tapping on the door, so I walk over to open it.

Kami is leaning on the edge of the door frame in a red silk nightie trimmed with lace.

"Hey hon, can I come in?" she asks.

"It *is* your house," I say, offering a welcoming gesture inside.

She sits down on the sofa in front of the fireplace and hits a button on the remote that turns the fireplace on. I close the door behind her and join her seated by the fireplace.

"Could we talk?" she asks.

"I assume this is about Zane?"

"Yes," she says. "I won't pressure you into getting back together with him, I promise. I was just hoping you'd take a moment to hear what I have to say."

"Okay," I say. "I can't promise anything."

"That's okay, I don't blame you. He did some incredibly idiotic things. I just thought you should know the whole story before you make any decisions."

I nod and hug a nearby pillow anxiously, unsure of what she has to say.

"When we were young, one of the first places we lived was in the Austrian Empire. I think it's technically Hungary now but at the time it was all part of Austria."

Of all the things I expected her to say, I didn't see this starting with a geography lesson.

"When we were about 19, we moved to a bigger city after people in our small town started noticing that we weren't aging like everyone else. Zane and I were both young and relied on our powers a lot to get whatever we wanted. Zane in particular was a bit wild, sleeping with every woman who caught his eye."

I feel an uncomfortable pang in my stomach at the thought.

"Do I really need to know this?" I ask.

"Sorry," she says. "It's relevant I promise."

"Okay… Continue."

"Anyway, there was this one girl in particular that drew his interest. She was young and she had a reputation in town because she had been engaged twice, but something had happened to both her fiancés. The first one was murdered and it was quite a scandal. The second just went missing and was nowhere to be found."

"Wait, is this like, a black widow situation?" I ask.

"Actually, a lot of people thought that. Some people bullied her and spread rumors because of it, but as Immortals, we had a hunch about what was really going on. There's a very well known, very powerful demon, one of the original seven of his species, named Asmodeus. He has a long history of latching on to a particular woman and then killing his rivals."

"Wait… What?" I ask. "Hold on, so he had a crush on this girl and just… killed the guys she was engaged to? Why didn't he just get engaged to her?"

"Well because Asmodeus is a Grade-A psychopath—all the original demons are. The originals aren't like Kieran, they're pure evil. Everything you've heard about demons comes from them. Asmodeus didn't even meet the women he decided he was supposedly in love with, he just stalked them and spied on them and killed anyone who tried to marry them."

"So you guys knew that this guy was really the one behind the girl's fiancés all dying?"

"We thought it was likely," she says. "But she was engaged again when we first met her, to Count Krisztian Schauberg. An arrogant bastard twice her age who just so happened to be a nobleman."

"She got engaged again? Even though people thought she was killing her future husbands?"

"Yep. Ilen—that's her name by the way—was considered the prettiest girl in the city, and apparently that's all it takes for men to risk death."

How pretty?

Don't be that insecure chick, just be cool.

"So she was really pretty?" I ask.

Nailed it.

"She was fine," Kami says. "She was a bit bland looking. She was brunette with delicate features and big eyes, bushy eyebrows—very forgettable. But the beauty standards back then were very different than they are today, and very white."

"Hmm," I say, trying not to come off too pleased at the idea that this girl was boring-looking.

Suck it, Ilen.

"Anyway, Zane decided he wanted her and he didn't care if it put him on Asmodeus's radar. He was young and reckless and I think he enjoyed the danger a little too much. Ilen pretty quickly fell for him and they had an affair behind her fiancé's back. It was particularly egregious because she was living in an outbuilding of the Count's estate."

"They were… doing that… in the guy's own house?"

"Yep," she says. "Men are idiots, Ava. Teenage men are basically one rung on the brain ladder above mosquitos."

I let forth a little burst of laughter.

"So, yeah, they were sneaking around right under her fiancé's nose, on top of Zane knowing very well that he could attract the wrath of a jealous demon. And Zane started developing feelings for Ilen."

I try not to look as insecure about that as I feel.

Where is this going?

"It was puppy love," Kami says, possibly to comfort me. "It was that young infatuation of sorts. She was ready to run away and get married to him instead of Count Schauberg, but Zane always deflected those ideas and insisted she marry the Count. He liked her a lot, but he knew he wasn't interested in marrying her himself and her fiancé was incredibly wealthy and would be able to give her a good life."

I nod in silence. There's so much going on in this story that I'm not sure how it's going to unravel, but it seems obvious that it will.

"So one day, we're on the way to the town center where we'd run our daily errands," Kami says with a soft, serious voice, "and we hear a big commotion and see a large crowd gathered outside the Schauberg estate."

Kami's body language has shifted and she looks pained just telling the story.

"They um," she says, pausing to clear her throat. "They were gathered around these big steps in front of the house. So of course we walk over to see what everyone's making such a fuss about. People are gasping and screaming and shouting, which in that town could have been over any local gossip. But then we get closer and we both notice it: the smell of death."

"Oh no."

"Zane realized it first and he took off running through the crowd. Ilen was-" Kami pauses a moment, her expression is somber and she almost seems to be choking on the words as they leave her throat. "Her body was covered in bruises and blood and she was sprawled naked on the steps. Her face was so swollen you could hardly recognize her, but Zane knew by her scent."

Kami takes in a deep breath before continuing.

"Everyone was just standing around. No one covered her, they just gawked. Maybe they feared getting on the bad side of Count Schauberg, who everyone suspected had done it. We knew he was making a point—he practically put her body on display. He wanted to prove he couldn't be messed with."

"Zane was devastated. He picked her up and held her. He shook her and rocked her, begging her to wake up. He couldn't stop crying."

"Oh my god," I say. No other words cover it.

"Schauberg had found out about the affair," she says in a solemn tone. "He beat her and he killed her because of it."

Kami stares down at her hands and takes a deep breath in.

"Something shifted in Zane that day. He blamed himself for seducing her. He truly believed he was evil and his powers were there to tempt humans to their death. He adopted this stoic persona and became obsessed over keeping himself in control. Zane decided he was a loaded gun and no one around him was safe unless he was in perfect control."

"Wow," I say. I'm at a loss for any other words.

"When he met you, he started acting like that naïve kid again," she says. "An old friend of mine is a Seer, which means she can see the future. She thought Zane needed to leave you—I disagree but that's a topic for another day. When he heard that, his worst fear became real: that something was going to happen to you because he got too close. He's terrified of losing you and he did the only thing he could think of to stop history from repeating itself."

"Does he know you're telling me this?" I ask.

"No. I know he'd be okay with you knowing, though, if it means you understand better why he did what he did. He doesn't even realize how much everything with Ilen affected him, but I see it in everything he does. You are the love of his life, Ava. You're it for him, he knows that. Which is why it scared him that much more that he might be harming you."

"I don't know what to say."

"You don't have to say anything. If you don't want to be with Zane because he hurt your feelings or acted like an idiot in a million other ways, then you do what you gotta do. But don't give up because you think he doesn't love you. Nothing could be further from the truth."

44

 ZANE

"Zane?" Ava's voice calls.

My eyes shoot open and I'm met with a view of the night sky, stars peeking through the haze caused by the city lights.

What time is it? Where am I?

I raise my head and see a bottle of brown rum in my left hand. It's cold and I'm outside lying on the pavement somewhere and my feet are wet.

Wait—why are my feet wet?

Through a groggy daze, I look toward my feet and see them dipped in Kami's pool. It looks like I decided to fall asleep right here.

"Zane?" I hear her voice call again.

I look to my side and see Ava seated next to me. I immediately sit up.

"Are you okay?" I ask. "What's wrong? What's happening?"

"I'm okay, I'm okay," she says. "I'm sorry to wake you, I just… can we talk?"

"Sure."

"I talked to Kami, and she explained what happened to… well what happened when you guys were living in Austria or Hungary or whatever."

I rub my eyes as I process what she just said.

Kami told her about Ilen? My eyes widen and I don't know where to start.

Why would she tell her that?

Ava's never going to trust me again. She's going to think I'm a monster.

I am a monster.

Why would Kami do this to me? Why would she ruin my chances with Ava? Please tell me this isn't happening.

"I think I understand a little better, why you did what you did," she says, biting her lower lip and looking down. "I'm sorry that happened."

"I... wha-... what?"

"I don't want you to protect me from anything, especially if that means hiding stuff from me. But if you can do that, if you can give me total honesty and let me make my own decisions..." she lets out a heavy sigh. "I'm willing to give it another shot."

I let my body drop back onto the pavement.

"Oh fuck off!" I say, covering my face with my arms.

"Excuse me?" Ava's voice responds.

These bloody dreams are a million times worse than the nightmares.

Sure, nightmares are awful, but it's worse believing the lies in my dreams—believing that she has come back to me—only to awaken to an empty room and a bottle of liquor... or two... or twelve.

"This isn't real," I say to myself. "This isn't real."

"Zane," her voice says. "What are you talking about? I'm real, this is real."

I roll to the side. I'd rather be tortured in a nightmare than have to suffer through more of this false hope.

"Go away," I say.

I feel a sharp tug on my shoulder but I stay put. Suddenly I feel a much heavier jab in my back and I leap to my feet.

"Owww!" Ava says, hopping on one leg. "What the hell! Are Sirens stuffed with rocks or something?"

"Wha-... Did you just *kick me?*" I ask.

"Well, you weren't listening to me and I tried to turn you over but you're this big ol' impenetrable lump of Siren-person so what exactly was I supposed to do?" she says defensively. "Besides, I probably still owe you a kick or two."

I can't tell if this could still be a dream, but the sensation was awfully convincing.

"So you're telling me that you want to get back together and this isn't a dream?" I ask.

Fucking idiot. Would a bloody dream actually tell you if you're in a dream?

"Okay, what's something that doesn't happen in dreams?" she asks.

"Well, you've certainly never kicked me in the back before."

"So there ya go—obviously not a dream."

"Then you're still affected by the venom," I say with a sigh.

"It's 4 am, Zane; the venom wore off before I went to bed."

"I…" I mumble, but can't find the words. I look at her sincere, grey eyes and I want so desperately to believe them, but I'm terrified of getting my hopes up. I look over to the pool, and in a split-second decision find myself diving in.

My body hits the water and my skin erupts in tiny bumps as the cold reaches deep into my bones.

This certainly feels real… *and bloody freezing.*

"Fuck!" I yell as my head emerges from the water, my nostrils flooded with the scent of chlorine. I shake my wet hair out of my face and comb it back with my fingers.

"Okaaayyy…" Ava says. "The heck was that about??"

I swim up to the edge of the pool beneath her and lean my elbows on the ledge.

"Well… I had to see if I was really awake," I say.

"And…?"

"I'm asleep for sure," I say with a smile.

Ava reaches a toe into the water and kicks to splash me.

My smile grows as I realize Ava is real, standing in front of me and ready to give me another shot. It feels like seeing the sun after an endless storm. I can't help but want to pull her in to join me for a middle-of-the-night swim.

"Come closer, love," I say as she stands above me.

"Oh no no no," she says. "I know how this goes and it ends up with me in the pool in Kami's nice silk PJs and that is *not* happening."

Busted.

"Okay, love, if I promise not to pull you in, can you kneel down closer to me?"

"Okay," she says, raising a brow in suspicion. "But if I end up in the water, so help me, I will drown your ass. I don't care how immortal you are."

"Fair enough," I say as she leans down.

"You're real?" I ask, taking in her face like I'm trying to memorize every detail.

"I'm real," she says.

"And you're giving me another chance?" I ask.

My heart is beating so hard, I'm surprised it's not sending waves through the water.

"If you don't screw it up," she says.

"I can do that," I say.

I lift myself upward toward her until my lips connect with hers. A warm feeling spreads through my chest as if this one kiss ignited a fuse within me. It's the first time I've felt alive all week.

"I love you," I say.

"I love you."

———

AVA

The sunlight is bright enough that it peeks through my closed eyelids. Despite drinking and staying up so late, I feel surprisingly content. I've missed having Zane's warm chest in place of my pillow and waking up to the rhythmic thumping of his heart and the slow rises and falls of his breathing.

I don't want to open my eyes, if only to bask in the moment a bit longer.

This is the last place I thought I'd be just 24 hours ago, when Jen was still trying to convince me going out drinking would be a good idea.

Oh god—Jen.

How the heck am I going to explain this?

My eyes open to the warm light of the mid-day sun filling the room and I watch Zane's fingers delicately twirl a lock of my hair.

"Morning, love," he says.

"How did you know I was awake?" I ask, turning upward to meet his deep brown eyes with mine. A wavy strand of his hair falls across his face and he brushes it away.

"Your breathing changed."

"That's one of the creepiest things you've ever said," I reply with a giggle. "You're not supposed to tell women you're watching them sleep and listening to them breathe. It may seem romantic in teen movies, but in real life you sound like a serial killer."

"Serial killer, eh?" he says with a goofy smile.

"Yeah, well, it's even creepier when you're smiling at me like that."

"I missed you so much," he says, looking deep into my eyes.

I giggle and my eyes dodge the sudden, intense eye contact.

"You're getting creepier," I say with a laugh.

"Really," he says in a more serious voice, lightly lifting my chin to look at him. "You are perfect. I'm never letting you go ever again."

The sincerity in his voice is overwhelming, and I can't decide if I want to kiss him or just awkwardly boop his nose to break up the serious moment.

Without my consent, my hand chooses the boop route.

Boop.

Zane blinks a few times in confusion.

"Wha-..." he says with a baffled expression. "I... What was that?"

"It's a boop," I say.

Obviously.

"What's a boop?" he asks with furrowed brows.

"You know," I say, repeating the action. "Boop!"

"Well that clarifies everything," he says with a laugh.

"It's like, a thing you do to cute things. You touch their nose quickly and you say 'boop.'"

He looks at me skeptically and raises one eyebrow.

"I can't explain a boop to you, okay?" I say. "It's just a boop. It's ineffable. It just *is*. And really, how do you not know what a boop is? Don't you have the internet?"

"Alright then, I guess I'll have to just take your word for it," he says with a smile.

"You're doing that creepy smile again."

"Get used to it, love. I got a second chance with you, I'm going to be smiling for a long time."

"Yeah, well, don't mess it up," I joke, playfully smacking his shoulder.

"No more making decisions for you."

"I should be involved in all decisions that involve me," I clarify. "We need to have conversations before you go off making rash choices."

"I can do that."

"Just don't hide stuff from me," I say.

"Mmm," he hums with a bit of a frown.

Uh oh.

"Don't make that sound; it seems like bad news. What are you not telling me?"

"Er... I'm not hiding anything, I promise," he says. "But I didn't tell you something, I'm not sure if this is the kind of thing you want to know about."

My heartbeat starts to pound in my chest.

"Oh god, did you sleep with someone while we wer-"

"No, no!" he says. "God no, nothing like that. Just, the night of Kami's party, when I went to pick up Kieran, I stumbled across him and uh… Shayna."

Oh shit.

That is not what I thought he was going to say at all.

"Do you mean they were kissing or like, full-on having sex?"

"The latter." He cringes slightly.

That bitch.

"Like, you're sure they were… doing that?"

"I mean, unless they were doing some pretty intense, half-naked yoga in the back room of the bar…"

"Oh god, okay okay," I say, cutting him off. "I could do without that visual, thanks."

Oh no, I'm picturing it. Oh god, why?

"And Kieran was…" I say, trailing off. "Why would he do that? That's so fucked up."

"I think Shayna gave him the impression that she and Jen had an open relationship."

I rub my forehead, trying to process it all.

"This is so bad."

"Should I have not told you?" he asks.

"No," I say. "I'm glad you told me. I just have no idea what to do with the information."

That's an understatement. Everyone knows the fastest way to get your friend to hate you is to accuse their partner of cheating.

"I appreciate that you're not censoring what you do or don't tell me," I say. "I don't want to be protected, I just want you to include me on anything that involves me."

"Hmm," he hums, sitting up on the bed.

"Can you stop doing that?" I ask, sitting up alongside him. "You're freaking me out!"

"Sorry, love. I just want to make sure everything's out on the table this time. There's just another thing I'd like to talk to you about."

"Okay, you're killing me here, what is it?" I ask.

"So, you remember what I told you that night after I punched your brother?"

"Um, when you said we were soulmates?"

"Oh bollocks," he curses under his breath. "Okay, I forgot about that one.

I guess there are two things we need to talk about."

"Holy crap, Zane, how much stuff have you been hiding from me?"

"I'm trying here, love," he says with a sigh.

"Okay, you're right. I'm sorry. Continue."

"So, I guess I should start with, er…" he says, tugging at his hair. "We are actually soulmates. At least according to the Seer who also thought I should break up with you."

My brain feels like a pinball machine with dozens of thoughts bouncing around inside.

"What??" I ask.

"She said we're soulmates. The real deal. You and I."

The thought is too bizarre to begin to wrap my head around.

"And she thought we should break up?" I ask.

"Er, yeah. She thinks I'm bad for you."

"Well then," I say, grabbing his hand. "She sounds like a dumbass."

A wide smile spreads across Zane's cheeks.

"Okay well, what I was trying to say was… do you remember talking about the mark?"

"Oh," I say. "Yeah, the Siren human-claiming thing."

"Well, the thing is, I've always been ready to do it," he says softly, looking down at his trembling hands.

I don't think I've ever seen Zane this nervous before.

"I was—well, am—worried about doing it because you're sick," he says. "And I think deep down, maybe, I'm a bit worried that you'd feel differently about me if you were immune to my powers. Maybe the effect is why you love me now."

It never occurred to me that Zane might doubt my feelings for him.

"Well then," I say. "You're a dumbass too."

He chuckles and looks up at me.

"We already know that, though, don't we?" he says with a smile.

"So," I say, slowly processing what he's told me. "What does that mean, then?"

"Well, I guess what it means is that it's your choice. If you'd like me to make you, more or less, immortal."

45

I stare at Zane with my mouth agape.

"What?" he asks.

"Really, Zane?" I ask. "You don't just casually offer your girlfriend immortality!"

"I didn't consider that particularly casual. Besides, I wanted to have a clean slate, be open and honest with you. Like you wanted."

"Okay well, yes, technically I did say I wanted that but… I didn't expect the secrets you were keeping to be, 'Oh hey, by the way, we're soulmates and I can make you immortal.'"

"I… fuck… I don't know. I'm trying to do this right."

"Zane," I say with a sigh. "You don't have to commit to this whole mark thing because you think you have something to prove to me. I'm not going anywhere."

"I'm not," he says, pinching between his brows and closing his eyes. "I've known for a long time that you're the one for me."

His eyes open to meet mine and he brushes a stray lock of hair behind my ear.

"I've been around a long time," he says, lightly brushing my jaw with his hand. "What I feel for you… it's so different—so much more—than I have ever felt for anyone in 200 years. Being without you and knowing that I hurt you, even for the few days we were apart, I couldn't stand it. I could hardly bear the pain. I knew taking lethe was stupid, but I was so desperate to make it go away."

I blink at him, struggling to find an adequate response.

"You are, without a doubt, the love of my life," he says, his voice shaking slightly. "There is no pressure for this. Honestly, I don't want you to do it. I'm not sure it's safe. But, it's a decision that affects you, so you should be involved."

"I… I don't know, Zane. This is a lot. We just got back together. Last night I was on a date with another guy and th-"

Zane interrupts me with a low, rumbling growl. His eyes turn bright green. His jaw tenses and he attempts to regain his composure, taking a tight breath through his clenched teeth. He swallows hard and his eyes narrow.

"Sorry, er, go ahead," he says, the green in his eyes slowly fading.

"It's just a lot to think about right now."

"You don't have to decide now, love," he says, running his fingers through my hair.

"What does it even do?" I ask. "I mean, what's the process? How does it work?"

"Er… It's a little grotesque, but basically, inside a Siren's wings there are… hmm… it's kind of like the supernatural equivalent of stem cells. They have the power to make human cells immortal, linking them in a way to the original Siren."

"So I'd be a Siren?" I ask.

"No, you'd still be human, you just wouldn't be able to age or die as long as I was alive. Unfortunately you'd still be sick, and my powers wouldn't work on you anymore, so I wouldn't be able to help make your pain go away. Kami thinks you might heal faster, but I'm honestly not sure. Not a lot of people do this."

"Why not?"

"Because Sirens don't often fall for humans, and in general the whole cutting off your wings thing is a big deal for some…"

Okay, hold up. *WHAT?*

"*What???*" I shout. "You're telling me you'd have to cut off your wings for this to work?"

"Oh uh, yeah," he says, as if we're having a normal everyday conversation. "I mean technically you only have to cut off one, but that would be really awkward and you can't use one wing anyway. Most Sirens go for both."

"I'm not letting you cut off your body parts for me, Zane," I say. "Just so I can live forever? No thanks."

He smiles slightly.

"What are you smiling for?" I ask.

"I'm kind of glad," he says. "I don't want to risk your safety. Even if your concern is for me, I'll take it."

"Oh, thanks," I say sarcastically. "What happened to you being certain I'm your soulmate?"

"Love," he scolds. "You know I don't mean it like that. I would happily give up any body part you happened to need."

He pulls me in for a hug and kisses me on the neck.

"Oh yeah? So you'd sacrifice your penis for me?" I ask with a giggle.

"You want it? Because I'd be happy to give it to you," he says with a devious smirk, grinding his hips into me.

"Pervert," I tease, sticking out my tongue at him.

He opens his mouth to say something but the vibration of my phone interrupts us. He grabs it off the bedside table and hands it to me.

It's Jen.

Oh boy.

"Heeyyy!" I say as I answer the phone.

"Don't 'heeyyy' me, girly," she says. "Where the heck did you disappear to last night?!"

"I told you I was heading home."

"Yeah, but whose home?"

"I, um…"

"Are you at Zane's?" she asks.

"No, I'm at Kami's."

"You bailed on us to go over to Kami's house? Why?"

"I'm sorry," I say. "I didn't mean to bail on you guys but I wasn't feeling… quite myself… and I had to talk to Zane."

"Girl, tell me you didn't."

Yep. I did.

"Um…" I say, having no response other than guilty silence.

"Oh my god, Ava!" she says. "You really are my little whoreball!"

"Shuuttt upppp," I whine.

"Well, this must've been one hell of a talk!"

All I need to do now is manage to explain this without using the word Siren or talking about his dead girlfriend or having to explain why he was alive in the 1800s.

Yeah. Simple.

"I found out about something personal that happened to him and… I can't really talk about it, but it explained some of why he is the way he is. Why he made the choice that he did and he thought he was doing the right thing. It's really complicated but I…" I pause, realizing Zane is right behind me listening to me talk about him.

I look over my shoulder to see Zane sitting up on the bed, his shoulders slumped and head hanging low. I mouth the word 'Sorry' and shrug my shoulders, unsure how else to address the situation. He gives me an understanding nod and gestures for me to continue talking.

"It's really hard to explain," I say with a flustered sigh. "Can you just trust me and not kill Zane the next time you see him?"

"So you're back together?"

"Yeah. We're back together." I look back to see Zane with a big smile on his face.

"Okay, hon," she says reluctantly. "I guess if it means that much to you, I won't kill him. For now."

"Why thank you," I say with a giggle.

"But I know somebody's gonna be real disappointed."

"Huh? Who?"

"Dreamboat Dave, of course!"

I hear another low growl from Zane. Apparently he can hear both sides of our conversation. I give him a quick glare and he shrugs in response. He walks over to the couch in his boxers, presumably in an attempt to give me more privacy, even though it's just a few more feet away.

"He was definitely smitten with you last night," she says. "He couldn't stop talking about you after you left. I didn't realize things were still possible with you and Zane, so don't be mad but I gave him your number."

A loud crack rings throughout the room and I turn to see Kami's marble coffee table split down the middle. My eyes widen at Zane but he won't look at me.

"Uh, that's okay," I say.

Zane turns around and looks at me with his eyes glowing green and one eyebrow raised.

"I'll handle it," I add.

I need to return the poor guy's jacket, anyway.

Zane seems to relax and turns back around, stretching out on the couch.

Personally, I'm less concerned with Dave and more concerned with how I'm going to broach the subject of Shayna with Jen. It's probably not the kind of conversation we should have over the phone; I need to time this delicately.

"Hold on," Jen says. "I'm getting a page from work."

"Okay," I say.

"Oh holy shit," she mumbles under her breath.

"What is it?"

"My boss is saying I need to come in to process some priority samples from a murder scene."

"Well, yeah, Jen," I say. "That's what your company does. Why does that surprise you?"

"The body was found behind Pike's."

46

 ZANE

Ava's eyes are wide as she hangs up the phone.

"Were you eavesdropping the whole time?" she asks.

"It's not eavesdropping if you have superhuman hearing," I say.

"So you heard about Pike's?"

"Yeah, still trying to wrap my head around it. I'll text Kieran to see what he knows."

I pull out my phone and send Kieran a quick message.

"That's so creepy," she says, sitting back on the bed and wrapping herself in the plush white comforter. "We were there last night. Do you think it's related to the other Siren?"

My fists clench and my nails dig into my skin at the thought of another Siren targeting Ava. Sirens don't usually kill—especially since they can get what they want without needing to. But one targeted Ava, and they did it by dosing her drink. Despite my arrangement with Kieran, that's not the usual way a Siren lures a human. They're usually more hands-on, approaching and charming their mark.

"It would be one hell of a bloody coincidence," I say.

A tapping sound turns our attention to the door.

"Z," Kami's voice calls. "What did you break this time?"

Ava slips on her pajama bottoms and buttons up the top.

"You can come in!" I say.

Kami barges in to inspect her guest bedroom. She pauses upon seeing her fractured coffee table and her hands move quickly to her hips.

"Z, you destructive man-child!" she screams. "That table was white

Carrara marble!"

"I don't know what that means," I say. "But I'll replace your bloody table, okay?"

She huffs in frustration and mumbles obscenities under her breath.

"Morning Ava," she says, turning to her. "Would you guys like some lunch?"

Ava looks to me and then to Kami again and blushes.

"I guess you can tell we've, uh…" she shrugs, "worked things out."

"Yeeaaah, hon, I kinda got that when you guys woke me up at 5 am with yo-"

"Oh my god!" Ava says, cutting her off.

A deep shade of pink fills Ava's cheeks and extends to her ears. She raises her hands to her face to hide.

"It's okay, Ava," Kami says. "We're 200-year-old Sirens. I've personally hosted my own orgies. I don't get squeamish about much."

Ava takes a pillow and holds it up to bury her face in.

"This morning is officially too much," she says, muffled slightly by the pillow.

I move over to sit with Ava on the bed and pull the pillow away.

"Alright, love, let's get some food," I say. "No more awkward conversations."

"If we can just avoid any more big revelations or embarrassing moments, that would be great," she says.

"Big revelations?" Kami asks, giving me a curious look.

"I told her about being soulmates," I say. "And about the mark."

Her eyes nearly pop out of her head and she gives a look that tells me that she's already filing away questions for me to answer later.

"Wow," she says, swallowing hard. "That is a lot of revelations for one morning."

"Yeah and then Jen calls and tells me they found a body at Pike's," Ava says.

"What?" Kami asks, rapidly turning toward Ava.

"Yeah, we were just there last night and I somehow got dosed with Siren venom," Ava explains. "Who knows what could've happened if I had stayed."

"Who was the victim?" she asks.

I'm surprised Kami glossed over the Siren venom so quickly. Does she know something I don't?

"I don't know," Ava says.

"I know who I'm personally rooting for," I say with a smirk.

Fucking Dave.

The scent from that lumbering oaf of a man still lingers in Ava's hair.

"Not nice," Ava scolds, narrowing her eyes and scrunching her lips in the most adorable way.

"I'm not a nice guy, love," I say with a smirk.

"Okay lovebirds," Kami says. "I'm gonna make lunch and then I need to go over to Pike's and look into this."

She gives me a suspicious glance that I can instantly read. It's obvious she's immediately expecting the worst of Kieran.

———•———

Finn sits across the table from me, perusing the menu.

"Man, I've missed proper food," he says with a longing sigh.

Kieran walks up to our table in a maroon leather blazer over a barely buttoned red dress shirt and jeans so tight it hurts just to look at them.

"Long time no see, my man!" Kieran shouts, gripping Finn's hand and pulling him in for a hug.

"Yeah, what's that all about?" he asks. "Everyone seemed to drop off the earth for a while there."

Oh. Yeah, we last saw Finn shortly before Halloween, when everything went straight to hell because I'm such a bloody idiot. Finn has always been a great voice of reason—maybe if he were there he would've stopped me before I broke up with Ava.

Finn chokes on air and his eyes go wide.

"What the hell happened on Halloween?"

"Ooh did you read his mind again?" Kieran asks. "Was he thinking about the lethe?"

Fuck.

"Lethe??" Finn asks, his hand covering his mouth. "A'right, what the feck did you do?"

"Oi, okay," I say with a sigh. "Long story short, I'm a total wanker. I thought that maybe the myth about Siren's venom was true and it was making Ava go crazy. It wasn't. But I broke up with her because I'm an idiot. Then I downed a bunch of lethe. That, expectably, made things much worse."

"Don't leave out the part where I tried to save your ass but you had to go say something stupid to Ava," Kieran says.

"And you thought I was a demon and tried to kill me," I add.

"Oh yeah, that too," he says with a chuckle.

Finn's jaw drops.

"Anyway uh, it's fine. We're back together, but I-"

"What now?" Kieran says with a shocked expression. "Shit dude, you just drop that on me like that?"

"Yeah uh, last night."

"And you're out to lunch with us?" Kieran asks. "Why are you not home, cashing in on that sweet, sweet makeup sex?"

I would've dropped this lunch in a heartbeat to spend more time with Ava, but she had a client meeting and work to do.

"So that's how it is, ay?" Finn's voice says in my head.

"Sorry mate," I say with a chuckle.

"What was he thinking?" Kieran asks. "Why'd he apologize?"

Finn shrugs and smirks at me.

"Man, Finn, you're no fun," Kieran says. "This power is so bitchin' and you won't even share it."

"You wouldn't find it so great if he could read your thoughts too," I say.

Luckily for Kieran—and more so really, for Finn—demons are immune to a Selkie's telepathy.

"It's not my fault I'm so complex and mysterious," he says with a smirk.

Finn rolls his eyes.

A waitress approaches our table. She has brown hair wrapped in a braid to one side and olive skin.

"Hi there! I'm Shandi," she says.

"Well, hello there, Shandi," Kieran says, taking a mere half of a second to decide he wants to have sex with this woman.

She reads off the drink specials and asks us what we'd like to drink. Finn orders a Guinness and I do too, Kieran orders a coke that he's undoubtedly going to spike with whatever alcohol is in the flask he has tucked in his jacket pocket. As the waitress leaves, Kieran's eyes follow her lower half.

"I'm personally relieved I can't read your mind," Finn says with a laugh.

"Hey man!" Kieran says. "With you two being boring housewives now, you know you want to live vicariously through my sex life. You just don't know what you're missing. You're not going to get that kind of dirty from Mr. Straight-Laced over here."

Finn looks awkwardly down at the table, avoiding eye contact with me.

Oh god. That's right, I completely forgot about the other night at the club. Finn certainly got an earful from my wandering mind.

Finn pinches his lips together, trying not to laugh.

"What's that look for?" Kieran asks.

Finn and I both shrug and silently exchange looks.

"Hey now, wait a minute," he whines. "Did Zane do something I don't know about? Is sweet little Ava a freak in the shee-"

Say the words and eat your tongue for lunch.

"I wouldn't," Finn says, stopping Kieran.

"See what I mean?" Kieran says. "He's so sensitive."

This lunch has already gotten wildly off-topic. I was supposed to be getting more info about the body at Pikes and yet I'm busy trying not to kill Kieran. Again.

Finn's eyes flick toward me and I realize he's wondering about what I've just thought.

Well, here goes nothing.

"So er, I wanted to talk to you about the body they found at Pike's," I say to Kieran.

"Body?" he asks. "What are you talking about?"

"You're telling me you don't know anything about the dead body they found last night?"

Kami is currently at Pike's investigating the scene, so part of my job is to keep Kieran away. I don't suspect him, but I do agree that his presence would be a nuisance.

"Shit," Kieran says. "That's gonna bring a lot of attention onto me. Just what I need."

His response seems genuine.

"Who was it?" he asks.

"I don't know."

"Pike's is Kieran's bar, right?" Finn asks.

"Yeah," I say. "I was there with Ava last night, too."

"Uh, technically she was there wit-" Kieran starts to say.

"Say it. I fucking dare you."

Kieran takes a heavy gulp.

"So um," Finn says in an attempt to change the subject. "You think this dead body is anything to worry about?"

"I don't know," I say. "There have been some suspicious deaths around. We think there's another Incubus in town. Not sure if this is related."

"Why do you think it's an Incubus?" Finn asks.

"Because they have that classic, drained Incubus-victim look."

"But I thought Incubi don't have to drain their victims," he says. "I mean, Kieran doesn't."

"We don't have to," Kieran says. "But we can. If I drain any random person on the street it will knock them out, or kill them if I take it a little further. But you get caught real easy that way."

"Wait, then why do you need to have sex with them? If you can just drain anyone."

"It's a lot easier to feed off sexual energy and there's a lot more of it to take. It sustains me a lot longer. Plus I can get off."

"I'm sorry I asked," Finn says.

My phone vibrates in my pocket as the waitress arrives with our drinks, setting them down on the table.

Kami

We have a problem. This is definitely an Incubus kill. But that's not all.

As I read her message, another comes through.

Kami

We know the victim.

47

I walk into the open courtyard at the center of a small shopping center. The place is relatively busy for midday; people carry armfuls of shopping bags, teens laugh while downing spoonfuls of frozen yogurt, a few men sit outside a women's clothing store with a look of boredom on their faces.

The click-clack sound of Kami's heels on the linoleum flooring catches my attention and I turn to see her walking toward me. She's wearing a black suit with a silk black top underneath and her hair pulled back into a low ponytail.

She walks up to me with a somber expression.

"Okay, what the hell is going on?" I ask.

"Here," she says with a sigh, gesturing to a nearby table and chairs. "Let's sit."

We both take a seat and I give her a questioning look.

"Why did we have to meet in person?" I ask. "What happened? Who is it?"

"Crime scene was already cleaned up when I got there," Kami says. "But I was able to charm my way into the PCPD offices. I made copies of all the files and checked out the victim's belongings."

"And??" I ask, pushing for more details on the victim that we are supposed to know.

She pulls out a deep purple cloth and unwraps it to reveal a gold necklace. The pendant is slightly wider than a business card and features two feathers stretching in opposite directions from a red center stone.

It looks familiar but I can't seem to place it.

I take a closer look at the object and slowly recognize a familiar scent.

The Seer. Lola.

"Shit," I curse under my breath. "Kami, I… I'm so sorry. I know you two were close."

"Thanks," she says softly, leaning onto my shoulder.

After a moment of silence, Kami sits up and continues.

"I don't know what is going on anymore, Z. If someone got to Lola, they have to know that I've been helping her investigate these killings. That's why I wanted to meet you in person. I don't know what's safe."

"Do you have any leads?" I ask.

"None that you're going to like," she says. She wraps the pendant back up with the cloth, along with a folded piece of paper and another small item I don't recognize.

"Are we seriously considering Kieran again?" I ask. "His reaction seemed genuine when I asked him about it. I don't think he even knew someone had died."

"The police said they interviewed him this morning," Kami says. "So if he pretended to be shocked, it's bullshit. He knew."

I stare at her, dumbfounded, trying to wrap my head around the new information.

Why would Kieran lie?

"Think about it, Z," Kami says in a serious voice. "Why would Lola be at Pike's? You think always-wears-couture, won't-drink-it-if-it-doesn't-have-bubbles Lola would go to a trashy pub in the middle of nowhere like Pike's?"

"I don't know. You know her better than I do."

"Why would she go to Pike's unless she had a vision? Unless she figured out it was Kieran and came there to confront him?"

"Fuck," I say with a sigh. "I know this looks bad, Kam, but Kieran isn't like that."

"He's a demon!"

"Exactly. He's a demon—that doesn't make him evil or a killer. You're making a lot of assumptions just because of who he is."

"That's a nice idea, Zane, and I wanted to believe in Kieran too, for your sake. But look at the evidence. At the end of the day, we all know where demons come from. Maybe they just can't change their nature."

The first seven demons—some call them the original demons or Demon Kings—created their own demonic legions. Original demons are intensely powerful, but each is as corrupt and vile as the last.

Their demon offspring, however, are individuals—not controlled by their demonic creators. They're no more destined to be like their makers than humans are to be like their parents.

"And what about us?" I ask. "Sirens are wild, aggressive, driven by their desires, uncontrollable… right? Are you and I just products of our design? Do we have any say in who we are?"

"That's different, Z. We weren't created by monsters."

"I owe him the benefit of the doubt. Kieran has never betrayed me. I understand things look bad, but I trust him."

Kami sighs and looks off into the distance.

"I made you copies," she says, handing me a stack of papers. "Whether it's Kieran or not, I'm gonna need your help on this. Look them over. We can talk more later."

She scoops up her things and walks away, leaving me with a pile of case files.

As if my life wasn't complicated enough.

AVA

After working out of a coffee shop all day, my hair smells like espresso and I look surprisingly disheveled for someone who has done nothing but sit for hours. I walk over to Zane's sapphire blue Charger, passing by a couple of girls sitting at a café table outside, flirtatiously waving in his direction.

Keep your eyes to yourself, ho-bags.

They're probably very nice people, and here I am slut-shaming them for checking out my boyfriend. I'm a bad person.

"I love your car!" one of the girls shouts.

Ho-bag.

Zane looks completely unfazed by their attention and smiles at me as I approach.

"Hey baby," he says to me out the window.

For a moment, the girl looks up as though Zane might be talking to her, but looks down awkwardly at her coffee when she sees me getting in his car.

I smile with delight.

Because I am a bad person.

"Hey," I say, as Zane leans and kisses me on my neck.

He seems to think by kissing me on the neck he's avoiding the arousing effect. But based on the way my body reacts to him, it's safe to say it is *not working.*

"Your place tonight?" I ask.

We've spent the last few weeks at my place, so I feel like it's only fair.

"Er, well…" he says suspiciously.

"Yeah, that wasn't a totally shady response," I say with a laugh.

"I may have… kind of… demolished my apartment."

I stare at him with a stunned expression.

"You what?" I ask.

"I er… So I may have trashed the apartment… and my landlord may be in the process of evicting me for the… erm… broken window and holes in the wall and the smashed sink."

"Holy crap, Zane!" I blurt out.

"Well, I told you I was a mess without you. To say I didn't take it very well is pretty much the understatement of the millennium."

"You're the one who broke up with me. Shouldn't I have been the one throwing stuff?"

"Love," he says with a sigh. "You know I didn't want to leave you. As we've already established, I'm a proper idiot."

"I know." I rub his arm with my hand. "I'm just kidding."

"But long story short, my apartment isn't the most habitable right now."

"Well, okay, but you're not allowed to go all Godzilla at my place," I say with a giggle. "I have a lot of irreplaceable artifacts in there."

Wouldn't want anything to happen to my collection of hand-assembled Swedish furniture or the Craigslist floor lamp that falls over without the heavy books I use to weigh the base down.

"Okay, love," he says with a smirk as we pull out of the coffee shop parking lot. "Can't promise the bed is safe, though."

He winks at me before turning his attention back to the road.

"So are you going to move then?" I ask, ignoring his flirty comment.

"Oh," he says, pinching his lips into a straight line. "So I was thinking about that. Been wanting to move for a while and there's a penthouse above Table. The last tenant just moved out and I've been thinking about taking it over. We already lease the space so it would make sense."

"Ooh, that sounds really cool. Why haven't you used it before?"

"Well, it's a little big," he says. "It's got a big office that I wouldn't really have any use for. A rooftop pool and garden. It's almost 300 square meters. Seems like too much space for one person."

"Oh," I say, pondering his words.

Oh.

OH.

Is he saying what I think he's saying?

"Okay, love, I'm going to need your help on this one," he says with a slightly nervous smile. "I've never done this before. I'm trying to, er… If you'd like… Should I ask formally or… Fuck. I'm rubbish at this stuff."

"You're trying to say that you want…" I start to ask, but then my courage abandons me.

Does he want me to move in with him? I don't want to be the one to say it if I've got it all wrong and then I'll end up being presumptuous.

"Would you like to see the place?" he asks. "And then, if you like it, we could live there. Together."

He tries in vain to hide his anxiety behind a subtle smile and unwavering expression, but there's a slight quiver in his voice.

"Um," I say, trying to think it over and come up with a response that will put him at ease without making an impulsive decision.

Do I want to move in with my extremely hot boyfriend and supernaturally destined soulmate into a fancy penthouse apartment overlooking the city?

If I respond with a 'fuck yes', will that make me seem desperate?

"Sure," I say. "I mean, we can look into it."

His expression softens and his smile widens into a genuine grin.

"Really?" he asks like a kid who was just told they're going to Disneyland.

"As long as you don't wreck this one," I say with a teasing grin

48

We step inside the swanky mirrored elevator and Zane scans a key fob before hitting a button that says 'P'.

I don't really know what that is supposed to stand for. *P… Primo floor?*

"P?" I ask.

"Penthouse, baby," Zane says. I suddenly feel ultra-dumb for not getting that one.

"Is someone going to show us the place or…?"

"My name's on the lease, love," he says. "If we want it, we just move in."

Oh. Right.

The elevator bell dings and the doors open to a small entryway with a set of doors. I look around expecting a hallway with additional doors but it's just the one small corridor.

"Where do we go?" I ask.

"Through the doors, love. Where else?"

He looks at me quizzically and opens the door for me.

"Okay, big spender, sorry if I don't know how these rich person things work." I say, my voice drifting as I look around at a massive open space with red brick walls and an upper floor surrounded by glass walls. Sunlight streams through five towering arched windows that extend to the loft level. The space is completely furnished.

"What do you think?" Zane asks.

"The fuck is this??" I ask in disbelief.

"You don't like it?" His expression falls.

"Of course I like it!" I say, slapping Zane on the shoulder. "But what is this?

This isn't an apartment, Zane, it's a fucking Pottery Barn!"

"I don't know what that means," he says with narrowed eyes.

"This is giant," I say, looking around. "Does this apartment take up the entire top floor?"

"That's what penthouse means, love," he says with a smile.

"Okay, well I told you I don't know how rich people stuff works."

I look to one window and realize that it's actually a door.

"Is there just a door to nowhere over here?" I ask, walking toward it. As I walk, I see a garden and an odd reflective surface.

"It's a garden," he says.

I step out into a beautiful green space flanked by trees. As I look around I catch the reflection again, and it's a pool.

A fucking pool.

"What the fuck!" I shout.

Zane looks at me cautiously.

"Is it too high? Do you not like heights?" he asks. "Is it the water? Are you afraid of water?"

"No," I say. "It's just, it's too much! How much money do you make, anyway?"

Shit. That was so rude. I can't believe I just asked that.

"A lot," he says with a smile. "Does that mean you like it?"

"Yes, Zane, but I kinda figured I'd be like… contributing to the rent. And this is… I don't think I could afford to pay the renter's insurance here."

"You know I don't care, right?" he asks, wrapping his arms around me and pulling me into his chest. "Perks of being a Siren, ya know."

"Yeah, perks of being a super-old guy," I tease.

"You know, love," he says with a glare. "I'd be glad to show you how young I really am."

"Oh it's okay, I believe you."

"Mmmhmm," he says, skeptical of my response.

"I mean, you are pretty immature," I say with a giggle.

"Is that so?" he asks with a cheeky grin that lets me know I'm in for serious trouble.

I try to dart away, but he has a firm hold on me.

"Well, if I'm so immature," he says, picking me up by the waist with ease and walking closer to the pool, "then I guess you'd be foolish to bring me out here and not expect me to do this."

Suddenly, we're submerged in the lukewarm water. The pool must be heated, and I'm grateful for it because my joints freeze up in the cold. Every time I'm cold, I end up awkwardly hobbling along like an arthritic Tin Man.

I emerge from the pool to see Zane laughing hysterically, his hair in loose wet curls and his T-shirt soaked.

Bastard.

I splash him in retaliation and he gives me a wicked smile as his eyes turn green.

Uh oh. Is he genuinely mad at me?

His eyes travel to my chest. My light grey blouse is almost completely transparent and clinging to my skin—and I'm not wearing a bra.

Oh.

"So, splashing, that's what mature adults do, eh?" he asks, stepping closer with a predatory expression.

Okay, Ava. You've got this. Don't be distracted by his hotness. Now's your chance to say something cool and sexy.

"I… uh…" I stutter.

Damn it.

His hands grip my hips and he leans in so that his lips are next to my ear.

"Well if you like it so much here…" he says with a low, rough voice. "Shall we break it in?"

I attempt to think of a clever or sexy response, but Zane's breath against my neck has completely shut off my brain.

My head nods as I struggle to grasp anything close to English.

His lips collide with mine and I feel the effects of his venom coursing through my body. In an instant, there's no pain or discomfort, just pure bliss; intense and electric.

Zane pulls away as if he suddenly remembered I have to breathe. He presses his forehead to mine and his eyes glow a radiant green. He brings his lower lip between his teeth and bites down hard, his eyes holding mine.

"Not wearing a bra today?" he asks with a devious smile, softly tracing his hands down the collar of my blouse. His hand undoes the first two buttons with ease.

It's totally unfair how cool and coordinated he is sometimes.

"Well, I wasn't exactly planning on getting pushed into a pool today," I say teasingly.

"I can't say I feel too bad about that," he says, his eyes following the outline of my body below the water's surface. His fingers delicately release another few buttons until the front of my top is completely open, my breasts falling just beneath the water's surface.

"I don't know if I should reward your bad behavior," I say with a smirk.

"You know you love me because I'm a little bad, baby."

He reaches his hands around my waist and up the back of my shirt, kissing and biting a trail along my neck as he pulls me into him.

He presses himself up against me, slowly rolling his hips into mine.

We're both in our wet jeans, and it occurs to me this may be more logistically difficult than I considered. The moment I get any jeans wet, they permanently suction themselves to my thighs.

"I'm not sure you're gonna be able to get my pants off," I say with a giggle.

"Oh?" he asks. He grabs the hem of my jeans and undoes the button, slides down the zipper, and with a sudden tug rips them down the center. After a few more tears, he lifts the tattered denim above the water and tosses the pieces onto dry land.

"You were saying?" he says with a smile.

"I was saying that it's a good thing you're rich, because you owe me new pants."

"I'll make it up to you," he says with another long kiss.

"You better," I say jokingly. "There ought to be some benefit to dating a Siren."

He subtly licks his lips, then pauses for a second before a wicked expression appears on his face.

I'm so doomed.

"Actually," he says. "I have wanted to try something."

He wraps a hand around the base of my neck, pulling me in for a kiss. His other arm lifts me up and I wrap my legs around his waist as he pins me against the edge of the pool.

I peel his T-shirt off, revealing his sharply chiseled muscles.

He brings his lips to my ear.

"Come for me, love," he whispers.

My heart begins to race and my breathing becomes shallow and rapid. A shiver travels down my spine and a warm euphoria spreads throughout my body. I sink my nails into his skin and he moans in response.

A jumble of expletives and nonsense sounds escapes my lips. My mind is completely wiped blank as I struggle to comprehend what just happened.

"I… I…" I stutter, struggling to catch my breath—or my brain cells.

"So I take it that worked," he says with a proud smirk.

"I didn't know you could do that. You've been holding out on me!"

"I've never tried," he says, kissing me and flicking his tongue across my lower lip. "But don't worry love, I'm sure we can make up for lost time."

49

My body is draped over Ava's in a blissful exhaustion on top of the dining table. My fingers grip tightly into the soft skin of her hips, unwilling to part with her body.

I lift my head up, a wet lock falling in front of my eyes. She takes a deep breath, staring back at me as though she's about to say something.

"Ow," Ava grumbles. "Okay, you're crushing my arm."

I quickly push myself off of her, chuckling to myself.

"Don't laugh at me, butthead," she says with a glare.

"I'm not laughing at you, love," I say, offering her a hand to help her up. She begrudgingly accepts and hoists herself off the table with a groan.

"Then what are you laughing at?" she asks with a pout.

"I thought you were going to say something profound or romantic and you say 'ow'."

"Yeah well, it's not my fault your big ol' buff Siren butt was busy crushing me to death."

"Ah, now there's that romance," I say with a chuckle, scooping her up and setting her down with me on the couch.

The room is littered with wet footprints and water droplets. Sopping clothes are scattered about like a trail of R-rated breadcrumbs leading away from the pool.

She lays down on my chest, her hand delicately tracing the edges of my tattoos.

"What's the deal with this one?" she asks, touching the marks at my waist.

"That's not a tattoo. It's my name."

"You got your own name tattooed on your body? Wow, narcissistic much?" She giggles and I ruffle her hair teasingly.

"Very funny, love," I say. "No, Sirens are born with their names written on their skin."

"Wait," she says, sitting up. "This is how you got your name? You didn't choose it or something?"

"Nope. I just read it."

"What is this language?" she asks with narrowed eyes, inspecting the ink on my abdomen.

"Not sure," I say, running my fingers across the characters. "I've just always been able to read it. All Sirens can."

"So this is how Kami got her name too?"

"Yep."

"So what does it mean?"

"It just means Zane. That's all it says."

"No," she says with a sigh. "I mean, what does your name mean?"

"Oh… er…"

"Have you never looked it up?"

Oh, I have. The answer is just incredibly pompous and she's definitely going to tease me over it.

"No, I have," I say. "It means Gift from God."

"Of fucking course it does," Ava replies with a fit of laughter.

"You asked."

"Do you have a last name?" she asks through restrained giggles. "Is it You're Welcome Ladies?"

"You're hilarious, love," I say, sticking out my tongue. "But no, I don't have a last name. It's just Zane."

"What do you have on your ID then?"

"Smith."

"Really? That's so boring. You could pick anything you want and you pick Smith?"

"I hardly ever use it," I say. "Kami used to change hers all the time."

"Used to?"

"Yeah, she sticks with her married name now."

"*Married name??*" Ava asks with wide eyes.

I guess I've never mentioned that before.

"Yeah, uh, she goes by Kami Selim. She got married a long time ago, kind of on a whim. He was an Immortal, but he got into some trouble and was killed. They had only been married for a month, but Kami took it hard. Decided to keep the name, kind of in tribute."

"Were…" Ava begins to ask, pinching her lips together anxiously. "Were you married before? Like… I mean… You've been around for a long time…"

"God no," I say.

I would have thought that would be comforting—I certainly wouldn't want to hear that she had a close relationship with anyone like that—but her reaction seems a little more disappointed than I would've expected.

"Well," she says. "I'm learning a lot today."

"Speaking of learning a lot," I say. "Have you decided what to do about Jen? It's been a while since…"

"You mean am I going to tell Jen that her girlfriend is also banging a demon?" she asks. "Well, since she's still working on not hating your guts, I don't really want her hating mine just yet."

"Fair dues."

"I'm secretly hoping they break up before I get around to dealing with it so I don't have to say anything."

I know the feeling. I have my own Kieran issues I'm trying to ignore.

"What?" she asks. "What's that sad face?"

"Oh, I…" I can't find the words. "Well, you know that body they found at Pike's?"

"Yeaaahhh…"

"Well, it was someone we sort of knew—an Immortal. Kami thinks Kieran had something to do with it."

"What?" she asks. "Why? Kieran doesn't kill people."

"I know," I say. "I've been trying to ignore it, come up with some kind of logical explanation. I've been avoiding Kieran, hoping that something would explain it all."

"Holy crap," she says softly.

"Yeah, I'm sorry I haven't mentioned it before. I've just been kind of processing it myself."

"No, I get it. It's complicated. Did you ask him about it?"

"I mean, no, but what's he gonna say?"

"I don't know," she says. "But it seems like you at least owe it to him to ask."

Well, she's got me there.

"As usual, baby, you're right," I say.

"What about your friend, Finn?" she asks. "Can't he just read his mind and tell you if anything is up?"

"Sadly, no. Finn's telepathy doesn't work on demons."

Come to think of it, even though Finn can't read demons, he does have a knack for telling if someone is lying; likely from a lifetime of hearing people's inner monologues. He may still be of use.

"Actually," I say. "It wouldn't be a bad idea to loop Finn in on this one anyway."

"If you fill me in on the details, I can help too," she says.

"Love," I say, lifting her jaw so that she's looking at me. "I do not want you involved in interrogating an Incubus."

"And I don't care what you want me involved with," she says, crossing her arms and giving me a death glare. "We talked about this."

"Okay, fine. You are your own person, but I really don't think we need to put you at risk."

"I don't think Kieran is dangerous," she says. "But even if he is—if you and Finn are there, and we're in public, am I at risk?"

"Probably not."

"Okay then, it's settled. Secret spy mission!"

What am I getting us into?

———•———

AVA

"Why am I agreeing to this, again?" Zane asks.

We're sitting in his car outside of Pike's, about to meet Finn inside while Kieran is tending bar.

"Because I'm my own person and you're not going to make decisions for me anymore," I say.

"Yeah," he says reluctantly, "and apparently you can't be your own person without risking life and limb."

"I'm not risking anything, Zane. This is Kieran. It's going to be fine."

"Well, if you start to feel sick, let me know and we can leave."

I'm already feeling really ill today, but if I give that away I know Zane will try to turn it into a reason I should go home. That's not going to happen.

"You're not leaving my side, right?" he says.

"Oh my gosh, here," I say, pulling out my phone. "I'll share my location with you and then you can make sure I'm not dead whenever you feel like."

"Wait, what's this now?"

"See?" I say, showing him on his phone where it shows my location. "Now you can know where I am and relax."

He looks confused for a moment.

"Why didn't we do this ages ago?" he asks.

"Because I don't want to encourage your craziness."

We both step out of the car and close the doors behind us.

"Is it really craziness to be concerned about your safety when you're surrounded by Immortals and demons?"

I ignore his question, in part because I don't have a good answer, and we head inside. Kieran waves to us and points to a set of open seats at the bar.

"So I guess you haven't sexed each other to death!" he says.

"Hilarious as always," Zane replies.

"Hey Ava," Kieran says. "How's cohabitation going?"

"We just got everything moved in," I say. "But now we're in that mountains of boxes stage."

"I'm happy to give you a hand if you need a real man to help lift the heavy stuff."

"I'm pretty sure technically neither of you are men," I add.

"Oh snap!" Kieran says, laughing. "Well shit, Z-Man, she's got us there!"

"'Scuse me, miss," a voice says from behind me. "Are these ugly blokes giving you trouble?"

I turn to see Finn as he wraps a friendly arm around Zane's shoulder.

"It's okay," I say jokingly. "I can handle these two."

"I'm sure you can," he says, his eyes slowly scanning the room as his eyes narrow.

"You okay?" I ask.

"Yes," he says. "Sorry, it's just awfully quiet in here."

"You're too used to Irish pubs," Kieran says. "Most bars don't have an endless soundtrack of loud, drunken singing and bottles breaking on heads."

"Oi," he says. "Don't take the piss. An Irish pub is a sacred place."

Finn's eyes continue to rake through the crowd, as if he's looking for someone or something.

Kieran gets us all our usual drinks and I decide to casually throw a question out there.

"So Kieran, what was the deal with the dead person here the other night?" I ask.

Probably not the most subtle route, but effective.

"I dunno," he says. "Nobody ever tells me anything. They didn't even tell me anyone was dead."

"Who didn't?" I ask.

"The cops, or the upper management," he says. "The cops just asked me if I heard or saw anything unusual or if I remembered a brunette Indian girl. I figured some girl got drunk and got into an accident or something. I had to hear from Zane that somebody died."

I glance over to Zane, whose guilty expression tells me he's feeling bad for doubting Kieran.

"Yep," Finn's voice rings in my head.

That still freaks me the heck out.

"Sorry," he says.

"Why is everybody staring at me like I just grew tits?" Kieran asks.

"Well, no amount of alcohol will wash away that particular visual," Finn says, taking a heavy gulp of his drink. "Cheers!"

"Oh you know you love it, you little Irish minx."

Finn laughs and points to his wedding ring.

The guys exchange banter for about 20 minutes. I'm starting to feel nauseous and lightheaded, but I don't want to interrupt the fun, so I try to push it out of my mind.

"Gonna hit the loo," Zane says, downing the remainder of his drink and heading toward the restroom.

"Okay, it *is* weirdly quiet in here," Finn says. "It's more obvious now that Zane's n-... Oh boy."

Finn cringes and shakes his head as a man approaches the bar and stands beside me.

"Could I get a whiskey, neat?" the man says to Kieran.

"Gotcha covered," Kieran replies, grabbing a glass.

Finn looks at the bathroom door as if he was expecting Zane to emerge.

"Play along, okay?" Finn's voice says within my head.

"Can I get you another drink, babe?" Finn asks, throwing an arm around my shoulders and pulling me in for an awkward side hug. It takes me a moment to understand that his question is directed at me.

"Uh," I start to say, watching the man grab his drink from the bar, giving us a suspicious glance as he makes his way back to his table. "No, I'm good, thanks?"

Finn pulls his arms back and eyes the bathroom door again. Kieran looks at Finn, then me, then back again, a smirk slowly growing on his face.

"What was that about?" I ask.

"Sorry, he was um… he was just a creep, basically. He was very interested in you. I thought I'd save us all from having to hold back a very angry Siren. I could see that pretending to be your boyfriend was going to be the quickest way to get him to leave."

"Oh, okay."

"Hey Finn," Kieran says. "Can I be the one to tell Zane about you canoodling his girlfriend?"

"Kieran," Finn says with a warning tone. "I'm trying to prevent a bloodbath, not be at the center of one."

"Bloodbath?" Zane's voice asks. He has suddenly reappeared over Finn's shoulder.

Finn and Kieran both flinch at the sound of Zane's voice.

"What?" Kieran asks.

"Shit," Finn says under his breath.

"You okay there, mate?" Zane asks.

"Hold on." Finn holds his hand up as his brows furrow. "This isn't right. It's way too quiet in here."

"Yeah, you said that before," I say.

"Because it's quieter than it should be for a room with this many people."

"Shit," Kieran says, his eyes widening.

"The only way that makes any sense is if…" Zane says with a pause.

"*If,*" Finn continues telepathically, "*about half of them are demons.*"

50

 ZANE

"Alright," I say, turning to Ava. "You guys wanna head to dinner then?"

I do my best to keep a calm demeanor and expression, even as I feel my blood pressure rise. It's one thing to bring Ava into a situation with one might-be-rogue demon, it's another entirely to bring her into a bar full of demons.

Ava's eyes are wide and questioning, but she nods silently.

"Well, then," Finn says with a surprisingly convincing air of calm. "I guess this is where we leave you, Kieran. Enjoy the rest of your night!"

Kieran says his goodbyes and I loop an arm around Ava, guiding her out.

"That phone thing is still on, right?" I ask.

"Yep," she says.

"Good."

If we have to be surrounded by demons, then I'm glad I at least have a way of keeping track of Ava if we're separated. Just the thought of someone taking her anywhere away from me makes me sick.

We get to my car and I invite Finn to follow us to our place.

"Oh my god," Ava says after a few minutes of driving in silence. "Why were there so many demons at Pike's? Are they always there?"

"I have no idea," I say. "It's not always easy to tell if someone's Immortal, demon, or human. There are some tricks, some are better than others at detecting things like that, but Finn's gifts are the only ones that could hone in on that sort of thing so easily."

"So is it safe to say one of our new demon friends is behind these mysterious killings?" Finn's voice asks in my head.

"Okay, that's really freaky," Ava says. "You're driving another car for Christ sakes!"

Based on her reaction, I take it he's talking to the both of us telepathically.

"Yeah," I say. "I think that's a safe assumption. Though I have no idea what kind of demons they are. But if there were that many, odds are at least one is an Incubus or Succubus."

"There are other kinds?" Ava asks.

"Oh sure… Ale, Shayatin, the Furies…"

Ava's eyes widen and her heart rate quickens.

Finn, God damn it, stop scaring her.

"Demons aren't all bad," Finn says. *"It's just… that many in one room without any logic or reason… it's not a good sign."*

"Can't be too careful," I add.

"Yeah…" she says softly.

———•———

Twenty minutes later, we reach the penthouse and we bring Finn up in the elevator.

"Well, that was interesting," he says as we head inside the apartment. "Got to admit, that's not how I saw this expedition panning out. We come in with Kieran being our only lead, Ava gets an answer from Kieran out of the gate, and we find ourselves up to our feckin' eyeballs in demons. I don't know about you lot but I've got more questions now than when we started."

"Same," I say, tugging at my hair. "I don't know what to make of it. What the hell are so many demons doing in Port Charlotte?"

"I'm pretty sure they didn't come for the quality theater," Finn jokes.

I look to Ava, who has been suspiciously quiet for the last ten minutes or so.

"Are you alright, love?" I ask. Normally I would try to ask privately, but we all know there's no privacy when it comes to Finn.

"Yeah, I um…" she mutters. "My stomach is hurting. Would you mind?"

"Not at all," I say, putting my hand to her cheek. "Your stomach feels fine. Everything feels fine."

Her expression notably softens and her muscles seem to relax.

"Thanks," she says softly.

"Nifty use of your powers, there," Finn says.

I nod. We spend another few minutes discussing possible explanations as to why all these demons are in town. None of them really make sense. I finally decide to text the only person who might be able to make sense of this: Kami.

AVA

I wake up to Zane's hand brushing hair out of my face. Nausea overwhelms me and my skin feels like it's on fire. The memory of last night hits me and thoughts of demons flood to the surface.

"Baby," Zane's voice says. "Are you sure you're okay alone today? I don't have to go to this appointment."

Appointment?

"My brain can't function this early," I say groggily. "What appointment?"

"It's 1 pm," he says with a chuckle. "I'm meeting with my accountant, remember? It's Friday."

"Oh yeah."

I totally don't remember.

"Go," I say. "I'll be home all day, anyway. No demons followed us home, Zane."

He nods and I let my eyes close again.

After a few minutes, the loud buzzing of my phone wakes me up. I fumble aimlessly until my hand finds the source and I look at the screen.

It's Jen. I completely forgot—I wanted to finally talk to her about Shayna today.

I raise the phone to my ear and answer the call.

"Hey," I say, my voice sounding faded and drowsy.

"Heyyyy," Jen's voice says over the line. "Where have you been? I've called you like eight times!"

I look at my phone again and sure enough, there are a bunch of missed calls from Jen.

"Shit, sorry, I slept in."

"Slept in?" she asks. "Geez, girl! It's 2 in the afternoon!"

I look at the time and, sure enough, it's 2:18 pm.

Crap.

"Did you still want me to come over today?" she asks.

I sit up in bed, rubbing my eyes, and I feel instantly woozy. The room spins and

I find myself falling back onto the bed.

This is just great.

"What?" I ask. "Could you repeat the question?"

"Are you okay, hon?" she asks.

"I'm fine."

"Bullshit," she says. "Is Zane with you?"

"Uh, no… he's at a thing."

"Alright, I'm coming over," she says. "You sound like crap."

"Well, that's not a very nice thing to say," I whine.

"Don't sound like crap and I won't tell you that you sound like crap."

I grunt in frustration.

"Do you have the address?" I ask.

"Yeah, you sent it the other day, remember?"

"Okay, um," I say, trying to pull my focus off the spinning ceiling above me. "The front desk guy can show you how to get up here. Tell him you're here to visit me."

"Okay," she says. "Just take care of yourself and I'll be there soon."

With that, I end the call and my view of the ceiling blurs before fading to black.

ZANE

"So I need you to initial here," my accountant says.

I get it, okay. This is the fifteenth fucking thing you've needed me to initial.

My mind drifts back to the events of last night. If there are so many demons in town, why are they at Pike's? And what are they doing here in town in the first place?

I've always been terrified that pulling Ava into my world would put her in danger, but this was something I hadn't accounted for. If we had never met, she'd still be at risk just living in Port Charlotte, maybe even more at risk.

I'm wondering if I passed over the mark idea too quickly. With all the crime and subterfuge in this town, maybe it *is* the best way to keep her safe.

My phone vibrates and, as I pull it from my pocket, the accountant gives me a judgmental, side-eyed look.

So help me, I will break this wanker in half if he says a word about me answering my phone.

I'm paying you to be here and bore me to death with your forms, and you're going to give me a bloody hard time over taking a call?

The screen lights up with Jen's name.

What?

Last I heard, Jen was still trying not to kick me in the bollocks every time she saw me. Now she's calling me for a chat?

If Jen's calling me…

My heart drops and I feel a violent gnawing in the pit of my stomach.

Something's wrong.

Something happened.

"Hello?" I answer, standing up out of my chair.

"Zane?" Jen asks. Her voice is high and breathy.

Fuck.

"What happened?" I ask, already assuming the worst.

"It's Ava," she says.

Her two words have me rushing for the door. The accountant is visibly flustered and attempts to follow me.

"Excuse me, Mr. Smith," he says. "You can't just le-"

A low rumbling growl erupts from my chest and my eyes must be flashing green because he stumbles backward in terror. I tear down the stairwell at full speed.

"Something's wrong with her," Jen says in a shaky voice. "When I showed up, she didn't remember even inviting me over and she couldn't stay awake. We're at the hospital. They won't tell me what's going on, they just took her back and now I'm just stuck in the waiting room and they're asking me all these questions and…"

"Which hospital?" I ask.

"Blackwell Memorial," she says.

My mind goes into a state of shock and it seems as if my body is operating on autopilot. I'm in my car before I know it and speeding to the hospital.

If the police want to ticket me for speeding, they'll have to follow me to the bloody hospital.

———

When I arrive, Jen is clearly in the midst of an argument with the woman at the front desk.

"I know that's what her record says, but I'm telling you it's an old record and you should under no circumstances call him," she says loudly. "I don't care if it's procedure, I…"

She spots me walking in and points to me.

"Actually, that's him right there," she says. "Mike, come over here."

I shudder upon being called by that scumbag's name.

What the fuck, Jen? I know she's still angry at me but that was uncalled for.

"Mike," Jen repeats as I walk up to the desk. "They were insisting on calling *you* because *you're* on record as her in case of emergency person and I was telling her that you and Ava broke up, but they apparently won't tell me shit. They will only talk to *you, Mike.*"

It bothers me to no end that he's still listed on her medical record, but I can hardly feel anything but panic right now. I reach across the desk and grab the woman's arm.

"Listen to me," I say before she can try to pull away. "You're going to tell me what's wrong with Ava and where she is. Right now."

51

Every inch of my skin is throbbing along with my heartbeat. I feel like I have the worst hangover of my life.

I try to remember if I drank very much last night.

What did I do last night? The bar with Kieran and Finn… was that last night? I only had one drink.

Why does the bed feel so uncomfortable?

I feel like our mattress was replaced with a lumpy bale of hay.

I try to pry my eyes open and am finding it harder than usual. As I do, the light seems unbearably bright and my dry eyes sting.

The room is white and unfamiliar, with styrofoam ceiling tiles like the ones you'd find in a dreary office building. I try to turn my neck to look around, but it's stiff and achy.

Where the hell am I?

My eyes catch the top of a light blue paisley-print curtain. Unfortunately, there's only one type of place that has curtains that garish.

Fuck.

"Ava?" a soft voice asks.

Jen's face appears over me. My vision is still slightly blurry and adjusting. Her voice was so shaky and weak, I almost didn't recognize it.

"Jen?" I ask. My voice is rough and dry.

"It's okay, hon," she says. "You're in the hospital. You're gonna be okay. We're here for you."

"We?"

I'm hoping she doesn't mean Zane. Being in the hospital and looking like death is bad enough when your boyfriend isn't an immortal paragon of hotness.

"Tell me you didn't call Zane," I say.

"Ahem…" Zane clears his throat.

I strain my neck a little further to see him standing in the corner.

Fuck my life.

"Hey," I say awkwardly.

I examine his face as he takes a step toward me. His eyes are bloodshot with dark circles beneath them. His hair is tousled and his white button-up shirt is untucked and wrinkled.

He looks devastated.

What the heck happened? Did I pass out during something important?

This is so embarrassing.

"What happened?" I ask.

"You um…" Jen says, her voice shaking.

I've never seen Jen this distraught. That doesn't bode well for whatever she's about to say.

"When I got to your place, you…" she continues. "You wouldn't wake up. You were barely conscious and disoriented. You tried to talk but you weren't making any sense. I had to get you to the hospital."

I sit up slightly, groaning in pain as I do.

A man with dark skin and a beard enters the room. Judging by the white coat, I think it's safe to assume he's my doctor.

"Hi, Ava," he says. "I'm Dr. Ellison. How are you feeling?"

"Um," I say. "Pretty bad. Everything hurts. My stomach especially."

"That's to be expected. You've experienced acute hepatic failure—liver failure. It's likely something you've taken or ingested. Have you recently taken any unusual medications or substances?"

"I already gave them your medications list," Jen says.

Jen is a godsend.

"Um, no, not really," I say. "Besides my usual prescriptions."

"Your friend said you recently stopped an experimental medication, Lornalaprozem?"

"Um, yeah. The doctor didn't tell me it was experimental, but yeah."

The doctor raises an eyebrow at me before continuing.

"Well, that drug can be rough on your liver. It could certainly be worse in combination with other medications, even if you stopped taking it for a while."

Of course. That just figures.

"Do you drink much?" he asks.

"Not much," I say. "I had one drink last night."

"Thursday," Zane corrects. He looks to me and adds, "It's Saturday morning."

I've been unconscious for over a day? Crap.

"What about acetaminophen? It's also known as Tylenol or Paracetamol?"

"Uh, yeah," I say. "I'm not sure how many. I take them for pain."

"Hmm…" the doctor says, narrowing his eyes. "That's one of the most common causes of liver failure we see, actually. If you don't remember how many you've taken, it's likely you took more than you should've. The good news is we've already got you on the right medication for it. Now we just have to wait and see if it works."

"Wha-… why did you say *if?*" I ask.

"We have to take it case by case. Everyone responds differently and your case is very advanced. Most people experience extreme nausea and pain before it ever gets to this stage. Unfortunately, for whatever reason, you didn't get the normal symptoms until the liver failure had progressed."

Zane clenches his jaw and his eyes fall to the floor.

I immediately know what he's thinking—that this is his fault. That using his powers to take away my pain has somehow hurt me.

"So if this treatment doesn't work…?" I ask.

"Well, um…" the doctor says. "We have other options, but not many. We're going to do everything we can for you. I wouldn't give up yet."

What?

"What do you mean?" I ask. "I feel like you're saying that like I'm going to die or something."

The doctor's face is serious as he stays silent for a moment.

"Am I dying?" I ask.

"Not… I…" he stumbles. "The treatment could still work. We just have to wait and see right now."

Jen and Zane both have disturbingly serious expressions. This must be news they've already been given.

"You really shouldn't be taking so many medications," the doctor says. "You're young, you're healthy, you don't need all this."

"Um… no," I say. "I'm not healthy. I have chronic pain and I get dizzy a lot and nauseous. My doctors have been working on figuring it out, they just don't have a diagnosis yet."

"Uh huh," he says. "Well, you know, sometimes just getting sunshine can be really good for you. It's certainly a lot better for you than all those drugs."

Oh good. Why thanks, Doctor Know-It-All. You just told me I'm fucking dying, but glad to hear that sunshine can fix all my problems.

"What?" Zane says to the doctor.

"Well," the doctor says, "a lot of times these things are really just emotional problems."

"Emotional problems?" he asks, his voice getting louder.

"Well, the body is just very interconnected and women can be particularly sensitive."

"Really? Did you just say women are overly sensitive?" Zane asks.

"I didn't mean it that way."

"I think you did," Zane says, his eyes shifting to green. "You're telling her that her problems aren't real. Why would you say that? You think she's popping anti-inflammatories recreationally?"

"No, sir, I…"

Zane quickly grabs the man's arm in his hand.

"Don't talk," he says. "Here's what you're going to do… You're going to get us the best doctor in this damn hospital and you're going to insist they come down here and handle her case because you're too bloody incompetent. You got that?"

The doctor nods and quietly leaves the room.

"Wow," Jen says. "You told that dick! I didn't even have to bust out my slappin' hand."

"You two are bad influences on each other," I scold.

"You think I'm going to let him talk to you like that, baby?" he asks.

I smirk and shrug. I don't really know what else I expected of him.

"Should I go grab Kami?" Jen says to me. "She's in the cafeteria. She's going to want to know you're up."

"Kami too?" I ask. "You guys, I don't want everyone making a big deal out of me. This is so embarrassing."

"Tough shit, whoreball. Lots of people love you so just shut up and accept our love."

With that, Jen makes her way out the door, blowing me a kiss before rounding the corner.

"So…" I say to Zane. "You don't have to stay here, I'm sure you have bet-"

Before I can register what's happening, Zane is beside me, our lips colliding.

"I'm not going anywhere," he says, pulling away just slightly and letting his forehead rest against my own, "but we need to talk."

"About what?" I ask.

You mean about me possibly dying? Pshh… That's no big deal.

Except it is. It's kind of the biggest deal.

Fuck my life.

"I can't lose you," he says.

His eyes are so close to mine that I can hardly focus, but I can still read the pain in them.

I try to run through the options, but only one comes immediately to mind. I never imagined having any part of this conversation, yet here I am about to say the words.

"Is immortality still on the table?"

52

I can't believe I'm actually considering this.

Fuck.

Ava is resting in her hospital bed. Her usually pink-speckled skin is dull and sallow, her delicate arms are covered with tape. She's tethered by tangled tubes and wires to beeping machines. Every element in this room is a reminder of the absurd fragility of human life.

Kami walks in with an iPad and closes the door, locking it behind her.

"Okay," she says softly. "I got the deets from Alek and he has a whole book on it."

Ava's eyes flutter open and she adjusts slightly to sit up. I stand and prop a pillow behind her back.

"Who's Alek?" Ava asks.

"He's a Siren friend of ours," Kami says. "He did the mark with his partner and he's got tons of info on it."

"You said he has a book?" I ask.

"Yeah, he scanned it for me." She holds up the iPad and waves it in the air. She hands it to me and I see a page of an old book, all in Greek.

"You know my Greek is terrible," I say. "You're gonna have to translate for me."

"Pshhh… okay," she says, grabbing the tablet out of my hands. "Well this says something like 'humans who are bonded to a Siren by blood are nearly immortal.' Blah blah blah… Ahh, here we go. How do I say this in English?… Basically, injuries are healed by the bond, but illnesses of the body are not."

"What counts as an illness of the body?" Ava asks.

"This seems to imply things that involve the body reacting to itself and imbalances. It's hard to really understand because they're talking about a lot of ancient medical concepts that we know now are definitely wrong. Like, they're talking about having too much blood—that's not a thing."

Ava chuckles softly.

"From what I can gather, the Siren blood will heal any wounds caused by outside things."

"Mmkay," I say. "What else?"

"So she won't be able to die until you do. When you die, she will become mortal again."

I feel insane even entertaining this idea, but I can't help but feel pleased with the idea of an immortal lifetime with Ava.

"It says the first year is particularly intense," Kami explains. "The body takes time to adapt to the bond. In the first weeks, the connection will be overwhelmingly strong, then over time you will become used to it."

"So what does that mean?" I ask.

"Well, Alek said that for them, they could feel the emotions and physical sensations experienced by the other person. Alek also said he felt particularly primal and was more possessive over David."

"*More* possessive?" Ava asks.

"Thanks, love," I say dryly.

She does have a point, though. I already find myself tensing every time someone looks twice at her. I've always been so good at fighting back those instincts, but now that I'm with Ava I can't help but want her to myself.

"They said it's weird initially but it starts to feel normal after a while," Kami says. "Plus I guess now David heals from injuries a bit faster, which is a nice perk."

"I'll take what I can get in that department," Ava jokes.

"Are you sure you want to do this?" I ask Ava.

Kami looks back and forth between us for a moment before handing me the iPad.

"Well you kids talk this over," she says. "I have a couple errands to run anyway."

She slips out quietly and leaves just me and Ava alone to discuss.

"Is this what you want?" I ask.

"What about you?" she asks. "This decision involves both of us."

I've wanted Ava since the moment I met her, even if I spent the majority of those first weeks denying it to myself. I can't imagine a life without her. The one time I tried, I demolished my entire apartment and drowned my sorrows in alcohol and lethe.

There has never been any point in pretending Ava is anything but the only person for me.

"I would do anything for you, love," I say. "I'm afraid of the risks. This is still something we don't fully understand. But the risks of mortality are seeming greater by the day."

Ava ponders for a moment before giving me a slight nod.

"What about your wings?" she asks. "They're a part of you."

"So are you," I say. "I can live without my wings. I can't live without you."

She gives me a sly smile as a slight blush washes over her face.

"Are *you* sure this is what you want?" I ask.

"I feel like it's the best option at this point."

"How romantic," I joke.

"I don't mean it like that. I mean, we already know we're soulmates. I know I love you. And being an immortal sounds pretty freakin' cool. I just wish there was a way to do this without all the complications."

"Well then, it's settled. I could never deny my baby anything she wants."

———◆———

AVA

We arrive at the parking structure of our building and Zane pulls his Challenger into one of our parking spots. Before I can even unbuckle my seatbelt, he's at the passenger side door, opening it and scooping me up from my seat.

"What are you doing?" I ask. "I can still walk, you know."

"If you think I'm letting you out of my arms while you're ill, you're mad," he says with a grin.

"You're ridiculous. When I'm immortal, I'm gonna kick your butt."

"Doesn't work like that, love. You may be immortal soon but you'll still punch like a kitten."

"Okay first off," I say as he carries me into the elevator. "Kittens have claws so they can scratch the shit out of you—don't disrespect kittens."

He chuckles in response as I attempt fruitlessly to wriggle out of his hold. I swear if someone else gets in this elevator and he still insists on carrying me, I'm going to claw him myself.

"Secondly, you don't know. Maybe I'll be different and get super strength."

"Okay, love," he says. "Sure. When you get your super strength, you go right ahead and kick my arse. Until then, though, fighting me is pretty pointless."

I let out a sigh of resignation and surrender.

I really shouldn't be surprised that fighting a hulking superhuman wasn't working out for me.

We arrive at the top floor and the elevator doors part to reveal Kami standing at our doorway with a large brown woven bag.

"Okay kids, let's do this thing," she says as we make our way inside.

"You're far too enthusiastic about this," Zane says, setting me down on the couch. "Should I be concerned about how eager you are to come at me with a knife?"

"We're doing this with a knife?" I ask.

"Yep," Kami explains. "Not a lot can cut through a Siren's wings."

"That's super intense. Are we sure this is a good idea?" I ask. "Isn't that going to be really painful?"

"I've fought in wars, been attacked by demons," Zane says.

"Got your butt kicked by a Minotaur," Kami adds.

"Yes, thanks for that, Kam," he says. "My point is, yes it will hurt a little, but I've handled much worse."

I sigh and nod.

"Okay then," I say. "If you're sure."

"You're the one thing I've always been sure of." He gives me a kiss on the forehead.

I feel the blood rushing to my cheeks at his sweet gesture.

"Why not give her a kiss on the lips?" Kami says.

"Do I really have to explain why that's not a good idea right now?" Zane says.

"I'm not an idiot, Z. I'm saying if she's already affected by venom then we'll know when it's working because the effect will go away."

"Oh," he says, looking back at me.

"Sure," I say. "Makes sense."

He reluctantly leans in and kisses me on the lips.

My body is instantly flooded with a feeling of euphoria and arousal. As he pulls away, I find myself trying to pull him back in, but as usual I fail to overpower him.

"Feeling affected, love?" he asks.

"Um, yep," I say with an embarrassed giggle.

"Alright, Kam, let's get this shit over with."

Zane rips his shirt off and I'm instantly distracted by his body.

What were we doing again?

Kami pulls a rather large, double-edged knife out of her bag and I'm suddenly shocked back to the reality of what we're about to do.

"Do I actually have to drink his blood?" I ask, feeling squeamish.

Is this really happening in my life right now?

"I brought mixers," Kami says, holding up a bottle of juice and a bottle of margarita mix.

That seems worse somehow.

I see a large shadow appear in my periphery and I turn to see Zane's wings spread.

Okay, it's official: my life is batshit crazy.

"Alright then," Kami says, grabbing the knife. "Um, I guess, uh… how should we do this? Maybe kneel?"

"You alright, Kam?" Zane asks, kneeling with his back facing her.

"Okay, Z, I'm a little freaked out here. It's not every day you chop off someone's wings."

Zane lets out a laugh.

"Is this the same woman who disemboweled that demon while he was still alive?"

I'm not even gonna ask.

"Yeah, yeah," she says. "Shut up unless you wanna be disemboweled too."

She takes in a deep breath before bringing the knife down in a clean, swift motion. The sound of the blade ripping through tissue is nauseating. Before I can even process it, his large black wing falls and she grabs it with her other hand.

"Argghh fuck!" Zane yells.

I'm stunned silent by the quickness of it all.

"Are you okay?" I ask Zane.

His eyes are pinched shut, but he looks up at me and smiles.

"I'm alright, love," he says, his voice slightly strained. "I promise, I can handle this."

I sigh with relief, but the sensation doesn't last long when I see Kami pouring a black fluid from the core of his wing into a cup.

Oh fuck no.

"Mixer preference?" she asks.

This is so gross.

I try to remind myself of all the disgusting medicines I've had to stomach over the years, but I can't think of anything that grosses me out more than this right now.

"Orange juice," I say, trying not to think of it much longer.

I look over to Zane who is still kneeling on the floor, one wing folded at his back. I feel so wrong about this. I'm to blame for hurting him, even if I'm not the one who held the blade.

"Don't," he says.

"Don't what?"

"I know the look you make when you're blaming yourself for something," he says. "As someone brilliant once told me, the person who knows what's best for me is me. I don't want you to protect me."

He gives me a knowing smirk.

"Oh shut up," I say. "You can't use my own words against me! That's cheating!"

"Yeah but you're feeling a little less bad for me, aren't you?"

I give him a glare as Kami hands me a glass of brown liquid.

I really shouldn't have looked at it.

Before my brain is allowed to think too much, I down it in one go.

That wasn't so bad, really. It's like metallic orange juice.

Except it's blood.

Oh god, eww.

Just stop thinking about it.

EWWWW.

I find myself coughing and gagging at the thought.

I try to stand up to go get water, but Kami appears with a glass at the perfect moment. I drink it down with a fervor.

Zane appears beside me, looking deeply concerned.

"How do you feel?" he asks.

"Like a little pathetic bitch of a vampire," I say. "I am not cut out for the blood-drinking life."

He carefully examines my face and smiles slightly.

"What?" I ask.

"Your eyes, they're not dilated anymore," he says.

"And your skin is getting its color back," Kami says.

Zane takes my hand and turns it over to examine my wrist. His eyes narrow and he brings up the other wrist to investigate.

"I don't see it," he says.

"See what?" I ask.

"The mark," he says. "It's supposed to show on your wrist."

"Maybe it's just obscured by the flower tattoo," Kami says, pointing to the ink on my right wrist.

"Maybe," he says.

As I look down at my tattoo to inspect it myself, Zane loses his footing and falls backward with a slight groan.

"Are you okay?" I ask.

"Your balance is probably thrown off from having just one wing," Kami says.

"ARHH," he groans loudly. "FUCK!"

"What's wrong?" I ask. "Are you okay? Is it hurting? Do you need venom to heal you?"

He lets out a loud, inhuman screech.

"What's happening?" I ask Kami, whose expression has morphed into one of concern and fear.

"I don't know," she says, trying to tend to Zane as his cries grow louder. "This isn't supposed to happen. Something's wrong."

53

Zane attempts to stand, but barely makes a step before he's reeling in pain. His remaining wing flaps erratically and he collapses into a nearby chair.

I jump up and rush to his side, placing a comforting hand on his shoulder.

"Talk to me," I say. "What's happening?"

"I don't know… fuck!" he groans. "It… fuck!"

"Do we need to heal him?" I ask Kami. Her usually unshakable demeanor is replaced by a frenzied panic.

"We haven't… the other wing… I'm not ready… I haven't set aside venom for him, I…" she stutters.

"Just kiss him, Kami," I say. "I don't care, I promise! Just help him!"

Kami nods and leans in to kiss him. Without warning, Zane sweeps an arm across and throws her backward across the room.

"No!" he shouts. "Don't fucking touch me!"

She manages to land on her feet in a crouching position, a bright flare of gold appearing in her eyes.

"What the fuck, Zane?" she asks.

"No one…" he says through labored breaths, "but Ava… kisses me."

"You're being ridiculous," I say to him, as Kami begrudgingly grabs a shot glass and fills it with venom. "I said I don't care. It's fine. You're in pain."

"Well I do care," he says. He grunts as he attempts to sit up further and Kami hands him the glass of venom and he downs it.

"Okay," he says. "That's definitely much grosser than the kissing."

"That's your own damn fault, Z," Kami says with an eye roll. "Feeling better?"

He turns around and his wound seals as he pulls his remaining wing back in.

"Fuck," he says. "Not really. Ahhh!"

He hisses in pain and lets out a spree of curse words, only half of which I've even heard before.

"Zane, talk to me," I say, holding his face in my hands. "What are you feeling? What's going on?

"It… fuck. It's like my nerves are on fire," he says.

"Where?"

"Everywhere—my skin, my muscles… fuck, I swear it's in my bones too."

Unfortunately, I know that feeling too well.

He tries to stand and staggers before dropping back into the chair.

"Can you not walk?" I ask.

"Bloody hell," he says. "I don't know… my vision is spinning and my head is throbbing. Is this what happens to humans when they get hung over?"

"Depends on the human."

Personally, I feel like that all the time.

"Maybe it's a side effect," Kami asks.

Wait…

I feel like this all the time.

"Crap," I mumble under my breath.

"What's wrong, baby?" he asks, dropping to his knees to be closer to me.

"I think this might be my fault."

He's feeling like shit because he's experiencing what I'm feeling. I should've known better. Kami practically said this would happen and I didn't listen.

I start sobbing and before I know it, I'm hyperventilating.

"Baby, look at me," he says softly, grabbing my hand. "It's okay. This is not your fault."

"But it is!" I sob.

Zane's eyes widen and his mouth falls open. Kami looks at me with the same expression.

"What?" I ask through choked breaths.

"Zane told you it wasn't your fault," Kami says in a faint voice.

"I know, but it is," I say, sniffling. "That's what I'm trying to say."

"No, baby," he says. "You should've believed me. I was touching you; you should have been charmed by that."

"It worked," she says.

Wait… *what?*

"I'm… I'm immune to your charm power?"

"It looks that way," he says.

I feel a stabbing feeling in my stomach. He sucks in a heavy breath as if he feels it too. Tears run down my face again.

"Listen, I understand you feeling guilty, but this isn't your fault."

"But it is," I say. "It's literally me—it's my pain you're experiencing."

"Wha-…" Zane starts to speak, but stops, as a knowing look washes over his face. "*This* is what you're feeling?"

"I'm so sorry! I didn't mean to do this to you. I didn't realize… I should have."

He grabs my face in his hands, firmer this time.

"Listen to me, love," he says. "I'm not blaming you. I didn't lie when I said I could handle pain, I just… didn't know you had been handling so much."

"I'm sor-"

"Don't you dare," he says. "I'm the one who's sorry. I'm sorry you're in so much pain."

"That…" Kami says. "What he's feeling… That's what you're feeling?"

"Yeah," I say.

"So, if it worked," she asks, "where is your mark?"

I look down at my wrists and see a few faint lines hidden underneath the ink of my tattoo that weren't there before.

"There," I say, pointing to my wrist. "It's hidden beneath my tattoo."

Kami flops down into a nearby armchair.

"Well I need a drink," she says.

"Bloody hell," Zane replies. "I'm gonna need about 80."

———◦———

Kami and I sit in the kitchen while Zane is resting in bed.

"So I had a little surprise that I thought would be fun after this but," Kami says, "I'm not sure it's a good idea now."

"A surprise? For who?" I ask.

"Mostly for Zane," she says, "but he's not dealing with things as well as I'd expected."

"I feel so bad."

"Don't. Men are just big babies. He'll learn to deal. If anything I'm just really looking forward to him having to experience 'that time of the month' with you."

"What's the surprise?" I ask.

"I asked Alek and David to fly in," she says. "I thought it would be nice to have a little cocktail party for you guys and give you a chance to hang with another Siren-and-marked-human couple. But he seems relatively under the weather."

"How about we do something smaller?" I ask. "They can come over here and we can just order pizza or something and hang out—something low-key. That way Zane can still rest but he gets to see his friends."

"Hmm," she says, as though she has just encountered the concept of low-key for the first time. "I guess we could do that. I'll text them, let them know there's a change of plans."

———◦———

I let Zane know we were going to have some people coming by, so he drank a bit of vodka to dull the pain and made his way into the living room.

"Hey," I say. "How're you feeling?"

"Apparently I'm feeling how you're feeling," he says with a fatigued smile.

"Very funny. You know what I mean."

"She means to ask, how are you coping with what she—a human—handles every day like a fucking champ?" Kami chimes in, putting out a spread of cheese and crackers.

"Ouch," he says. "That's cold."

"Yeah, well, you threw me against the wall earlier, so you'll have to forgive if I'm a little unsympathetic."

"Yeah, er," he says, tugging at his hair between his fingers. "Sorry about that. I'm not really sure why I did that."

"Don't think I won't get you back for that, by the way," she says, narrowing her eyes.

Zane and Kami both turn their attention to the door, and a moment later we hear a knock. Zane seems skeptical over who our surprise guests could be.

Kami opens the door to reveal a stunning man, well over six feet tall, with wide shoulders, a flawless dark-brown complexion, and a shaved head. Beside him stands a much-scrawnier man with pale skin and short, dark brown hair. In comparison, he looks remarkably plain.

It isn't hard to tell which one of them is the Siren.

Oh god. Is that what I look like next to Zane?

Kami welcomes them inside and Zane seems pleasantly surprised, getting up from the couch to greet them.

"Oi, who invited these cunts?" Zane asks with a smile.

The giant man, who I assume is Alek, holds out his hands for a hug.

"C'mere ya cranky ol' git," he says in a deep British accent, pulling him in for a hug.

"This your girl?" Alek asks, gesturing toward me.

"Yep," he says. "Alek, this is Ava."

"So great to finally meet you, Miss Ava," Alek says, giving me a hug as well.

Zane lets out a low, rumbling growl.

"Ahh, so you're at the 'I'm going to kill everyone who touches my partner' stage," Alek says with a laugh. "Adorable."

Zane rolls his eyes and glares at him.

"This is my love, David," he says, pulling David in to his side.

We exchange introductions and David opts for a handshake, which only seems to irritate Zane mildly.

"I never thought I'd see the day Zane found his match," Alek says with a smile. "She's beautiful by the way—far too good for you, mate."

"That's a proper fact, right there," Zane says, kissing me on the cheek.

"Oi, c'mon then, you didn't go through all this so you could kiss her on the cheek. Give her a proper kiss."

Zane looks to me with trepidation.

I just go for it, leaning in and kissing him on the lips. I don't feel the instantaneous high, but I still find myself enraptured and wanting more. I guess he doesn't need venom to have that effect on me.

As he pulls away and opens his eyes, he seems genuinely surprised.

"I can't believe I can do that all the time, now," he says with a huge smile. He goes in for another long kiss.

"Aww," Alek says. "Okay, stud, how bout you let her up for air now, ay? Humans still need oxygen you know."

Zane's lips part from mine and I find myself unable to tear my eyes from his. He's still just as captivating as ever.

We chat for a while before David pulls me aside to talk on the patio.

"So how does it feel?" he asks.

"Kind of crazy," I say. "After the whole marking, I was really expecting him to be less… I dunno…"

"Stupidly hot?"

"Yeah," I say with a chuckle. "I wasn't sure how much of it was his powers and stuff."

"I know what you mean. Sirens, they just can't help it. Everything they do is intoxicating."

"Do you ever feel…"

"Like a basic bitch?" he asks.

I giggle at his comment.

"Pretty much," I say. "I mean, how do you even begin to have self-esteem when you're around these Greek gods all the time?"

He laughs.

"I know what you mean," he says. "But a man doesn't cut off his wings for you because he sees you as anything less than perfect. Remember that. It's a big deal to them. Culturally, it's saying that they've chosen you as their one lover for life. Most Sirens could never fathom having just one partner for even a few months, let alone for life."

It hits me just how big of a deal that is—and how much Zane must love me to have even considered it. He puts on a cool, unaffected act, but I should have considered that this meant more than I realized.

"Wow…" I say. "I never really thought about it that way."

"But I guess your Zane has never been a 'normal Siren', has he?" he says.

"So they tell me."

"You know, if you want, there are a few tricks I could teach you."

"Tricks?"

"Yeah, you know, these beautiful bastards can still be brought to their knees every once in a while."

I can't help but delight at the idea.

"For instance, you know how he can feel everything you feel now?" he says.

"Yeah…"

"Well, if you feel something good, he'll feel something good."

I nod, pretending like I understand what he means so I don't look super naïve. He chuckles to himself.

"When you touch yourself, your partner feels the sensation," he explains.

I guess my nod wasn't very convincing.

"Oh, and if you want to drive him really wild," he adds. "You know the spot where his wings would come out?"

I nod.

"Dig your nails into his skin there," he says. "They're ultra-sensitive there, especially without their wings."

"But wouldn't that hurt?" I ask.

"Babe, you literally can't hurt him. You're immortal now but you're still not a Siren. You could punch him in the face and he would hardly feel it."

"Are we talking about punching Zane in the face?" Kami asks, walking out to join us on the balcony.

"Yep," David says.

"Good," she says. "I call first dibs."

54

 ZANE

Kieran walks up to my table on the restaurant patio. He's wearing ultra-tight, distressed grey jeans, black trainers, and a black shirt with cut-off sleeves. The shirt is emblazoned with big white text that says "I like my men how I like my women."

"Alright, Z-Man, care to explain to me why you had me meet you at fuckin' House of Soup here?" he asks, pointing to the restaurant sign with a laugh.

He takes a seat across from me and his eyes narrow as he looks at me.

"Okay, yeah, I was already pretty confused by your choice of restaurant, but that creepy-ass smile on your face is giving me the heebie-jeebies. Why are you in such a good mood? Is the soup spiked? Is it people?" he asks.

"Oh my god!" he yells, far louder than anyone should in a restaurant. "THE SOUP IS PEOPLE!"

I grab his wrist and shoot him a glare.

"Stop being a knob, mate."

"Damn!" he exclaims. "You're getting really strong. Somebody's been eating their Wheaties!"

"Why did I agree to hang out with you again?" I say with a smile.

"Probably because your girlfriend is busy."

"Good point."

"Speaking of which… you… smell different."

"And that has something to do with Ava being busy?"

"You smell like her," he says. "Like a lot. And not just in the usual way of having been constantly up in that pussy."

A growl resonates from deep in my throat and my hand finds its way instantly around his throat, tightening as I pull him toward me.

"You talk about Ava like that again and I'll free your eyeballs from your skull."

"Whoa!" he says, his voice strained under the pressure of my grip. "Shit, Zane, you're… really… fuck… can I breathe, please?"

"Technically you don't need to breathe," I say as I release him.

"Okay, man, but I do consider it a personal preference," he says, coughing slightly. "Damn, being with Ava has turned you into The Hulk. A really grumpy, territorial Hulk."

He rubs his throat and takes a sip of my water.

Shit. Maybe he's got a point. That was a bit of an intense reaction, even for me.

"Fair dues," I say. "Er, sorry. I uh… may be affected by uh… the marking."

Kieran chokes mid-drink and coughs water onto the table.

"What??" he shrieks. "You did it? You did the mark thing? No fuckin' way!"

"Yes fuckin' way," I say. "Ava ended up getting really sick and, well, long story short, it's done."

"Damn!" he says. "That's why you smell like Ava, then? And why you're so damn cheery? Minus the trying to squeeze my head off, of course."

"Maybe," I say, feeling a smirk stretch across my face.

Okay, he's right. It feels good. Really good.

She's mine—forever.

"Still doesn't explain the sudden soup interest," he jokes.

"Oh yeah, well… Ava's across the street meeting one of her web design clients," I say, pointing to the coffee shop opposite the restaurant.

"And she needed a chaperone?" he asks.

"No," I say. "I just… the mark has heightened my, er, protective instincts. I just wanted to make sure she was okay. This was as close as she'd agree to let me get."

"Oh shit, you're full-on stalking her?" he asks, snickering.

"I'm not stalking her, wankface," I say.

"Wankface?" he asks. "I like it. I can't decide if it's insulting or sexy. It's perfect."

I roll my eyes. The waitress appears just long enough to hand us the menus and step away again.

"So does this mean I'm totally fucked now?" Kieran asks. "Or rather, *not fucked?*"

"How so?" I ask.

"You've already been crazy attached to the missus. Now that she's marked, I feel like you're never gonna wingman for me anymore," he says. "Then again, I guess you're a wingless man now?"

He laughs at his own joke as I glare at him.

"Technically I still have one," I say. "Things got complicated and I decided to leave it. Feels pretty weird, honestly."

"I wonder if it's like having one testicle."

I ignore his comment in favor of answering his original question.

"If you need my assistance, I'm still here," I say. "Just let me know when."

"Feel like coming by Pike's tonight?" he asks.

"I'm not letting Ava anywhere near Pike's until we figure out why there were so many demons there."

"No offense to Ava, but you could just come by yourself. Or are you afraid you have no game now that you're her lil bitch?" he teases, giving me a knowing smirk.

"You forget who you're talking to," I say. "There's no human on this planet I can't seduce, end of story. Or have you forgotten our bet at Pike's?"

"As I recall, I took her home."

"You fucking cheated!" I say.

"Please, like you were going to step out on your lovergirl anyway."

"We weren't… It wasn't…" I stammer. "That's beside the point. That girl was eating out of the palm of my hand and you know it. I'll show you tonight. Nobody can resist a Siren's charms, I fucking guarantee you."

Kieran's eyes widen as his expression slowly morphs into a concerned and intimidated one.

Took him long enough, but maybe he's finally got it through his thick skull that he's a fool to question a Siren's abilities.

"Excuse me?" a voice says from behind me.

Fuck.

Ava is definitely right behind me.

———•———

AVA

"So what's happening tonight, then?" I ask, my lips pursed and my arms tightly crossed.

"I uh… I didn't mean it like that, love," Zane stutters.

I've never seen such an imposing, tattoo-covered man look quite so submissive.

"We're cruising for chicks at Pike's," Kieran says, fighting back a smirk.

"I hope you're not too attached to breathing after all," Zane threatens.

"Welp," he says. "It's been fun knowing you, Ava."

Zane rolls his eyes.

I can't believe his nerve, talking about how freakin' smooth he is with the ladies after getting so macho over me meeting with a male client.

"I told Kieran I would help him get a meal tonight," Zane says.

"A meal?" I ask.

Aren't they at a restaurant right now?

"His kind of meal," Zane says, raising his eyebrows.

"Oh."

Ohhh.

That kind of meal.

"So you guys are going cruising for chicks then?" I ask.

"Chicks or dicks," Kieran says.

"Chick or dick," Zane says. "Singular. For Kieran."

"If it's for Kieran then why were you talking up your skills so much?" I ask. "I believe your words were 'No one can resist a Siren'?"

"Well, love," he says with a suave voice. "You certainly couldn't resist me."

He pulls me into his lap and goes in for a kiss, but I pull away.

"Remember, love? We can kiss on the lips all the time now."

"Oh I know," I say. "I just don't quite feel like kissing you right now, playboy. Somebody's in need of a serious ego check."

Zane wraps his arms around my waist and kisses my neck.

"If you say so, love," he says.

What an ass.

As he smirks, a devious idea begins to form in the back of my mind.

ZANE

As we walk into Pike's, Kieran is already scanning the room for his prey.

"You're lucky I came with you tonight after what you pulled with Ava earlier," I grumble.

"That's what you think," he says. "I like to think of it as *guaranteeing* you'd come with me."

"How do you figure?"

"Because you're already in the dog house so you have nothing to lose," he says with a chuckle.

"It's a miracle I haven't killed you yet," I say as we each pull up a seat at the bar.

"You know you love me," he says, wrapping an arm around my shoulders.

I roll my eyes as Kieran orders drinks from Shayna.

"So who's on the menu tonight?" I ask.

"I haven't decided yet," he says. "I'm debating if I'm in the mood for a double."

He gestures over to a couple making out in a booth along the wall. The man is tan with a scruffy beard and is wearing a very loose long-sleeve T-shirt and an equally oversized pair of shorts. The woman has bright blond hair with brown roots and is wearing a sweatshirt, tight shorts, and high-heeled boots. Much like her outfit, these two are an odd combination.

"That's what does it for you?" I ask.

"Hey, everyone enjoys a good double dip every once in a while."

Just when I start to remember why I like Kieran, he says disturbing shit like that.

I decide to move on rather than respond to that.

"Threesomes are tricky," I say. "Especially with men. They're not too great with sharing."

"What happened to Mister Irresistible Siren?" he teases.

"Alright," I say. "Challenge accepted."

We grab our drinks and approach the couple and I put my hand on the man's shoulder. He turns to me, pausing their snog session.

"You don't mind if we join you, do you?" I ask.

He gives me a dazed nod as his girlfriend looks confused by his invitation.

"I'm Kieran," Kieran says. "This is my buddy Zane."

"Tim," the man says. "This is my girlfriend, Joss."

Tim puffs up his chest as he emphasizes the word girlfriend. If he's this territorial already, this is going to be a real challenge.

"Nice to meet you," I say, reaching out to shake each of their hands.

"What's your accent from?" the girl asks, slurring slightly from drunkenness.

"England," I say, taking a sip of my drink.

"I've been to London before," the girl says. She begins to drone on about London as I try my very best not to roll my eyes.

As she's talking, I suddenly feel an unexpected sensation that I can't quite place. A warm, pleasurable feeling awakens my nerves and pressure builds in my jeans.

Fuck.

What is happening to me?

I try my very best not to shudder at the feeling, tightly gripping the edge of the table with my hand.

"…is it?" the woman asks.

She's looking at me as if she expects an answer, but I completely missed the question.

"I'm sorry," I say. "Can you repeat the question?"

"Is England close to Britain?" she asks.

Bloody hell, this woman is an idiot.

"England is part of Britain," I say.

"Oh, so it is close then," she says.

I take a sip of my drink, trying to ignore my growing bulge in my trousers.

What the fuck is wrong with me?

I've spent a lifetime being in control of my body and emotions, now I'm getting hard in the middle of a conversation with two strangers I have no attraction to?

The only person I've ever had this kind of instantaneous arousal for is Ava, and she's at home. Just the thought of her makes all kinds of dirty thoughts flood to the surface.

I take another sip of my drink as a feverish heat rises under my skin and my pulse races. I can feel her hands touching me, moving up and down in torturously slow strokes.

I choke on my beer, spilling it onto my lap. I instinctively grab a napkin and go to dry it off, but the additional touch compounds the distraction and I find myself biting my lip to hold back a moan. Kieran turns to me, giving me a baffled look when he looks down and sees the clear outline of my dick through the denim.

"You okay?" he asks.

"Ye-… yeah…" I stammer. It comes out as more of a moan than I intend.

"Yeah, we're gonna go," the girl says.

My unusual behavior has clearly not won them over, and the couple rushes out of the booth.

"The fuck was that?" Kieran asks with a laugh. "Did you seriously just get a stiffy just talking to those two?"

"Shut up, K-... Kieran," I say, stifling a growl. My hands grip the table so tightly that the wood begins to compress under my fingertips.

"I didn't realize you were so desperate for Ava that if I separated you, your dick would explode," he jokes.

Just the mention of Ava has obscene thoughts racing through my head.

My mind is racing and I stumble onto a realization: *Ava. The mark.*

I pull out my phone and text her.

Me

What are you doing?

"I have to go to the restroom," I tell Kieran, trying and likely failing to mask my arousal as I race to the restroom stall.

I slam and lock the door behind me, leaning my back against it as I free myself from the tension of my jeans.

I feel the vibrations of my phone in my pocket and pull it out.

Ava

At this point, my dick is throbbing and my impulse to touch myself is overridden by the sheer intensity of sensation when I do.

I can't stop picturing Ava touching herself and the visual alone has me near orgasm.

My hands clutch the top of the stall door behind me, my elbows pointing in front of me as my hips involuntarily thrust forward. My breaths are staggered and heavy.

The pressure builds until it overflows and surges, sending pleasure to every cell in my body. I fail to fight back growls and inhuman moans as I ride each wave.

My muscles relax and I collapse against the stall door, my grip just barely keeping me upright.

I take a moment to compose myself and clean up. My reflection in the mirror looks wild. My T-shirt is soaked in sweat and my hair is in messy, damp curls, with a single lock stuck to my forehead. I run my hands through it a couple of times to make myself more presentable before leaving the restroom.

When I return to the booth, Kieran is already chatting up another girl. He smirks at me as I walk up, giving me a knowing look and fighting back a laugh.

"Zane, this is Tamra," he says.

I introduce myself and take the seat beside Kieran.

He mumbles under his breath at a level only an Immortal would hear.

"I guess it did explode."

55

The scent of coffee and toast wakes me from a deep sleep. I stretch my arms above my head and my joints pop like they're made of bubble wrap.

Ow.

I reluctantly roll myself out from under the covers and onto the floor, letting out a groan when my body thunks onto the floor less gracefully than I intended.

Ow.

I pull myself off the ground and make my way to the kitchen, where Zane is standing in his boxers and pouring himself a cup of coffee.

"Morning, love," he says, leaning in for a quick good-morning kiss. "Long night?"

He looks at me with a mischievous grin, clearly recalling the sexy little prank I played on him last night. I smile to myself.

"Nope," I say, stealing a slice of toast from his plate. "You?"

He wraps his arms around my waist and pulls me in until my chest is flush with his.

"Cheeky girl," he says

"I don't know what you're talking about." I smirk at him and innocently bat my eyes.

"Of course you don't. You definitely didn't try to distract me last night or anything of the sort." He playfully rolls his eyes and smiles.

"Well, I mean, you are a Siren—God's gift to women and all that—so I'm sure you can't possibly be distracted by little ol' me."

He gives me a playful spank.

"Yeah, maybe I did deserve that," he says. "But you know, the only reason my ego is what it is… is because I won the only girl that really matters."

He places a soft kiss on my lips. Even without the effect of the venom, his kisses send shivers down my spine and through to my fingertips.

I'll never get tired of this feeling.

"You know, there's just one problem with your plan," he says. "Now that I know I can feel it when you touch yourself… I know it will work in reverse too."

I blush as he thrusts his hips forward, grinding himself into me. A soft moan makes its way past my lips, but we're quickly interrupted by the sound of our doorbell ringing.

"Oh crap," I say. "What time is it?"

I look at the clock and see it's almost noon. I told Jen she could come over at 11:30 and I'm still in my pajamas.

"Are you expecting someone?" Zane asks.

"Jen," I say. "I woke up so much later than I thought."

Zane steps away to put on clothing while I make my way to the door. As I open it, Jen bursts in with her usual enthusiasm.

"Ava, light of my life!" Jen yells, throwing her arms around my neck and pulling me in for a hug. "I'm so glad you're doing better! Never do that to me again, okay?"

I hear a low growl from Zane and turn to see him with his eyes slightly narrowed and his arms tightly crossed. It looks like he's still working on the extra possessiveness brought on by the mark.

"Zane, other light of my life!" Jen exclaims. She runs over to Zane and gives him a big bear hug. The expression on his face is of pure confusion as she squeezes him and rocks him back and forth.

His eyes widen as he looks to me for an explanation. The last he had heard, Jen was still pissed at him for our short-lived breakup.

"I explained to Jen how your family friend was able to get me that experimental treatment for my liver failure," I say with a bit of a wink.

"Yep," she says, releasing Zane from her hug. "You are responsible for saving my boo over there, so you are officially one of my favorite people ever."

He continues to look skeptical but nods nonetheless.

"Happy to help," he says, giving me a knowing smirk.

"So are you not feeling well?" she asks, pointing out that I'm still wearing pajamas.

"No, I'm actually doing alright today," I say. "I just slept late."

"Well, good," she says. "Then you can give me a proper tour this time."

"Okay," I say. "But let me get some actual clothes on first."

———◆———

"Well, this place is fucking amazing," Jen says as she plops herself down on the couch in the living room.

"I know, right?" I say. "I feel like such a poser living here."

"Hey, there's nothing wrong with being a gold-digging ho."

I giggle and sit down in the armchair beside her.

"Thanks for bringing me to the hospital, by the way," I say. "I never really got a chance to say thank you."

"Oh hon, no thanks required. You're my favorite person on the planet; I've always got your back."

"When I got my chart back there was a note that said the person who brought me in was 'distraught and has potential for violence.' At first, I thought they meant Zane, but they also said it was a woman."

We both laugh.

"Well they wouldn't let me see you or know what was going on. I came this close to slapping a bitch, but Zane showed up and I just told them he was Mike," she says.

"Oh god, why?" I ask.

"He was the only person they had listed as a contact for you—you should really change that by the way. They were so close to calling him, despite me telling them a million times that you weren't together. You're welcome for that, by the way."

"I totally forgot I had him listed on my records there," I say. "I haven't been to that particular hospital in ages. That would have been so embarrassing."

"Speaking of Zane," she says. "Where did he disappear to?"

"Oh, he's probably taking a nap. He's been dealing with some stuff lately and it just wears him out."

What's the right way to say he's experiencing my symptoms and he has to take breaks to deal with it?

I feel a tightness around my heart as I try to ignore the feelings of guilt.

He would be fine if it weren't for me.

Stop it, brain.

"I'm fine," Zane's voice says as he emerges from the other room. "Just took a nap."

He walks over and sits in the chair next to mine.

"So what's new with you?" I ask Jen. "Anything exciting?"

"Not really," she says. "Shayna has been super busy at the bar lately and working a lot of long nights, so we haven't gotten to see each other much."

I try my best not to react to her statement, but I immediately wonder if Shayna's affair with Kieran is still ongoing.

I am a horrible friend. I need to tell Jen and I need to tell her soon.

"And we may have discovered a new element at the lab," she adds.

"A new element?" I ask. "What does that even mean?"

"Well, we don't really know yet. But you know that murder at Pike's the other night?"

Her comment immediately catches Zane's attention and he leans further toward her, listening intently.

"Well they found a vial of clear stuff in the victim's purse, and they sent it to us for testing," she says. "But all of our results have been inconclusive. Its spectral signature doesn't match anything in our database. Nothing like this has ever happened before."

Zane's eyes narrow and he purses his lips.

"A vial?" he asks. "Are you sure that was part of the Pike's case?"

"Yeah, it's definitely that case. I remember because this lady had a crocodile-skin Berkin bag and there was trace evidence of crocodile scales on everything. Why?"

"Oh uh, no reason," he says. "I just thought I remembered hearing about the case on the news and there was nothing about a vial."

"Well, that's probably because someone lost it," she says. "We requested another sample of the liquid for re-testing and they told us several items from the evidence box had been misplaced—which is usually code for some dumbass put them in the wrong box."

"Several items?" Zane asks. "What else?"

"I'm probably not supposed to tell you this, so don't mention it to anyone, but it was like an old necklace, the vial of liquid, and a folded piece of paper with a drawing on it. Even the photographs of the items went missing, so all we have to go off is the written descriptions. We can't even re-test the liquid, which is super frustrating because we used the original sample up during the first round of testing. Personally, I was quite looking forward to naming my own element."

"Jenium?" I ask.

"I was actually thinking 'Jubileenium,'" she says.

Of course. Only Jen would name an element after a comic book character.

"What's that?" Zane asks.

Oh, now you've started something you'll never be able to stop.

"Jubilee is only the greatest superhero of all time," Jen explains. "She can shoot fireworks from her hands and blow shit up and she's Chinese and she can do sick backflips and…"

I look over to Zane, who seems to be struck with the realization that he's just committed himself to listening to the entire elaborate backstory of Jubilee.

KAMI

There's a loud thumping at my front door.

Why is it that no one ever uses the bell? This estate is giant. If I weren't a Siren, there's no way I'd be able to hear a knock, and yet people refuse to push the big glowing button next to my door.

I walk down the corridor and open the door to Zane. He looks like he's in an unusually bad mood, and walks past me without even saying hello.

"Wow," I say. "Okay, Z, just let yourself in why don't you."

"We need to talk," he says. His voice is stern and rough.

"Um, okay," I say, closing the door behind me and following him into the foyer. "What's going on?"

"The case documents you gave me from Lola's murder… they're incomplete."

Shit.

"Oh," I say. "Are they? What's missing?"

"Really?" he asks.

Shit shit shit.

"What are you getting at?" I ask, doing my best to maintain a sincere tone of voice.

"You know exactly what I'm getting at," he says, a rumbling growl emerging beneath his words.

Until he tells me what he knows, I can't let on anything.

"No," I say. "You're going to have to tell me."

"Well, first off, I'm missing a page from the evidence inventory," he says. "I'm also missing the part where you stole evidence that you didn't fucking tell me about!"

Shit.

My shoulders pull inward, my head lowers, and I back up as he steps toward me. I've never been afraid of Zane before, but I find myself shaking slightly.

"I kept trying to think to myself, why the fuck would Kami take evidence from a police case?" he says. "I mean, why? Because you don't work for the Council yourself. You're not trying to protect the Immortal world. That's not your schtick. You sure as hell wouldn't protect Kieran. And if you needed something, you would just put it back once you were done, not steal it outright. No, the only reason you'd get rid of evidence—and the only reason you'd hide it from me—is if it would implicate *you*."

56

 ZANE

The guilt in Kami's eyes is unmistakable. I've known her long enough to know that I've pushed the right buttons. Though apparently she's been sneaking lies past me for a long time. I guess I don't know her as well as I think.

"Zane," she says with a shaky voice. "I know that sounds bad."

"You're bloody right it sounds bad!" I shout. "It sounds like you fucking killed Lola and lied to me about it!"

Her mouth shuts rapidly and her eyes widen.

"I…" she mutters. "You… You really think I killed Lola?"

I know Kami wouldn't kill someone without a reason. But then again, I also thought I could trust her not to lie to my face.

"I don't know," I say. "How would I know anything when you've been intentionally keeping things from me?"

"Fair," she mumbles, her eyes falling to the floor.

I walk over to her and put my hands on her shoulders.

"What is going on?" I ask in the calmest voice I can muster.

"I… Shit, Z, I fucked up. I fucked up big time."

Kami has made her share of mistakes, but I don't think any of them had her acting like this.

"What did you do?" I ask.

"The murders that have been happening around town… I made a big mistake," she says, a tear rolling down her cheek.

"Fuck, Kami," I say. "Now is not the time for drawing this out. What the bloody hell did you do??"

"I sold my venom!" she blurts out.

I blink and step back. I can't even comprehend what she's just said. The concept is so incredibly reckless.

Kami has never been one to avoid trouble, but she's also never done something quite so negligent. This is more than a minor cock-up. Siren venom can be very dangerous in the wrong hands. As much as I've trusted Kieran, I still wouldn't give him some of my venom.

"That's what Lola had in the vial—venom?" I ask.

"Yeah," she says with a sigh. "I knew it wasn't related to her death so I didn't think it would matter to take it. I didn't want it ending up in the wrong hands."

"You sacrificed the right to make that argument when you sold it!"

"I know that, okay! Would you cut it out with the 'I told you so's already? I'm well aware I've made a mess of things!"

"How did you even end up selling your venom?"

"I needed information from a demon," she says, sitting down on the marble staircase and dropping her head into her hands. "I had the vial of venom I got from you in my purse. When she spotted it, she said she'd trade the information for it."

"You sold *my* venom?" I say, a growl building in my chest.

"No!" she says. "I swear, Z, I didn't. I told her I needed it for emergencies. But I was at a dead end and I needed her intel, so I gave her a couple drops of my own venom in a vial. It was so little."

She sighs and continues.

"Anyway, word got around and demons kept showing up trying to buy venom off me. I kept telling them no, but…"

"But what?" I ask.

"The night of my party, someone stole the vial."

I stare at her blankly.

"Someone stole," I say through my teeth, "my venom?"

She pinches her eyes shut and nods.

"They diluted it and now they're dealing it like a drug. That's what Lola had in her bag. I have no idea how Lola found out or procured any, but…"

I can't even believe what I'm hearing

The Council would kill her if they thought she was trafficking a substance from an Immortal source for profit. Lola could've told the Council herself, but if she had, we would know. They're not known for their patience or leniency.

"So you killed her to keep her quiet?" I ask.

"No!" she shouts. "I didn't kill her, Zane. I didn't know she found out until I found the vial in evidence."

"Kami, if your venom brought demons here," I say, slowly working it out in my head, "these murders could be anyone. There could be multiple killers even. And yet you insisted on accusing Kieran."

"I guess maybe that was unfair. Obviously I've been making mistakes."

"You lied to me and accused Kieran of murder and sold your venom and stole evidence…"

"Okay, I get it," she says. "I only took it because I knew it wasn't relevant and I didn't want the cops having venom in their evidence locker."

"But that's not all you stole, is it?" I ask.

"The necklace?" she asks.

"And the paper? You stole a paper too."

"Oh," she says, her voice falling as her eyes dodge my own.

"No more fucking lies, Kami," I say. "Or I will walk out this door and be done with you for good."

"Okay," she says, standing up and heading upstairs.

I'm not sure if she expected me to follow her, but she returns rather quickly with a folded sheet of paper in her hands.

"This is it," she says. "I didn't know what to do about it. After her little prediction about you and Ava, I didn't want you to take too much from Lola and her visions."

She hands me the page. Unfolded it's a bit larger than printer paper and has a thick, handmade texture to it. The sheet is covered with scribbled words, a couple crossed out, and a sketch of an ornate, silver tube. I read a few of the notes, trying to make sense of it.

Demons + Sirens? 2276 Elder
Kami? Why?

I turn it over and immediately one drawing in particular catches my eye—because it looks a lot like me.

The writing next to it says "Don't trust Zane, warn Kami" followed by one underlined and circled word:

Dangerous

"What… what is this?" I ask.

"She writes down notes about her visions," Kami explains. "To keep track. Please don't panic over this, okay? A Seer's visions are very complicated…"

"I mean, I'm not going to panic. I know I'm not dangerous, and I've sure as hell learned my lesson about jumping to conclusions," I say, flipping the paper over again. "But why would she say that?"

"I don't know. She told me her visions were often misleading. She must've got some wires crossed."

"You should have told me," I say, looking over the paper.

"You're right, I just panicked. Please don't hate me."

"I don't hate you, but this is the end of it. The secrets end here."

She frowns slightly and nods.

This new information certainly complicates things. I just hope this is the last surprise Kami has in store.

57

 ZANE

The county permit office may very well be my least favorite place in town. The space is cramped, with a ceiling so low it feels like the room is slowly collapsing on you. The walls are painted in a color I can only imagine is called 'Depressing Corporate Beige' and employees are separated by cramped cubicles. It looks like a warehouse where they store miserable government workers.

I'm here for another operating license for one of my commercial buildings in town. I look at my numbered ticket: 431. They're currently calling 380.

Bloody hell.

I consider charming my way to the front of the line, but it doesn't feel fair to everyone else here.

Damn.

In a way, dealing with a human problem like this is almost comforting right now—if only to get a break from the Immortal drama. Between the mark and Kami and living in a town infested with demons, it's kind of nice to be able to get irritated over waiting in line. It's one of the most normal-boring-human things you can possibly do, like complaining when Starbucks spells your name wrong.

An odd sensation pulls my focus. I feel a cold spot on my neck and chills run down my spine.

What the hell was that?

I would assume it was the mark if I didn't know Ava was asleep in bed.

The sensation grows, dozens of soft touches along my neck—almost as if Ava were kissing me.

She's not.

She can't be.

I feel more light touches on my neck and shoulders. This time I'm certain it feels like lips to my skin.

I'm suddenly drowning in panic at the possibility that Ava could be with another man right now.

Okay, I'm officially fucking insane.

Ava is not cheating on you, you idiot.

My mind floods with images of another man kissing her, touching her. I try to shake off the thought and focus on literally anything else.

A tight feeling around my wrist and then the other has me distracted again—it's as if someone is grabbing my arms.

My chest begins to tighten and I feel a panic rising in me.

I flash back to memories of gripping her wrists and holding them above her head while I…

WHAT THE FUCK.

Without even thinking, I bolt out of my seat and head to my car at lightning speed.

This can't be happening. Ava wouldn't do this to me. She wouldn't.

What about that guy she was seeing, Dave?

Stop it. No.

Dave is fucking your girl, touching her, kissing her—right now.

I let out a frustrated growl and tug aggressively at my hair, as if I could pull out the intrusive thoughts.

I slam my foot on the gas pedal and peel out of the parking lot.

What about that blond nurse, Trevor?

Bloody hell. Why am I doing this to myself?

Is Nurse Trevor playing doctor with Ava?

Fuck off.

Are they in your bed?

"God fucking damn it!" I scream.

My window is open and I catch a judgmental look from a pedestrian with their child as I speed by.

The permit office is just minutes from our building, but right now it feels like an ocean away.

When I arrive at our building, I toss my keys to the valet and race to the elevator, frantically pushing the button for the penthouse floor.

She's probably fine. She's probably fine.

This all feels wrong.

Fuck.

My fists tighten as I watch each floor number light up. When I hit the penthouse level, I practically force the elevator doors open and frantically race through the front door.

I hear Ava's voice softly mumbling from our bedroom. She's quiet, almost inaudible.

"Ava?" I call. "Baby, are you okay?"

I'm terrified and my chest feels like it's being crushed. As I head to the bedroom, I hear her whimpering and can just make out my name.

I find her alone in bed, her eyes closed and her body thrashing.

"Baby," I say, stroking her cheek. "It's okay, it's me. You're having a bad dream. Baby, wake up."

How can I feel what she's feeling in a dream? That hasn't happened when she's dreamt before.

"Help…" she mewls.

My heart breaks at the pain in her voice.

How long has she been alone and in fear, calling for me?

And I was thinking she was cheating on me.

I am such a prick.

"Ava," I call again, squeezing her hand. She continues to shake and shudder.

I grab her shoulders and shake her until she launches at me and begins to beat her fists against my chest. Her eyes are pinched shut and tears are streaming down her face.

"Stop it, Kieran!" she screams.

My heart drops into my stomach as she opens her eyes.

She wasn't having a dream.

———⋅———

AVA

"Ava," a voice softly calls, waking me from a dead sleep.

I open my eyelids just enough to see the room lit in a dim red light.

Where is that coming from?

I groggily rub my eyes and reopen them. I see Kieran seated at the edge of the bed beside me, looking down at me with a slight smile. My body feels heavy and my vision is foggy. The air is hot and dry.

"What time is it?" I ask.

"Does it matter?" he asks.

"Well, I'm going to kill you either way, so I guess no."

He chuckles and I sit myself up at the head of the bed.

"What are you doing here?" I ask. I look to my left to see Zane isn't in bed with me. "Where's Zane?"

"Shhh," he says, placing a finger to my lips. "So many questions."

I slap his hand away from my mouth.

"Kieran, cut the crap, what's going on?" I ask. "Why are you here and why are you waking me up?"

"You don't tolerate anyone's bullshit," he says. "I like that."

"Zane?" I call loudly. "Why is Kieran bugging me?"

I receive no response.

"He went out," he said. "He asked me to keep an eye on you."

"That's weird," I say. "And it still doesn't answer my other question: why are you waking me up?"

"Well it's no fun if you're asleep," he says. "I wanted to get to know you better. You're intriguing."

"I'm really not," I say, rubbing my eyes again. "Especially not fresh out of bed. I'm a more-boring, more-grumpy version of my awake self, with the hair of a troll doll."

My muscles are weak and I find myself not resisting when he grabs my wrist and turns it over to look at my tattoo. His skin is cold as he traces his finger lightly over the lines where the mark peeks through.

"And yet, Zane was willing to give up his wings for you," he says. "Do you have any idea what that means? He isn't just any Siren."

"You mean the whole *Iron Siren* thing?" I ask, drowsily tugging my hand away. "Why is everyone so obsessed with that?"

"Because he's an anomaly," he says. "You know that he's known for being immovable. That he's spent his entire existence never letting himself get too close to anyone. Did you know he was the only Siren employed by The Council? Sirens usually aren't trusted to hold positions with them at all. They lose their cool too easily. It's bad for business."

"Kieran," I say. "I'm really tired… Can we skip the story time and you just explain to me why you woke me up?"

"Where's the fun in that?" he asks.

"Well it'll be more fun when I slap a demon in the face and go back to sleep."

"Ooh, feisty little Ava," he says, placing a gentle hand on my cheek.

"If you woke me up to have some banter, I'm really not in the mood."

"That's not why I'm here," he says with a mischievous look, stroking my cheek.

"Then why are you here?"

"I'm more of a show than tell kind of guy."

In one swift motion, he's on top of me, propped up by his elbows resting on either side of my head. He lowers himself down and I feel his torso press down onto mine as he kisses my neck. His cold lips shock my system and I attempt to push him off me.

"Stop!" I shout. "Get off me!"

He lets out a sinister laugh and his eyes fill with black from edge to edge. I've never seen this side of him before.

"Kieran, you're scaring me!" I shout, attempting—unsuccessfully—to push him off.

"Really?" he says. His voice is calm and menacing, with a hint of amusement. "You're fighting a demon? Do you understand how weak you are in comparison to me?"

He grabs my wrists and pins them to the bed with hardly any effort, tracing his icy tongue along my collar bone.

"I thought we could do this the easy way," he says. "I just want to have some fun. I'm due a test run."

I struggle against him, but a feverish heat washes over me. My muscles are responding less and less to my mind's commands. Every inch of my body slowly feels like it's being weighed down by an impossible force, dragging me into the mattress.

"That's better," he says. The look on his face is not remotely human.

"Zane!" I scream. "Help!"

His wicked laugh echoes throughout the room. I try to move, but I can barely twitch a muscle. My arms and legs are frozen in place.

I scream louder, which only seems to encourage him. Kieran's face is twisted into an expression somewhere between delight and hunger. He's familiar, yet so unrecognizable in this moment. It's as though he's been stripped of his soul.

"Stop it, Kieran!" I scream, struggling to free my arms.

Suddenly, the world around me shifts and I find myself opening my eyes to an unexpected face—Zane.

58

"I'll kill him. I swear to fucking god, I'll cut his hands off so he can never touch you ever again. I'll send him through a fucking wood-chipper, see how he heals from that."

Zane paces back and forth, his eyes glowing a brilliant green and his fists tightly clenched. A deep growl rumbles behind his every word.

"Zane, it was just a dream," I say. "You're making a big deal out of nothing. It wasn't real."

"Yes, it bloody was real!" he yells. "He's an Incubus! He's a literal sexual predator! You think it's a coincidence that you have a dream about an Incubus trying to assault you?"

"What does that mean? I don't understand… you think he was actually there in my dream?"

"Do you not know what an Incubus is?" he asks.

"I mean you guys said he's a demon and he feeds off sexual energy."

"Fuck," he says, resting his head in his palm. "He has the power to enter and control dreams. You didn't know that?"

He says that like it's common knowledge.

Maybe it is for Immortals, but not humans.

"No, how would I know that?" I ask. "They don't teach demonology in public school."

"I'm sorry, baby," he says with a sigh, wrapping his arms around me. "This is all my fault. I didn't warn you. I should never have trusted him."

"It's okay. I'm fine, really."

"I don't get it, though," he says. "Why now? Why is he just now going after you?"

Now that I think about it, this may not be the first time.

But if I tell him that, will Zane spontaneously combust?

"Um…" I say. "There may have been another time."

"WHAT??" he roars, pulling away from me. The veins in his neck bulge outward and his skin has turned a deep red.

"Just once. When we first started dating, I had a dream about Kieran. I didn't think anything of it at the time. I'm not even sure I knew you were a Siren at that point."

"I'll bloody gut him," he says. His voice is soft and eerily calm.

"It wasn't like this time," I say. "He was more normal and friendly. He didn't force anything on me. He just kissed me, but he stopped when I said no."

Zane rails his fist into the brick wall and chunks of brick fly everywhere, leaving red dust hanging in the air.

He walks out onto the patio and closes the door behind him.

I'm not sure if I'm supposed to go after him or if he needs to be alone. I decide on giving him space and I slump onto the couch with a sigh.

Did Kieran really attack me?

If he's so truly evil, how did I not see it before?

I don't even know who to believe anymore. It seems like all people ever do is disappoint.

I can only imagine how Zane feels. Kieran is his best friend. He trusted him. He defended him. I feel almost guilty for having come between them. But if Kieran is really evil, I'm glad we found out now.

I look out onto the patio, but can't see Zane from this angle. I stand up and look out the window, scanning the rooftop for him, but I can't find him anywhere.

He wouldn't have just left—*right?*

Uh oh.

I quickly pull out my phone and dial Kami.

"Hey," I say when she answers. "We have a problem."

———•———

ZANE

I pull my car halfway up onto the lawn in front of Kieran's place and throw it in park. My feet are practically on the ground before the car stops moving.

As I approach his front door, it occurs to me he might be at work already. If he's not here, I'll head to Pike's next. I ponder if I should knock, but my body decides for me when my foot collides with the door, sending it off its hinges with a loud crackle.

I hear Kieran's voice cursing and a high-pitched scream. As I step inside, I see Kieran and a redheaded woman both sitting naked on his couch playing video games.

His eyes widen and he slips on a pair of boxers, quickly throwing a pile of clothes at the woman. He takes one look at me and his expression morphs into one of panic.

"Zane… Don't… She's human…" he says, raising one hand up as if to hold me off.

"Human??" the woman shrieks, frantically slipping her dress on. "Kieran, what's going on? Who is this guy?"

"It's fine, babygirl," he says. "But you need to go. Now."

I let out a growl. It's taking all of my strength to wait for this woman to leave. She scurries out, stepping over the collapsed door and shards of wood.

"Now, Z-Man, hear me out…" he says, stepping back slowly.

"Did you think I wouldn't find out?" I ask.

My blood is boiling and my skin feels like it's on fire. Every second my fist is not connecting with his face feels torturous.

"I…" Kieran says. I can see his eyes darting back and forth, looking for an exit.

He launches toward a back room, but I tackle him to the ground.

I grab him by the neck and smash his head back into the floor. My other hand delivers a blow to his face, his bones making a satisfying crunching sound upon impact.

"Fuck!" he curses, grabbing my arm zane extending his claws deep into my skin.

He pulls his feet inward and kicks me in the chest, launching me backwards. He jumps back up to his feet, now in a fighting stance with long black claws at the end of each finger.

"Okay, I probably had that coming," he says, spitting blood out onto his carpet.

"You have a bloody lot more than that coming," I say. "You fucking demon scum."

I fire toward him again and we struggle in a lightning-quick barrage of fists and claws.

"Z… Fuck!" he huffs through ragged breaths. "God damn fucking… listen… fuck!"

He lands a hard punch to my abdomen and I fall to the side.

"Jesus, you're too damn strong now," he says with a sigh. "This thing with Ava has turned you into a fucking beast."

"Don't you fucking say her name," I say, throwing a punch as he dodges it.

"It was harmless!" he shouts, stepping behind his kitchen counter for cover. "It's not even real, Z, not really. It's just a dream!"

His mouth is so full of blood it's not clear if I've left him with any teeth. His face is swollen and bloodied with the skin split across one eye.

"It's real to her, you sick fuck," I say. "And it's real to you and you bloody know it!"

I break off a chunk of the ceramic countertop and hurl it at his head. It collides with his eye with a sharp crack and he stumbles back.

He runs for it and I chase him to the bedroom, which he now seems to realize is a dead end. I step closer and closer as he coughs and pants.

"Zane, I didn't mean anything by it," he says. "You know how many times you told me you weren't interested in her? All you did for weeks was tell me you didn't like her. You made it out to be this fling."

I have tunnel vision and there's a deep desperation in me to have my hands wrapped around his throat.

"You think that justifies attacking my girl?" I say, each word rolling off my tongue with a particular venom. "She's always been mine. And you're just some demon prick who conned me into thinking you could ever be anything better than *vermin*."

A flash of hurt appears in his eyes, but it's gone in an instant and replaced by a deep black nothingness spreading across each eye from edge to edge.

"Is that so?" he says with a wicked smile. "Because I'm pretty sure I got there first."

I swipe at him but he dodges to the other side of the room.

"I wanted her first," he says. "So don't give me your bullshit about staking some kind of claim to her."

Those words ignite a fury in me. My fist strikes his chin and sends him backwards into a short wooden dresser. He springs back up and lands a blow to the side of my head, sending a shock wave of pain through my skull. My ears are ringing as I stumble, struggling to maintain balance.

"If I hadn't backed off and let you have her, she would've come home with me that first night and you know it!" Kieran taunts, knowing precisely which buttons to push.

I've been foolish to not see that he's been after Ava this whole time. Who knows what else he's lying about.

Maybe he really did kill all those people.

Especially with vials of Siren venom circulating out there. For all I know, that could be the real way he's been getting his meals without me.

A thought hits me and I feel like all the air has been knocked out of my chest.

"That night when you called me to the bar…" I say, my mind processing the words as they leave my lips. "What are the odds another Siren really targeted Ava?"

His facial expression shifts so subtly, anyone who didn't know him well would've easily missed it. I, however, immediately clock his accidental show of guilt.

"You dosed Ava with venom??" I ask, diving toward him with my hands headed for his neck. "You motherfuc-"

"Idiots!" a woman screams from the doorway, interrupting my attack.

We turn to see Kami standing with a hand on her hip and a look of judgment. She grabs me by my sleeve and pulls me away from Kieran.

"Kami, I'm not finished with th-" I say.

"Yes, you are," she says abruptly. "I have Ava in the car outside."

Naturally, she has said the only words that might actually be able to stop me from obliterating Kieran in this moment. I freeze in place and examine the damage I've done. His face is so covered in blood that his only distinguishing features are his pitch-black eyes. Behind the blood and bruises is just a hint of a smirk still plastered on his face.

"We're leaving," Kami says.

I reluctantly allow her to pull me out of the room. As soon as I exit, she turns to speak to Kieran, blocking the doorway.

"If you *ever* come near Zane or Ava again—dream or otherwise—I will grind you into dust and use your remains as demonic fertilizer for my lawn, you got that?"

He lets out a cold laugh in response and Kami guides me out of the house.

"How could you be so stupid, Z?" Kami curses as we walk toward her car. "You know, I miss the days when I was the reckless one and *you* were the one cleaning up *my* messes."

"Do you know what he did?" I ask.

"Yes, I do," she says, opening the driver's side door. "Do you know what *you* did?"

She gestures to the back seat of her car where Ava is lying down, her knees up to her chest as she clutches her head.

"Fuck, baby," I say, kneeling into the car and reaching for her hand. "What happened?"

"It's okay, I'm okay," she says softly. "Are you alright?"

Her voice cracks ever so slightly and, despite her best intentions to convince me otherwise, I know she's in pain. Leave it to Ava to try and worry about me when she's suffering.

"What happened?" I ask again, this time turning to Kami for an answer.

"You're bound to each other, you clueless moron," Kami snaps. "So *what happened* is you just got your human girlfriend into a fistfight with a demon."

Guilt grips my heart, flooding my body until every drop in my veins is tainted with self-loathing.

That's what happened.

I'm what happened.

59

After Kami made sure Zane was healed, she left in her car and Zane drove us home in his Challenger. He was quiet during the ride back to our place—the kind of quiet that told me he was drowning in guilt below the surface. He looked like his heart had been ripped from his chest and an empty shell was left in its place.

I understand how he feels. Since the marking, he's been coping with my own pain and pretending to be fine, but every time he'd cringe or grunt, the feeling of responsibility would weigh on me. No one wants to be the cause of a loved one's pain.

He remained quiet on our ride up the elevator and as he unlocked our front door.

When we enter the house, I close the door behind us and Zane drops his keys unceremoniously onto a table near the entryway. He shambles into the living room, his arms hanging wearily at his sides as he kicks off his shoes and collapses face-first onto the couch.

I take a seat at the edge of the couch and rub his back with my palm.

"Are you okay?" I ask.

He rolls over and looks at me with glossy red eyes.

"Am *I* okay?" he asks. "No, Ava, I'm a bloody monster."

"Hey, stop talking like that. You're not a monster."

"Of course I am, Ava," he says as tears begin to fall down his cheeks. "I brought Kieran into your life. He was my friend, so I let my guard down and then he attacked you. If he's a monster, then what do you call the person who let him get to you? What do you call the person who went in there to fight a bloody demon without even thinking about how it would affect you?"

"I'd call them human," I say. "Okay, you may not technically a human, but that doesn't mean you're not allowed to act like one every now and then. You deserve to let yourself off the hook sometimes."

"I just saw red," he says, raking his hands through his hair in distress. "You were so scared, baby. The way you looked at me when you woke up, I can't get it out of my mind. You were staring into my eyes with this panic I had never seen before. I wish I had lived my whole life never seeing you look at me like that. Like a monster. And then I became one."

I can feel sorrow radiating from him. The weight of everything he's dealing with—betrayal, the loss of a trusted friend, deep self-loathing, anger—is overwhelming. Seeing him like this is far worse than any physical pain. He looks broken.

"Stop it!" I snap, feeling the need to defend him—even against his own words. "You are not a monster! You made a mistake, okay? You wanted to protect me and you messed up and that's okay. Mistakes happen."

He takes in a jagged breath, struggling to look me in the eye.

"I should have known better," he says. "The mark… we knew it worked both ways. I wasn't thinking and you got hurt."

"Zane, don't do that to yourself," I scold. "You are not judged by your worst moments. The next time I make a mistake, will you label me a monster?"

"Ava," he says softly.

"Would you?"

"No," he says. "But yo-"

"No buts, Zane," I say. "You have it in your head that you're this horrific creature that needs to be kept chained up. That you need to hide yourself away from the world to avoid harming me or anyone else. But that's bullshit, okay?"

I grab his face and look him in the eyes.

"You are a good person," I say.

He looks like he's about to argue with me, but I lay down on his chest and wrap my arms around him and repeat it.

"You *are* a good person."

He lets out a heavy breath and his chest falls.

"Okay," he mumbles. "I… I'll try to see it that way."

"Good."

"I'm still sorry you got hurt."

He sits up, lifting me up with him as he pulls me tighter into his arms.

"Do you wanna tell me what happened?" I ask. "With Kieran?"

"I beat the shit out of him," he says with a rough, despondent voice. "He basically admitted it, that he had done it. He brushed it off like it was no big deal."

"Really? He admitted it?"

The idea that Kieran was really that person in my dream was hard to wrap my head around. He was so different, so inhuman.

"Yeah," he says with a sigh. "I should have never let him near you. I didn't know. I bought his rubbish about just trying to get by and not wanting to be a killer."

"Does that mean Kieran is the killer you guys have been looking for?" I ask, not sure if I really want to know the answer.

"I don't even know anymore. He's probably one of many. We had no idea so many demons were in town, and now with venom being spread all over the place, who knows how many more demons are in the city."

"You really think Kieran is killing people?" I ask.

"He attacked you," he says, exasperated. "He dosed you with venom. I have no idea what he's capable of."

"Wait… what?"

He closes his eyes and nods slightly.

"So that night, when you and I…" I start to ask, trying to piece together what he's saying. "But didn't you tell me *he* called *you* about that?"

He pinches his mouth in a tight line as he ponders my words.

"I don't know," he says. "Maybe he felt remorse. Maybe he was afraid he'd get caught."

"Maybe he didn't do it."

I still can't imagine Kieran dosing my drink or attacking me, and even if he did, calling Zane wouldn't make sense.

"He did it," Zane says. His tone of voice is too defeated to be anything other than certain.

"Okay," I say quietly, allowing the weight of the words to sink in.

"Okay, I can't carry these bags and walk and drink this at the same time," Jen says, holding up five shopping bags in one hand and her smoothie in the other.

"That's why you don't buy more things at the mall than you can carry," I tease.

"Oh shush your big ol' judgey face. I'll have you know I desperately needed these shirts, jumpsuit, candles, comic books, and hair ties."

"I'll agree about the hair ties," I say, plopping myself down on a nearby bench as she joins. "You ask me to borrow one literally every time I see you."

"See!" she says, lifting her bags and shaking them in the air. "Necessities!"

She places the bags on the ground and sits down beside me. I let out a sigh as I take solace in the momentary break from walking and carrying bags.

"Are you okay?" she asks. "You're sighing a lot today."

"Yeah, sorry," I say. "I'm fine."

"Okay, not buying it." She turns her shoulders toward me and takes a sip of her smoothie through the straw. "Spill. What's up?"

"It's Zane," I say with a sigh. "He had a falling out with Kieran."

"Oh shit, really? I thought those two were inseparable."

"I feel terrible. He's clearly miserable and it's all my fault," I say before I can consider how I'm going to explain this without using the words Siren or Incubus.

"How so?"

"Kieran, he um…" I say, struggling to find a non-supernatural explanation.

"He has a thing for you, doesn't he?"

"Yeah, pretty much."

"I kinda figured," she says, taking another drink of smoothie. "That guy was all over you when we first met. Honestly, I thought he had just gotten over it."

"Apparently not…" I say, trying to run through everything again in my mind. It still feels wrong to me that Kieran could have really been this way all along, but I can't argue with it if he flat out admitted it. "I feel like I broke up the dynamic duo."

"Well if he can't respect bros before hoes, then good riddance," she says with a chuckle. "I guess that means no more Pike's for a while, eh?"

"Yeah, probably not."

I figure I won't bother explaining that I'm avoiding Pike's anyway due to their demon infestation.

"Eh, it's alright," she says. "I've been kind of avoiding it myself. There's only so much you can watch your hot bartender girlfriend get hit on."

Oh god. Shayna.

With everything going on with demons and me almost dying, I never told her what I knew. I still have no idea how to handle it, and I've definitely let it go too long. I open my mouth to respond, but Jen narrows her eyes, clearly distracted by something.

"Well, speak of the devil!" she says.

I follow her eyes to a woman in a white T-shirt and jeans in a shoe store across the corridor. It takes me a moment to recognize her as Shayna.

Oh no.

"It's my boo," she says with glee in her voice. "Let's go say hi!"

It breaks my heart to hear the joy in her voice when I know this woman isn't being faithful to her. I owe Shayna a good slap to the face.

Jen scoops up her bags and stands up, but then pauses with a confused look.

"What?" I ask.

As I turn back to look at Shayna, I see her wrapping her arms around a short, blond woman in a dress, who is leaning back into her embrace.

Oh god.

Jen is frozen in place, her bottom lip wavering slightly and her eyes welling up with tears.

Shit.

I look back and forth between them, unsure of what to say. It's clear Shayna still hasn't spotted us as she cuddles with this other woman.

I owe this bitch a lot more than just one slap.

"Jen, I-" I start to say, but she interrupts me.

"Let's go," she says, dejectedly. "I don't feel like shopping anymore."

She quickly turns on her heels and makes a beeline for the nearest exit. We trek across the parking lot to Jen's car and jump in.

I don't know what to say. This is the second time in a week that one of my favorite people has been crushed by the betrayal of someone they've trusted and I just want to break down and cry. She doesn't deserve this.

The moment the car door shuts, she starts bawling. I reach over to give her a hug and she cries into my shoulder.

I desperately want to run back inside and beat Shayna into the ground. Sure, she's bigger and stronger than me, but fuck it—I'm immortal now.

"Wh-... why d-... she sa-... but I lo-... am I such a loser... pretty... she di-..."

Jen tries to speak, but between her sobs, I'm only making out every eighth word.

"Honey, you're a goddamn catch and Shayna is the dumbest woman in the world for not seeing that," I say.

"I… she… we… why d-… some blond bitch… an-… such a… douchecanoe…"

I chuckle a bit at her colorful terminology.

"I'm so sorry, Jen," I say. "She doesn't deserve you."

"What am I su-… she di-… why…?"

I can't understand much of what she's saying, but I know Jen well enough to know what she needs right now. So I say the only thing I can think of that might make her feel better.

"All I got was something about…" I say. "Hebrew Butterfree?"

She looks at me and instantly bursts into laughter.

"See, this is why I love you," she says, burrowing deeper into my hug.

She laughs between sniffles and at moments I can't tell if she's giggling or crying.

"Why?" Jen asks, her voice calmer yet still heartsick. "Why wasn't I enough?"

My chest tightens at her question. I hate that she's feeling like this.

"Some people don't know what a great human being looks like," I say, stroking her hair. "You're more than enough. She just doesn't know what enough is."

Her breathing is staggered but settling.

"I just wish I had found out any other way than this," she says.

My heart shatters into a million tiny pieces at her words.

60

AVA

Earlier today, the café was buzzing with people. Sounds of idle chatter, the whir of the coffee grinder, and the clanging of dishes echoed against the walls. But as the day wore on, the noise and activity crept to a halt. Now it's just me and my computer with a few café staff members cleaning up.

I've been sitting here all day and I'm not sure I've gotten anything done. I had come here for a change of scenery because I wasn't productive at home, but my plan seems to have failed. All I can think of is how I want to comfort Jen. How I want to take care of Zane and make his sadness go away. How I want to punch that damned Shayna in the face—and Kieran too.

In fact, this is really all Kieran's fault.

Note to self: Punch Kieran.

So what if he's a demon? He hurt Zane and he slept with Shayna and I'm pissed. I don't care if I break my hand in the attempt.

Actually, I'd prefer not to break my hand.

New note to self: Buy brass knuckles.

I hear a vacuum running and I take that as a cue that I've definitely stayed here well past my welcome. I pack up my laptop and other things and make my way out.

I walk to the door and push, but the door doesn't budge.

"We lock the front doors at closing," the woman at the front counter says. "You'll have to use the back."

She points to the other side of the café before wiping down a nearby table.

I weave through empty tables on my way to the back exit. It lets out into a dimly lit alleyway that leads to the parking lot.

If I were looking for a great spot to be serial-murdered, this would be it.

Two men are standing a little further down the way, smoking cigarettes. One of them has a beer bottle in his hand. They're yelling and laughing loudly, clearly wasted off their asses.

Great.

As one talks, his voice makes a chill run down my spine. I could swear I know that voice. I freeze for a moment and peek at the two men again. They're both tall, relatively well-built guys in their late-twenties. The shorter of the two is a blond in an oversized olive-green zip-up hoodie, baggy jeans, and a knit cap. The other is a brunette in a metallic silver puffy jacket that I recognize instantly: it's the guy that came after Jen and me in the bookstore.

The last time I saw this guy, my knee had just gotten up-close-and-personal with his testicles.

Crap.

I step backward to head back into the café, but the door seems to have locked behind me.

Double crap.

I pull out my phone to call Zane. My phone is at 10% battery, which is not ideal, but I'll take it.

After several rings, his voicemail picks up.

Triple crap.

"Hey," I say quietly to Zane's voicemail, so as not to be overheard by the creep and his friend. "Um… so I'm coming home from the café and I'm in a bit of a tricky situation. I'm stuck in the alley behind Café Allegra and that guy from the bookstore is here and I can't get back into the café so um… could you come get me?"

I hang up and try to think over my strategy.

The penthouse is about 15 minutes away. Of course, that's if Zane is in fact at home and not somewhere else. And then he still needs to get my message. Do I just wait here?

There's a solid possibility this guy won't even recognize me, right?

Pike's is only a few blocks from here, but if I call Kieran and he turns out to be the monster than Zane thinks he is, I could end up trapped in an alleyway with a demon who tried to attack me in my dreams.

I am so screwed.

I pull out my phone again, thinking maybe my best approach is calling the cops, but all that shows up is a black screen.

My phone is dead.

Fuck. So much for that 10% charge.

Okay, okay. So what are my options?

Walk past the creep and his friend and hope he doesn't recognize me from our last encounter? No thank you.

Wait here until Zane or someone else comes along to escort me past them? Also not great. Plus, awkwardly standing in this doorway might draw more attention to me.

Yep. I'm screwed.

My eyes scan the alleyway and I see the creep looking at something on his phone. I make a split decision to seize the moment and just go for it. I put my head down and pretend to be talking on my phone. I keep my eyes on the pavement as I attempt to nonchalantly walk past the two men.

"That's the stupidest shit I've ever seen," the blond says to the creep.

"Hey!" one of them calls.

I'm hoping that wasn't addressed to me, but I rather not look up to find out, so I continue along.

"Hey!" the man repeats, his voice getting closer as I hear the clomping of his footsteps behind me.

This was a terrible plan.

I bolt forward in an attempt to reach my car, but I feel myself being railed back by my arm.

I let out a very unimpressive yelp as the man tugs me backwards. I'm immediately met with a pair of bloodshot eyes. The guy I've unaffectionately named 'Creep' is staring back at me with a sinister smile. His face is flushed, his eyelids are heavy, and he staggers closer to me. This man is a walking failed sobriety test.

Okay. Need new options.

Kick to the balls? It worked last time…

Take off running? That would be more feasible if Mr. Creep would let go of my arm.

I tug my arm back but he just grips tighter

I was kind of hoping being immortal would make me stronger and more badass, but not being able to die isn't particularly comforting when you encounter a creepy, homophobic jackass in a dark alley.

"What do you want?" I ask. That definitely sounded more antagonistic than the cool and casual tone I was aiming for.

"I remember you," he slurs. "You're the lesbian bitch who kicked me in the nuts."

"Oh shit!" his friend says with a laugh.

Hmm… is it too late to pretend I don't speak English?

"You must have me confused with someone else," I say, keeping my eyes trained on the ground.

"Oh, are you some other purple-haired lesbian bitch?" he asks. He looks back to his friend and the two of them laugh.

I slip through his grasp and take off running, but he grabs my sleeve and pulls me down hard. I fall into the brick wall beside me, scraping my hand and face against the rough surface. My heartbeat thrums in my ears and my body begins to shake.

"Going somewhere?" he asks through a hoarse laugh.

I attempt to stand up but he pushes me back down with a foot to my chest. With my options limited, I decide on a new tactic.

"Help!" I scream.

The creep leans down, grabs me by the throat, and tightens his grip until I no longer have enough air to scream. I attempt to pry his fingers off without success and dark spots begin to appear in my vision.

In a quick motion, he tosses me to the side.

"Not so tough without your girlfriend around to hit me from behind…" he says with a sneer.

I look around, desperately scanning my surroundings for someone or something to get me out of this. His friend steps closer, his eyes full of the same sadistic glee.

"What do you think?" the blond asks. "Should we cure a lesbian tonight?"

Before the creep has a chance to respond, both men vanish before my eyes. In a flash, they appear on the other side of the alley with a man holding them both up by their necks. My eyes catch his familiar silhouette and long brown-black hair in a ponytail.

"These Queer Eye rejects giving you a hard time, Aves?" Kieran asks, both men flailing their legs and attempting, fruitlessly, to wrestle free from his grasp.

I stumble slightly as I stand up, holding onto the wall to prevent myself from falling. Our encounter has definitely triggered a bad dizzy spell.

Kieran throws both men to the pavement and turns around to look at me, his eyes entirely black.

"You okay?" he asks.

"Yeah, uh…" I say with a hoarse voice. "I'm okay."

The blond man swings at Kieran from behind, his fist hitting Kieran's temple with an unimpressive thud.

Kieran is completely unaffected by the strike, but his eyebrows lower in irritation and he slowly turns around.

"If you wanted my attention," Kieran says, "all you had to do was ask."

He grabs the man by the collar and pulls him in until their faces are nearly touching. He tugs him forward into a rough kiss.

Wow, okay, that's not how I saw this going.

As he pulls back, a wisp of glowing smoke flows from the blond's mouth into Kieran's. He breathes it in as the man collapses to the ground.

Whoa. Wait… He's not dead, right?

The creep looks at Kieran in horror as his friend's now lifeless body rests on the concrete.

"What the hell did you do to him?" the creep asks, his voice shaking despite his attempt to sound intimidating.

"Oh don't worry, sweet cheeks," Kieran says with a devious smile. "You'll get a turn too. I just want to take my time with *you*. Wouldn't want to be accused of being a minute-man, now would I?"

He grabs the creep's shirt and quickly launches him across the alley into the opposite wall. His body makes a disturbing 'thwump' sound as it collides with the brick wall.

As he slumps to the ground, I'm startled by the high-pitched screech of rubber tires on the road. Kieran and I turn to see the bright lights of a low car stopped at the end of the alley.

"Loverboy's here," he says, turning to me with a bit of a grin.

61

 ZANE

Kami has a point. I really have to stop breaking shit.

I scrape out the last of the remaining bits of dried mortar from the missing chunk of our living room wall. Next time I punch a hole in the wall, I'm aiming for an area that's easier to fix.

I bring in the bucket of mixed cement, slip a pair of work gloves on, and use a trowel to apply a thin layer to the space where the new bricks will go. My phone buzzes on the coffee table, but I can't exactly answer it with my hands covered in blobs of grey sludge.

After the new bricks are placed, I pull off the work gloves and take a look at my phone.

The screen says: **New Voicemail - Ava**.

I hit play on the voicemail and put it on speaker so I can listen to her message while I clean up.

"Hey, um… so I'm coming home from the café and I'm in a bit of a tricky situation," her voice says through the speaker.

I immediately freeze upon hearing the shaky, apprehensive tone in her voice.

"I'm stuck in the alley behind Café Allegra and that guy from the bookstore is here…"

My palms clench and a cold sweat washes over me. In moments like this, my heart usually pounds, but instead, it feels like it has just stopped.

I grab my phone and keys before heading out at lightning speed.

"And I can't get back into the café so um… could you come get me?" her message continues.

I opt for the fire escape over the elevator, knowing that I can make better time on foot. The fire escape rattles and shakes as I race to the bottom, the steel reverberating with each step. In an instant, I find myself in my car, speeding out of the garage.

My mind attempts to calculate how long it will take me to reach Ava. Café Allegra is one of a few she frequents for business meetings or when she needs to get out of the house. It's about fifteen minutes away, but I think I can make it less than ten if I double the speed limit and completely disregard traffic rules.

I attempt to call Ava back while driving, but instead of the ringing I expect, her voicemail picks up immediately.

Fuck.

I try again, but again it goes straight to voicemail.

FUCK.

I can't help but feel responsible. If I hadn't been moping around the house like a bloody arsehole over this shit with Kieran, she wouldn't have felt like she needed to work from the café. Sure, she didn't say that was the reason, but I'm sure it didn't help.

I watch the time tick forward another minute as I blow through a stoplight, leaving a chorus of angry horns in my wake.

My stomach drops and I feel an intense fear overtake me.

Something is wrong. Ava is in trouble.

I look at the clock. It's been a few minutes since Ava's call, and I'm still at least five minutes away.

Another thought hits me, and it's one that turns my stomach.

There is one other option.

Fuck.

I pick up my phone and call the only number I can think of.

"Oh, so you're talking to me again?" Kieran's voice says through the speaker.

He sounds truly baffled as to why I've called him after our less-than-amiable last encounter.

"Kieran," I say sharply. "It's Ava, she's in trouble."

"What?" his voice says quietly.

"She called me, she's in the alley behind Café Allegra. She ran into that guy who attacked her. I know you're close. Please, she's not answering her phone."

There's no response but the soft background sounds of a crowded bar, as if he's debating helping me after everything that happened between us.

"Bloody hell, Kieran, I know we have our issues but if you ever cared for me or for Ava—please—she's in trouble."

He still doesn't respond and I bring my hand down hard onto my dashboard, creating another large indentation.

"Fuck!" I curse, whipping the phone into the back seat.

I feel a sharp, stinging pain in my hand, then again on my cheek.

A mix of rage and fear rises in my chest. The terror and fury in me merge into a remarkable clarity. A black cloud fills the edges of my vision until I see nothing but a small circle directly ahead of me and I press the gas pedal hard into the floor.

———•———

AVA

I see the door open and Zane's familiar silhouette emerges from the car, not even bothering to close the door behind him. He appears in front of me with a motion so sudden, I'm pretty sure I heard the sound barrier break.

He's out of breath and disheveled, his eyes ablaze.

"Are you okay?" he asks, holding my face delicately in his palms as he investigates the scrape on my cheek.

"I'm fine," I say.

"You're bleeding," he says as his face turns stern and cold.

He scans the scene before him. The creep is slumped against the wall about ten feet behind me. Kieran leans against the opposite wall with his arms folded across his chest and one ankle crossed over the other. Just to his side is the unconscious—hopefully not dead—body of the creep's friend.

"Hey man, you gotta help me," the creep whimpers, begging Zane for help.

If only he knew just how much he was barking up the wrong tree here.

Zane takes a few steps toward him. This is far beyond his typical reactive rage—this was cold, calculated, sinister. This isn't the hot-burning fury of an enraged animal. This is a time bomb: patient, quiet, deadly.

"This oughta be good," Kieran says with a mischievous smile, glancing between Zane and the creep.

"This psycho and this bitch fucking attacked me," the creep says as Zane steps closer. "There's something wrong with him! I think he's on PCP; his eyes are crazy!"

"Bro," Kieran says to the creep with a small chuckle. "You do realize that I'm *Good Cop* in this situation, right?"

The creep grips the side of his ribcage as he sits up further against the wall, groaning in pain while Zane looms over him.

"I think I have a broken rib," he moans.

"Only one?" Zane says, throwing a devious glare in Kieran's direction.

With a fast yet disturbingly controlled motion, Zane's foot collides with the man's chest. He folds over with a grotesque crunch that I can only imagine is the sound of several more ribs cracking.

I gasp as Kieran bursts into laughter.

"Okay, when you're not on the receiving end of Zane's Hulk-out rage," he says, "it can be pretty entertaining."

It's somewhat invigorating to see the man who attacked me and Jen get his just desserts, but the actual violence of it is a little nauseating. I step between Zane and the man now wailing on the ground. He doesn't deserve to make himself into any more of a monster in his own eyes.

"I know he's a dick, but he's not worth it," I say. "Let's go home."

Zane's eyes meet mine with only a glimmer of recognition. He seems to be battling internally over whether to kill the man or not. He nods and gently moves me aside, kneeling to speak to the man face to face.

"You see this woman right here?" he says, pointing to me. "The woman you attacked for no reason other than your own dodgy ideology?"

"You're all fucking nuts ma-" the creep says, cut off by Zane's hand to his throat.

"This woman is the reason you're alive. This woman is the reason I'm not strangling you with your own intestines right now. She's the reason you don't look like a bloody Picasso painting. So the next time you think it's a good idea to attack someone weaker than you, I want you to remember that you need good people like her. Someone to tell a person like me not to rearrange your bloody body parts."

The man struggles against Zane's grip. He might as well be fighting against a god, because Zane remains perfectly still.

"Now you're going to go to the police station," Zane continues. "You're gonna tell them that you tried to assault a woman. You're gonna admit everything illegal you've ever done. And if they don't lock you up right away, you're going to go up to every cop in that place and tell them to fuck themselves until somebody arrests you."

The man nods and Zane releases his neck.

"Now get the fuck out of my sight," he growls.

The man takes off running, limping and holding his side as he does. He stumbles away until he's out of view.

"Are you really okay?" Zane asks me, his eyes fading in intensity as he pulls me in for a hug.

"Yeah," I say.

Sure, I'm dizzy and I feel like crap, but I didn't get murdered in a dark alley so I'm counting that as okay.

Zane pulls me into his chest and kisses the top of my head.

"Thank you," he says, looking over at Kieran.

Kieran's face suddenly becomes more serious.

"I didn't do it for you," Kieran says, giving me a nod.

"Is he…?" I ask, pointing to the blond man's collapsed body.

"He'll be fine," Kieran says. "I just fed off him enough to knock him out."

I nod. Apparently these are just the kinds of things I accept in conversations now. *My life is so weird.*

"So does this mean you're over your little shit fit?" Kieran asks Zane with a smile.

I swear Kieran has a death wish or something.

"We're never gonna be good," Zane says.

"Oh my god, really?" Kieran asks. "You're such a drama queen!"

"Are you serious?" Zane asks, breaking away and stepping toward Kieran. "You assaulted my girlfriend, my marked mate. You're bloody lucky I left you with all your limbs, you sick fuck."

"Oh please," Kieran says with an eye roll. "Kissing someone counts as assault now?"

"Bollocks! Did you forget that we're bonded by the mark? I could feel everything. I know exactly what you did."

"Wait, what?" he asks. His brows furrow and his lips part slightly.

"You didn't realize I would be able to feel it?" Zane asks, his voice laced with animosity. "Of course you didn't."

"Wait, hold on, that doesn't make any sense…" Kieran mumbles.

I see Zane's eyes glowing brighter by the moment, so I pull him toward the car before he does or says something he'll regret.

"Zane, babe," I say softly. "Let's go."

"Something is wrong," Kieran says, his face contorted in confusion. "None of this makes any sense."

"The only thing that's wrong is that I ever trusted you in the first place," Zane shouts. I continue to pull him back to the car until we both step in and he slams the door. I plug my phone into his car charger as he starts the engine.

As we drive away, I send a text to Kieran.

Me

Thank you for tonight. Zane needs to calm down. We'll talk soon, ok?

62

AVA

I pause for a moment in front of the bathroom mirror. A small bruise is forming on my cheek beside a wide abrasion.

I look like I lost a fight with a cheese grater.

"We should take care of that," Zane says from the doorway, his eyes soft but plagued with guilt.

He reaches into the cabinet and pulls out the first aid kit, grabbing a handful of equipment.

"I'm sorry, this is probably going to hurt," he says, bringing an alcohol wipe to the wound.

As he brushes it across my face, the alcohol stings each and every nerve while I try not to cringe.

Ow fuck fuck fuck.

Stupid face. Stupid cut. Stupid Zane with his stupid alcohol trying to save me from stupid germs so I don't get a stupid infection.

"You're making that face you make when you want to kill me," Zane says with a smile.

"I don't want to kill you," I say. "Okay, maybe a little bit. That crap burns."

"Yeah, I know," he says, rubbing his cheek.

Oh, that's right… he could feel that too.

Not gonna lie, it does somehow feel better knowing that someone else has to suffer your pain too. That probably makes me a bad person, but it's just the truth.

He applies a bandage with an extra-gentle touch.

"You're a pretty good doctor, you know that?" I say.

"Well, I was a medic for a while, way back when."

"What?" I ask. "What kind of medic? When?"

"For Her Majesty's army," he says with a smirk. "About 80 years ago or so."

It's moments like these I remember I'm not having a sane, normal, human conversation and this is—in fact—totally batshit crazy.

"A lot of the first aid stuff holds up, but technological advances have changed a lot. At this point, I just know the very basics."

"Yeah, you're not into much newfangled technology, are you gramps?" I tease. "I still haven't gotten you to figure out video chat."

He wraps his arms around me and carries me to the bed.

"Hilarious, as always," he says sarcastically, lying himself down beside me and smiling. His expression falls as he inspects the bandage on my cheek.

I can tell by his expression he's feeling guilty.

"I'm sorry I didn't get there sooner," he says, lightly stroking my cheek.

"It's okay," I say. "Kieran got there in time. I'm alright."

His face twists and tenses at the mention of Kieran's name.

"You should talk to him."

"Why?" he asks. "What could he possibly say to me that would justify attacking my girlfriend in her sleep?"

"I… I don't know," I say with a sigh. "But something here isn't adding up. You need to sit down and talk. You know, the thing you do with your voice and not your fists?"

He rolls his eyes at me.

"Would you be so quick to forgive if his victim were me? Or Jen?" he asks, tension rising in his voice.

He's got a point. If he had come after someone I loved, I'd probably be more inclined toward the punching idea. I guess it's a good thing that's not the case, because I'm not really in demon-fighting shape.

"Do you know for sure?" I ask. "Because it sounded to me like he didn't know what you were talking about. Maybe it really was just a dream."

"He just didn't want to admit it to your face. He's a coward."

Zane's eyes begin to flicker green and I know I shouldn't escalate further. Instead, I lie back and sigh.

———

Am I really doing this?

I tried to give Zane a few days to cool off after the incident behind the café, but he's still refusing to talk with Kieran.

He may not want to know what Kieran has to say, but I do. So here I am, having snuck out of bed to meet Kieran when he gets off work, which happens to be at 1:00 am. I watch a few straggling patrons stumble drunkenly out of Pike's in the dim light of the parking lot before making my way inside.

Pike's has emptied out and Kieran locks the entrance door behind me.

Kieran wouldn't really try to hurt me… Right?

"Hey there, Aves," he says with a smirk. "How's the wifey? Grumpy as ever?"

"Uh, yeah," I mumble. "He's stubborn."

Kieran invites me over to the bar and offers to pour me a drink. He's visibly disappointed at my choice of drink: water.

"You're no fun," he says, pouring me a glass from the tap and sliding it across the bar.

"Kieran, we need to talk," I say.

"Yeah. I'm a bit confused about what I'm in trouble for exactly. So you told Zane about the dream, I take it?"

"Yeah. Well, sort of. He could feel it through the mark bond and he woke me up."

"What?" he asks, furrowing his brows. "How could he have possibly… Wait, when was this?"

"The day of your fight," I say.

Kieran's expression morphs into one of seriousness and panic, two things I had never associated with Kieran.

"You had this dream *then*?" he asks with wide, questioning eyes. "Shit, Ava. *Shit.*"

"What?" I ask.

"What did I do in your dream?"

"You, uh…" I stammer, uncomfortable reliving the details of a rather unpleasant nightmare. "You talked about Zane at first a bunch; you wanted to know why he marked me. Then you tried to kiss me and touch me… and when I fought you, you held me down and then… I couldn't move."

Kieran's jaw tenses and his hands begin to shake.

"Ava," he says. "I'm so sorry. That… that wasn't me."

His words seem so genuine, but I don't know what to believe.

"So you didn't visit my dreams or slip me Siren venom that time at the bar?"

"Well, I'm not entirely innocent," he says with a shrug. "The venom thing—I'm guilty of that one. I wanted to give Zane a reason to talk to you, and I was offered venom from another demon, so I took advantage of the opportunity."

"Kieran!" I shriek. "That's not cool!"

"I was watching to make sure you were okay," he says. "I just knew you two needed to talk, but you were both too stubborn to figure it out yourselves."

He's not entirely wrong.

I roll my eyes as he continues.

"And I really did visit your dream once… soon after we had met. I don't know if you remember."

"In my bedroom," I say. "You kissed me."

"Yeah," he says, looking suddenly bashful as his eyes trace shapes on the floor. "But Ava, I didn't visit you again, I promise. And I would never…"

He seems disgusted with his words, choking on them as they exit his throat. It's as if he is desperate to get the taste off his tongue.

"I've never used my powers to stake anyone," he says, his pupils growing until his irises are completely black.

"Stake?" I ask. "What does that mean?"

"It's… How much do you know about Incubi and Succubi?"

"Not much. Until recently, I didn't know you guys could enter dreams."

He pours himself a shot of vodka that he quickly downs and refills, only to down again.

"So, some of us were created from scratch…"

"By the original demons, right?"

"Yeah, so you know that bit," he says. "Well, the originals didn't exactly get along. They were all power-hungry bastards, so one started creating a legion to overthrow the others and before you know it, all of them had created their own particular brand of demon. Abaddon created Furies, Lucifer created Daeva…"

Did he just say Lucifer? What the heck has my weird-ass life come to?

"…and Asmodeus created us—Incubi and Succubi."

"Asmodeus? I feel like Zane told me about him," I say.

"Yeah, they have a bit of a rivalry going on," he says. "They were both into the same chick way back in the day. He doesn't like to talk about it, but I know it ended pretty badly."

Oh. That was the demon who was interested in Ilen, before she was killed by her fiancé. That's why I know the name.

"Anyway, Asmodeus gave us the power to enter dreams so we could seduce our victims, but the guy was a real sick fuck. So he gave us the power to immobilize our prey and manipulate their dreams. It's called staking because it's as if you staked someone to the ground. It's fucked up."

"Oh," I say. It was the only response my mind could come up with.

"Asmodeus considers himself the patron demon of lust, but what he considers arousing, most people would consider grotesque. I only met him the once, but let me tell you, that was enough."

"When did you meet him?" I ask.

"He converted me. Some Incubi were born purely of Asmodeus, others are converted from human volunteers. A Succubus recruited me, but Asmodeus is the only one with the power to transform a human into an Incubus."

"So, it was just a dream?"

"I wish," he says with a sigh, pouring and downing another shot. "But from your description, it was real. It just wasn't me."

"Then who was it?"

"Well, it had to be someone who knew you, knew me, knew Zane, has the powers of an Incubus, and had motive to pretend to be me."

"That definitely just makes you sound more guilty."

"Thanks for the faith, Aves."

"I'm just sayin'…"

"Honestly, only one person makes sense," he says, resting his head on the bar. "And that m-"

We're interrupted by a knock at the pub's front door. Kieran breathes in heavily before his eyes shoot wide open. In an instant, he has grabbed me and set me on the floor behind the bar. He takes my phone from my pocket and rips out the battery.

I start to respond but his hand quickly covers my mouth. He looks at me with gravity in his eyes and mouths the words "Don't move."

The door creaks open and I hear Kieran telling someone that the bar is closed.

"Just one drink, friend?" a man's voice says.

"I'm actually heading out," Kieran says. There are a few shuffling sounds before the lights turn off and I hear the door shut and lock.

What the fuck is happening?

I consider putting the battery back in my phone and calling Zane, but I know there must have been a reason Kieran did that.

The men's voices outside are growing louder. I peek out from behind the bar and can see Kieran talking to three men outside the narrow front window. With as little sound as possible, I slide along the floor until I'm close enough to the window that I can hear what they're saying.

"I should've known sooner," Kieran says.

"I don't know what you mean," another says, his slight smirk giving him away.

"You guys have been out here every night when I leave the pub. At first, I just thought you were just losers who got your kicks hanging out in parking lots, but you blew your cover. I stay a bit late tonight and, next thing I know, you impatient goons are knocking on the door? Rookie move. Why is Asmodeus having you watch me?"

Oh god. These are Asmodeus's men?

"Alright boys," a voice says from the shadows. A tall, slim man in a long black trench coat emerges seemingly from nowhere, clapping slowly. He has an eerily sinister presence and exudes power. His spiky bleach-blond hair practically glows as he steps into the light.

"You figured me out, big boy," he continues, stepping within a few feet of Kieran. "Congratulations. Would you believe me if I said I just wanted to check up on one of my favorite little sex demons?"

"No," Kieran spits.

"Fair enough," Asmodeus says with a smile. "Can't blame me for trying."

"You're trying to get to Zane," Kieran says. He lets out a growl and I watch as claws extend from his fingertips.

"Ooh, feisty! I like that!" Asmodeus teases. "But I'm not trying to get to anyone. Maybe Zane did rob me of my lover. Of course, it's probably even worse that he robbed me of my revenge. But I'm not one to hold a grudge."

"Bullshit!" Kieran says.

Asmodeus holds his palm up and Kieran instantly falls to his knees with a groan.

"Are you accusing me of lying?" he asks.

Kieran lets out a pained grunt.

I try to move slightly to see what's happening. As Kieran comes more into view, I can see him digging his claws deep into his opposite bicep, blood pouring from the wounds. He continues to claw and dig at himself and I can see Asmodeus's wicked grin growing as he watches.

He's making him do this to himself somehow.

"Ye-… Aaagghhh fuccckkk…" Kieran screams. "You motherf-… AAAHHH!"

His claws tear until I see bone and muscle tissue and have to look away.

Okay, I'm going to be sick.

I feel hot tears run down my face as Kieran's screams grow louder.

"Tell me, where *is* your friend Zane?" Asmodeus asks. "Or better yet, where's his precious little woman?"

"I don't know where he is!" Kieran screams, his voice thick with agony.

"And the girl? Tell me…"

Instead of words, Kieran responds with a mix of growls and gurgles that are truly sickening. The sound alone is enough to trigger my gag reflex.

I don't really want to see what's going on but I need to know. I peek out again and see blood gushing from Kieran's mouth like a fountain as he spits out a large piece of what looks like ham.

Oh fuckity fuck fuck fuck.

It's his tongue.

63

I slink down behind the bar with my back to the window. My eyes have already absorbed enough nightmare fuel to last me at least five years of therapy.

"I'm very disappointed in you, Kieran," Asmodeus says with a disturbing laugh. "I thought we were friends."

I hear a thud as Kieran lets out a guttural cry that chills me to my core. He screams through a series of coughs, gurgles, and chokes. The noises alone make me gag.

"Do you hear that?" one of Asmodeus's men asks.

Crap.

I cover my mouth with my hand in an attempt to stifle my gagging.

There's silence for a moment as I hold my breath. I don't know if they can hear something as quiet as my breathing from where they are outside, but I don't really want to take that chance.

"I see you called in reinforcements," Asmodeus says with a laugh. "Tsk tsk, what a bad boy. I guess we're out of time then."

Kieran continues to wheeze and moan as I begin to hear a faint sound in the distance. After about thirty seconds, the sound becomes clearer—it's the wailing of police sirens.

I finally let out a breath.

Thank God.

ZANE

I see flashing red and blue lights outside Pike's as I pull into the car park. I pull hard on the parking brake and exit the car in a quick motion.

"Ava?!" I call, my eyes searching the lot for a glimmer of purple hair.

"Excuse me, sir," a police officer says as he approaches me. "This is a crime scene. We need to close off the parking lot. You can't be he-"

I grab his wrist and speak before he attempts to shake me off.

"I'm supposed to be here," I say, eyeing his coworkers behind him. "Tell your fellow officers I'm authorized to be here."

The policeman nods and shouts, "He's alright."

I open my mouth to call for Ava when I spot her kneeling on the pavement with a blanket around her shoulders and a group of emergency workers surrounding her.

Fuck.

"Ava!" I yell, sprinting towards her. "Baby, are you okay?"

I drop to my knees to meet her on the ground. She's covered in blood.

"I'm okay," she says through tears, pulling me in for a hug.

I feel anger rising in my chest, but something interrupts the feeling.

I don't smell her blood. I don't feel any pain from her. Since I woke up and found her side of the bed empty, all I've felt is fear. Whose fear, I couldn't really say for certain, but I didn't feel anything else.

My eyes travel to the group around her. Four paramedics are tending to a muscly bloke on the ground who is covered head-to-toe in blood. It takes me a moment to recognize the man is Kieran.

His skin is stained crimson, strands of hair are pasted to his forehead, and there's a plastic tube down his throat. As the emergency crew raises him up on a stretcher, his eyes flicker open and he looks at me. He gives me a wink as he's lifted into the ambulance.

"Where are you taking him?" Ava asks. She writes down the address and we agree to follow them to the hospital.

"What the hell, Ava?" I ask. "What happened?? *What were you thinking?!?*"

"I… we just talked…" she mumbles. "I didn't know, I couldn't…"

I feel instantly guilty as I can hear the remorse in her voice.

"I'm sorry, baby," I say, pulling her into a hug. "I'm sure you were just trying to help."

She follows me to my car and we get in. Her car is still parked out front, but I rather she not drive home tonight.

As we pull out behind the ambulance, I let out a sigh.

"What happened?" I ask, more calmly this time.

"I just came to talk," she says softly. "I knew you wouldn't approve, but something didn't make sense with Kieran and you refused to hear him out, so I did."

I grip the steering wheel tighter.

"Talking doesn't usually end in bloodshed," I say. "And I'm gonna guess you weren't the one who did all that damage to Kieran."

If a five-foot-four human girl got the best of Kieran, I would never let him hear the end of it.

"Asmodeus," she says. I feel instantly sick at the mention of his name. My body stiffens and my foot reflexively slams on the brake.

"What?" I ask, the car now at a complete stop in the middle of the street.

"He showed up outside. I'm not sure what he did—it was like he was forcing Kieran to hurt himself."

Fuck.

I slowly release the brake and press my foot on the gas pedal.

Dozens of contradictory feelings swirl within my chest. I hate the idea that someone hurt my friend—let alone that someone being Asmodeus. At the same time, I hate Kieran for attacking and threatening Ava. I hate him for bringing her into a dangerous situation. Up till now, I've never simultaneously wanted to protect someone and kill them at the same time.

"Well, the thing about Asmodeus is," I say, "he can control Incubi and Succubi. All the originals can command their own creations. If Asmodeus tells one of his demons to jump, they have no choice but to jump."

"So Kieran and others like him are always under the control of the original demons?" she asks.

"No, Asmodeus can't just control them whenever he wants. His powers only work in close proximity."

"Is he going to be okay?" she asks.

"He'll be fine, love. Demons are next to impossible to kill. You basically have to restrain them until they starve."

"That's lovely," she mumbles.

My chest tightens with each passing minute. I almost don't want to know the rest of the story, but I have to ask.

"Did Asmodeus say anything to you?" I ask. "Did he hurt you?"

"Kieran told me to hide in the bar, so I did. I don't think he knew I was there."

Thank god he kept her safe.

"Do you…" I ask, the words almost catching in my throat. "Do you know why he's here? Does he know I'm here?"

"Yeah, um… sort of. He asked where you were and where I was."

He asked about Ava.

He knows about Ava?

Oh god, I'm going to be sick.

We reach the Emergency section of the hospital and I park the car.

"Kieran didn't attack me in my dream," she says, staring ahead to avoid eye contact with me.

All the anger I felt toward him is back in an instant and my chest burns at the thought of him touching her—hurting her.

"Ava, he told m-"

"No," she cuts me off. "He told me he did do it once, the first time, before you and I were officially a thing. But he didn't know anything about the second one."

"And what, you just so happened to have a dream where Kieran, an Incubus, attacks you in your sleep? And you expect me to believe that's a coincidence?"

"No, Kieran didn't think it was either. He thought it was someone else bu-"

"Someone else?" I snap. "Who else w-"

I stop as a disturbing thought hits me.

Who would want to attack Ava? Who would even know who she was? Who would have the power to…

Fuck.

———◆———

AVA

Zane managed to charm us back into Kieran's room in the ER. As we walk in, several doctors and nurses are huddled around Kieran.

I expected chaos—flickery fluorescent lighting, machines beeping at high speeds, frantic doctors throwing around words like 'bilateral' and 'pulmonary'. But the reality is something very different.

Three people in scrubs mumble quietly to each other while looking over his chart. Another looks perplexed while fiddling with the buttons on the machine.

"The EMT who brought him in said we were looking at multiple deep lacerations," a woman says as she reads over his chart.

"When he got here, we were looking at a Class III hemorrhage. His blood loss was substantial. He absorbed two units of O-neg faster than I've ever seen."

Well, there's the medical terminology I expected.

I see Kieran's eyes open slightly and he lifts his arm to give us a little wave.

"I'm sorry," one of the doctors says as she spots Zane and me. "We can't have vis-"

"You can make an exception for us," he says, his fingertips lightly resting on the back of her hand.

"Okay, well, sit over there please," she says, guiding us to a set of chairs.

We sit down and Kieran smiles at us. His teeth are covered in blood, and it's both humorous and unsettling to see him smile through this situation.

I spot the wound on his shoulder and see that it has already healed substantially. When they loaded him into the ambulance, he had torn a major chunk out of his shoulder and all that was left was a gnarled mess of tissue and bone. The once-deep slashes have closed until just minor cuts and scrapes remain.

Zane begins chatting with the doctors and nurses. One by one, he charms them, until we're alone with Kieran in the room.

"So how you feeling, mate?" Zane asks, anxiously combing a hand through his hair.

Kieran points to his mouth and shrugs.

"Oh right," I say. "His tongue, he um… he doesn't have one."

"Bloody hell," Zane says. "He cut your tongue out?"

Kieran shakes his head.

I don't actually know what happened to Kieran's tongue, just that one minute it was in his mouth, and the next minute it wasn't.

"Asmodeus was asking him where you and I were," I explain. "I'm not sure wh "

"You bit your own tongue off? Intentionally?" Zane interjects.

Kieran nods with a slight smile.

What??

"Oh my god, Kieran! Why would you do that?" I shriek.

"To protect us," Zane says, his eyes falling to the ground. "If Asmodeus compels an Incubus to tell him something—anything—he can't resist. His body would force him to."

"Unless…" I say, slowly putting the pieces together. "He couldn't speak."

Kieran gives us both a thumbs up.

"Thank you," Zane says, the two of them locking eyes for a moment. "For the text. For protecting Ava. For everything."

"The text?" I ask.

"Yeah, I was already on my way when I got it," Zane says. "I woke up to this bad feeling you were in trouble. I guess I could feel it through the bond. So when you weren't there next to me, I checked your phone's location. It said 'offline' but showed Pike's as your last known location. I swear when I read the word offline, I nearly lost it."

My head sinks with guilt. I should've at least left a note or something.

"This was the text he sent me," Zane continues.

He pulls out his phone and shows me the message.

Kieran

911 @Pikes - Ava here, bring pigs

"Pigs?" I ask.

"Kieran has never been a big fan of coppers, not than any non-humans are. I figured it had to be pretty serious if he wanted to get the police involved."

Kieran reaches for a pen and paper at his bedside. He writes for a moment, then turns the paper toward us.

Does this mean you've changed your mind on castrating me?

"For now," Zane says with a bit of a smile as Kieran writes something else.

Good, because I'm really gonna need my dick now.

We both look to Kieran with confusion. He holds two fingers up in a V-shape and raises them in front of his lips, then sticks out the small stub of his remaining tongue and wags it from side to side.

Oh god.

That's an image I won't be able to get out of my head.

64

The doorbell rings as Ava grabs a beer for Kieran from the fridge. As expected, it's Finn, in his go-to navy varsity jacket over a grey t-shirt and jeans.

"Come on in, mate," I say, gesturing inside.

"Oi, whole gang's 'ere!" he says, opening his arms to invite Kieran in for a hug.

"C'mere you beautiful bastard!" Kieran says, jumping over the couch and pulling him in.

"Hey Finn," Kami says with a smile. He separates from Kieran and greets Kami, then turns to Ava.

"Ava, lovely to see you again," he says, spreading his arms again for a hug.

I feel a creeping displeasure as his body touches hers.

Finn has a lifemate. A mate for life. He is not interested in mine.

A small growl exits my lips, but quietly enough that no one seems to hear before Ava and Finn separate.

I swear I used to have self-control, but you'd never know it now.

"So why the secrecy? I feel like I'm in a Bond film," Finn says as we all take seats around the coffee table. "Based on your messages, I assume we aren't gathered for a birthday party."

"Unfortunately no," I say. "An old *'friend'* is back."

"So by your tone, I'm hearing… not really a friend," Finn says with lowered brows.

"Asmodeus," Kami adds.

"Bloody hell," Finn says, his mouth falling open and his eyes widening.

"Yeah, pretty much," Kieran says.

"He found Kieran at Pike's and was asking about Ava and me," I explain. "He used his powers over Kieran to try and force it out of him."

"Christ!" Finn says, quickly bringing a hand to his forehead and shoulders to make the sign of the cross.

"He didn't tell them," Kami mutters, her eyes glancing to Kieran before quickly falling to the floor.

"Hey, you're leaving out the part where I bit off my fucking tongue to save these two like a fucking hero," he says, grinning as he gestures to Ava and me.

Finn's eyes grow wider still and his brows raise in horror.

"Heroes don't call themselves heroes," I say. He responds by holding up his middle finger and giving me a glare.

"Okay, I think we're getting off track here," Ava says.

"Ava's right," Kami says. "We know he's here. We know what he wants. Now, what the hell are we going to do about it?"

"And what he wants is Zane and Ava?" Finn asks. "Why?"

Kami looks at me, as if to ask my permission to explain, so I give her a slight nod.

"When we were young, Zane and Asmodeus were both interested in the same woman—Ilen," Kami says.

I look to Ava and notice her slightly shift in her seat. She stares at her hands as Kami speaks.

"Well, we didn't know per se, but we had a feeling," she continues. "It was his classic M.O., the mysterious deaths of a woman's suitors and all. He was always one for controlling things from the shadows. But she was pretty and we were young. Zane started, well, um… sleeping with her."

My head falls into my hands. Ava strokes my back and gives my arm a tight, reassuring squeeze. In one simple touch, it's as though she has lifted all the weight off my shoulders.

How did I ever live without her?

"Anyways," Kami says. "She also had a fiancé—Count Krisztian Schauberg, total d-bag. The spineless bastard, he… he killed her."

I close my eyes and take a deep breath as I try to fight off the flashbacks.

"Oi," Finn says softly. "That was not your fault. Humans can be… well, they can be fucking monsters. You aren't responsible for what they did."

"That's not the whole story," I say with a heavy sigh.

Ava turns to me in confusion. I knew Kami didn't tell her everything. Honestly, I did my best to hide it from Kami too, but I've always wondered if she knew and just never said anything.

As I look at Kami, she gives me a soft, knowing look that tells me we didn't have as many secrets between us as I had hoped.

"I killed him," I say, my voice low and flat. "I killed Krisztian."

I'm terrified of what Ava will think of this new information. Will she now see me as the monster I know myself to be? I can't bear to look at her. I don't want to live with the memory of what it looks like when she falls out of love with me.

I feel a hand at my back, that same familiar gesture of comfort. She rests her head on my shoulder and the tightness in my chest instantly subsides.

"For Asmodeus, that was an unforgivable offense," Kami adds. "He was angry, but had no one to take his rage out on. So he did what in his mind was the next best thing: he burned the city to the ground."

Kieran and Finn both look at me with solemn faces and uncharacteristic silence.

I look to Ava, who is looking up at me with the same love and devotion as always. It's the first time in a long time I've considered that my sins may not be so unforgivable.

"We had already left town," I say. "I thought I had covered my tracks. Now and then, I would hear rumors about Asmodeus—his new lovers, acts of gruesome torture—and some of them would mention his interest in me. It was never more than a passing thought, only that he was asking about me or keeping an eye on me. After decades passed, I got the impression he had let go of his grudge."

"Asmodeus never lets go of a grudge," Kieran says.

"But why now?" Finn asks. "What changed?"

"Ava," Kami says, confirming my worst fear.

"Me?" Ava asks. "What did I do?"

"You didn't do anything," Kami says. "Asmodeus likes to think of himself as a sort of patron saint of marriage."

"What?? Marriage?"

"He likes to claim that he is responsible for the modern institution of marriage," Kami explains. "It's bullshit, but he's one of the oldest living beings so it's not like anyone can question him."

"But what does that even mean?" Ava asks.

Fuck. I don't even want to think about this.

"Since he's the demon of lust, he feels that he's entitled to a taste of every newly married woman," Kami says. "Basically he's a fucking creep."

"But we're not married," Ava says, gesturing between us.

"To him you are."

She takes Ava's wrist and turns it over, tracing the lines of her mark beneath her tattoo.

A growl rumbles through my chest at the uninvited touching and Kami pulls her hands back.

"To Sirens, that's as meaningful as marriage. Maybe more," Kami says. "And it tells Asmodeus that Zane has a vulnerable spot."

"So he wants to—what—have sex with me?" Ava asks skeptically.

"I can't fucking talk about this anymore," I interject. "Can we get to the part where we throw chunks of him into the ocean?"

"If only it were that easy," Kami says, pulling an old book out of her purse. "This was not easy to find, by the way."

"What's this now?" Finn asks.

"It's a very old bible." Kami sets the book down on the table. "Let's just say it's got a lot in here that the modern-day version doesn't."

"Like Adam getting his bone on with Steve?" Kieran asks.

"Like how to kill Asmodeus." She smirks at him and opens to a page with an illustration of Asmodeus himself. He hasn't aged in all these years.

"*Demon of lust…*" Kieran reads over Kami's shoulder. "Blah blah… *penchant for vengeance… Kings of Hell…* Wait, does this say the woman was marrying her cousin because he had cousin-dibs? This is the kind of shit happening in the Bible and they say demons are the bad guys?"

"Give me that," I say, pulling the book toward me. I scan its contents for any indication of how to kill Asmodeus.

He is known as the king demon of lust, the originator of fornication and adultery.

…Sarah had been married seven times, but the evil demon, Asmodeus, killed each husband before the marriage could be consummated.

…the progenitor can only perish at the hands of his progeny.

I pause a moment to parse the sentence.

"You read it?" Kami asks.

I nod, narrowing my eyes as I re-read the passage.

"Come on then, share the secret!" Kieran says.

"He can only be killed by a dagger to the heart," Kami says, her eyes fixed on Kieran, "in the hands of an Incubus or Succubus."

Kieran's jaw drops and his eyebrows raise. For once, he has no witty comment.

"Oh helllll nooo," Kieran says. "I mean, I love you guys, but how the fuck am I supposed to kill someone who's a fucking million times stronger than me and has the power to control my every move?"

"Well, that," Kami says, "is the big question."

———✦———

I grab everyone a round of drinks from the kitchen before returning to the living room where Kami, Finn, Kieran, and Ava sit looking perplexed and defeated.

"Is there a way to sever your connection to Asmodeus?" Finn asks.

"Don't you think I would've done that already if I could?" Kieran replies.

"What we need is a plan," Kami says.

"What we need is a miracle," Kieran replies.

Kami rolls her eyes and ignores his comment.

"Well, first thing we need to do is protect Ava," Kami says. "I think she's gonna need some immortal protection until we figure out a way to get rid of Asmodeus."

She's right. Ava is the priority.

"Guys, I know I'm a human," Ava says, "but I can't expect you all to uproot your lives over me."

"Ava, you're so sweet, but this isn't just about you. Asmodeus is a danger to everyone he encounters. If he's in town, no one is safe. We all need him dead," Kami says.

"She's right," Finn says. "Not that any of us would let him hurt you, but one way or the other, Asmodeus is a major threat to all life. Burning down a city is just a whim for him. His powers are nearly limitless."

"Not making me feel better about being your sacrificial lamb here," Kieran says.

"Sorry," Finn replies. "I think we're all in over our heads here."

"Why don't you bitch-slap him with your seal tail, huh?" Kieran jokes.

Finn lets out a laugh.

"You know I would support you guys," he says. "But I'm pretty useless in battle, unless you wanted me to seduce him. Though I doubt my powers would work on him."

"Seduce him?" Ava asks. "*That's* your power? Is every Immortal's power something to do with sex?"

"No, love," I say. "Us kindred spirits just tend to hang around together. In Immortal culture, not everyone gets it. But Sirens, Selkies, Encantados, Satyrs, Nymphs—we understand each other, so we tend to be friends."

"Oh, okay," she says with a nod. "I was starting to think the supernatural world was just really kinky."

Kieran and I burst into laughter, joined shortly after by Kami and Finn.

"You have no idea," Kieran says with a smirk.

"So then what are our options?" I ask, steering the conversation back to our goal.

"Well, I have a lead on some, uh… demonic handcuffs," Kami says. "We could basically use Kieran as a weapon."

"If you wanted me in cuffs, gorgeous, all you had to do was ask," Kieran jokes. Kami instantly whips a throw pillow at him and he dodges.

"And we're going to need a lot more firepower than we have now," I say.

Kami nods.

"I might have something for that," she says. "I'll let you know."

"Then what?" Kieran asks. "Duct tape a dagger to my hands and jab me at him like a demon swordfish?"

Finn chuckles.

"Pretty much…" Kami mumbles. "We'll have to work out the finer details."

"But Asmodeus will know whatever you plan, won't he?" Finn asks. "He can just compel Kieran to sell you out."

"I really rather not bite my tongue off again," Kieran says. "To say that was unpleasant would be an understatement."

"We could not tell him the plan," Ava says.

"True," I say. "But at this point, he already knows part of it. We can't take back what he already knows."

"But you can, can't you?" Ava asks. "What about the stuff that made you forget me?"

"Lethe!" Finn says. "It's brilliant."

"So we need lethe, which we've already got," Kami says. "Some handcuffs that can hold back a demon. And then we just need to find a Fury."

"A Fury??" I repeat.

If her plan is what I think it is, I'm really not gonna like it.

65

Ava rests in my lap while Kami walks in circles around the kitchen island and talks on the phone to one of her contacts. She's been bouncing from lead to lead for hours now.

"If I knew a Fury, don't you think I would be contacting them instead of you?" she snaps.

"Kami is still on the phone?" Ava asks, stirring from her nap.

"Yeah," I say. "We expect it to take a while. Fury smoke is relatively hard to come by."

"Because it makes people stronger?" she asks.

"Not exactly. It makes people, well… angry."

"Then why did Kami say you needed it for strength?"

"Sirens get their strength from their passion—love, hate, lust—and that intensity is at the core of our powers. That's why I've gotten stronger and faster since I met you. Being in love, especially with your soulmate, is a hell of a power boost."

A few years ago, if I had gone toe-to-toe with a demon, they'd wipe the floor with me. Now, I can overpower Kieran, which he's not very pleased about.

"So why not try to increase the other good emotions instead?" she asks. "Taking something that makes you angry seems like the worst option."

I smile and stroke her hair.

"Because, love," I say. "No one could love anyone more than I already love you."

Her cheeks redden and she gives me a shy smile.

"Okay, shut up and stop being so sweet," she says. "I can't handle it."

"Alright!" Kami says, setting her mobile down on the kitchen counter. "Do you want the good news or the bad news?”

“Oi, just tell us,” I say.

“Good news is I have located someone who has Fury smoke,” Kami says, joining us on the couch. “The bad news is it’s your old friend Dionysus.”

Bloody hell.

Dionysus is one of the few Immortals as old as Asmodeus. The Greeks worshipped him and other early Immortals as gods.

“I take it we don’t mean an *actual* friend?” Ava asks, sitting up from my lap.

Not even close.

“Dionysus would consider Zane a friend, but…” Kami says.

“But in reality he just likes to toy with people, and I’m his favorite plaything,” I explain. “He has the power to free people of their inhibitions. Kind of like Siren venom mixed with alcohol, at a thousand times the potency. After I got a reputation for being well-controlled, he was desperate to test his powers on me.”

“Did they work on you?” Ava asks.

The last time I saw Dionysus, I woke up in a phone booth in the middle of East London wearing nothing but one boot.

“Um, yeah,” I say. “They worked.”

“Dionysus isn’t dangerous,” Kami says. “He’s just the immortal equivalent of too many Jägerbombs.”

“Sounds like he and Kieran would get along,” Ava says.

“Oh I’m sure they would,” Kami replies. “But what Dionysus really loves is the bottled-up, repressed types like Zane.”

“I’m not repressed,” I grumble.

“Maybe not anymore,” she says, “but we both know he has a special fondness for ‘liberating the oppressed.’”

It’s true. Dionysus has gone by many other names—Bacchus, Zagreus, Liber—but one of his favorites was Eutherios, aka The Liberator.

“Fine,” I say. “Call him. But don’t tell him anything about Ava. I don’t want her dragged into this.”

“Okay,” Kami says. She grabs her phone and steps away.

As she does, I hear Ava’s mobile ring.

“Sorry,” Ava says, picking it up. “It’s one of my clients. I have to get this.”

Kami leans on the kitchen counter while waiting to be connected to Dionysus. Ava steps out on the porch to handle the call from her client.

I lay back on the couch, watching the ceiling fan spin.

"Okay, no problem," Ava says, speaking to her client. "What about it isn't working for you?"

She's a little too far away for me to hear the voice on the other line.

"You mean the scroll bar?" she asks. "I mean, technically yes, we can remove that but you really need…"

I can see her face scrunch up in irritation.

"You do?" Kami's voice says from the other room. I turn to her and she gives me a thumbs-up gesture. "And exactly what would this social call entail?"

"Well, the scroll bar is supposed to move," Ava says, the subtle frustration growing in her voice.

"One hour seems reasonable," Kami says, looking to me for confirmation. I nod.

"Yes, he'll be there," she says. "And you'll have the smoke ready?"

"It really can't be in the center of the page beca-" Ava says. "Yes, I un-"

"What??" Kami asks. Her tone immediately draws my attention and I stand up.

I listen closer, attempting to pick up the other voice.

"I don't know what you're talking about," Kami says.

"Kami, darling," Dionysus says through the phone. "News travels fast… gossipy demons…"

I can only understand bits and pieces of what he says.

What exactly is he getting at?

"Well, don't believe everything you hear," she says, looking at me with concerned eyes.

"…both visit… only fair…" he says. It's too quiet to make out his exact words, but it seems he wants both Kami and me to drop by for a visit.

She looks at me with questioning eyes, which I return with a shrug and a nod.

"Okay, agreed," Kami says. "We'll call to arrange details."

She hangs up and lets herself fall over the side of an armchair and collapse into it.

"Well, that ought to be interesting," she says with a sigh. "Honestly, I'm surprised you agreed to it. But it's good, because it's pretty much our only lead and Dionysus is a powerful friend to have in a crisis."

"Why are you surprised?" I ask.

"Because you're so crazy protective of Ava and Dionysus is, well… he is who he is."

"What??" I ask, a slight growl trailing behind my voice. "Nobody said anything about Ava."

"Shit, Z, I thought you were listening to our conversation!"

"I was! I heard most of it. I thought he was asking you to come too."

"No, he insisted Ava come," she says. "He found out about you two through the demonic grapevine and he wants to meet her."

"He doesn't give a shit about meeting her, Kami," I spit. "He wants to use her to torture me!"

"He won't hurt her," Kami says. "You know Dionysus isn't evil, he's just a troublemaker. He's all about wine and sex and partying. It won't kill you to spend an hour with him."

"It just might," I say. "You're bloody lucky we're desperate."

I exhale and flop onto the couch, burying my face into a pillow.

"Well, that was a clusterfuck of a phone call," Ava says with a sigh as she walks back in from the patio. "Hopefully you guys have some good news."

Kami and I both look at her silently.

"What?" she asks. "What did I miss?"

———·———

AVA

You would think the "God of Partying" would live in Las Vegas or New York or something, but here we are—a short flight later—in the middle of friggin' Utah.

Yep. Utah.

Zane is driving our rental car—a grey sedan that he looks completely out of place in.

"I can't believe I agreed to do this," he says through his clenched teeth.

"Are you sure you're not overreacting?" I ask. "I mean, Kami seemed to think it would be no big deal."

"That's because she's Kami. Getting pissed off your arse, sticking your tongue down a stewardess's throat, and demonstrating naked backflips would be her idea of a good time."

"That was oddly specific."

"My point is," he begins to say.

"You don't like being out of control," I say, giving him a reassuring pat to the shoulder. "I get it."

Zane is always so sure that he is a monster. That if he loses control of himself, he'll hurt people. He says he's worried about Dionysus hurting me, but I think he's far more worried he'll hurt me himself.

"Try not to resist him," he says. "His powers are strongest when you try to hold yourself back. And he can sense lies, so don't try to deceive him."

"How do his powers work? Does he have to touch me?"

"No, his powers don't have the same limitations mine do. He can use them intentionally if he feels so inclined, but otherwise his power will just radiate from him and affect everyone within 20 feet of him."

I nod as we pull up to a rather large strip club in the middle of the dessert. It's so in the middle of nowhere that it almost seems like a mirage. The building has a large, grey exterior and a big flashing neon sign on its roof. The sign features the shape of a red apple with a snake wrapped around it and pink lettering that reads "Garden of Eden."

"Fuck," Zane curses as he comes to a stop and pulls the parking brake.

"You can do this," I say. "Maybe it'll even be good for you. Maybe you'll see that it's not that bad."

He shrugs in response as we both step out of the car and toward the front entrance.

The club interior has no windows and dim lighting, despite it being midday. The room is sprawling and filled with plush, white couches surrounding multiple circular platforms with poles, several of which are occupied by male or female dancers. The patrons are completely wasted, some dancing with their limbs waving wildly in the air, others having aggressive make-out sessions with their hands down each other's pants. In the corner, a woman is singing karaoke while her friends seem to be involved in a fistfight.

This place is like Octoberfest if in place of beer there was nudity. And more beer.

"Hello, gorgeous!" a voice calls.

A grey-haired man with bronze skin approaches Zane and gives him a tight hug.

"Dionysus," Zane says stiffly.

That's Dionysus?

I'm not sure what I was expecting, but I wasn't expecting a forty-something hipster with a pompadour haircut.

"And this is Ava?" he asks, pulling me in for a hug too.

I expect Zane to growl, but I don't hear him. Maybe he's finally becoming less possessive.

"Hi," I say. "It's nice to meet you."

"Well come, sit, enjoy!" he says, guiding us to a white couch in front of a podium beneath a purple spotlight.

He gestures toward a man and woman, both in risqué clothing, who walk over at his command.

"Zane, my dear," Dionysus says, bringing the woman forward. "I know you enjoy women in particular, so I brought her for you."

"No thank you," Zane says with a clenched jaw.

"No?" Dionysus asks with one brow raised. His eyes rake over Zane before turning to me.

"Don't worry, lovely, I got you one too," he says with a smile.

Oh good. This is awkward.

"I wasn't sure what you liked," he continues, pulling forward a towering, buff, blond shirtless man in low-slung pants. "But Charles here can be anything your heart desires."

"Um, I'm good, thanks," I say. "No offense Charles."

Charles nods and Dionysus purses his lips.

"Well, she clearly goes for the dark and brooding type," he says, waving a hand at Charles.

In a moment, the man's overbuilt body morphs into a trim and fit physique. Tattoos appear on his chest and arms as his hair turns jet black.

Damn.

Okay, I'm not saying 'dark and broody' is my type, but the makeover is working on this guy.

"He's a shifter?" Zane asks, his jaw tight.

Shifter-Strippers are actually a really good idea.

Strip-Shifters? Shippers? Stripters?

"They both are," Dionysus says with a smile.

"We're not interested," Zane says.

"Yes," he says, looking Zane over again. "I see that. Perhaps your tastes have gotten a bit more… specific."

Dionysus leans over to whisper in the stripper's ear. She begins to transform, her skin lightening, and her hair shortening as it becomes… purple. *Oh wow.*

The woman now stands before us with an identical face and body to my own in a very intense lingerie set, fishnet stockings, and impossibly high heels.

I turn to Zane, whose eyes have gone wide and turned bright green.

Should I be jealous of myself right now?

Dionysus laughs, seemingly pleased with himself.

The woman walks up to Zane and attempts to give him a lap dance, but he pushes her away with so much force she lands several feet away.

"Dick!" she shouts at him, standing up and dusting herself off.

"Zane," Dionysus says in a warning tone. "Are you denying my hospitality?"

"No," he says, his jaw clenched. "I'm just not interested in this type of entertainment. I've made that clear."

"Well," Dionysus says with a smirk. "Guests in my club either receive dances or give them. No exceptions."

Wait… is he trying to get me to strip?

Actually, that sounds kind of fun.

"Fine," Zane huffs, standing up and approaching me. He stands in front of me and puts his hands on my knees, leaning in to whisper in my ear.

"Ready for a show, baby?"

66

A few strippers are dancing on the various podiums around us, with several patrons gawking at them. This section is in the middle of everything but is cleared out—probably reserved for Dionysus. Music with heavy bass plays in the background.

Zane takes a few steps back from me as I sit on the leather couch.

Wait—what's happening?

He's not doing what I think he is… right?

Zane starts to rock his hips forward to the beat.

Yep. He is.

"About time," Dionysus says, leaning back in his chair with a grin.

Zane looks insanely attractive under the purple and pink lights. He moves with surprising ease as he approaches me and puts a leg on either side of my knees so that he's standing with his abs at my eye level.

Damn.

He gives me a smirk and bites his lip as he rolls his hips to the rhythm.

Holy crap.

Zane has always been ridiculously attractive and he's certainly been a decent dancer when we've danced together, but I had no idea he could do *this*.

Has he practiced this before?

He starts to draw a crowd and I feel a bit of jealousy bubbling in my chest.

Zane grabs the top of the couch on either side of my head and pulls himself to me until his lips are at my ear.

"This is just for you, baby," he whispers, as if he could tell what I was thinking.

As he pulls back, his eyes are glowing slightly. I guess I'm not the only one his dancing is having an effect on.

He straightens up and grabs the bottom of his shirt, lifting it just enough to grab it with his teeth. He continues to dance with his abs now on full display. I'm pulled in by his every move as if I have tunnel vision that allows me to see only him.

"So Zane," Dionysus says as a server places a bottle of wine and several glasses on the table. "You've never had any problem with getting a lap dance before. Why the sudden change of heart?"

"I told you, I'm not interested in getting a lap dance," Zane says, stepping back as he slowly pulls off his shirt to cheers from the people around us.

I don't know what's more impressive: how perfect he looks or that he can dance and hold a conversation at the same time.

"Tsk tsk tsk," Dionysus scolds. "You know better than to lie to me, darling."

So... he did want a dance?

Zane sighs and gives him a quick glare.

"Fine, I don't want a lap dance from one of your strippers," he says.

"That's better," Dionysus says with a chuckle.

I can hardly keep track of the conversation with Zane shirtless and gyrating in front of me. My eyes gravitate toward the growing bulge in his pants. Though my instinct is to look away, for whatever reason I don't care as much as I usually would.

This must be the effect of Dionysus's powers.

Honestly, it feels kind of nice. I don't know what Zane was so afraid of. Inhibitions suck anyway.

Zane takes his T-shirt and loops it behind my neck, using it to pull me closer to him. He rests his knees on the couch, still straddling my legs. His vivid green eyes practically burn into my own as he licks his lips.

"So Ava," Dionysus says, interrupting our moment. "What is this effect you have on Zane?"

"I... um... what?" I ask. My mouth is dry and my brain has left the building.

"What did you do to conquer the Iron Siren?" he asks with a chuckle. "Because, from the looks of it, Zane is well and truly under your spell."

"I have no idea," I say with a shrug. "Apparently we're soulmates?"

"Last time I saw Zane, I just barely got his Siren eyes to flash," he says. "Look at him now—he's full Siren."

I look back at Zane, whose eyes are trained on my chest.

"Are you particularly adventurous in bed?" Dionysus asks.

Before I can respond, Zane has him pinned against a pillar in the center of the room. Zane's eyes are even brighter and his grip on Dionysus's neck looks impossibly tight. A deep rumbling growl reverberates through the floorboards.

"You'll never fucking know, mate," Zane says.

"Zane, it's fine. It doesn't bother me. Let's calm down," I say.

Zane's grip slowly loosens and he releases Dionysus, who looks almost disappointed.

"No no no," Dionysus says. "Where's the fun in calming down? I want to see how far we can push the Iron Siren. Jealous type, are we?"

"Don't," I say.

"Thank you for the suggestion, Miss Ava, but I do as I please. Always."

Dionysus looks to Zane, whose hands are still in fists at his sides.

"Naya," Dionysus calls to someone across the room. "Come here."

I turn to see my shifter doppelgänger, still with my face and body in leather lingerie. As she approaches, I can only think one thing: *Is that what my boobs really look like?*

"Would you dance for us please, darling?" Dionysus asks the woman.

She nods and steps up on the platform with the pole. She begins skillfully spinning around it, her legs managing to support her entire body weight.

I kind of want to record this to post on my Instagram.

Zane's eyes are ablaze and his every muscle is tense.

"Tell her to stop," he says, as others gather to watch her.

"Why would I want to do that?" Dionysus asks.

"Because you don't want me to murder every bloody person in this room for eyeing my girl," he says with a growl.

"Look at you, darling," he says, stepping towards Zane. "You're a true Siren— defending your claim on your lover. It's adorable."

Dionysus gestures to the woman and orders her to shift to another form.

"There, see," Dionysus says. "I can be agreeable. Besides, I have other things I'd like to try."

Zane gives him a murderous glare.

Dionysus waves a hand toward me, but I don't know what it means. As I turn to Zane, his eyes are focused intently, raking up and down my body. I look down at myself to see I'm now wearing a lacy black lingerie set with lots of crisscrossed straps.

It's a good thing he magically put this on me because there's no way I'd be able to figure out what to do with all these ties and strings.

Zane is now immediately in front of me, looking at me like a lion looks at a zebra. A low, clicking growl emerges from his lips and his single wing extends from his back.

Oh boy.

In an instant, there's a rush of air and we're on the couch, his body on top of mine as he peppers frenzied kisses along my neck.

"Zane," I moan.

He growls again and his lips crash into mine with fervor.

I see something out of the corner of my eye and glance quickly to the side. Dionysus sits there with a smile while sipping his wine. The unexpected visual shocks me back to reality.

"Zane, stop," I say.

Zane pushes himself backward off of me and stumbles slightly.

"Shit," he curses.

"Oh, don't stop on my account," Dionysus says.

Zane pulls out his phone and shows it to Dionysus.

"It's been an hour," he says, his wing folding back into his body as he replaces his shirt. "We met our end of the bargain. You owe Ava her clothes and me some Fury smoke."

"Once a party pooper, always a party pooper, aren't we Zane?" he asks.

Zane doesn't reply and simply holds out his palm.

Dionysus pulls an object from his pocket and places it in Zane's hand. It's a small golden sphere about the size of a grape attached to a chain like a necklace.

"Careful where you open that," Dionysus says. "It's potent like you wouldn't believe."

"And Ava?" he asks.

Dionysus waves his hand again and my regular clothes are back. Zane grabs my hand and pulls me toward the door and I quickly wave goodbye.

"Have fun!" Dionysus calls as we reach the doors and step outside.

Zane picks me up in his arms and rushes to the car, placing me in the passenger seat as he appears in the driver's seat and speeds away.

"Whoa, Zane," I say. "We got the smoke, everything's fine. You need to calm yourself."

His head snaps toward me, his eyes looking almost radioactive. He rails the steering wheel to the side and we veer off the road into the dirt. I hear the click of his seatbelt being undone, shortly followed by my own.

He lets out a guttural sound that I could only describe as a roar.

"I can't think straight… you… fuck…" he says. Instead of finishing his thought, he pulls me in for a deep kiss.

I already felt lightheaded from his dance earlier, but with his kiss I swear like I'm floating.

ZANE

Ava crawls over the center console as our tongues intertwine. Her movements are not particularly graceful and yet this may be the sexiest thing I've ever seen.

She straddles me and I grab two handfuls of her arse. Grinding on her at the club was torturous and I was dangerously close to fucking her in front of everyone in that room.

"Fuck," I hiss as she rolls her hips, kissing and sucking at my neck.

My dick is straining against my jeans as I watch her tits bounce behind the thin fabric of her T-shirt. Purple strands fall into her face and she bites her bottom lip and moans.

Fuck.

I look down at her denim shorts and decide they're not going to make it. I unbutton the first button and then quickly rip them down the middle, tearing until the fabric falls away.

"Zane!" she says with a gasp.

I'm sure she's trying to scold me for ruining her shorts but all I can think is how good my name sounds on her lips.

I graze my fingertips down her stomach and between her legs, touching her through the silk fabric of her panties. She shivers as her body collapses forward into me.

She nibbles at my neck while I pull her panties to the side, sliding a finger into her. She lets out a slew of beautiful noises that bring me to my breaking point.

Fuck this.

I unbutton my trousers and sigh with relief. Her hands begin immediately stroking me and I shudder at the sensation. I desperately grab for the condom in my wallet and quickly slip it on, mentally praising myself for putting one in there before we left the hotel—you know, just in case.

I pull her closer toward me until our bodies align and slowly lower her onto me.

"Zane," she moans, pushing me further toward the edge.

I grab her hips and move her up and down. Her breasts bounce with every thrust. I pull her in for a kiss as she continues riding me.

She begins to shiver and her muscles tense as her orgasm pulses around me. A mixture of curses and moans pours out of her mouth and that's all it takes for my own release to follow. My limbs fall to my sides as Ava's body drapes atop mine.

"Fuck," I say through heavy breaths.

"Yeah," she says.

"Did we just fuck in the car like bloody teenagers?"

"Actually, my high school boyfriend had a motorcycle," she says.

I growl in response.

"Just kidding," she says with a giggle.

"Not funny, love," I say. "Not funny."

67

I wake up to the sound of my pulse hammering in my head. My limbs are sore and impossibly heavy and the room is spinning. I groan and bury my head under a pillow.

I should know better. If you have chronic pain and have the audacity to do anything other than lie down and sigh, you're basically asking for trouble. Ever since we returned from Utah yesterday, I've been paying the price for trying to be a normal person.

Through the pillow, I hear the familiar lull of Zane's voice but can't quite make out what he is saying, so I begrudgingly lift it from over my head.

"What?" I ask. My voice is hoarser than I expected; I sound like a chicken with a sore throat.

"Are you feeling okay?" he asks.

I open my eyes to see him looking back at me with wrinkled brows and his lips pinched into a thin line.

"I'm technically alive," I grumble.

'Okay' is complicated for me. Some days I can't tell if I feel worse or I'm just not as up for coping with it all.

"Yes, love," he says, sitting beside me on the edge of the bed. "I could tell you're alive because corpses don't usually do a lot of talking. But I'm getting the distinct impression that doesn't actually mean you're feeling well."

He flashes me a sarcastic smile.

"Can you feel it?" I ask. "Is it hurting you too?"

"Sort of," he says. "The feeling isn't as strong as it was when we first did the mark, but I can still sense it. I can feel that your pain is intense, even if I don't feel it to the same degree."

"Yeah," I mumble, though it comes out as more of a groan.

"I take it you're not feeling well enough to join me today?"

"Join you for what?" I ask, rubbing my eyes as I sit up slightly. Just this small action has my head pounding.

"Remember? I got a call about a possible lead on Asmodeus. I'm leaving to meet the guy in about an hour."

"Oh, was I supposed to come for that?"

"Honestly, it's probably better that you didn't. I don't know too much about this bloke. I just didn't want to leave you alone."

"Well, I'll be fine here, anyway. I think you're being paranoid about me always needing bodyguards."

"You're going to have 'bodyguards' as you call it regardless," he says with a teasing glare. "I was going to have Finn come with us, but if you're staying home I can have him stay with you."

"Wow, only one bodyguard?" I ask jokingly. "You really like to live dangerously."

"Nice try. I'm calling Kami too."

I sigh and flop back down onto the bed.

At least I'll get a chance to sleep.

———•———

After spending most of the day lying in bed while Finn and Kami hung out in the living room, I finally dragged myself out at about 6 in the evening.

"Oh good, you're up!" Kami says, eating potato chips out of a bag. "Girl, you can really sleep."

"I wasn't sleeping so much as I was just lying there cursing life," I say.

"Okay then, sunshine," she says with a laugh. "Well, I'm glad you're here. There's only so much of listening to Finn's old-man stories that I can take."

"Oi!" Finn snaps. "I'm not an old man. I'm not even 400."

"You're almost twice my age, old man," she says teasingly, throwing a chip at him. He manages to maneuver himself in such a way that the chip lands in his mouth.

"Thanks, love," he says with a smirk.

"Well, I see you two are a bit stir-crazy," I say, pouring myself a glass of orange juice.

"I'm not really made for babysitting," Kami says. "No offense hon, happy to help you of course."

Ouch. Offense definitely taken.

"Just to be clear," I say. "This is entirely Zane's insistence. I'm pretty sure I'd be perfectly fine at home on my own. We have security and massive locks and whatnot; I don't think even Asmodeus could break in here."

"I wouldn't underestimate him," Finn says. "The Demon Kings are incredibly powerful, and Asmodeus has a truly insidious mind."

"Well thanks, Finn," I say. "You're making me feel a lot better."

"Speaking of leaving the house," Finn says. "I'm sorry, but I need to head out soon. I have family business to attend to this evening. Since Kieran's working tonight, I've arranged to take you and Kami to Pike's."

"Isn't that more dangerous than being at home?" I ask.

"It's better to have two of us looking after you than just one," Kami says. "Besides, Pike's is a public space with lots of humans. The last thing Asmodeus wants to do is make a scene."

"He's the methodical, patient type," Finn adds. "He won't just strike in a room full of people without a plan. That's not his game."

"But isn't Kieran kind of useless against him?" I ask.

"Not if you have these," Kami says, pulling a set of ancient-looking handcuffs from her purse.

"Uh, do I want to know?" I ask.

"They're not for kinky things, Ava," she says. "Get than dirty human mind out of the gutter! They're immobilization cuffs. Anyone in them can't use their powers or move anything but their head. In an emergency, we slap these on Kieran and he can't be used by Asmodeus."

"Okay, sure, but he can't help us either," I say.

"True," she says. "That's if Asmodeus shows up. But he's not usually that straightforward with his attacks. He's more of a devious, in-the-shadows type. If he sends his demons or anyone else for you, Kieran can help us fight."

I nod slightly, hardly acknowledging that my life has become a series of these really bizarre conversations.

Finn encourages us to get going, so I get dressed in my most comfortable yoga pants and sweater, plus a big puffy coat since it's absolutely freezing outside lately.

We make our way to the parking garage and Finn hops in his car. I join Kami in her car and we head to Pike's.

After a 20 minute drive, we pull into the relatively empty parking lot of Pike's and head inside.

"Hey! Who let that man in here?" Kieran shouts from behind the bar, pointing at Finn. He steps around the bar and walks up to us. "Excuse me, sir, we don't allow seafood in this establishment."

Finn gives him a playful slug to the gut.

"Oh really?" Finn asks. "Then what's a little shrimp like you doing here?"

Kieran and Finn both erupt in laughter and greet each other with a big hug.

"Boys," Kami says with a sigh, rolling her eyes.

"So how's 'Ava Watch'?" Kieran says. "You look like you're still in one piece. Good job, you two."

I try my best not to cringe at the thought of being babysat by my boyfriend's friends.

"*Oi, love,*" Finn's voice rings in my head. "*We're your friends too.*"

Sometimes I forget he can do that. Oh god, what other awkward things have I been thinking?

Finn gives me a subtle smile.

"What's the word on the patrons?" Kami asks.

Finn looks around at the other people in the bar. One man sits alone at the other end of the bar, sipping what looks like a whiskey on the rocks. A couple across the room is getting cozy in a booth while a group of frat boys is playing pool.

"I can read everyone except shrimpcakes over here," Finn says with a smirk.

Kami rolls her eyes.

"So what're you heading home for?" Kieran asks Finn. "Must be pretty good if you're skipping out in the middle of all this Asmodeus crap."

"I uh… um… well…" Finn stutters.

"That's not suspicious at all," Kami says.

"Well, right now is… I haven't said anything so far but… well…"

"Holy shit," Kami says, her eyes wide.

Finn nods with a smile.

"Can someone let me in on the secret?" Kieran asks.

"I need to head home for the Zenith," Finn says. "Because it's the one time every few years when Selkies can, well…"

"Oh shit," Kieran says. "You and Marella are gonna make a baby?"

"Yep," Finn replies, slightly blushing.

"Gross." Kieran scrunches his face in disgust.

"Well, I think that's really cool," Kami says. "I know you guys have always wanted to have kids."

"Might as well," Kieran says. "Since you're old now and have no game."

Finn flips him off and they both laugh.

"At least I had game to begin with," Finn says with a grin.

"All you Immortals think you're hot shit, but when push comes to shove, it's me going home with the hotties."

"Is that why you need Zane's help to get laid?" Finn asks.

"Ohhh, damn," Kieran says. "I don't need Zane's help to get laid. His venom just makes it more potent. Besides, Zane and I have already competed and I won."

What? When did this happen?

"I would hardly say you won," Kami says. "You pretended Ava was here to make Zane panic. That's cheating."

"Wait—this happened when Zane and I were already together?" I ask.

"No, no," Kami said. "This happened shortly after he met you when he was all piney and obsessed with you."

"He's like that now," Kieran says.

"Which just further proves beating Zane doesn't mean anything. He was a lost cause."

I can't tell if that's a compliment to me or not.

"What is it about Immortals? Every time we get together, somebody makes it a big power play," Finn says with a laugh. "Can't we just agree we're all capable of turning humans into putty and call it a day?"

Pshh… rude. I'm right here.

"Bollocks, sorry Ava, that's not how I meant it," Finn says.

"It's okay," I say.

"Well, unfortunately my loves, this is where I leave you," Finn says.

"Alright, bro, go stick it to your woman and make some mer-babies," Kieran says with a wave. Finn flips him off before giving us all a wave on his way out of the bar.

"The bromance between you two is the worst," Kami says with an eye roll.

The jingle of the door lets us know that someone has entered the bar. Zane should be back soon and a little part of me hopes it's him. Instead, I turn to see another familiar face: Shayna.

Anger burns through my chest at the sight of her. It's the first time I've seen her since Jen and I saw her cheating at the mall—since she broke my best friend's heart. She doesn't seem to see me as she approaches the bar to talk to Kieran.

"Hey," she says. "I'm here to pick up my paycheck."

Without thinking, I walk over to her. The blood rushes to my face as I contemplate what to say to her.

I finally settle on going with the first thing that comes to mind: a hard slap to the face.

My palm makes a sharp 'smack' sound as it contacts her cheek, leaving behind a red handprint.

She looks at me in shock as she touches her sore cheek with her hand.

"What the fuck, Ava?" she asks.

"Really?" I ask. "You cheated on Jen! First with Kieran, then with that bitch at the mall. You don't even bother being discreet about it! Not that you should've hidden it better—that's not the point! The point is, you broke her heart, you big… giant… ho-bag… bitch-face… bitch."

Nailed it.

In hindsight, I really should have planned what I was going to say.

She raises an eyebrow and pinches her lips between her teeth as if she's holding back a laugh.

This isn't really going as I planned.

Suddenly an idea occurs to me.

"Kami, can you help me?" I ask. "I need a redo on this."

Kami smirks and walks over to a slightly confused Shayna and reaches for her hand.

"You don't remember anything about this encounter with Ava," Kami says. "Everything she says from now on will be the first time you've spoken today."

Kami steps back and Shayna nods before giving me a confused look.

"How could you cheat on my best friend?" I ask, my voice getting louder with each word. "You broke her heart. I have no idea what she ever saw in a cheating, garbage, basic bitch like you, but you know what? Good riddance!"

"This is none of your business, Ava!" she says with a glare. "You think Jen is so innocent, but she was living with her ex and kept it from me for weeks."

"Yeah, Jen's not perfect, but she deserves someone a million times better than you. And you deserve exactly what you got. You lost a sweet, wonderful human being who actually cared about you. God knows why she did—you are clearly not worth her time or kindness."

I turn on my heels, rather pleased with my rant, before turning back around.

"Oh yeah," I say. "One more thing."

My palm connects with her cheek again, the force radiating through my hand and Shayna's face even harder than before. I turn around as she stares in shock and sit myself back down at the bar.

My hand hurts like hell, but I'll be damned if I show that while she's watching.

"Bitch-face bitch?" Kieran asks with a sly smile.

"Oh, shut up."

68

Well, today was a bloody waste of time.

Of course my informant was a no-show. Either he got spooked over the idea of Asmodeus finding out he was talking to me, or worse—Asmodeus already found out and made an example of him.

It's more likely that the bloke panicked and skipped town. It isn't Asmodeus's style to just make someone disappear. He loves to make a big show of his kills.

I swear, going after Asmodeus is just one dead end after the other.

Signs and lampposts flicker by as I drive back home. My Challenger is the only car on the road and the windows are fogging in the frigid night air.

In my rear-view mirror, I see a cloud of vapor rising from the back of my car.

Bollocks, is it really that cold?

The engine starts to make a strange whirring sound and I can feel it running roughly. It churrs and sputters as I pull over to the side of the road. A sign ahead says it's 40 more miles back to Port Charlotte.

Fuck me. Today is really not my day.

I fall back into my seat and let out a heavy sigh. The heater starts to wheeze before slowing to a stop.

Perfect.

I ponder a moment before giving Ava a ring.

"Hey!" she answers.

"Hey, love," I say with a sigh.

"What's wrong?" she asks, immediately sensing the defeat in my voice.

"Oh, it's fine. My lead didn't pan out and I'm having car troubles a ways outside the city. I think I'm going to have to call for a tow, so I'll be later than expected. Are you fine to stay at Pike's for a while? Are you safe?"

"Sure," she says. "There are lots of people here and it's totally safe. Just take care of yourself, it's freezing out."

"I'm fine, baby. You think a little cold would affect me?"

"Okay, Mister Macho. I love you!"

"I love you too," I say. "Talk soon."

I end the call and look at the many engine warning lights currently flashing on my dashboard and shiver.

Fuck. It's bloody freezing.

AVA

A few drinks in and the pain in my muscles has eased substantially. Sure, I'm going to regret this tomorrow, but when you're friends with the bartender, why not enjoy the perks?

"You guys are getting along a lot better," I say to Kami, my speech only slightly affected by the alcohol.

"Who?" Kami asks.

"You and Kieran," I say, pointing to him as he pours drinks for two women down the bar.

"Yeah, well…" she says, taking a heavy swig of her drink. "I guess I feel a little bad for judging him all these years. I was so ready to jump on him the moment something seemed up, but he came through for Zane. He always does. Zane deserves that."

"Yeah." I nod and watch as Kieran flirts with the girls he's serving.

The door jingles as it swings open, letting in a burst of cold air. We both turn to see a heavily bundled Zane making his way over to us.

"Well, look who it is!" Kami says. "How's the car?"

Zane sighs and scoops me into a hug from behind.

"Missed you, baby," he says, before turning to Kami. "The car should be fine. I had it towed to the shop and I'll have someone check it out in the morning. It was running pretty rough, I think the cold took its toll."

"You didn't take very long, cute face," I say, giving him a quick kiss.

"Yeah well, after the tow truck came, I decided to say fuck it and called a rental car," he says with a shiver. "How many drinks have you had, love?"

I hold up three fingers.

Wait, was it three or four?

"I'm shocked," Kami says with a laugh. "I feel like you never let that car out of your sight."

"Yeah well, I figured I'd rather be with my baby," he replies, giving me a kiss on the cheek and squeezing me into another hug.

"By your baby, do you mean Ava or the Challenger?" Kieran asks, reappearing from behind the bar.

"You'll never get your hands on either, mate," Zane says with an eye roll.

"Hey, why so salty Z-Man? We can't share?" he asks jokingly as he pours Zane a beer.

"I wi-" Zane starts to say.

"I know, I know," Kieran says, cutting him off. "You'll kill me. Something about tying my intestines into balloon animals or roasting me on a barbecue, yada yada. Gotcha."

Zane ignores Kieran's comment and takes a drink of his beer.

"Thanks for looking out for Ava today," he says to Kami.

Translation: thanks for babysitting the poor pathetic human.

"Yeah, thanks for indulging Mister Paranoid over here," I say, sticking out my tongue at Zane.

"On that note, I'm fucking exhausted," he says with a sigh. "Ready to head home, love?"

I nod and gather up my things. We say our goodbyes and head on home.

<hr />

Zane scoops me up and carries me out of the elevator.

"You're like, really really pretty—you know that, right?" I say with a giggle. "You've got… like… a really good face."

"Thanks love," he says with a smile as we approach the door. "Ahh bollocks."

"What?" I ask.

"The bloody tow place has my keys. Do you have yours?" he asks.

"Yep," I say. "They're in my purse. Where's my purse? Did I leave it at Pike's?"

"Love, you asked me to carry your purse, remember?"

He laughs as he sets me down, my legs slightly wobbly. My usual dizziness is only enhanced by the effects of the alcohol and I stagger a bit as I rummage for my keys.

"Aha!" I say, pulling out my jumble of keys and unlocking the door.

Zane picks me back up and brings me inside.

"I can walk on my own," I say with a giggle.

"You're pissed, love," he says.

"No, I'm in a super good mood." I pause for a moment. "Oh you mean drunk, yes I am that."

I giggle as he drops me onto the couch and kisses my forehead.

"Yes, you are quite *that*," he says, smiling.

He sheds a couple of layers of jackets and picks me up onto his lap. He pretends to be so tough, but with his extra coats, shivering, and chilly hands, I know better. I pull a blanket over the both of us and cuddle up to him.

"You're amazing," he says with a sigh. "Do you know that?"

"Yep," I reply. He wraps his arms tighter around me and laughs.

"Could we take a picture?" he asks.

"Of what?"

"You and me."

"Why?"

"I don't know, I just don't have many and I missed you today," he says, giving me big pleading puppy-dog eyes.

"Alright," I say.

He scoots me up further onto his lap and pulls out his phone. Before I can properly pose, he pulls me in for a kiss. His lips are still cold but they move with desperation, his tongue dipping in and out between my lips.

I look over at his phone. It doesn't look like the picture has been taken and there's a little red circle on the screen.

"You're not taking a picture, you're filming!" I say, slapping his chest. "You butthead!"

"What?" he says with a smirk. "Oh, oops! Did I push the wrong button?"

"If I look like a dork on that, you're required as my soulmate to delete it. It's the law."

"Aww, but what if I want to show all my friends what a fox my soulmate is?" he asks, his lips pinched into a pout.

"Oooh you're smooooth," I say, sticking out my tongue.

"But isn't that why you love me?" he asks.

"No, I love you because of the whole free immortality schtick," I tease.

Zane narrows his eyes then suddenly his hands begin to tickle my sides.

"Is that so, my love?" he asks. I laugh as I attempt to wriggle loose from his grasp.

I break free and jump up from the couch.

"Come at me, wing boy!"

———•———

ZANE

This whole day was such a bloody disaster.

I wish I had just spent the entire day with Ava. Instead, I spent most of it frustrated, cold, and alone.

I open the door and am instantly hit with the heated indoor air.

Thank fuck.

I look around but don't immediately see Kami or Ava.

"Hey," Kieran calls. "What are you doing here?"

"What the bloody hell are you on about?" I ask. "I'm really not in the mood for your cheekiness. I'm here to pick up my girl."

Kieran narrows his eyes before they widen suddenly.

"Did you forget something?" Kami's voice says from behind me. She seems to have been making out with a buff bald guy in the booth behind her. "Where's Ava?"

"The bloody hell do you mean, 'Where's Ava?' Are you taking the piss?" I ask. "You're supposed to be watching her."

Is this their idea of some kind of twisted prank?

I turn to look back and forth between them, their expressions both frantic.

"I... it... oh my god," Kami stutters. "*That wasn't you.*"

69

Zane playfully stalks me around the coffee table as I slowly step backwards to avoid him. The alcohol in my blood is affecting my coordination and I stumble slightly.

"You should know better than to fight an Immortal, love," he says with a smirk.

"What you gonna do 'bout it, Mister Siren?" I tease, stepping back slightly.

"You're not afraid of me, are you?"

"Of course not."

"Why is that?" he asks with a raised eyebrow. "I mean, you're human. I'm infinitely stronger than you, faster than you. You should find me terrifying."

His serious expression tells me we're no longer having the same playful conversation. Zane is so caught up with this feeling that he's a monster. Sometimes it still creeps into the little moments.

"I know you're afraid of hurting me," I say, stepping closer to him and wrapping my arms around his torso. "But I know you never would. I have faith in you. Deep down, I know who you are and *you are good*."

"Hurting you… is my nightmare," he mumbles as he looks at me with a furrowed brow. His eyes scan my face as if he's working something out in his mind.

"Well, you won't hurt me, so you have nothing to worry about."

He smiles and steps back, reaching into his back pocket and pulling out his cell phone.

"Do something for me, would you?" he asks.

"Sure," I say. "What's that?"

He holds out his phone as if he's trying to take a picture of me.

"Say that again for me," he says softly.

"What?" I ask, rolling my eyes. "I'm not sure I understand. Are you filming me again?"

What is with Zane and the videos today?

"Please?" he asks.

"Okay," I say, looking into the phone's lens. "I uh… You are good. You are a good person and I have faith in you."

"Faith in what? The whole thing…"

His expression is solemn and dark.

"I know that you will never hurt me," I say. "I trust you."

He looks at the phone's screen for a moment before looking back up at me.

In a flash, I feel intense pressure against my cheekbone along with a loud ringing that reverberates in my ears as Zane's fist connects with my face. I tumble to the floor and hold a hand up to my cheek as my jaw goes slack in horror.

"What about now?" he asks, a smirk growing on his face as he looks me dead in the eyes. "Still so sure?"

"I…" I mumble, unsure of what to say. I feel like I'm hovering outside of my body, unable to speak or react.

This isn't right. Zane wouldn't hurt me.

"Oh, come on, Ava," he says with a chuckle. "A moment ago, you were so sure of me. So much faith. Where did all that go?"

My mind runs through every moment of the night so far and nothing is adding up.

Kami's words echo in my mind: *"You never let that car out of your sight."*

"Where's your car?" I ask.

"That wasn't the response I expected," he says, his voice slightly higher than usual. "All you have to ask is about the damn car?"

It wasn't just his voice, everything about him seemed off. Maybe the drunkenness made it harder to notice, but now it was all hitting me. There was an undeniable undertone in his voice that made every word seem wrong. Even the way he moved was *off*.

"Whatever's happening, Zane," I say. "This isn't you. We can fix this."

"Oh really?" he asks with a smirk.

He types something into his phone before throwing it onto the couch. In the blink of an eye, he has me pinned against the wall by my shoulders, my head snapping back with a hard thunk. The rapid motion alone makes me nauseous.

His deep brown eyes stare back into mine. There's a shallowness in his eyes that I've never seen before. There's nothing but emptiness behind them.

Brown eyes…

In all the times Zane has even been angry or aggressive like this, his eyes would glow their usual vivid green, but in this moment they are brown.

It's a kind of detail you might get wrong if you were pretending to be someone you're not.

He left his car behind with the tow truck driver?

And his skin feels so cold.

What is with the sudden desperation to take these videos?

His words from earlier come back to mind: *"what if I want to show all my friends…"*

He didn't say *mates*.

Oh crap.

He's a demon.

I can feel my heart pounding in my chest and the room suddenly feels way too hot.

"What's wrong with you?" he asks.

Well that's just a rude thing to ask. What's wrong with you, *dickhead?*

I decide my best bet is to let on as little as possible until I figure out how to get out of this.

"Well, you did just hit me in the face and stuff, so I'm pretty sure I'm not feeling too great about that."

He chuckles at me as he picks up a glass of water. He takes a sip before flinging it across the loft. The glass loudly shatters against a far-off wall and I flinch.

"What gave me away?" he asks, his voice suddenly shifting to an American accent.

"I… uh…"

"You're panicking. I can hear your heartbeat speeding up, the blood running faster through your veins. Something has changed. You're onto me, so let's cut the crap," he says with a small laugh. He grabs me by the front of my shirt and throws me very easily onto the floor. His frame then appears above me and a sinister smile stretches across his face.

"I… You said friends…" I mumble. That wasn't the entire truth, but I found myself panicking to give him an answer before he decided to throw me out the window of our twenty-some story building.

"Friends?" he asks. "Oh damn it. You know, I thought the accent would be the easy part. End every sentence with 'love' or 'mate', throw around a 'bloody' or two and you've basically got Zane."

He sighs and sits down on the couch as I sit myself up and lean back against the wall.

"I speak 23 languages for hell's sake, yet I can't properly imitate a single Siren?" he says. "Well now, that's just embarrassing."

"Who are you?" I ask.

"Oh Ava, after the moment we shared together, you still don't remember me?" he says with a smirk. "Everyone is so disrespectful these days."

My eye catches a fork on the table beside me. He's currently rambling to himself. Maybe I can catch him off guard and make a break for it?

Okay it's not a great plan, but I don't have another one.

I jump up and grab the fork with the fastest motion I can muster and jam it into his shoulder. His hand is around my wrist instantly and, despite my best efforts, I can't even come close to breaking free. He pulls out the fork with his other hand and grunts.

This is bad.

"There's that feisty little Ava I expected," he says with a laugh. "Now that was not disappointing. We're going to have a lot of fun, aren't we darling?"

Only one other person has called me that. It was the demon from my dream that was pretending to be Kieran. *It was Asmodeus.*

"It's you," I mumble.

"In the flesh," he says, raising his palms up. "Well, in *someone's* flesh."

His body shifts into a different form: the one I saw torturing Kieran outside of Pike's. His hair shortens and lightens to a platinum-blond and his build becomes leaner, almost skeletal. His true form is slimmer and less imposing than Zane's, but somehow more terrifying.

"There," he says with a sigh. "That's better."

"Why do you insist on pretending to be someone else?" I ask.

The shift between being attacked and having a seemingly normal conversation is jarring.

"I don't usually, but this was a special case. I was being watched," he says with a smirk.

"Watched?" I ask. "By who?"

"Your darling Seer friend," he says. "She was quite powerful, couldn't risk her catching on to my activities. I'm quite a private person, really."

"So you decided to look like Kieran?" I say.

"Pretended to be Zane too. I thought I had thrown her off my scent, but she caught on anyway. She was going to tell Kieran, and I wasn't quite ready for the big reveal at that point. So she had to die. Shame, too. She was quite powerful. Why is it that the Seers can never see their own death coming, huh?"

Asmodeus lets out a sigh and relaxes into the couch slightly.

"I guess you know what they say about best-laid plans," he says. "Oh well, it all worked out, though."

"Why are you here?" I ask, mostly to keep him talking. Of course, delaying will only work if someone is coming for me.

Another disturbing thought comes to mind: *If he's here, where is the real Zane? What if something happened to him and he can't come?*

"I'm just here to congratulate Zane's new bride," he says.

"And by congratulate, what are the odds you actually mean kill?"

"Relax, Ava. I have no desire to kill you."

He pulls out a cigarette and lights it before taking a big puff.

"I will, of course," he says. "Kill you, that is. But it's not personal. You're a means to an end. An eye for an eye so to speak."

I know he's telling me he's going to kill me, but all I can think about is how this asshole is smoking in my apartment.

I'm never getting that smell out of the couch, am I?

"So you kill a bunch of random people around town, then you kill me, and that somehow gets you your revenge?" I ask.

"Of course not," he says. "I do not get my hands dirty, especially not to kill random humans."

He takes another heavy puff of his cigarette and blows the smoke toward my face. I try not to react, but I end up in a coughing fit.

"My demons got to town and started having their fun long before I knew anything about this place. Turns out the city has a Siren venom problem—wonder how that could have happened. But then word got back to me that not only was Zane in town, but he had a lover. I had to see for myself."

"Okay, well you've seen me," I say. "You can go now."

"You should be honored, really. This is a rare occurrence. The personal attention of the one and only God of Lust."

"I've met the God of Lust and you're not him," I say.

"Oh please, you mean Dionysus?" he asks, his eyes narrowing. "He's a wannabe—a poor man's version of me. I am curious what brought you to meet Dionysus, though."

I pinch my lips shut, realizing I may have given a part of the plan away. Not that the original plan was really valid anymore.

He stalks toward me and I stumble backwards onto the rug at the base of the stairs. I try to run up them but he instantly grabs my ankle. My chin hits one of the wooden stairs with a hard thunk, my teeth biting into my tongue hard. The taste of iron fills my mouth and I see little red droplets landing on the floor beneath me.

"You think Zane loves you so he'll just magically save you?" he shouts, rolling me over to face him. "You think his 'love' matters??"

He holds both my arms over my head with a single hand and I struggle as the stairs dig into my back.

"He supposedly loved Ilen, didn't he?" he says. "And what happened? He was selfish, and she suffered. If he really cared for her, would he have let her die? And now look at you—the same fate. But where is your lover? As usual, he's nowhere to be found."

My eye catches a slight movement from the open patio and a dark figure appears behind Asmodeus. The figure appears dark even as it steps into the light; black smoke swirls around, consuming their body from head to toe. The only thing I can see through the smoke is a pair of vibrant green eyes.

70

Time slows to a near standstill and a ringing in my ears blocks out every other sound.

This can't be real. She can't be gone.

My stomach is in knots.

Fuck, I'm nauseous. I don't even get nauseous.

"How could you have let this happen??" I ask as Kieran and Kami exchange panicked looks.

Is it Asmodeus? Did he take her somewhere?

"Okay, just calm down, Z," Kami says, her voice rife with anxiety. "He looked like you and we had no way of knowing."

"Except we did," I say. "Lola told us. '*Don't trust Zane.*' She warned us and I was too bloody clever to listen. She knew."

And of course, this happens during the Selkie Zenith, eliminating Finn from the equation. He was the only person who would've known it wasn't really me.

We were given every sign—how did we not see what he was planning?

I pull out my phone to see if I can track Ava. Her phone pings at a familiar location: the penthouse.

He took her home.

"Damn it," I curse. "They're at our flat. We need to get there *now*."

"You think it's Asmodeus?" she asks.

"Of course it is. This is exactly his game and he's got us right where he wants us."

"Okay, this is okay," Kami says.

"How the bloody hell is this okay??"

"The plan can still work. We just need to accelerate the timetable into however much time it takes me to drive between here and the apartment."

Kieran and I follow Kami out to the parking lot.

"Get in the back," Kami says, gesturing to her purple sports car.

"The back?" I ask.

"God damn it, Zane, just go!" she shouts.

I crawl into the back seat and Kieran rides shotgun. Kami peels out of the parking lot and onto the main road.

"First thing, Kieran," she says, handing him a small vial of lethe from her purse.

"Oh boy, so we're really doing this, huh?" he asks. "How much do I take?"

"A little goes a long way," I say.

"Down the hatch," he says, nodding and sipping about half of the vial. "What now?"

"Now it's your turn," Kami says, catching my eye in the rearview mirror.

This wasn't the plan. We were supposed to have time to prepare. We were supposed to fight Asmodeus on our own terms. Ava wasn't supposed to get anywhere near this.

The Fury smoke has been on a chain around my neck since we got it from Dionysus. I pull out the gold orb from underneath my shirt and open the clasp. A black smoke begins to pour forth from it and I inhale.

Tendrils of smoke find their way into my mouth and nose until I'm overcome with a feeling of sinking darkness. I feel the rage running through my veins and oozing out of my every pore.

"How ya feelin'?" Kieran asks.

"Like I'm walking on fucking sunshine, mate—how the fuck do you think I'm feeling?" I growl.

"Okay, okay," he says. "Honestly, it's hard to tell what's the Fury smoke and what's your usual cranky self."

"No more witty banter, Kieran," Kami interrupts. "We need to kick this into high gear. Okay um, Zane… you left Ava with us and we let you down. We were supposed to protect her."

She's trying to help by riling me up to enhance the effects of the Fury smoke.

"Come on, Zane," she says. "You trusted us, doesn't that make you mad?"

"No, Kami, it just makes me realize what a fucking arsehole I am for pulling you guys into this in the first place."

"Okay, now," Kieran says. "Kami, you suck at this. I'm a certified professional at pissing Zane off, trust me."

Kieran flips around in his seat so that he's facing me.

"Hey Z-Dawg," he says.

"Don't fucking call me that," I hiss.

"What? Z-Dawg? Meh, I like it…" he says. "So, Z-Dawg, what the hell happened to your car anyway?"

"My car ran out of antifreeze and the engine shut down. I just bloody topped it up."

As the words leave my lips, I realize it's probably no coincidence.

Someone sabotaged my bloody car so I wouldn't make it home on time.

"You really need to take better care of your car, Z-Dawg. Haven't you ever heard of maintenance?"

"Piss off," I snap, a growl rumbling in my chest. "Someone must've set me up—fuck!"

My mind runs through the details. The whole thing could've been a setup. Who's to say the informant I was there to meet even existed. Just an excuse to get me out of the way.

My phone vibrates in my pocket and I pull it out. It's a message from an unknown number, but in the thumbnail I can clearly see Ava.

I let out a hoarse scream and nearly launch my phone through the windshield, but Kieran grabs it away from me.

He looks at the screen for a moment before looking back at me.

"Okay man, I'm gonna play you this 'cause if anything's gonna piss you off, I'm pretty sure it's this, but don't shoot the messenger."

He turns the screen to me. A video is playing of Ava kissing me—but it's not me. Asmodeus's vindictive eyes are staring back at me through the lens, enjoying the torture he's putting me through. This is all a sick game to him. A small smirk appears on his face as he nips at Ava's bottom lip.

I'm going to bloody kill the bastard.

A guttural scream resonates from my chest and I begin to shake.

"Whoa shit," Kieran says, his eyes widening. "Dude, your eyes are black."

"Keep going," Kami says.

"Oh yeah, let's fucking torture Zane some more," I snap.

"Hey guys," Kieran says. "Did I take some really heavy-duty drugs because I have no idea why we're here and Zane has black eyes and I think his face is like… smoking?"

"Yeah, you took something," Kami says, rocketing the car around a tight corner. "All you really need to know is that we're killing Asmodeus and you just need to sit there and do nothing."

"Sweet," he says, leaning back in his seat with his legs crossed. "Wait, so why are we killing Asmodeus?"

"Because he's a psychopath obsessed with getting back at Zane over an old stupid grudge. And now he kidnapped Ava," she says. "We've got to stop him before he kills her."

"Ahh gotcha," he says. "And who's Ava?"

A low growl vibrates from my throat.

"Oh and why am I getting text messages from this random number?" he asks, holding up my phone.

Asmodeus seems to have sent another video.

"Play it," I say.

He hits the button and Ava appears on the screen. She's smiling and batting her eyes shyly at the camera. Her cheeks are flushed and she seems slightly inebriated.

"You are good," her voice says in the video. "You are a good person and I have faith in you."

Her words feel like a knife to the chest.

She believes in me—like she always does. She has no idea.

"Faith in what? The whole thing," a man's voice says.

His English accent is shite.

"I know that you will never hurt me," she says. "I trust you."

Suddenly she's struck with a fist from behind the camera.

My whole world stops in a single second.

When I was 18, I was kicked in the ribs by a horse. As a soldier, I lost a leg from a landmine in the Hürtgen Forest outside Belgium. In 1942, a demon slashed my abdomen open in a bar fight. But I've never experienced pain like this until I saw the look of betrayal in her eyes at this moment. She had faith in me. And I watched that faith shatter.

"Shit, I didn't know that was… is that… Ava?" Kieran asks.

My whole body shakes as I seethe, my jaw clenched so tight it could break. A fire burns in my veins and I feel an extreme clarity spread to the once-clouded corners of my mind. My singular focus is ending Asmodeus—for good.

As if on cue, Kami pulls up to our building.

"We should take the fire escape," Kami says, jumping out of the car. "It's our only shot at catching him off guard."

She grabs a knife and a roll of duct tape from the trunk and slips the binding cuffs onto Kieran's wrists. Placing the dagger in his hands, she runs the duct tape around them until the knife is firmly secured.

"Oh yeah," Kieran says. "This is definitely a great plan. It's probably too late for a bathroom break, eh?"

I see deep black smoke covering my hands and creeping up my arms.

"Okay, Z, this is it," Kami says. "Right now, it's time to be the monster. *Ava needs the monster.*"

71

In an instant, Asmodeus is ripped off of me and launched across the room, his body smashing through a decorative glass panel. I grab the stair railing to pull myself up. The smoke-veiled figure is standing steadfast between Asmodeus and me.

I can just barely make out the familiar shape of Zane's curly hair and broad shoulders beneath the thick fog of opaque black smoke.

"Are you okay?" Zane asks. His voice is rough and angry, but unmistakably his.

"I… I'm okay," I stutter. I don't sound nearly as reassuring as I intend to.

Before Zane can respond, Asmodeus rises to his feet. His clothing is tattered and covered in blood; several large glass shards protrude from his skin.

"Took you long enough," Asmodeus says with a vicious smile. "Did you not get my messages?"

Zane lets out a deep, terrifying growl as tendrils of smoke crawl forth from his fingertips, creeping along every floor and surface until they reach Asmodeus and wrap around him.

"Your problem is with me," Zane says. "You let her go, and we'll do this—you and me. You don't get anything from killing a human and you know it. You blame me for Ilen and that's fine. But it's about me—not her—me."

"Fury smoke, hmm?" Asmodeus replies, seemingly ignoring his request. "Clever. I mean, I'll still kill you, but I can appreciate the creativity."

The smoke shifts and swirls, tightening around Asmodeus's chest. He begins to squirm and cough under the increased pressure.

"And where is the rest of the Scooby Gang?" Asmodeus asks between wheezes.

"They didn't come with me," Zane says. "They let you take Ava. You think I'm going to trust them now?"

He can't really mean that. He left Kami and Kieran behind?

"Aww," Asmodeus says teasingly. "So ready to abandon everyone over this unimpressive human girl."

Asmodeus begins to turn red and sweat as the black smoke reaches his neck and squeezes. He hardly struggles, and instead begins to laugh, even as the blood rushes to his face.

He throws his head back and his muscles tense, sending a wave of pressure surging forth from his body. It ripples out across the room, tearing through the layers of smoke and shattering every glass surface in the house. Zane is knocked backward but stays upright.

"You want to die for her?" Asmodeus says, appearing before Zane and pinning him to the wall. "I'd be happy to make that happen for you."

Asmodeus lands several blows to Zane's jaw in quick succession. Smoke swirls around their bodies, twisting and churning like a tornado. My own face stings and my ears ring as I feel Zane's pain through our bond.

I can't just let him do this on his own.

I look around for something—anything—that I might be able to use to fight a demon. I never thought it would get to this point, so I hadn't really made an in-case-of-demon-fighting plan.

Beside shattered glass and a few thick books, there aren't a lot of great options. But something else catches my eye: a slight reflection of a silhouette outside the window.

There's someone else here.

Zane and Asmodeus continue to struggle, trading strikes and slamming each other into every surface. To my human eyes, it looks more like a frenzy of swinging fists and smoke than an actual fight.

I see another quick blur in the distance and my eyes follow the motion to a figure mostly obscured by the dim light in the corner. Maybe my brain is working faster than normal or maybe I'm just seeing what I want to see, but I could swear I'm watching Kami sneaking up behind Asmodeus as he fights with Zane. She seems to be carrying a very large object but I can't tell what it is.

Before I have time to process what I'm looking at, Kami lunges out of the shadows at Asmodeus. He dodges Zane's fist in one motion while simultaneously sweeping a hand backward toward Kami with enough force to throw her to the ground.

The object rolls into the light and it's not really an object at all, it's Kieran, with his wrists wrapped in duct tape.

Asmodeus breaks into a sinister laugh before sending out another wave of energy that throws both Kami and Zane backward.

Asmodeus stalks over to Kami.

"I should've known you two were hiding around here somewhere," he says with a smirk. "So this is the grand plan? A bit of tape and a particularly unremarkable demon?"

"Unremarkable? Now that's just rude," Kieran says.

Kami attempts to sweep a leg under him but he reaches down and grabs her calf in his hand, digging his claws into her skin as she screams in pain.

Smoke snakes around his legs and rips them out from beneath him. Kami seizes the opportunity to kick him in the gut before scrambling backward.

Zane runs toward him but is launched back by another wave of force from Asmodeus. The impact of his body hitting the wall sends a deep crack through the layers of brick.

Asmodeus vanishes and my eyes scan the room for him. Zane seems to be looking too, his eyes glowing green through the haze of smoke. Kami rises to her feet, limping slightly as she too searches for Asmodeus.

Kami begins to cough and sputter. Blood drips down her lips as she stares at me with wide eyes. She clutches her stomach, which is now seeping blood through a large gaping hole.

As I struggle to even process what's happening, Asmodeus emerges from behind Kami, his black claws extended and his arm coated in blood to his elbow.

Kami shudders and collapses to the floor as Asmodeus lifts Kieran's limp body by his shirt collar.

"Get away from them," Zane snarls, smoke spiraling toward Asmodeus.

"Ah ah ah," Asmodeus cautions. "You wouldn't want to lose another loved one tonight, would you?"

He wraps his hand around Kieran's neck and digs his claws into his skin.

"Fuck this guy, Z," Kieran spits. "Kill the bastard."

"So ungrateful," Asmodeus says, looking down at Kieran. "You think I can't still control you, demon? You exist solely to serve my will."

"On second thought, Z," Kieran says. "Is it possible to kill this fucker twice?"

Asmodeus digs his claws deeper into Kieran's neck until blood is gushing from the wounds.

"Tell me, was this the grand plan?" Asmodeus asks, throwing Kieran to the floor. "Is this all they've got? Is there anything else I need to know?"

"Joke's on you, bitch," Kieran says, coughing slightly. "I've got no fuckin' idea."

"Is that so?" Asmodeus asks, his eyes narrowed in confusion.

Asmodeus grabs a fistful of Kieran's hair and drags him closer. He kneels down and grips Kieran's chin in his hand.

Zane seems to be contemplating his next move, slowly inching closer as Asmodeus carefully inspects Kieran. Asmodeus rifles through Kieran's pockets and pulls out a small glass vial with a black lid.

"I knew there had to be a trick," Asmodeus says, his eyes now pitch black from edge to edge. "What are we looking at here?"

He unscrews the lid and sniffs the contents.

"Lethe…" Asmodeus says with a snicker. "Simple, but effective. Well done."

"Thanks, babe," Kieran says with a smirk. "It's nice to be appreciated."

"There's just one problem with this plan," Asmodeus says, looking at Kieran with a grin so wide it would make anyone nervous. "You're no longer of use to me."

In a swift motion he rips Kieran's throat open, throwing him to the ground beside Kami.

Zane rams into Asmodeus with tremendous force, tackling him to the ground. The two exchange blows in an eruption of power. Blood splatters across every wall as smoke and debris fly through the room. Guttural sounds assault my ears as pain and rage flood my senses.

I run over to tend to Kami and Kieran. I know Kami usually keeps Siren venom in her purse. If she has any on hand, I can help her.

"Do you have venom?" I ask her in a whisper.

She attempts to speak but finds herself coughing up more blood. Her skin grows paler as she looks at me with panicked eyes and shakes her head no.

Crap.

I look to Kieran, who seems to be unconscious.

Double crap.

72

Zane and Asmodeus continue to struggle against each other—their grunts and heavy breaths punctuated by the sounds of every object they break along the way.

I pull Kami's weakened body up onto the couch as she wheezes, then I lift Kieran up into a nearby desk chair. For magical beings in extraordinary shape, they're both a lot heavier than they look.

Either that or I'm way more out of shape than I thought.

Let's go with the 'heavier than they look' theory.

A vibration shakes the room and knocks me over. My balance was already pretty terrible, but the residual effects of alcohol are not making anything easier.

I turn to see Asmodeus land a heavy blow to Zane that sends him backward, his head snapping hard against a concrete post. In a flash, I feel a cold hand around my neck, pulling me back into a firm body.

Asmodeus laughs softly as his lips just barely touch my ear. The feeling of his breath on my neck sends chills throughout my body and I feel nausea wash over me.

"Don't fucking touch her, Asmodeus," Zane growls.

His eyes are as vibrant green as they've ever been, but the black smoke around him masks any other expression. There's a slight quiver to his voice that most people probably wouldn't notice, but I recognize as fear.

"A little late for that, isn't it Zane?" he asks. "Or did you not have a chance to watch our little video?"

Video?

Oh god. That was Asmodeus.

I kissed Asmodeus. On video.

I want to wash my mouth.

Is there such a thing as mouth sanitizer?

"I swear to god, you touch her again and it will be the last bloody thing you ever do," Zane snarls.

"Well, I was going to kill her…" Asmodeus says, his claws extending slightly into my skin. "But now I've got a better idea."

Zane is seething, but Asmodeus has the upper hand now and he knows it.

Asmodeus reaches into his pocket, keeping one hand around my neck. He pulls out the vial he took from Kieran and pops the cap off.

Lethe.

The stuff that made Zane forget me. The stuff that I suggested they use.

I mean, sure, that's not good. But lethe is temporary.

Right?

The smoke around Zane dissipates just enough that I can see through it.

"Don't," he says to Asmodeus. It's not his usual threatening tone, but rather an almost pleading one.

The way Zane is reacting makes me think this isn't nearly as harmless as I had hoped.

"You prefer I kill her then?" Asmodeus asks.

"No, please," he begs. "I'll do whatever you want."

"Ahh, sweet Zane," Asmodeus says, holding the vial to my lips as I close my mouth tightly and struggle unsuccessfully to free myself from his grip. "This *is* what I want."

In a split-second decision, I go for the only thing that makes sense to me at the time: I elbow him in the stomach.

I seem to have caught him by surprise, as the bottle is jostled from his hand to the floor. The liquid splashes onto my face and mouth in the struggle. I quickly spit and sputter in an attempt to avoid swallowing any.

"Oh Ava," Asmodeus says with a sigh. "Usually, I would appreciate that kind of foolishly brazen move from someone so weak. But you've ruined a rather delightful plan, haven't you?"

"Fuck you," I snap.

Was that a smart thing to say to an all-powerful demon?

No.

But I just said it.

"I'm not bloody kidding, Asmodeus," Zane says in a rough, low voice. "Let her go. You've got me, you can have your fun. She never wronged you."

"Ahh, but you forget one thing," Asmodeus says. "Why hurt one of you, when I could hurt both of you?"

An unbearable pain shoots through my leg as a grotesque crack echos through the air. I scream and collapse to the ground and watch as Zane does the same.

Tears flood my eyes in an instant as my heart thrashes against my ribcage, as I try to wrap my head around what has happened. I grasp my calf with my hand. The bone is unmistakably snapped in two. The thought alone has my stomach reeling.

Asmodeus stalks over to Zane until he is hovering above him. Zane lies on the floor, the thinning smoke revealing his battered and bruised frame.

Asmodeus laughs and kicks Zane in the stomach as he lies on the floor.

This is it. We're going to lose.

I glance over to Kami. Her eyelids are fluttering as she struggles to maintain consciousness. As our eyes meet, she mouths the word "go" and looks out to the balcony.

Our building has a fire escape. *Is that what she means?*

And then what? Leave Zane and her and Kieran here to be tortured by Asmodeus?

She can't possibly think I'd be okay with that.

I drag myself closer to her. The couch has now collected a pool of her blood and she's tightly gripping her abdomen. Kieran is still unconscious in the office chair next to her.

"What do I do?" I whisper.

"Run," she wheezes. Some of her words are obscured by her weakened voice, but I manage to make out bits and pieces. "You're… human… you're the… get out… You are not a threat."

"I can't," I say. "I won't leave you. Any of you."

Being the weak one isn't usually a positive, but in this moment I know what she means. Asmodeus has spent most of the night ignoring me, when he wasn't using me as a prop. If anyone could slip through the cracks, it would be me. I'm human, a particularly weak one at that, and now I have a broken leg. I couldn't be less dangerous to someone like Asmodeus if I tried.

But maybe that's the point.

I'm the only one who can slip through the cracks, because I'm the only one he doesn't think he has to pay attention to.

Zane attempts to fend off Asmodeus, but seems to be weakening by the second.

"Why are you so hung up on Ilen, anyway?" Zane asks. "You were nothing but a pathetic fucking stalker to her!"

Asmodeus growls and pounces onto Zane, striking him again and again.

Zane is goading him. He knows we've lost and he's making sure I have a chance to get away.

Screw that.

He wouldn't leave and neither will I.

I tug myself up onto the couch and over to Kieran, who is still slumped in the office chair with a knife duct-taped to his hands.

Asmodeus stands up over Zane and turns back to look at me for a moment.

"Don't think I've forgotten about your girl, Zane," he says with a smirk, before focusing again on Zane. "I still have a lot of ideas for her."

A thick cloud of smoke suddenly launches Asmodeus back, falling to the floor just a few feet in front of me. He rises to one knee and growls in response, his back to me as he faces Zane.

If I'm about to die, I hope they cut this part out of my obituary.

I leap to my feet. The immediate excruciating pain in my leg sends shock waves throughout my entire body, but I'll be damned if a little pain stopped me now. With all the effort I can muster, I wheel the chair holding Kieran's unconscious body at full speed toward Asmodeus. The knife in Kieran's hands plunges into Asmodeus's back.

Asmodeus turns around to look at me, almost offended at the audacity of my attempt.

"Really?" he mumbles. With no further sound or spectacle, Asmodeus shudders and falls onto his chest and his body immediately crumbles to ash.

The pain suddenly overwhelms me and I crumple onto the ground.

Oh yeah, that's right.

Broken. Friggin. Leg.

———•———

ZANE

I examine Ava's swollen and bruised face and I can't help but cringe knowing that, at least for a moment, she thought it was me who did that to her.

She has deep scratches across her neck. Her poor leg is swollen and stark white—you can tell it's broken just by looking at it.

"I'm so sorry," I say. "It wasn't su-"

"Go kiss Kami, already," she interrupts.

"But I promised you."

"Oh my god, life and death here, Zane," she says with a smile.

I give her a quick kiss before moving over to Kami. She's unconscious but her heart is still beating softly.

I place a long kiss on Kami's lips before stepping away. Slowly, she begins to regain color as her wound begins to heal.

"You with us, love?" I ask.

"Shit… What the hell happened?" she asks, shooting up in her seat,. "Did you get him? Asmodeus? Is he dead?"

"I didn't get him," I say, looking over to Ava. "She did."

I can't help but smile as I look at the very tiny woman who just managed to defeat one of the world's oldest and most powerful demons. If I wasn't certain it would get Ava killed, I'd have all the details printed on the bastard's gravestone.

Here lies The Almighty Asmodeus. Killed by a tiny human girl with a wheely chair.

"You're kidding me," Kami says. "Oh my god, Ava, you are such a little badass but that is soooo not what I meant when I was telling you to go. I meant to get the heck out and save yourself!"

"I know," Ava says, groaning as I help her into the armchair. "But I wasn't going to leave you guys here to die."

"Well, I guess I'm grateful," she says. "Even if that was a totally insane thing for you to do."

"Um, guys?" Kieran's voice calls from behind me, coughing between breaths. "What did I miss?"

"Ava killed Asmodeus," Kami shouts.

"No shit?" Kieran says. "Sweet! Who's Ava again?"

Kami and Ava both laugh as I walk over to untie Kieran.

"Is that going to wear off soon or does he just not know who I am anymore?" Ava asks.

"It'll wear off," Kami explains. "It's hard to say when, but eventually he'll get his memories back. Lethe is real tricky and it affects everyone differently."

"Is that why you were afraid of me having any?" she asks, turning to me.

"Well, with humans the effect is permanent," I say.

"Oh. I guess I'm glad I didn't know that at the time."

"Oh, hello there, gorgeous," Kieran says as he eyes Ava.

I rip the duct tape off Kieran along with a fair amount of his arm hair as he throws a bunch of expletives my way.

I smirk to myself before grabbing the key to Kieran's cuffs and unlocking them.

"So what was the deal with the 50-Shades schtick?" Kieran asks. "Kinky post-murder after-party?"

"No, you were the murder weapon," Kami says.

"Sweet," Kieran says. "Like… Mrs. White in the library with the sexy demon?"

"Yeah, except instead of a sexy demon, it was you," Kami teases.

"That was hurtful," he says, holding a palm to his chest.

"How are you doing, love?" I ask Ava, who is lying quietly in the armchair.

"I'm okay," she says. "Really tired and my leg is definitely broken. I should probably go to the hospital."

Fuck.

I'm such a prat.

Of course she needs to go to the hospital. I've gotten so used to her telling me that she was fine that I started to forget what the hospital was even good for.

"Sorry love," I say. "Kami, get your keys. She needs a hospital."

"Oh, of course," she says. "Ava, do you want me to grab anything for you or do you want to just go?"

"Could you grab me a change of clothes?" Ava asks. "I've got a lot of blood on these. I'm not even sure what is whose."

Kami runs to the bedroom to grab Ava some clothes while I stay with her.

"Are you okay?" she asks.

Leave it to Ava to ask if I—the self-healing Immortal—am okay.

"Yes," I say. "As long as you're okay, I'm okay."

"That's good," she says. "You're not quite so smoky anymore."

I chuckle at her description.

"Yeah, decided to quit. Heard it was bad for you."

"That was a really lame joke," she says with a bit of a giggle.

"I'm so sorry I couldn't protect you," I say, the words pouring out of me faster than I can even think them. "I should've known he would've done something like that. I hope you know that I would never, ever hurt you."

"I know," she says with a smile. "You're the only one who took so long to figure that out."

"Not sure if I can say the same for you, though," I say. "Turns out you're a pretty vicious killer."

"Yeah, you better watch out. I'm a demon slayer."

"Yes you are, baby," I say with a smile.

Ava's expression softens for a moment as she looks at me. Her eyelids flutter and her skin goes pale.

"Ava?" I ask. "Are you okay?"

"I… I'm not sure…" she stutters. "I don't feel…"

"Baby? Talk to me."

Her eyes lock into a far-off stare and her eyelids begin to droop.

"Wh-…Do I know you?"

Ava and Zane's story continues in...

Siren's Fall

Available now at most online retailers.

A Note from the Author

First of all—sorry for that cliffhanger! I know, I know. But I promise this won't be one of those stories where the couple is torn apart and spends an entire book trying to find their way back to each other. That's not my style.

The second book, Siren's Fall, is the final book in this journey and has a guaranteed happy ending. The story picks up right where this one leaves off. There will be twists, surprises, and plenty of emotions along the way, but trust me—it will all be worth it.

Thank you so much for reading this far! Your time and support mean the world to me. I hope you'll join me for the next (and last!) chapter of this adventure.

See you in book two!

Acknowledgments

First and foremost, thank you to Nick—for being my first reader, my first fan, and my person. This book literally wouldn't exist without you. None of them would. You're the best happy ending this sick girl could ask for, and I don't even care that you don't have wings.

Many thanks to Shannon French, an awesome fellow author who helped me out with an early-days beta read. Your keen eye saved me from many a typo and your insight was greatly appreciated.

And a huge thank you to my awesome Wattpad fans—you created the most positive, loving, and supportive corner of the internet, and I'm endlessly grateful. You spent your time cheering me on, and that means more than I can ever put into words. This book is published because of your encouragement, and I hope it brings you as much joy as you've given me.

About the Author

LUX RAVEN writes paranormal romance with brooding bad boys, strong-but-vulnerable heroines, and a heavy dose of spice. As a chronically ill writer, she got tired of never seeing heroines like her in romance—so she created her very own disabled protagonist who goes on adventures, has hot sex with a winged bad boy, and finds the swoon-worthy love we all deserve.

Lux first unleashed her stories online on Wattpad, where they racked up over 3.5 million reads and even won a Watty Award in 2022. Now, she's bringing her debut duology to print, ensuring more readers can escape into a world where love always wins (because if it doesn't have a happy ending, it's not romance, and she will absolutely die on that hill).

A lifelong paranormal fangirl, Lux spent her teen years obsessing over *Charmed*, *Sabrina the Teenage Witch*, and *Big Wolf on Campus*, so naturally, her books are full of supernatural drama. These days, she lives in Los Angeles with her partner and their dog, where she's living her best basic-millennial-bitch life going to weekend brunches and drinking her body weight in green tea.

You can find her on Instagram at @LuxRavenWrites or at LuxRavenWrites.com, where she's probably rambling about book tropes or raging against the patriarchy. (Probably both.)

LuxRavenWrites.com

Available Now:

Siren's Fall

**Ava & Zane's journey isn't over yet.
Find out how it all ends in Book 2.**

The last year of Ava's life is a complete blur. She wakes up in a demolished apartment with a broken leg, surrounded by unfamiliar people who insist they're her friends. How did she get tangled up in this chaos?

She doesn't remember Zane—the gorgeous man claiming to be her boyfriend—or the truth he's hiding: he isn't human.

Zane refuses to give up on her, but restoring Ava's past is only the beginning.

When Sirens across the globe start turning up dead, Ava and Zane are forced back to London to hunt whoever's behind the attacks. The deeper they dig, the clearer the truth becomes: these murders are no accident. Killing the Demon King unleashed ancient enemies— and now, they're out for blood.

Get it now at most online retailers.

www.ingramcontent.com/pod-product-compliance
Lightning Source LLC
Chambersburg PA
CBHW011122190726
48289CB00012B/2874